THE
DOWNEASTER
DEADLY VOYAGE

PAUL THOMAS FUHRMAN

The Downeaster: Deadly Voyage by Paul Thomas Fuhrman

Copyright © 2015 Paul Thomas Fuhrman

This is a work of historical fiction. While based upon historical events, any similarity to any person, circumstance or event is purely coincidental and related to the efforts of the author to portray the characters in historically accurate representations.

All ship illustrations were reproduced from *Masting and Rigging and Sailing* and *Sailing Ships Rig and Rigging* by Mr. Harold Underhill by kind permission of the publishers Messrs Brown, Son & Ferguson, Ltd.

Cover image: *The Downeaster 'Alexa'* courtesy of Irving Gerrardo Ferral. http://irvinggfm.deviantart.com/

ISBN: 978-1-61179-331-4 (Paperback)
ISBN: 978-1-61179-332-1 (e-book)

BISAC Subject Headings:
FIC002000 FICTION / Action & Adventure
FIC014000 FICTION / Historical
FIC047000 FICTION / Sea Stories

Address all correspondence to:
Fireship Press, LLC
P.O. Box 68412
Tucson, AZ 85755
info@fireshippress.com

Visit our website at:
www.fireshippress.com

ACKNOWLEDGEMENTS

Donna Mewha Fuhrman
Mary Miley Theobold
Josh Caine
Libby Armitage Hall
Jennifer Fisher
Thomas W. MacNamarra, RADM, USN, Ret.
Susan M. Reverby
Captain Daniel Moreland
The Mariners' Museum, Virginia
Mystic Seaport, Connecticut
The San Francisco Maritime Museum
The Maine Maritime Museum, Bath
The Argentine Naval Hydrographic Office
Watermen's Museum, Virginia
James River Writers
Virginia Commonwealth University School of Nursing
The National Archives
The Friday Docents, The Mariners' Museum
Bill Picklehaupt
Brown, Sons and Ferguson, Glasgow
University of Connecticut
Tom Richardson & Tom Warrenton
Chris Paige
Marguerite Wainio
Sister Norberta, Sisters of Saint Francis
(My rhetoric teacher and beloved life coach)
Miami University, Oxford, Ohio
(Miami was a university before Florida was a state)

INTRODUCTION

The Downeaster has three main characters and thus three stories linked to the voyage of the wooden New England-built ship *Providence* from New York to San Francisco and around Cape Horn in 1872.

The details of this voyage were taken from the 1854 log of the clipper ship *Hurricane*. Captain Stephen Very Junior prepared the log for Lieutenant Mathew F. Maury, USN. Maury is considered the father of oceanography, and it was his route the *Hurricane* followed.

The process of turning this log into a fictional account of a voyage involved making use of both modern and antique aids to navigation. The daily positions of the ship were plotted on modern paper and electronic charts. Active reference was made to both modern and historical *Sailing Directions*, the *Atlas of Pilot Charts*, *Admiralty Pilots,* and a perpetual nautical almanac. The weather is as it actually occurred. No imagination, however fertile, can equal the reality of being at sea. Detail about the ship is based on the *Benjamin F. Packard*, the *Balclutha*, and the *Joseph Conrad*. The reason the ship is *Providence,* and not *Hurricane,* is that this novel is fiction. It departs from strict history for the sake of storytelling.

There are several historical characters involved in the story as well as historical buildings, events, and weather. I've tried to portray these people as accurately as I could and with a sympathetic understanding for the time in which they lived.

My sailors drink, swear, use tobacco, and enjoy the company of women. Their real voices are reflected in the shanties you'll see on *The Downeaster*'s pages. Cast off and enjoy your passage around Cape Stiff, and beware of Shanghai Brown when you get there, Dauber.

"The captain was a drunkard, the mate a Turk; The Boatswain was a bastard with the middle name Work."

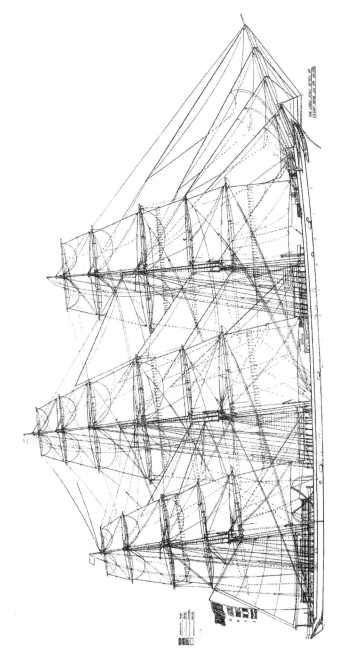

IRON SHIP 'CORIOLANUS'

'Coriolanus' illustrates the type of sail plan that would be used on a Downeaster such as the fictional 'Providence.'
Split topgallant sails and yards were not commonly used.

Illustration Courtesy: Messrs Brown, So & Ferguson, Ltd.

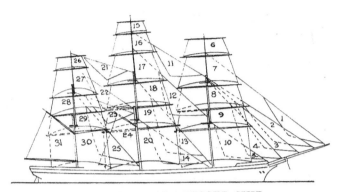

SAILS OF A FULL-RIGGED SHIP.

1. Flying-jib.
2. Outer-jib.
3. Inner-jib.
4. Fore-topmast-staysail.
5. Fore-staysail.*
6. Fore-royal.
7. Fore-topgallant.
8. Fore-upper-topsail.
9. Fore-lower-topsail.
10. Fore-sail or fore-course.
11. Main-royal-staysail.
12. Main-topgallant-staysail.
13. Main topmast-staysail.
14. Main-staysail.*
15. Main-skysail.
16. Main-royal.
17. Main-topgallant.
18. Main-upper-topsail.
19. Main-lower-topsail.
20. Mainsail or main-course.
21. Mizen-royal-staysail.
22. Mizen-topgallant-staysail.
23. Mizen-middle-staysail.*
24. Main-spencer.
25. Mizen-topmast-staysail.
26. Mizen-royal.
27. Mizen-topgallant.
28. Mizen-upper-topsail.
29. Mizen-lower-topsail.
30. Mizen or cro'jack.
31. Spanker or driver.

* These sails are not common to all ships.

SAILS OF A FULL-RIGGED SHIP
Illustration Courtesy: Messrs Brown, So & Ferguson, Ltd.

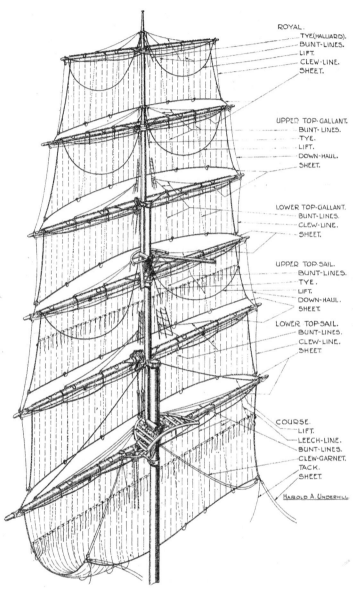

ROYAL.
TYE (HALLIARD).
BUNT-LINES.
LIFT.
CLEW-LINE.
SHEET.

UPPER TOP-GALLANT.
BUNT-LINES.
TYE.
LIFT.
DOWN-HAUL.
SHEET.

LOWER TOP-GALLANT.
BUNT-LINES.
CLEW-LINE.
SHEET.

UPPER TOP-SAIL.
BUNT-LINES.
TYE.
LIFT.
DOWN-HAUL.
SHEET.

LOWER TOP-SAIL.
BUNT-LINES.
CLEW-LINE.
SHEET.

COURSE.
LIFT.
LEECH-LINE.
BUNT-LINES.
CLEW-GARNET.
TACK.
SHEET.

HAROLD A. UNDERHILL.

PERSPECTIVE DRAWING OF MODERN SQUARE-RIGGED MAST.
Showing sails set and lead of running rigging.

PERSPECTIVE DRAWING OF A MODERN SQUARE-RIGGED MAST
Illustration Courtesy: Messrs Brown, So & Ferguson, Ltd.

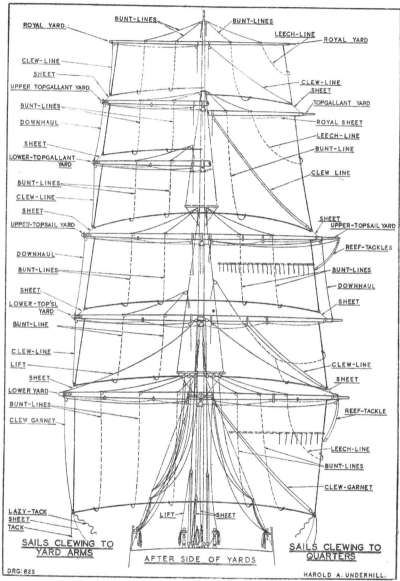

ROYAL YARD
BUNT-LINES
BUNT-LINES
LEECH-LINE
ROYAL YARD
CLEW-LINE
SHEET
CLEW-LINE
SHEET
UPPER TOPGALLANT YARD
TOPGALLANT YARD
BUNT-LINES
ROYAL SHEET
DOWNHAUL
LEECH-LINE
BUNT-LINE
SHEET
LOWER-TOPGALLANT YARD
CLEW LINE
BUNT-LINES
CLEW-LINE
SHEET
SHEET
UPPER-TOPSAIL YARD
UPPER-TOPSAIL YARD
REEF-TACKLES
DOWNHAUL
BUNT-LINES
BUNT-LINES
DOWNHAUL
SHEET
SHEET
LOWER-TOP'SL YARD
BUNT-LINE
CLEW-LINE
LIFT
CLEW-LINE
SHEET
SHEET
LOWER YARD
BUNT-LINES
REEF-TACKLE
CLEW GARNET
LEECH-LINE
BUNT-LINES
CLEW-GARNET
LAZY-TACK
SHEET
TACK
LIFT
SHEET
SAILS CLEWING TO
YARD ARMS
AFTER SIDE OF YARDS
SAILS CLEWING TO
QUARTERS
DRG: 825
HAROLD A. UNDERHILL.

PLATE No. 34.—RUNNING RIGGING ON SQUARE SAILS.
(Sails Set.)

Running Rigging on Square Sails
Illustration Courtesy: Messrs Brown, So & Ferguson, Ltd.

THE
DOWNEASTER
DEADLY VOYAGE

PAUL THOMAS FUHRMAN

FIRESHIP PRESS

PART ONE

Paul Thomas Fuhrman

One

Isaac Griffin

Some years ago—never mind how long precisely—
having little or no money in my purse, and nothing
particular to interest me on shore, I thought I would
sail about a little and see the watery part of the world.

—Herman Melville

Monday, March 25, 1872
Boston

Isaac Griffin stood on the porch of the Christison home on Beacon Hill. Looking toward West Church and a cluster of people in the churchyard, some still singing a hymn, Griffin heard their words, "Come, sinners, to the gospel feast," and laughed quietly. "Gentle fools," Griffin muttered, stamping the soles of his shoes on the stoop to free them of the gray slush.

Griffin had been summoned to meet with his friend and business partner, William Christison Sr., whom he had not seen in more than two years. Master and part-owner of the fully rigged ship *Providence*, Griffin had spent twenty-six months and eleven days at sea; his mind still expected the ground to rise and fall beneath his feet and teased him with nausea. He had been ashore only three days.

He looked up at the azure blue sky. Fair-weather cumulus clouds trailed behind a cold front. He exhaled loudly to watch his breath

3

condense in the cold air. He savored the comfort of his wool overcoat while remembering the frost etchings on *San Matias*'s port lights that morning. He kept his gloved right hand in the pocket of his coat to prevent pain in his injured fingers—pain caused by the cold.

He set his mind to the task at hand. Removing the scarred hand from its sanctuary, he reached for the brass knocker on the Christison door. It was at this moment that the smell of coal smoke and the odor of sulfur from a nearby chimney entered his consciousness, reigniting the memory, but he ignored it, or so he believed. He did not accept that his hand would always be useless; the doctor said there was hope, but his eyes told him what his fingers touched. His fingers told him nothing. When he grasped the knocker, pain shrieked from the damaged tendons and injured nerve endings. He wanted to flinch, to yelp, to let his eyes tear, but he did not. Forcing his hand had become so practiced, a ritual of exorcism. Laudanum had been a last resort, and once past Cape Horn and into the Atlantic, he vowed never to use the opiate again. He had triumphed over his addiction, as he could not accept defeat. But today he used his left hand to knock.

The door opened. "Captain Griffin, it's good to see you again, sir. The Commodore and Mr. William are in the library. They are expecting you. May I take your coat and hat?"

The butler made no comment as Griffin stretched his left arm across his stomach, wedged the gloved left hand under his right elbow, and pulled his hand from the glove. Griffin saw no response, not so much as a blink, on the butler's face as he placed only the left glove inside his tall derby hat. That Saturday, a woman in the horsecar had turned her head away from him when she saw his naked right hand. The glove must remain on. No one must ever see it.

"Commodore, Captain Griffin is here."

Little had changed in the two years since his last time there—Billy's massive desk, the walnut paneling, the half-empty book shelving, the paintings of past and present Christison ships, the old red leather couch and mahogany table where he and Billy had planned voyages and examined sail plans while drinking Kentucky

4

bourbon and smoking Cuban cigars. Billy sat lumped behind his desk now motioning for Isaac to sit in the chair. William Jr. was in the room.

His friends addressed William Christison Sr. as Kicking Billy or just Billy. His business acquaintances and staff addressed him as Commodore. He had inherited a shipping line from his father, Alva, and the title was honorific and not at all naval. The name Kicking Billy was well-earned, bestowed upon him by the men before the mast, at first in anger as victims of Billy's fits of rage, and then with respect and affection as his youth passed and his wife quenched his anger by tempering his heart with her own.

Kicking Billy spoke laboriously, occasionally slurring his words. "Isaac, I've sold the old *Cambridge* and *Portland.* They're salmon packers now. I've only two ships left: the *Providence* and the *Natick.* There's not enough shipping in New England to keep even these. If I let them ride empty at anchor, fallow, I'm bankrupt."

Billy continued, "I'm on the verge of mortgaging the house. I've got to send thee to sea when the *Providence* is ready, when she's finished her repairs. I can't give thee time ashore as promised."

Griffin turned to listen to William Jr., but the son remained silent. He examined William Jr.'s face to determine the extent of his participation in the decision, but he stood away from them by the cold fireplace. Then William Jr. adjusted his spectacles and began to speak: "I've analyzed trends since the Civil War." A smile flicked across his face.

"The information's in the *New York Times*, from Lloyd's—not hard to get at all. I think all that's left for deep-water sail is the grain, coal, and guano trades. The difference in speed between steam and sail is negligible over those distances, and the cost per ton hauled is to sail's advantage. Simple analysis, really. Things change. So must we."

And me?

William's analysis was irrelevant. Only his reference to change caught Griffin's attention. Both Griffin and Billy knew that the American merchant marine, thanks to Congress, would never recover from the Civil War. The world was changing. Confederate raiders had driven American shipping from the sea and the products of New England manufacturing into British bottoms. Steam was eradicating sail from the seas. They had discussed the Suez Canal when it opened in 1869. They saw passenger traffic disappear with the transcontinental railroad. Change would come. It had to.

Griffin watched William Jr. leave the room at his father's insistence. When the son reached the door, he turned and glanced at Griffin. Griffin had seen the face before on mates, hands, and day men. The face burned with resentment.

When the library doors closed, Billy spoke. "I've had a stroke, Isaac. It's frustrating. I talk so slowly. Now I can't walk without a cane." Billy then noticed Griffin's hand.

"What happened? That was not in thy report."

Griffin flinched. "Burned. Not a true hindrance, though."

"Who dost thou think I am, Griffin? It is a hindrance. The men treat thee differently now. How do the mates react? Can thou do chart work anymore? Art thou dependent on the mate? Let's sit over there, on the couch. I've never liked sitting here." He stood, then walked slowly, steadying each stride with his cane.

"Thy report covered the accident, the repairs, the bottomry bond. Thee said nothing about thine hand. Talk to me. I need to know how it has affected thee. I have plans for thee."

Billy became less agitated. "Sometimes, Griffin, it helps to talk. I know thee as well as mine own image in a mirror."

Griffin saw something in Billy's eyes. He recognized it although he had never seen it before. It was something his own father had denied him.

"They made me load coal in the rain in Newcastle," Griffin began. "Said do it now or wait ten days. I knew I should have refused. Damned if I didn't know better! Then, two weeks later, as I stood over my chart desk working the noon sight, looking in my almanac for the declination of the sun, I heard shouts: 'Captain, there's a fire in the cargo hold by the foremast. She's smoldering below. Smells like rotten eggs, sir.'"

"So the fire burned thy hand."

"I don't remember the explosion or the fire that maimed my hand. I first saw my hand in my cabin. The mate and boatswain were holding me upright."

"Many maimed souls go to sea. How it happened is well past thy wake."

"My hand was in hell. I ordered a combination of six drops of laudanum mixed with red wine. God, I wish I had never taken the laudanum. I also had a poultice applied to my hand. When the laudanum dulled the pain, I went back on deck and led flooding and jettisoning the coal. I didn't want my crew to see me weak, ever. Then afterward I said, 'Pump her dry.' No emotion, just 'Pump her.' I walked slowly to my cabin. I remember each step. I had to concentrate. My knees were shaking, Billy. I collapsed into unconsciousness on the reception area rug. Then more laudanum. I hate sulfur. It's hell. My impatience caused all of it."

"Didst thou see a doctor?"

"Yes. He told me my hand puzzled him. That I should be able to use it. Not all of the burn went deep into the hand. I had to exercise it despite the pain. If I didn't, it would stiffen up. I told him I could not move my fingers. He said I could but that I had to force myself despite the pain. I had to convince myself that I could."

Billy had heard enough. "And now thee thinks thy hand is a punishment. Well, all of us make mistakes. Hast thou learned from thy mistake?"

"I have. I have questions too. What happened to you, Billy? Why are we talking behind closed doors?"

"It's William. He can be bril...smart with figures, but he's never wanted to go to sea, just sit at a desk and buy and sell with men like him, like he is at the Mercantile Exchange. He has no..." The words stopped for a moment, then continued. "Even my father, Alva, had a soul. Thee owns a third share of *Providence*. Now I need thee to be half partner in the firm. That's why I sounded your mind. I can't manage by myself. God knows we are not worth that much now, two ships left. I have to ask that. I'm asking for thy money and thy help."

7

Griffin saw that Kicking Billy's struggle with his words was more than just the stroke. He was ashamed.

"William can't run the company by figures. He needs help from a mariner. Someone shippers will respect as a man and listen to— hell—understand without words being spoken. Go with him when he sees the lawyers. I can trust thee."

"When?" Griffin asked.

"Wednesday at two. I won't be there. Can't climb the stairs anymore, damn it."

Griffin's mind was already thinking about raising the money. "Yes, I understand." He paused. "The money—I've put my life savings into my share of *Providence.* I've not much left, just *San Matias.*"

"No choice, Isaac; I'm standing here with my hat in my hand."

Griffin looked directly into Billy's eyes. "I'll do what I have to. I'll mortgage *San Matias.* Selling takes too long. I may not be here to sell her."

Griffin hoped to hear the word "thanks" form on Billy's lips. But this was not forthcoming. Instead, Griffin saw Billy's eyes water and heard, "I'm ashamed."

"It's all right, Billy."

Billy was a desperate man, pushed to his limits by his finances, his son, and his failing body.

Kicking Billy's face straightened and then formed a wry little smile. Griffin was pleased; Billy still had confidence in him and the money was less disturbing to him than his friend's loss of pride.

"One other thing. I can't send thee to sea an em...emaci...sack of bones. Come have dinner with my family. Thee will, won't thee?"

"You amaze me, Billy. First you ask me to go to sea while I've scarcely recovered my health. You dress me down. Then you pick my pockets and, without taking a breath, invite me to dinner. Miss Hanna will be there, won't she?"

Billy's jaw moved again in circular motions to form his words.

"Damn it, why not, Griffin? There's seaway enough to laugh a little, to lie-to a spell then do... Let's remember the good times, get a little drunk together, and then get on with this sorry business. Hanna wants the dinner. She's planned a feast, invited one of her friends to be thy partner."

"A woman?" Griffin's expression showed surprise and his discomfort with the idea of a female dinner partner. "Hanna's idea?"

Billy smiled. "Thee could say that, I guess. I mean a woman. They knew each other at Vass...school. She's a spinster and a suffer-ra-gette. She's no more interested in thee than thee art in her by my reckoning. Hanna says this woman is very intell...pleasant." He laughed. "Thee loves to quarrel with me. Thee will love to argue with this woman! She's all the Woman Question. Thee will be safe, coward. No entan...getting fouled by a swooning beauty. Thou won't lose thy damned inde...bachelor."

Griffin smiled. "You better have some bourbon and a Cuban cigar, a Partagás, for me."

Griffin watched Kicking Billy slowly rise to his feet, and Griffin stood out of respect. Billy's full beard was still there, though now completely white. His pride still showed in his clothing: charcoal gray worsted wool jacket, high collar, silk paisley tie, and subdued windowpane-checked medium gray trousers. Griffin saw tears form in the old man's eyes. It took Billy a long time to speak, but each word was clear. "Isaac, I never wanted this to happen. It's beyond me. I'm watching the worth of two generations disappear, my father's and my own."

Seeing exhaustion from speaking overtake his friend, Griffin said, "Back your main-yard." His voice was as soft and comforting as years at sea permitted. His hand, his left hand, gently patted Billy's shoulder.

Kicking Billy took a handkerchief from his pocket and dried his eyes. He then gripped Griffin's left biceps. In Griffin's memory, it was the first time Billy had ever touched him save for shaking hands.

"I'm not going out with a whimper, Griffin. I fear ruin more than death."

Griffin did not even ask Billy where he was to take the *Providence*.

Two

Nicholas Priest

*But the father said to his servants, Bring forth
the best robe, and put it on him; and put a ring on
his hand, and shoes on his feet: And bring hither the
fatted calf, and kill it; and let us eat, and be merry:
For this my son was dead, and is alive again; he was
lost, and is found.*

—Luke 15:22–24

Wednesday, March 27, 1872
Boston

"Nick, I wanted to get you out of the house. I can't see how you'll
ever get well sitting on the edge of your bed sawing away on Uncle
Johan's old Cremona or with your head buried in some book all
night. We're near the India Wharf building, do you see it?" George
Priest offered his son a piece of horehound candy from the paper bag
he held in his hand.

"Thanks, Father. The candy helps my cough. I like my violin."
The boy's voice emphasized the word "like" with a rising inflection
as well as extending the word itself. "It's like a friend to me, my
only friend. Oh, I can make it out. I see the sail loft sign right in the
middle."

"You've got to start being with people again, Nick. Not everyone
is like those boys at school. Besides, you need fresh air. Your mother
and I would love to see you smile again."

10

The father placed a hand on his son's shoulder.

"You'll find this meeting interesting. I don't think you've ever met people like these men before. Remember what I said about making good decisions? You'll see why lawyers like you'll be one day are indispensable."

The boy asked, "Who is this William Christison Jr.?"

"His father owns Christison and Son Shipping. I'm doing this as a favor to the father. My friends Richard Henry Dana and Captain Isaac Griffin will be there also. I'm not impressed with the son. I'm sorry to say that. Remember what I told you to say. Be polite. We need to get off the horsecar."

The India Wharf building was a long multistory brick building occupying an entire wharf on Atlantic Avenue. It did capture Nicholas Priest's imagination. He had never seen, heard, or smelled anything like it in his life. The boy counted nearly thirty small stores on its first floor facing the street. They sold everything imaginable from China, India, and the rim of the Indian Ocean. Silks and thousand-year-old eggs from China, and brass trays from India that reflected the morning sun and warmed an otherwise chilly day. The street was perfumed with spices and tea and pealed with the voices of both men and women filled with the hope of finding treasures—at a price. Nicholas felt his father's hand tousle his hair.

"See, Nick? What did I tell you?"

Nicholas Priest saw that the street was full of merchants, ordinary people, sailors, and even extraordinary people in flowing costumes, men with turbans, and Chinese men with long braided pigtails hanging to their waists.

His father asked, "Enjoying yourself? We'll have lunch here when the meeting is over. We'll get a tandoor meal. The bread is wonderful and the tea is strong and aromatic. The spices wake your mouth up.

"In the summer months, Nick, you would think you were at a bazaar. Musicians play for the money you toss them; there are street acts, comedians and magicians, dogs and cats trained to jump through hoops and to dance. See, it's better than a stuffy bedroom

11

and scratching away on that violin. We'll go here again. Promise. Next time we'll try Chinese food, beggar's chicken."

The walk up to the third-floor Christison and Son office seemed all too short when his father introduced him to William Christison Jr.

"This is my son, Nicholas. I thought he might enjoy seeing how his father makes a living. There's a lesson in torts in the lawsuits you're considering, Mr. Christison. A very important lesson the boy should know."

William Jr. smiled at the word "important."

Nicholas nodded to the thin businessman sitting in a swivel chair positioned between his desk and the head of the table where he, his father, and the others sat.

The thin man had arranged his desk, swivel chair, and meeting table so that all he had to do was remain seated and turn around to face the table or the desk. It was obvious that he would allow himself no loss of time whatsoever. He even remained seated to greet Mr. Dana, a man approaching sixty and his senior.

Does Mr. Christison even bother to eat? I hoped he might offer us tea.

Isaac Griffin smiled at the boy. "Let him ask an occasional question, William. He just might spare me the embarrassment of having to betray my ignorance of the law. I don't even know if your suit is federal or a matter for the courts in San Francisco."

The boy saw Griffin wink at Mr. Dana.

The elder Priest turned to his son. "Well, what do you say to Mr. Christison, Mr. Dana, and Captain Griffin for allowing you to be here?"

"Thank you, sirs." Nicholas turned to see if his father approved of his answer.

Throughout the exchange, Nicholas Priest had watched Richard Henry Dana. His father had told him Dana was one of the preeminent attorneys in the country and a good friend. He had a long and highly successful career practicing admiralty law. He was also known for championing the rights of sailors. Dana's eyes sparked with immense energy and inquisitiveness. It did not surprise Nicholas Priest that Dana would question him. The directness of those questions, however, upset him.

"What happened to you? Your complexion has no color. Your face shows bruising, and you are thin and emaciated. Are you sick? Why aren't you in school? Did someone assault you?"

William Jr. interrupted. "The *Providence*?"

"Let the boy answer my questions. It angers me to see anyone mistreated. Something terrible happened."

"My appearance, sir? That's why you are asking me these questions?"

Dana smiled. "Yes, of course. I know your father, and he would never allow you to be so badly mistreated. Never."

George Priest interceded. "Enough's happened to the boy, Dana. I brought him here to get him out of the house. I wanted him to see me at work."

Dana was visibly upset. "George, the last thing I want to do is embarrass the boy. I want to help him and you if I can. Besides, if you want him to practice law, to be a litigator, let him answer my questions. Let's see how he handles himself. After what happened, words and questions must be a nuisance to your son by now, surely?"

Nicholas looked toward his father. Dana was correct; a thick callus had started to form. The headmaster, the doctor, the school nurse, all had questioned him. When he returned home the questioning continued: his father, his father's doctors, the nurse hired to care for him, and, most intensely, his mother. He vowed he would never again be abused, if only he knew how to prevent it. The telling was routine by now, but the betrayal and physical pain still lingered.

"I'm not a street musician entertaining people for the money they throw, Mr. Dana. I don't want your pity either. This"—he pointed to a bruise—"happened because people have no respect for me."

"You've got sand, Nicholas. I can see that." Dana's smile left Nicholas wondering if he might, in fact, admire him for not succumbing to the desire for pity.

Isaac Griffin turned, looked Priest straight in the eye, and said, "I admire sand."

If these men admire me—

William Jr. was becoming irritated. "I brought you here to discuss recouping some of the money I spent for the *Providence*'s repairs in San Francisco, shoddy repairs. Had I known, George, I would have asked you to leave your son at home."

George Priest took a breath and composed the rhetoric of what he was about to say. He responded, "Mr. Christison, here are your options: You can sue your underwriters for breach of contract; you can sue the ship surveyor for inaccurate or biased work; you can sue the shipyard for shoddy work. One, all, or some combination of them. It's up to you. The real question is your chance of succeeding in any of this. Do you agree, Mr. Dana?"

"Yes, of course."

Isaac Griffin listened and added, "William, let me remind you that my life savings went into the bottomry bond for those repairs. That's why I own a third share in *Providence*. You could not repay me! Despite that, despite the Commodore asking me to be half partner, I'd like to hear what Nicholas has to say. Besides, this suit isn't going anywhere."

Nicholas seemed to inflate within his clothes. He then straightened his back and looked at each man sitting at the table. "If all you want is to know what happened, I'll tell you. It's not a pleasant story. I don't enjoy recalling it."

The younger Priest composed himself. "They came for me after midnight. My roommate, Charles, had to be part of it, had to have known about it. I trusted him. I hoped he was my friend. Then, suddenly, they hurled me out of my bed, threw a sheet over me, and started to beat me with their fists. They forced me out of Mosby Hall, out beyond the quad, beyond the parade ground, to the edge of the woods. They threatened me; they said they would club me if I screamed out."

Emotions pooled at the lower lids of Nicholas Priest's eyes, reddening them to the brink of spilling over. His sinuses started to drain. He felt his father's hand on his shoulder. His father handed the boy a handkerchief.

The Downeaster

Why does this crying always happen? I hate it... It's why... I don't want them to see me cry.

The boy lowered his eyes and concentrated on the floor. It was worn pine; no two boards were the same width or length. The floorboards were held to their joists with cut nails. His nose stopped dripping and he sniffed briefly.

Nicholas then remembered his mother painting the portrait the thin man was so proud of, the old Quaker—the man with painted eyes that followed you throughout the room, staring at you, never blinking.

He rubbed his eyes and said, "I read too much."

He remembered his father calling the man old Alva, the Quaker; he was the thin man's grandfather. When the boy had regained control of his emotions, he jammed the handkerchief in a trouser pocket and continued.

Dana asked, "You knew these boys, then. You trusted them?"

"I did trust them. I'm not sure I can trust anyone now. They stripped me naked, tied me to a tree, and pissed all over me." Nicholas Priest saw that his father did not approve of the word "piss."

"Yes, they urinated on me. They were laughing, calling me Priestie. Charles seemed to enjoy it as much as the rest. He called me Priestie too. It was the first time he did that. Then someone yelled, 'Someone's coming, let's get out of here.' No one was coming. They were afraid someone might catch them. It was well after midnight. They left me there until sunrise, maybe an hour, not much more. I was wet from their urine, and naked, and my lip was bleeding. It was freezing. I was tied to a tree. My body shivered. It was bad. That was my sixteenth birthday, the seventeenth of February."

Nicholas Priest saw a flash of disgust on Dana's face.

"The groundskeeper found me and wrapped me in his old gray army coat—my nightclothes were torn—and took me to the headmaster's house. The headmaster sent his butler to get my clothes and gave me hot tea to drink. He then sent for Dr. Metzger, the school's doctor, who came and examined me. He had this funny instrument that looked like a wooden recorder, only smaller. He

15

listened to my chest. He took my pulse and my temperature. He said I was too cold. He said my lips were blue.

"Dr. Metzger then took me to the infirmary. I was wrapped in blankets. He put me into a warm bath and then put me in bed under heavy blankets. He took my temperature after the bath. The next day, I started to cough."

"Are we here to discuss my ship or shall we all just go home?" William Jr. interjected.

Dana ignored William Jr. and asked, "Where did this take place?"

George Priest remained silent and let his son answer the question. "Saint Alcuin Military Academy in Virginia."

Dana continued his questioning. "What happened in the infirmary?"

"I became weaker. I developed a cough, my chest hurt; I had a fever and coughed up mucus. I still do. It's yellow. The cuts are healing, but the bruising isn't. I've bruises on my body too."

"And Dr. Metzger?" Dana asked.

"He saw me every day for a week, often twice a day. He listened to my chest, felt my pulse, and took my temperature. He said my chest was gurgling. I wheezed too. He had the nurse, old Mrs. O'Conner, take care of me. Mrs. O'Conner encouraged me to drink flaxseed tea. She's a widow. All the boys in my form called her Mom. The doctor made cough drops for me but insisted I not be fed too much, just broth. He said too much food was bad for me. Mrs. O'Conner snuck me bread rolls and butter, and even a piece of her mince pie."

"Why did they send you home?"

"The school didn't. One day, Father came and took me home. He was angry."

George Priest added, "They thought it was consumption or pneumonia. The doctor wanted to drain his lungs. That's quackery, in my opinion."

Nicholas Priest was puzzled. His father shook his head as if to say no when he spoke the words "consumption" and "pneumonia." The men nodded, even Mr. Christison.

Dana asked, "What did you do, George?"

"I had words with the headmaster. He offered me an apology of sorts, but he refused any responsibility, personal or for the school. I asked if hazing was common. He said no but that it was traditional. I then asked if that meant he turned a blind eye to it. He took offense at my question. His evasiveness was enough to disgust me. I threatened to sue. I wanted to hit him with my fists. I said I'd see the place closed."

"What did you say to your son?"

"What can you say, Dana? I said be brave. I held him in my arms. I'd not held him since he was little. He's been away at school. Do you see how much weight he's lost?

"The trustees settled out of court. The headmaster was sacked, the boys expelled. I've set up a trust for Nicholas with the proceeds. He'll have at least a modest income for the rest of his life."

Dana replied, "Do you know my story, Nicholas?"

"No, sir."

"I was a student like you. I started to go blind from measles. I thought going to sea was my only chance to regain my vision. I spent two years before the mast as a common seaman. It was rough work and dangerous, too, but it cured me."

William Jr. asked again, "My ship?"

Dana then looked at William Jr. and spoke. "Yes, yes, and the business at hand. You used a Salem underwriter. George and I will need to examine the policy carefully, but I don't want to raise your hopes. Do you agree, George?"

George Priest replied, "I do. In my experience, the Salem people know what they are doing. I don't think we'll catch them in an error. Besides, they employ lawyers too."

Dana resumed speaking. "That only leaves the insurer's agent who surveyed the ship for damages, and the shipyard. We must prove deliberate falsification or incompetence. Did you dicker over the shipyard's price or challenge the insurer's survey of damages? Did you hire an independent surveyor to do an inspection? Are the insurer's agent and shipyard even worth the cost of a lawsuit? Did you look at criminal proceedings? You seem to think you were defrauded. How much money do you think they are worth? Probably not much."

Griffin added, "Everything seemed on the level until the work began."

William Jr. laughed. "It takes a lawyer to tell you that there's no hope, no chance of recouping any money, and then charge you for the dismal news."

Griffin's face showed anger. "Your money?"

Dana looked at William Jr. and replied, "My retainer covers reading the underwriting documents. I'm sure that's true for Professor Priest also."

The elder Priest nodded his head in agreement. "Let's see what it says; then you can litigate or just lick your wounds. I won't accept this pro bono, ha! Neither will Dana."

William Jr. replied, "My decision?"

"Yes, your money." He chuckled while looking at Griffin.

Then Dana asked William Jr. a totally unexpected question.

"Do you employ apprentices on your ships?"

"I do. My ships have berths for four boys."

Dana turned to the elder Priest. "Send this boy to sea. I think he needs to get out in the world and learn about men, and maybe even become one himself."

Isaac Griffin nodded his head. "Send him with me. I like him already. The sea is a teacher, a hard one, but I'll keep an eye on him for you."

Griffin then addressed Nicholas Priest. "You'll need to work hard and never, ever complain. Do you understand me? Can you do that?"

Nicholas Priest realized the ship captain was not joking. "Yes, sir. I'll do that."

George Priest was quick to reply. "His mother will not be happy about this."

"Neither was mine." Dana laughed.

Dana turned to the boy. "Are you agreeable?"

Priest answered, "I'll do what Father tells me."

"But are you agreeable?"

Dana then addressed both the father and the son. "This boy needs fresh soil to grow. Going to sea will either make him strong or kill him. If he lives, no one will ever treat him like that again. They'll respect him."

George Priest saw his son smile. "I think he is, Dana."

Nicholas Priest's father signed the apprenticeship agreement and tendered thirty dollars to Christison and Son.

Isaac Griffin looked at the boy and said, "You're bound to go now."

He then told the father, "I'll make sure he's safe. But I'll not coddle him. He'll be a horned shellback before he becomes a lawyer."

The boy looked puzzled.

"You'll have crossed the line and rounded Cape Horn. What you tell your missus is your business, Mr. Priest, but I promise you and her that I'll watch out for this boy. Might we speak in private? There's something needs looking into."

***

Nicholas Priest did not speak to his father during their horsecar ride from Atlantic Avenue to their Back Bay home. He remained silent despite his father's efforts to persuade him that it was for the best that he should leave his home and go to sea. He was told to ignore the agony his father would suffer because of that decision. When they reached their home, his mother, Niesgin, greeted them in the parlor, where she had set up her easel.

Niesgin was a popular portrait artist in Boston. Her customers were wealthy businessmen requiring suitable portraits to hang in their places of business. In fact, the portrait of a bald man in his late sixties with a long nose, a long face, an imposing gray Francis Joseph mustache, and cold eyes dominated the canvas despite the impressive granite textile mill occupying the background. His dry-plate photograph rested on a table. This man could not pose for the painting because he had little time for things other than business and the obligations of his class. It was Niesgin's insight and memory that colored his eyes and toned his cheeks.

These portraits paid well but were not her favorites, as so little imagination was required to render them. She preferred to paint dogs—large, imposing dogs with faces showing canine dignity and affection. Canine eyes fascinated her, wolves' eyes. Today she wished she owned a dog, an angry Rottweiler or Pinscher to attack her husband.

Nicholas Priest stood some distance from his parents, who had forgotten he was in the room. He could hear every shouted word, could see every facial expression, every arm wave, and every belligerent pose.

"What have you done? How could you do this without asking me? I regret the day I met you, George. Don't you care about Nicky at all?"

"How can you say that? Do you remember the doctors? Who hired the nurse? You recall none of that? You stand there and tell me I don't care?" George Priest turned his back on his wife to hide the anger in his face. "I worry about the type of man he'll become. How he'll earn a living. If he'll even live. Hell, I told you what that man said—the hazing was traditional, built character. I didn't need to ask you; I knew your answer anyway. No. *Nein.* Always, *nein.*"

She touched his shoulder to force him to look at her. He stood with his back to her until he felt her hand drop; then he turned again, his eyes avoiding hers.

"Don't you realize there will be no one on that ship to take care of him, to comfort him when he's sick? And those men—have you ever seen a sailor? They are crude men. They swear. They smoke foul tobacco and even chew it. Disgusting."

Niesgin's arms were straight down at her sides and her hands formed tight fists.

"Their officers treat them like criminals. Do you think these men will care about Nicky? Those officers, all they care about is working the sailors hard; that was the way it was when I crossed the Atlantic on that packet. Those sailors stared at me, my breasts, down my dirndl, when they thought I wasn't looking. They'd whisper and laugh. You've sent Nicky…is it too late?"

George Priest had thought about this moment. From the instant he made the decision to send his son to sea, he'd known this argument would occur. He replied, "I'm not going to stand here and argue with you. Do you think I like it any more than you?"

His wife raised her hands from her sides and placed them on her hips as her face reddened.

"The decision's made; the money's spent. It's been well spent. He's going on the *Providence*. The captain is Isaac Griffin. William Christison Jr. assures me that Griffin is a fair man. I could tell he is; I looked into his eyes. He'll watch out for Nick. Our son will not be berthed in the forecastle with the rest of the men. That's not done, never done unless a boy is at least eighteen."

Niesgin's mouth gaped. "Pederasts!"

"No!" George's face grimaced in pain. "Nick and the other apprentices have their own berthing space. I've been assured the mates will be responsible for the boys. Give the boy a—"

"You said boys. How many will there be?"

"Three along with Nick."

"Where is this ship going?"

"To San Francisco. From there to England and back to Boston."

"*Mein Gott!* Do you know that involves rounding Cape Horn, George? Don't you read the papers—ship after ship sinking there?"

George replied, "So? I send him to Virginia, to an expensive school, and what happens? Those boys may have killed Nick. These are the sons of rich men, the best families. And that pompous headmaster—traditional. Our son has consumption! The doctors don't know how to cure it. Damn it, give Nick a chance to fight for his life."

Nicholas Priest shuddered at the words "fight for his life."

So that's why he—

"Don't swear at me, George! I'll not have it!"

"The money's spent. That's that. I have to lecture tomorrow, torts. I need to prepare."

Niesgin Priest screamed, "Do you know what it's like to suckle your infant at your breasts? Do you know the pain I suffered when he was born or the happiness when he was first placed in my arms? Do you know what it is like to lie awake at night waiting for him to cry? That's why I feel this way."

Her husband turned to walk away, then stopped. He turned back and saw that his wife was crying.

"When, George? When did we stop? Did you notice when?"

George Priest saw the anguish on his wife's face. He wanted to speak because he did remember. He wanted to comfort Niesgin, to promise her a tomorrow once more, to share expectations with her, but Nick must go. So, not finding the words, he turned his back on her to seek the familiar sanctuary of work. The house echoed the sound of his heavy oak study door slamming against the doorframe, forced shut by his frustration.

"Nicky, come to Mama. Come to Mama, little *zaubermaus*." Nicholas Priest obeyed his mother, who gathered him in her arms, holding him close to her. She stroked his black hair while crying, "*Mein zaubermaus*." He sensed the warmth, the softness, and safety of his mother's arms, the comfort of her scent, but despite this he thought: *I won't have to watch them fight anymore.*

Three

Kayleigh MacKenna

*A charge we bear i'th'war, and as the president of
my kingdom will appear there for a man. Speak not
against it. I will not stay behind.*
                              —William Shakespeare

Monday, March 25, 1872
Boston

Kayleigh MacKenna stood at her table so as to be seen amidst the
crowd of women as her friend Hanna Christison entered the tearoom
in Wellesley.

"I'm here!"

The sun streamed through the bay window in the front of the
room and framed Hanna in gold for a moment, highlighting the
rivulets of her blond hair, catching the flow of her white polonaise,
illuminating the lace trim in a golden sheen. Even the cacophony
of the room complemented Kayleigh's friend. It was as if she was
glorified by the room's noises; as if wrapped in applause by the
sudden rise and fall of the voices of women enjoying themselves,
a chorus, a melody measured by the percussive notes of silver and
fine porcelain. Kayleigh's small table sat in the back of the room, in
a dark corner, near the kitchen door.

Before Hanna could take her seat, Kayleigh exclaimed, "The
meeting was such a success, Hanna. There were nearly two hundred
women in the parish hall, and we raised two hundred thirty-three

dollars in donations."

"I wish I had been there. Who was there?"

"Dr. Zakrzewska spoke about the New England Hospital for Women and Children. She told us how it was founded to provide clinical experience for women physicians. She spoke of her school for nurses and how limited the opportunity for such training was in Boston."

Hanna's nodding approval drew a smile from Kayleigh.

"She first spoke about how she began her career in Berlin as a midwife and how there were no other opportunities for women in medicine. Then she spoke about how medicine itself is changing, becoming increasingly scientific."

Kayleigh paused to breathe.

"Dr. Zakrzewska has such eyes, Hanna. She inspires me."

Leaning forward across the table and without thought, Kayleigh touched the top of Hanna's hand to make sure she could share her excitement.

"Then she spoke about how Harvard and other medical schools were now requiring student physicians to pass examinations to demonstrate their competence. She said all of this creates a need for nurses who do more than change dressings and clean. Now body temperature must be measured and recorded to track the course of treatment; now organs must be listened to for diagnosis. Dr. Zakrzewska spoke, too, of the growing use of microscopes."

Hanna's face reflected Kayleigh's rising level of excitement.

"She said nurses would become the eyes and ears and hands of the physician when the physician could not be with the patient. This, she said, was why nurses should be educated and licensed, why it is a profession and not a mere occupation."

Kayleigh smiled.

"I could just feel the hope and pride she gave to the young women there. Oh, that I could do the same."

Hanna smiled now in turn. Her friend was happy. Her smile encouraged Kayleigh to continue.

"Next, Phebe Walton told everyone about the New England

Women's Club efforts. I was so embarrassed by what she said about me. She saluted me for my willingness to take up nursing at Massachusetts General Hospital. She said I sacrificed so much to set an example for others. Then she said I was courageous to be seen as a modern woman without fear of how society might regard me. I thought she would go so far as to say I had abandoned the company of men and hope of marriage, but—listen, Hanna—she didn't. Instead, she called me a lone woman, a maiden crusader."

It did not matter to Kayleigh that Hanna had seen and heard many times before what was to come. Harsh or not, the words burned in Kayleigh's bosom. As her anger rose and sparked in her green eyes, her voice would drop a chord at a time from mezzo-soprano to a near dark and malicious contralto. Then the curve of Kayleigh's lips would flatten; the meter of her words would increase. Kayleigh's instincts would reveal themselves in a moment's flash of bared teeth.

"I'm not...We're not helpless. Freedom, Hanna, comes from independence and equality with men. They won't just give it to us either."

Hanna spoke calmly and with the slightest hint of sweetness, "Easy."

Kayleigh saw that Hanna's face was calm, unaffected by the passion now driving her.

"I didn't know, Hanna—my voice? Was I too loud? I just cannot comprehend why she accepts such nonsense—and marriage!" Her teeth flashed. "As if I should make that my life's goal: dependence on men, obedience."

The flash of anger discharged Kayleigh's emotion. As she breathed, her voice returned to its normal octave.

"Still, I must thank her for her contribution, for the money she raised with the club."

Hanna lowered her head slightly, blinked both eyes dramatically in unison, and grinned. Kayleigh saw this and laughed.

"Phebe knew you years ago, Kayleigh. You were so delightful when we were in college together. We had adventure after adventure. Remember? Young men sought our company. Do you remember sitting in that tandem shell with that blond boy? It was such a beautiful April day."

"Oh, yes." Kayleigh laughed. "We were chaperoned; the dean sat in the stern. My boy—that delightful boy—couldn't even brush my hand with his."

Hanna's face changed before Kayleigh's eyes. She saw vertical lines appear on her forehead's center and the smile disappear from her lips.

"Now—for years—it's been nothing. You're no longer Kayleigh; you're Joan of Arc, the brave warrior for all causes of women. Instead of armor, you wear starched gray and brown travel dresses. Your red hair, pulled back into a tight bun, is your helm. You work at the hospital; you raise money; now you are trying to create a nursing school and organize a demonstration in Fall River. You work to exhaustion—never for yourself. Your eyes are sunken. You do avoid men. Admit it."

As Hanna's remark registered in Kayleigh's mind, she lowered her head and closed her eyes. Kayleigh then opened her eyes and focused them on Hanna's. She did not realize that her eyes begged Hanna to stop. Hanna was always compelled to ask why Kayleigh had changed.

"I suppose even your father worries when he finds time away from making money. Did he and your mother see the transformation? Do they notice the dresses, your hair? Women call you a spinster behind your back. It's no secret. Phebe said nothing new. It had to be that Beacon Hill boy. Tell me, Kayleigh. We call each other sister. Why do you leave me to guess? Trust me, please trust me."

Kayleigh MacKenna continued to look into Hanna's eyes. She saw both love and concern within them, but there was only one choice for Kayleigh; she must remain silent and hide her shame.

Hanna pleaded, "Come to dinner this Friday, Kayleigh. Come have fun with me and stay overnight; we'll spend Saturday together. We'll shop and have tea in Boston."

"And I suppose," Kayleigh replied, "you'll have a dinner partner for me? Some shining example of manhood you hope will sweep me off my feet? "

"Kayleigh MacKenna, Kayleigh, Kayleigh," Hanna gushed. "Yes, I do have a dinner partner for you. He's handsome too, but so silent; you'll labor all evening to draw a single word from him. Oh, Isaac Griffin's polite, but he'll not say a word unless it's with Billy, and then they'll talk shipping rates, recall old sailors they knew who have long since passed away. Yes, I think he's shy. Oh, he'll gather your interest up like a ball of yarn when he mentions something called the Cunningham patented topsail jigger bumpkin."

Kayleigh giggled, repeated the words "jigger bumpkin," and then smiled like a cat. Hanna ignored the smile and pressed her invitation.

Hanna began stroking an imaginary beard. "He's handsome of course, bearded. He's educated too. Those eyes, Kayleigh, those eyes. They're gray. Oh, my. He'll beguile you with them because there is a soul somewhere in him. There's such a mystery just waiting to reveal itself."

"Really?" Kayleigh was puzzled. "He sounds boring. I can imagine Griffin and me talking. He could tell me what he's read, and I could tell him what I've read. Does he read, Hanna?"

"He buys a new almanac every year—Billy said so. Please don't turn me down. I'll lend you one of my dresses; I have a wonderful polonaise that matches your complexion and your red hair. It's turquoise blue. Remember how we used to borrow each other's dresses? You'll be so stunning in the turquoise polonaise. Even Isaac Griffin will notice."

Kayleigh replied, "I don't know. By the end of the week, I'm exhausted, and I wouldn't be at the hospital Saturday to take care of my ward."

"We'll have fun, Kayleigh. As for Saturday, I'd rather you go shopping with me. You owe me, too. That was some lecture you gave to the Employment Committee. You apologized for embarrassing me."

While unconsciously shaking her head no, Kayleigh replied, "I do owe you. I suppose once wouldn't hurt. Will you have a good fish course? It's Friday."

"What would you like?"

"Salmon or trout."

Then Kayleigh protested, "Those committee women had a lesson coming. They think they know everything, including the needs of workingwomen. They want respect for their thoughts, their poems, while mill girls only want a sixty-hour workweek." Kayleigh sat erect in her chair. "I just couldn't be silent. Such earnest hypocrisy."

Hanna's voice became distinctly feminine, the voice mothers use to calm crying infants and irate men. "We're all women. Freedom is also the right to have a mind and show it for the world to see."

***

The James Bliss and Company ship chandlery, conveniently located next door to a sailmaker, was on Atlantic Avenue and was well-known as the oldest of its kind in Boston. Israel Dunrow, the clerk, held court with two customers, Captain Isaac Griffin and Captain Stephan Bray Jr.

Bray barked out, "Israel, do you have the 'sixty-nine *Coast Pilot for California and the West Coast of North America*? The Coast Survey one? I tell ya, Isaac, you have to treat those things with caution. Thankee, Israel." He quickly flipped through the pages to find the recommendations for the approach to San Francisco Bay.

"This is what I mean. See, Point Año Nuevo, Pigeon Point. What these don't say is that the sailing directions given are for steamers! I know of three wrecks there, the *Carrier Pigeon*, the *Sir John Franklin*, and the *Coya*. All sail. They picked *Coya*'s bones clean. All of them were broken up on those black rocks in the fog. Men's bones are still there between the rocks. Steamer directions! Those smoke belchers don't have to wear. Just you keep a good reckoning and an alert lookout."

Griffin raised his gloved hand to Bray's face. "Still have my common sense, Bray."

"How in blazes can you use a sextant?" Bray's curiosity exceeded his sense of civility.

"I let the first mate do it! Ha-ha. That's his job, ain't it?"

Griffin continued, "No, I had a Norwegian carpenter. Shipped him in Frisco. Knew his trade. He built me a pine plank that straps onto my forearm. It's got a bulge that slips between the sextant handle and the frame. The sextant slips over, then fits down in a notch. Had trouble using it at first—I mean a second or two error." He winked.

Israel Dunrow interrupted. "Show him the pistol I sold you—go ahead, Captain Griffin." Dunrow was proud of his sale.

"Can you take it out of its box for me, Israel?" He held up his gloved right hand.

"See? It's a Smith and Wesson Russian, big .44 caliber. You can club a man with it or shoot him. Here's what I like."

Griffin took the heavy blue steel revolver by its walnut stocks, holding it in his left hand. He then jammed the barrel down between his shirt and trousers on his right side. "Watch this."

Using only his left thumb and index finger, he opened the break-top mechanism and showed Captain Bray how the case ejectors worked. "All I got to do now is pick a few cartridges from my pocket, and it's loaded. That's not all. I'll ask a saddlemaker to fashion a shoulder harness for me. The barrel will go straight down under my armpit and tie onto my belt."

"Can I show you something, Captain Bray?" Israel Dunrow asked.

"Naw, not today. Got my old Navy Colt. Converted it."

"I'll take a trade."

Not sharing the clerk's enthusiasm for selling firearms, Griffin asked, "Bray, do you know Peleg Carver?"

"I do. He's a full fathom tall, fists as big as hams, and carries them down at his sides like he's ready for a fight; you know, his shoulders lean forward like this, like he's saying, 'Come on, lad, try me.' "

Griffin nodded gently to let Bray know he understood him.

"What kind of sailor is he?"

Bray replied, "First-rate. Proud of his ship, too. Has had a master's ticket for years."

"Why doesn't he have his own ship?"

Griffin saw nothing on Bray's face to indicate surprise or deceit.

"He and his family are all deep-water men. About all that's been available are coastal schooners. His damned pride! He could have a big five- or six-master if he wanted but says he's a ship-rigged man and goes to sea. He's concerned about his family's tradition, all Searsport men for generations, all masters. Carver ain't starving as a mate."

Bray chuckled as he said "ain't starving."

"Is that it, Bray?"

"Well, no. I've heard he's got a superstitious streak in him like an old johnny. I've also heard he won't abide someone crossing him. But as long as we have to ship men by American rules, he's as good as it gets. He can make them see the light about deserting ship before payout, and he can make a sailorman out of a mule."

Griffin nodded. "He's going to be my first mate going round the Horn. Lennon will be second mate, but he doesn't know celestial. He's learning, though."

Captain Bray smiled. "Well, Carver's a Maine man. He'll suit you fine. By the way, a group of us is going to the Belle and Maiden Friday; an association dinner is what I told my missus, no business, just cards and cigars."

Griffin smiled toward his friend. "Can't. Kicking Billy's having me over for dinner. Miss Hanna, Junior's wife, will have a suffragette friend for me to meet."

Captain Bray looked at his friend and winked. "A real looker, I'll bet."

Griffin smirked.

Four

A Dinner Party

Whenas in silks my Julia goes,
Then, then, methinks, how sweetly flows
The liquefaction of her clothes.

Next, when I cast mine eyes, and see
That brave vibration each way free,
Oh, how that glittering taketh me.

—Robert Herrick

Friday, March 29, 1872
Boston

Griffin looked at his pocket watch to assure himself he would be neither late nor too early for the dinner party. His day had been busy. Besides meeting with William Jr., he had taken his chronometers to be cleaned and registered. He had bought a new set of oilskins and sea-boots from James Bliss and Company. He had bought gifts for Hanna Christison and Kayleigh MacKenna, a novel by an English author, a woman. The bookseller's attractive clerk had assured him it would please any gentlewoman. So of that much he was confident; it was his favorite bookstore.

Jimmy Meehan, his cook and yacht keeper, had helped him into his evening clothes, particularly with his white tie. Jimmy also had reminded him, to his irritation, what his mother had taught him. A gentleman always approached the plainest or the most elderly

31

female first. He assumed he would approach her first and tell her of his delight in meeting her. All the better, he thought, if she happened to be a redhead. His only concern, nay fear, was his inability with polite but meaningless talk.

The butler opened the double doors to the parlor and announced, "Captain Isaac Griffin."

Perhaps it was the light in the parlor, perhaps habit from ships—low overheads—but he ducked his head. When he brought his head up again, his eyes were focused directly on a redheaded woman's eyes, the green eyes of Kayleigh MacKenna. Griffin stumbled with the words—"Good evening"—but at least he had spoken first.

***

Kayleigh MacKenna helped Hanna Christison endure that great nightmare of all mistresses of the house: the half hour spent in anticipation of her guests' arrival and the anxiety of making sure everything was perfect. She watched Hanna confer with the housekeeper, then sit at the table to see if the height of the fresh flower arrangement obscured the vision of the person sitting across the table. She heard Hanna insist on candlelight because of its ambiance, its intimacy, and dreaded the romantic implications intended for her.

She followed Hanna to the kitchen to oversee each course in its preparation. The footman's livery was correct; Missus looked impeccable in her black uniform. However, most of Hanna's attention prior to this, indeed, nearly the whole morning and the better part of the afternoon, had been directed toward Kayleigh MacKenna herself.

"No. No. I will not wear a corset. Not that one or that one. None at all, Hanna. Don't you have something from the artistic dress movement? Something intelligent?"

"You mean something shaped like a circus tent? No, I have nothing of the kind. I've never had anything of that kind, nor will I ever have. I'm so sorry the turquoise dress doesn't suit you. You know, as thin as you are, you just barely need the corset—no tight lacing."

"No, I would have to wear that thing under it, the baleen stays, no, thank you. How shall I bend or breathe?"

"Well, dear, how about this?" Hanna then showed Kayleigh an emerald green ball gown by Worth. She held it next to Kayleigh's arm.

"Oh, that is wonderful." Kayleigh was pleased.

"Yes, it accents your complexion brilliantly—even better than the turquoise dress. Try it."

Hanna and a maid helped Kayleigh undress.

"Try this tournure; it's muslin."

The two women stood in front of Hanna's full-length mirror. Kayleigh turned slowly, looking at herself first from the front, then from the back, peering over each shoulder. Then she turned to Hanna and smiled. "I do like it."

Once the choice of dresses was determined, Kayleigh and Hanna turned their attention to their hair. When a woman gazes upon herself in a mirror, she alone has the clarity of vision to see how the tiniest of curls or the subtlest of layers affects the faring of her beautiful face. "Oh, no, Hanna. It makes my face too long."

Despite such pronouncements, Kayleigh welcomed Hanna's suggestions. In the end, the red and blond crowns of glory proclaimed the strikingly wholesome beauty of the two women. This achievement was obtained with the help of *Harper's Bazaar*, two maids, and much cast-iron technology devoted to making of hair something that nature had neglected to do. The women were delighted despite the doubts they raised with questions to each other and the anxious moments spent in front of Hanna's mirror.

***

The half hour before dinner: The plate! Kayleigh watched as Hanna summoned the butler and a mismatched fish fork was replaced with a matching one. Every detail was now in place; every detail was perfect, including Kayleigh MacKenna.

At last the hour came, the minute arrived, and the exact second passed. The butler escorted Griffin through the great hall and to the parlor doors and announced his arrival.

Kayleigh thought she would laugh at first. He ducked his head as he passed through the parlor doors. When he raised his head, he caught her staring at him. He formed a smile. She formed a smile. His gray eyes were indeed mesmerizing. They were not the eyes of a youth or a fool but bore witness to what he had seen, where he had been. His black hair was lightly grizzled with gray well before its time. He wore a well-trimmed beard and mustache that seemed to hide his mouth. It was his eyes that revealed the smile, the instant and honest delight he experienced at seeing her.

He's shy.

William Jr. stepped forward to introduce Griffin to her. She had already determined that she would extend her hand to him. It was then she saw his right hand was covered not with a formal white glove worn with evening clothes, but in black kid leather, immobile black leather.

A wooden hand?

***

It was only a handshake of gloved hands. Griffin extended his left hand to her right. Their eyes met again. They smiled. The significance, the momentous effect, came when he realized that their hands remained clasped longer than they should. His left hand seemed supremely sensitive to him. He savored her warmth and the length of her fingers pressing his palm. He felt the delicious smallness of her hand, a woman's hand. He felt her fingers grip his, relax, and then grip them again in an embrace. He should have felt uncomfortable. He should have wondered if anyone saw them do this, as should she. If anyone saw him behave so boldly with a gentlewoman he had just met. He did not care. He waited to release her hand when he felt her hand relax in his, when he saw her smile, blink her eyes quickly, and refocus their warmth on his.

***

She was stunned. It was his left hand. She realized that she initially relaxed her grip from the surprise. Then she gripped his fingers with hers. Her fingers sensed the strength of his. Her palm told her how pleased he was with her. He wished to caress her, to hold her. She smiled and relaxed her grip but held the hand in place, letting his fingers trace its contours as he withdrew his hand. Once her hand and his were no longer clasped, they remained unconsciously poised to grasp each other again. Her eyes glanced to the side to see if the others were watching and returned to his eyes. She smiled. She abandoned concern for who might be looking and what they thought.

Kayleigh knew it had taken place in a moment, many seconds short of a minute. Kayleigh was overcome with surprise and the sensations of her body reacting to this man. These instincts were both frightening and pleasant. Their warmth pushed aside her fear and stirred a hunger for more. This was the most wonderful moment of her life.

Could he feel this way too?

***

"Miss MacKenna, I'm delighted to meet you."

"It pleases me to meet you, Captain Griffin."

"Miss Hanna, Miss MacKenna, I hope these novels offer you some enjoyment. I was assured they would." The butler gave each woman her gift, looked to Hanna for permission to leave, bowed slightly, and left the room.

Hanna Christison spoke first. "Thank you, Captain Griffin. I can't ever remember seeing such a lovely leather-bound edition of *Pride and Prejudice*. Miss MacKenna and I will treasure our gifts always." And, with a noticeably different tone, a tone betraying apprehension, or so Griffin thought: "You will, won't you, Kayleigh?"

Griffin saw Hanna turn her head to watch her friend's reaction.

Griffin had no barometer, no sextant, not even a lead line; nothing to discover what was happening within these women's minds. He did see Hanna raise her right hand to cover her mouth.

What?

35

Kayleigh extended her hand to touch Griffin's forearm and gushed, "Thank you so much, Captain Griffin. This novel has always been a favorite of mine. I don't think Mr. Darcy himself could have bought so beautiful a gift for a woman. It will always remind me of you and this evening."

Griffin heard Hanna exhale. The butler, who had quietly reentered the room, took the novels and set them aside.

Again they held each other's hands as he bowed slightly towards her. She was his sole focus. Dinner was announced. Griffin was pleased that Kayleigh took his left arm so readily and let him lead her to the dining room and help her take her seat.

Five

The Dinner

But as all several souls contain
Mixtures of things they know not what,
Love these mix'd souls doth mix again,
And makes both one, each this, and that.
　　　　　　　　　　　　　　—John Donne

Friday, March 29, 1872
Boston

Kayleigh MacKenna thoroughly enjoyed the split pea soup and poached salmon with egg sauce. She was virtually unaware of William Jr.'s attempt to maintain polite conversation as he summarized the news so far for March. Her attention was focused directly across the table, over the top of the flower arrangement.

William Jr. commented, "I don't recall a colder March or as much snow in my lifetime. I'm ready for spring. What about you, Griffin?"

"I won't see much of a New England spring. It will be winter in Antarctica and the Southern Hemisphere."

Kicking Billy interjected, "Keeps the fast ice frozen up to the shore of the South Shetlands. The pack ice starts to form in late August."

Isaac Griffin replied, "Yes, that's my recollection."

William Jr. again took the conversational helm. "Wonderful dinner, Hanna. Don't you agree, Miss MacKenna?"

Kayleigh replied, "The salmon was magnificent, and the

Chablis—a Droin?—it pairs so well with the salmon. I think the dinner has been wonderful too."

She addressed Griffin almost silently. "How do you cope with being so separated from the news while you're at sea? I would feel marooned, I am sure."

William Jr. droned on about a railway accident in Maine caused by the heavy snow.

Griffin raised his eyes to hers. "The news isn't that important, unless we declare war. We do speak with other ships at sea and exchange information. I always have at least one newspaper aboard. If the other ship is bound for New England or the Eastern Seaboard, we may give him letters to post for us. My mates often do this."

He watched for her response and smiled. "I do read when I can. I'm interested in ideas and questions, very few novels. When I'm ashore, I spend much time at the library—there's so little room for books aboard ship and so little time to read."

Kayleigh was delighted. She now could engage Griffin in spoken conversation, a discussion to encourage further unspoken exchanges between their eyes.

"What do you read, Captain?"

"I bought *The Descent of Man* in Bath and almost finished it on the train. His ideas will be shocking to some. The book is not an altogether enjoyable read, too much biological detail. Needed, I suppose?"

William Jr. overheard Griffin and Kayleigh. "Darwin, eh, Griffin?"

Kayleigh noticed that Griffin looked in William Jr.'s direction and then began drumming the table slowly with the index finger of his left hand. Kayleigh addressed William Jr. "I asked the captain what he reads. Perhaps, given his circumstances at sea, he should be allowed to discuss Darwin if he pleases. Would you be offended, Hanna?"

"Oh, no, not at all. My William has come to some interesting conclusions about Darwin. He's read several articles on this latest book and attended a lecture at Harvard Divinity School. He speaks of it all the time." Then she added, "I'm so proud of him."

Kicking Billy was not shy at all. "I'd rather talk about the Apaches and the Black Hills of Dakota—there's the next gold rush."

The wild rice with chicken liver pilaf and the vegetable courses were served with a chilled Trimbach gewürztraminer.

Kicking Billy smiled. "Hanna knows how much I love this wine. The spice! The chicken's good too. Never had a cook or steward at sea that could do this well. Maude tried, though."

Kayleigh's eyes shifted to Kicking Billy. "Maude?"

"My wife. She's passed on. Consumption." He labored with the word "consumption."

"I'm so sorry for you, Commodore."

"Maude went to sea with me. Still haven't gotten used to sleeping alone in bed."

William Jr. looked around the table and gently shook his head in obvious embarrassment for his father. "Darwin has interesting things to say about the place of men and women."

Kayleigh asked, "He does?" Her voice was mezzo-soprano.

Hanna smiled; she assumed polite agreement with her husband's opinions.

"Yes, Miss MacKenna, he certainly does. Men are superior to women in so many uncontested ways; we are the stronger, more aggressive, and more intelligent of our species because our brains are larger as well as our trunks and limbs. Why, that woman's ideas—I mean Miss Claflin's—are ridiculous. It is indeed my duty to protect Hanna, to provide for her and provide a home in which she can attain her natural happiness, which is to bear and nurture our children."

Griffin lowered his head and spoke in a near whisper. "I don't understand his reference, this Miss Claflin? Who is she, Miss MacKenna?"

"She believes women should have the vote." Kayleigh motioned for Griffin to move his head closer to hers so she would not be overheard. "She's a Libertarian and believes in free love. She's even attempting to run a brokerage on Wall Street. They ostracized her for her ideas."

Griffin replied, "Free love? So? The men on the HMS *Bounty* mutinied because love was free in the South Pacific islands and they did not want to return to England, where it wasn't. They took native wives and risked hanging."

Kayleigh asked, "You don't consider the native women's behavior immoral?"

"I'm not sure morality has anything to do with it. For them, it's simply natural. If a woman there wants a man, she is free to pursue him. If a man wants an island woman, he knows he must please her."

"Captain, are those your beliefs?"

"Don't you think denying nature is wrong, perhaps even harmful?"

Kayleigh replied, "I'm Catholic, which is to say I'm bound by the gospels and the doctrine of the church. However, my mother and father are from Ireland. They have more questions about the church than I do. Father says there's mud on the church's boots. Your ideas fascinate me. I never expected to hear such ideas, and it would please me to hear more; would it please you to discuss them with me, Captain?"

Griffin spoke with excitement. "I have no one—"

"Dr. Acton anticipated Darwin." William spoke with authority; the tone and volume of his assertion signaled his desire to direct the conversation. He had overheard Griffin and Kayleigh's aside.

"This anticipation is a fact not surprising to any educated, progressive man. The doctor states that woman's nature is directed toward the home, the nurture of children. That is her natural state. That is the source of her happiness, indeed, natural happiness, if I too may use the word. Can't you see? Women are the equals of men, but our spheres of influence differ. Women, as do men, satisfy their own natures, thus bringing that nature to its highest development, generation by generation. So man and woman must occupy their own place to find happiness and fulfillment. Each must be respected and encouraged, but in different ways."

Hanna Christison turned toward her husband. "William is a wonderful husband. He has always protected me. You saw how he courted me, Kayleigh." She hoped Kayleigh understood her intent to change the topic of conversation.

Kicking Billy smiled and held Hanna's hand momentarily. "I loved my Maude. She brought me happiness. When I was sick in bed, she took my place on the *Natick* as its master. Truth be told, she was a better navigator than I am—understood Bowditch better and made sense out of Maury. She brought a black cat aboard to amuse the crew."

Griffin chuckled.

William Jr. remained serious. "But was she happy, Father?"

"As a clam, William."

Griffin smiled at Kayleigh, and then addressed a question to William. "Have you considered the most salient issue with Darwin: that we are descended from the apes?"

Kayleigh watched William Jr.'s face contort and then redden before he answered Griffin's question. She felt an odd sense of satisfaction.

"The Bible is divine revelation. It cannot be in error since it is the word of God. Darwin is wrong. Such ideas are dangerous. God put the rings on petrified trees at Creation. These are the very same rings that lead some to assert that these trees were living more than six thousand years ago. He placed rings there as well as fossils, and for his own good purposes, perhaps to test us."

Griffin was startled, "Ex nihilo?"

Those words puzzled Kayleigh, although she understood Latin. She sensed conflict. "I'm sure the Bible is correct, William. It is we who do not comprehend God's work. What does it matter to Him if a day is a day or a million years? Time is mere thought to our Eternal Father."

Griffin turned his head toward Kayleigh momentarily and made sure her eyes met his. He smiled. He then resumed staring at the white tablecloth while drumming the table slowly with the index finger of his left hand. He stopped drumming to speak to his dinner partner in a subdued voice.

"Does it matter? Really? Creation is no more than clockwork set in motion; so is life. We spin for a time without intervention like gears in a watch, nothing more."

Kayleigh thought he looked into her eyes to see if she understood what he had said. She hoped he had chosen to reveal his mind to her, to trust her, to see her reaction. Had he wanted to know if she would reject him?

Kayleigh momentarily glanced at the people sharing the table and then focused on Griffin. As their eyes met, she slowly moved her right hand toward Griffin's left hand. He responded. His left hand inched toward hers. She smiled; he smiled, in unison.

We can be totally open with each other.

Hanna also observed the wordless exchange.

The remains of the meal, the mincemeat and custard pies, were removed. Hanna invited Kayleigh to the parlor while the men remained in the dining room for cigars and liquor. Kayleigh stopped Hanna abruptly at the parlor door.

Six

A Matched Pair of Carriage Horses

Dancing is the poetry of the foot.
—John Dryden

Friday, March 29, 1872
Boston

Kayleigh stood directly in front of the parlor door with the serious face of a sentry challenging an approaching stranger. "No, Hanna, we're going to the dining room. Aren't you insulted that women aren't invited to stay? Haven't you felt it unjust that they are allowed to drink and smoke while we must confine ourselves to tepid sherry and *Harper's*? Don't you want to go back? I do. Isn't it time?"

To Hanna's surprise, Kicking Billy and Isaac welcomed them warmly. William Jr. said, as if under duress, "Hanna, Miss MacKenna, you are welcome to join us. Please stay." He then frowned in Hanna's direction.

Kicking Billy offered a round of Kentucky bourbon whiskey served without ice or water. "It's called sour mash. I like it as well as a good brandy. Griffin likes it too."

Kayleigh responded, "My father taught me to drink whiskey this way. He has a snake and a pot still from Ireland. I like its fire and spice. It's a little raw, like life itself."

William Jr. whispered to Hanna, "What next, cubeb cigarettes?"

Kicking Billy winked and asked, "Kayleigh, do you know 'Whiskey for Me Johnnies'?"

43

"Oh, no, I don't know that song. You men just want to sing. Hanna warned me."

William Jr. looked anxiously at his wife and interjected, "Let's go to the parlor. I'll play the piano so we can dance." He then raised his eyes beyond the room's ceiling, beyond the sky itself.

***

William Jr. took his seat at the piano, then ruffled through some sheet music and chose a waltz. It was obvious that he played well and took pleasure from entertaining at the piano. Hanna stood behind him for a moment and placed her hand on his shoulder, then bent close to his ear and whispered, "Thank you, Sweet William."

Kayleigh saw Isaac smile and then bow gracefully from the waist to Hanna. He turned and asked Kayleigh to dance.

Hanna attempted to dance with Billy, but he was able only to turn slow, jerky circles with her. Hanna steadied the elderly man and buoyed his spirits by appealing to his mischievousness. "We must take turns watching Kayleigh and Isaac and tell each other what we see. They mustn't know we're watching."

The old imp smiled.

Kayleigh and Isaac waltzed. Kayleigh was able to teach him little flourishes. Dancing gave them an opportunity to talk about themselves as well as holding each other and having no more than a dozen or so intimate inches between their faces. Kayleigh wondered if he was aware of her perfume, a blend of flowers and nutmeg. Hanna had given the perfume to her. Then Griffin spoke.

"Kayleigh, 'ex nihilo' means 'from nothing.' William as much as said God is capable of lying."

Kayleigh was taken aback. "I'm sure that wasn't his intention. He doesn't seem to question things, Captain. Perhaps he simply believes what he hears and reads. So many do."

She then asked out of the blue, "A clockwork? Are you an agnostic?"

"I've read Huxley. I don't know. Maybe I am an agnostic. I don't see God intervening in our lives; there's no need. The only time I feel God is at sea. The sea feels no..."

Griffin paused to consider his words. Kayleigh had asked him a question whose answer he had never fully realized.

"It can bless or kill without caring or even conscious thought. In so many ways—I just don't know—that seems godlike. In seminary everything was reason, corpse-cold reason—no majesty, no awe, no love. Then I'd sneak off to the little churches, where the preachers ranted and stomped and drove their congregations into frenzy. An emotional peak would occur, then a release of these emotions. There was no substance and a seeming glorification of ignorance; the Bible was the lone authority and absolutely inerrant. I was lost to religion. Reason and emotion seemed irreconcilable.

"The sea involves you and challenges you to survive it. It lives but doesn't. These challenges, and courage, have to give our life meaning and insight into our purpose."

"Captain, you are a puzzle. For a man who seems to doubt God, you think so much about Him. It seems God trickles through your fingers like water. You seem content, but you are not."

Griffin replied, "I am? Please call me Isaac."

"Kayleigh." She smiled. "Just cup your hands and drink."

"That seems so simple, Kayleigh."

She smiled. "It is, Isaac. Just open your heart."

He spoke before she could finish. "I am an actor on a stage. Everything I do is for others, the sailors and my ship—would you feel less of me if I told you I felt fear? Would you reject me if I have doubts about my decisions? I'm sorry. I finished your sentence. That was rude."

Kayleigh moved closer to him. "I'm glad you did. I would be hurt if you felt you could not share with me. May I share with you?"

Words were not needed to answer her question.

"You must feel alone aboard ship, Isaac. Is there anyone to confide in? How lonely it must be to have no one in whom you can seek comfort."

Gripping his hand more firmly, she continued, "All you can seek is counsel; all you can show is confidence in your decisions. How lonely you must be. We both pretend to be brave. There's something I must show you."

Kayleigh took his arm, let him take her to a pair of parlor chairs sitting by a small table, then reached into her reticule and pulled a folded letter from it and showed it to him. She summarized the letter for him. "The doctor is warning me against continuing my work as a nurse at Massachusetts General. He says it will ruin my reputation and disgrace my family."

Griffin took the letter, read it quickly, and returned it to her. "I don't understand this at all; he acknowledges that you accept no money for your work, but you will ruin your reputation?"

"Yes, he believes nursing should be done by matronly married women or by elderly widows. Then, too, so much of the work is drudgery, cleaning."

Kayleigh removed a glove to show him what such work had done to her. Griffin took her bare hand in his and with the thumb of his left hand unconsciously stroked her knuckles.

Kayleigh continued, not withdrawing her hand. "Do you realize what this reveals about how he regards women? He's saying a single woman should not nurse the sick and injured. He thinks it's below my class. He also implies drudgery is the lot of ordinary women."

Griffin responded, "That's so much in so few words. I never realized." He paused to think. "He amazes me. Why doesn't he respect your courage and compassion? I do, and I don't share his ideas about women's lot in life either. I've seen too much."

Kayleigh saw Griffin's anger surface in the color of his complexion and the whites of his eyes and placed her hand gently on his forearm and smiled. "He thinks no one would marry me. He's a kind man; he truly is."

Griffin responded honestly but without thinking. "I'd marry you."

Kayleigh quickly caught her breath. "Well, I'll certainly not show this letter to my father now."

"You've confused me—your father?"

"You seemed surprised."

"Why—are you afraid of your father?" Griffin extended his

hand to hold hers, and then, realizing what he had done, withdrew it quickly.

"No, of course not." She again took his hand in hers. "He does have a temper, though, like you. I would worry for the doctor."

Kayleigh felt Isaac's hand gently pressing her own. He then moved closer to her.

"We were talking about being alone, Kayleigh. Maybe we share more than we realize. I'm glad you showed the letter to me."

Kayleigh replied, "Let's dance again. These things can wait. William is playing a waltz now. Dancing makes me happy."

He helped her to her feet without ever letting loose of her hand.

They danced silently, their bodies closed to within no more than a hand's breadth from each other, and periodically brushed together. The focus of their eyes betrayed that these gentle collisions were not accidental.

The dance ended. They found themselves so absorbed in each other that they remained in each other's arms. Kayleigh had noticed Griffin glance at the tops of her breasts and was sure it was not intentional. Her nipples hardened. It was the same reaction she'd had when she let her eyes first linger on his.

I wish I could chide him. Make him feel uncomfortable. Then I could smile and let him know I was just teasing him.

"Must you look at your feet so often?" She giggled, breathed in, and exhaled slowly.

He blushed.

Hanna noticed how they still held each other and said, "Oh, William, you must play another waltz."

Kicking Billy laughed quietly.

William played on.

Isaac and Kayleigh slipped easily into the embrace of the music and continued.

"I'm impressed with the relationship you have with Commodore Christison."

"That's a long story, Kayleigh. Do you want to hear it? Sailors are famous for long yarns."

"I'll listen if you tell it. Is it famous or infamous?"

They stopped dancing momentarily to laugh. Their foreheads touched briefly.

"Commodore Christison and I are old, old friends. It was he who brought me from before the mast. It was he who guided me, promoted me, and is like a father to me. He did this despite being a tyrant. The men call him Kicking Billy."

He looked into her eyes and found no reason to stop his story.

"He rescued me from being shanghaied in San Francisco by crimps and runners." Griffin paused. "He became my mentor. Billy is the reason I am the master of *Providence*."

"Why is he called Kicking Billy?"

Griffin replied, "Before Maude, he needed little provocation to kick a man who appeared slow to do his duty. He did kick people."

"My goodness. I don't understand runners and crimps, Isaac."

"They're parasites. They like to slip on board a ship in harbor when the officers are not looking and steal the crew." Griffin's face showed disgust and anger. "It's slavery. Crimps, shanghaiers, or boarding masters get sailors as soon as they leave their ships, drug them, then sell them to ship owners or captains for the sailor's dead horse—that's his advance on his wages. Sometimes they'll steal sailors before they even get ashore.

"Once on board the ship, the sailors are beaten into submission and forced to sign articles but are paid no money for their work. There's so much money in places like San Francisco or Portland, the legislators, the police, the mayors. All turn a blind eye to it. It's slavery; that's all. Sixty dollars for a seaman, one hundred for a cook in San Francisco. It's done here in Boston too."

Kayleigh asked to hear more, although she was less interested in what he had to say than in what it told her about his character.

"Sometimes, these men reappear after working their way back from China or Australia; sometimes they just disappear and are never heard from again. That's why Billy rescued me. No one asks about sailors lost at sea."

Kayleigh smiled and squeezed his good hand lightly. "But you're here with me."

William Jr. played a polka. Since Isaac could not do the bold steps, he asked Kayleigh to sit with him.

When seated, Kayleigh looked directly into Griffin's eyes. "Will you show me your hand when we're alone? Does it cause you pain?"

He replied, "I've tried to hide it. It's badly scarred and discolored, an ugly white. I've seen people's reactions to it."

"I'm not afraid to see it or to hold it in my hand, Isaac, not at all."

Hanna's back was turned to the couple. She and Kicking Billy were a few feet away, near the piano. Hanna looked at Kicking Billy and asked, "What are they doing?"

Billy stopped and composed his thoughts. He then replied, "What Maude and I did when we realized we wanted each other."

Hanna asked her husband to play another waltz.

Kayleigh and Isaac resumed dancing together. Hanna observed that with this waltz they had not quickly resumed conversation. They were watching each other's eyes. Toward the end of the waltz, Hanna caught a brief snippet of conversation. Kayleigh had just giggled. "That would please me even if we are to marry." Hanna could not hear Isaac say, "Is that so impossible?"

It was getting late, and time for the event to wind down.

Kicking Billy turned to Hanna and whispered, "They are a matched pair of horses. Damned if they won't pull well together."

Hanna laughed quietly and smiled at her father-in-law's remark. "I never expected it. Who would?"

Seven

Joy and Consultation

O, gather me the rose, the rose,
While yet in flower we find it,
For summer smiles, but summer goes,
And winter waits behind it.
　　　　　　　　—William Ernest Henley

Saturday, March 30, 1872
Boston

Kayleigh MacKenna and Hanna Christison were seated in Hanna's small sitting room. Breakfast was over, and the ladies were, at last, out of earshot of the men and the servants. Hanna exclaimed, "Jane Austen! *Pride and Prejudice*! What happened last night? You despise Jane Austen."

"I like Isaac, though. I like him, and may even love him. It's incredible. Oh, Hanna, it was like being struck with lightning. The first time our eyes met. We both knew it. We both felt so restrained. We wanted to talk. The talk about Darwin—he revealed something to me. I don't think he wanted to embarrass your husband. He was really saying 'See, by revealing this to you, I'm saying I trust you.'"

"Kayleigh, this joy is so sudden. I've not seen you so happy in years. You're like a child."

"I am a child now, no more than sixteen. Ha. Dickens could write about me, *A Christmas Carol of Kayleigh MacKenna*. The sad ghosts of yesterday, the wonderful, the bright and shining spirits of

50

today, and tomorrow."

She rose from her chair.

"Come on, Hanna, no one will see us."

She took Hanna's hands in hers, formed a circle with their arms, and together they twirled round and round until their laughter overcame them.

"I never thought I'd see such a thing, Kayleigh. Please, tell me more."

"You know the letter from the doctor? The one I showed you?"

Hanna nodded her head.

"I let him read it. I explained it to him. He really didn't understand. I told him the doctor was politely saying that no man would marry me if he knew I was a nurse, a single woman nursing rough men. He still didn't understand. He said he admired courage and compassion. Then, can you imagine this? He said marriage was not so impossible. It became a joke, our little joke, that he would one day marry me."

Hanna replied, "That's bold. No one would joke about a marriage proposal in Boston—in all of New England; such a contract is so serious."

"We did. Can you believe it? He said he would marry a courageous and compassionate woman. He meant me, yes, me!"

"I don't believe it. I can't imagine any man in New England ever saying such words so casually." Hanna raised a hand to her mouth mimicking shock.

"That's not all. Darwin—he told me about women in the South Pacific."

Hanna eyes widened as she replied, "Did he tell you women wear no clothes from here on up?"

"We didn't talk about clothes. It's—well—better; yes, even better than that. It's natural for a woman to pursue a man and to want to sleep with him."

"Kayleigh, if I were your mother I'd wash your mouth out with soap. That's shocking. If people knew you repeated what he said, the word would spread all over Boston."

"That's not all. He said island women expect a man to please them."

51

Hanna was nearly out of her seat. "He's been at sea too long. He's becoming a savage."

"He says it's a perversion to deny our nature."

"Oh, my."

"He told me about seminary. I told him he could show me his hand."

"My dear Kayleigh, my dear sister, the last time something like this happened, this joy, this being moonstruck by a boy, was when we were at Vassar together. It was that boy from Mount Vernon Street. Remember? Something happened to you with him. I'm afraid for you. What happened? You've never told me anything."

"Don't ruin it for me, Hanna. I'm not that girl anymore. "

"Tell me, please."

"Hanna, things happen. Things like Isaac's hand. You can't change anything. It's best to forget and go on with your life."

"Oh, Kayleigh, don't do anything rash. Control your impulses. Talk to me when you feel you must do something risky."

"Hanna, I do need your help. We can't just meet each other. People would talk. I don't want that kind of trouble. Would you and William help us meet again? Perhaps we could picnic together or just play cards here at your house. We want to see each other. You and William could watch us and tell people—"

"Oh, and tell them what? That we leave you and Griffin alone together in our parlor?"

"Weren't you and William Jr. ever alone together? Wasn't it something you both wanted? Didn't you know it was time to sit together at the piano with no eyes watching you?"

Hanna reluctantly smiled. "I'll see, Kayleigh. William needs time—I need him to get away from his work. Seeing Griffin court you might even inspire him."

***

It was only after sleep had overcome Kayleigh that the memory came again. It came to her home, to her bed, to her dreams. She felt her sweat run cold and pool at the nape of her neck. She felt fear. She dreamed of running, sprinting down a path only to find it closed over with brambles and twisted vines, and then running again in another direction. She was running away from him, that man. Each time she thought she could stop and rest, his footsteps and breathing snatched sanctuary away and set her sprinting in terror.

He was gaining on her. As she forced her mind into consciousness of her bedroom, she saw him. He stood over her, leaning by the side of her bed. She saw the anger on his face once more and knew he had exposed himself; he was erect, grotesque; he would beat down her resistance and force himself within her. As she awoke he faded until there was nothing but his face, and then only the darkness of her bedroom and her terror.

Kayleigh remembered the rape. She remembered the fear, his hands, his words—"Bitch, cunt"—his fists, and her helplessness, how soiled and ashamed she felt. Again he threatened her; he threatened to tear away the joy she'd discovered with Isaac. Now she felt guilt. She had brought this upon herself. If Isaac knew, would he want her? Could any man ever want her? She could not bring herself to answer her own question. Everyone would blame her.

Sleep came over her again, mercifully. It was a few hours before dawn. She remembered the gentleness of Isaac's fingers, his laughter with her, the joy she would fight to keep. She felt Isaac's hand in hers and remembered how he drew her hand to his chest—sleep at last. She dreamt of islands, dreamt of sunlight, warm sand on her bare back and legs, and dreamt of the sounds of tropical birds and the sweet taste of tropical fruit.

***

It was now Monday, noon. Isaac Griffin had arranged a carriage to take him and Kicking Billy to an old roost, the Belle and Maiden Tavern. The two seamen sat at a corner table with glasses of cold porter and beefsteaks.

"I know what I'm talking about." Kicking Billy was mildly frustrated with Isaac. "It happens." He struggled with the words. "Something tells thee she's the one; it happened to me. I knew I wanted to marry Maude"—he struggled with his words—"the second I saw her. Don't expect me to tell thee to be cautious."

Isaac did not expect cautious words. Kicking Billy had taken Maude to sea with him. Isaac knew how she had charmed her husband, taken the edge off his tongue and his temper, and made meals pleasant for the mates by sparing them from long periods of silence and occasional angry outbursts from her husband.

"She's bold and beautiful, Billy."

He stuttered, "Thee lets her boldness bother thee? If she came from Tahiti or Java or Spain, her brass...wouldn't...hell, thee'd like it. I remember when thee chased women. Go after her, damn it. Don't be surprised by what thee learns about her; she'll test thee. She has to know she can depend on thee, that thee are not playing her along. Women got to be sure. As sure as hell, so she'll test thee. Thee will not see it coming. I'm warning thee."

Griffin looked at his friend, hoping for an answer, an insight. "Those women I chased after—it isn't like that now. A week or two and I would be bored with them and ready for another. Some no more than a night. Kayleigh's different.

"Sure, we are attracted to each other. She even joked about it. There's more. I can't explain it. I've never had such hunger before. It was like we were slowly becoming part of each other. My thoughts were hers; hers were mine."

Billy smiled warmly, "Son, I firmly believe I...thee needs a woman. Miss Kayleigh is pretty." He paused in order to form his words. Then he said clearly, "I like her, Isaac. Damn it, I like her. If thee must have concerns, fear that thee will lose her."

***

Later that week, both Kayleigh and Griffin received an invitation to join William Jr. and Hanna for a picnic aboard a chartered catboat. Isaac Griffin responded by inviting Kayleigh, Hanna, and William Jr. to a day of sailing on Griffin's yacht and home, the *San Matias*.

Hanna had succeeded in bringing them together again; she and William would soon—by mid-April—depart from their parlor to give them privacy. Isaac and Kayleigh realized they could not stay apart. They soon met alone. Kayleigh had ignored Hanna's warning as she had ignored her mother's.

Eight

Luncheon Aboard San Matias

Here, a little child I stand,
Heaving up my either hand:
Cold as paddocks though they be,
Here I lift them up to thee,
For a benison to fall
On our meat, and on us all. Amen.
—Robert Herrick

Thursday, April 11, 1872
Boston

The Belle and Maiden was open and doing its usual brisk business of catering to the needs of harbor pilots and older seamen. These men loved it for the food, the conversations maintained around the clock, New England fare, and porter. The wood for the paneling was said to have come from a British prize taken by none other than the *Constitution* herself. The patina bore convincing evidence of its history.

The tavern common room was enveloped in the blue-gray smoke of pipes and cigars, and the rolling cacophony of the patrons when Isaac Griffin and Jimmy Meehan walked through the door. The word "sir" greeted Griffin, as he was a ship's master, and Jimmy Meehan was greeted with a wink and a slap on the back based on numerous past visits, memorable philosophical arguments, and his willing laugh. They were shown to their table and offered coffee or tea. Neither man needed a menu, and Griffin, being in a good mood from last night's visit with Kayleigh MacKenna, offered to buy the breakfast.

Eileen Meagher brought Griffin his usual slice of ham, buckwheat pancakes, and syrup and set them before him in a gracious style. "Here's your breakfast, sir."

The widow Meagher was in her early forties and compared well to a Glasgow-built steel bark for sheer and for weatherliness. She made a point of displaying her ample bosom to Jimmy Meehan when serving him his bacon, eggs over easy, johnnycakes, and coffee. "Top of the morning, Mr. Meehan. I hope you'll find these to yer liking."

Jimmy, all too aware of what "these" were, replied, "They wud please a bishop." He gave her a lingering pat on her rump to emphasize his pleasure with what she had offered. "I'll see you t'evening, Eileen."

Griffin did not believe in wasting time, money, or words. "We'll be having a guest for lunch today, Jimmy. Maybe some bean soup, small beefsteaks, beets, and soft bread would do, but do your best."

The old sailor muttered an "Aye" to his captain, while restraining both a smile and a chuckle. He still knew how to read the wind and box a compass. Jimmy noticed that his captain was aware of anything out of place, anything less than shipshape on *San Matias*, and had spent the prior week on hands and knees with Griffin putting her in a fine state of shine and order. The old sailor knew something was unusual; he had noticed a strand of bright red hair on the captain's dark wool jacket earlier this morning. The hair had not been there before Friday when he had brushed his captain's shore clothing.

"So who will be our guest, Captain? The commodore from the navy yard? Or is it Miss Kayleigh?"

Isaac laughed. "Of the two, who would you prefer?"

"Have yer ever seen a pretty commodore?"

***

Kayleigh MacKenna was excited. She could consume barely a single piece of buttered toast and only one cup of coffee for breakfast.

57

She fussed with her maid while the maid helped her dress in one of Hanna Christison's dresses borrowed for the occasion.

"Miss Kayleigh, you do look fine. Your sea captain will be pleased. Yes, miss, he will."

Now Kayleigh paced nervously in her parlor, in the small townhome her father had provided for her near the hospital. She wanted to address Griffin with some small word of endearment, but thought "dear" was too common and "darling" too bold. Perhaps with just the right inflection, the right tone, letting the word linger a bit, "Isaac" would do. She paced, she fretted, and she adjusted her hair.

The brass knocker on her door rapped. She did not wait for the maid but opened the door herself. There he stood before her with his derby in his left hand and in his best suit of clothes. She thought of all she had rehearsed but instinctively rushed into a quick embrace followed by an impulsive kiss.

"Have you had breakfast, Kayleigh?"

"I had one earlier."

"Are you wearing comfortable shoes, no French heels? We are going to walk a little today."

She made sure she had eye contact, and with a slight flutter of her lids, and with her sweetest tone, she said, "Are we going to the country?"

"You'll see."

Griffin had hired a carriage and driver to take them to *San Matias*. It was a beautiful ride on a beautiful day in a city they both loved. She was happy and fairly bubbled with excitement. She talked about the week to come. She looked forward to observing a surgery. Her questions had impressed the young surgeon. Isaac listened without hearing but with absolute absorption in her facial expressions, the arc of her eyebrows, and the magic flush appearing and disappearing across her nose.

"You're taking me to Broad Street. We're going to the *San Matias*!"

The carriage stopped at the base of a pier, and the two continued down the pier to its head. Along the way, a few sailors showed their appreciation for Kayleigh with "Good mornings" and beaming faces. Some cheered encouragement to Isaac, calling him "Captain." The sailors respected their limits and the mate on duty.

Kayleigh was delighted, and her bright red blush announced it.

Upon reaching the end of the pier, Kayleigh squealed like an excited girl. She fairly flew across the gangplank and went straight to the tiller. "I love her. She's so beautiful and fast."

"She is beautiful. I saw a Le Havre pilot boat I liked and had *San Matias* built on her lines."

"I'm jealous of her." Kayleigh feigned seriousness.

"Well, I'm glad of that!"

They climbed down the companionway. Upon seeing Kayleigh, Jimmy Meehan beamed with delight and muttered under his breath, "Aye, Captain, she's going to pull you in and keep you a happy paddy, if you're man enough to keep her."

The light streamed into the saloon from the butterfly hatch. The teak gleamed. The cabinetry all had louvered doors with polished brass hardware. Jimmy had rigged the dining table and placed a blue-checkered tablecloth over it with a coffee cup serving as a vase for flowers.

"Is this your idea, Jimmy?" Kayleigh asked as she pointed to the flowers.

"Yes, miss, and I have a grand meal for us, too." He began to take the sturdy earthenware plates from racks over the galley sink and set the table for three.

"You'll eat with us, Jimmy?"

"Yes, indeed. This is my home too. I have a bunk in the fore-peak cabin."

"Will you be going with the captain on the *Providence*, Jimmy?"

"No, miss. Me job's right here with this boat. I have to pump out the bilge twice a day. When the captain goes to sea, I take care of her. When the *Providence* clears soundings, *San Matias* will go into the yard for repairs and will be laid up in September for the winter."

"What will you do then?"

Her question reflected true concern. Jimmy Meehan delighted

her with his humor and with the kindness he had shown for Hanna on the sail and picnic aboard *San Matias*.

"I stay with the boat and see that things are done right."

"Do you still live on the boat?"

"I stay on her as long as she's in the water. Otherwise, I stay at the Seamen's Bethel. It's safe there."

"Are you hungry, Kayleigh?"

"Aye, Captain!" Kayleigh laughed.

"Well, Jimmy, bring it to us smartly, if you please."

The meal was well prepared, an obvious tribute to her and a clear sign of Jimmy Meehan's approval of her, perhaps even with his captain for bringing her into their lives.

She found it surprising that although the flatware was just the essentials, Jimmy had correctly arranged the setting.

Kayleigh ate with gusto. Both men silently wondered how she could remain so slim.

Jimmy asked, "Have you had grog, miss?"

"No."

Jimmy took a bottle of dark Jamaican rum from the cabinet, poured a measure into each of the three earthenware mugs, then added two measures of water and squeezed a little lime juice into each mug. "Some put sugar in it, miss, some don't. Well, here's to sweethearts and wives, as they say in the navy."

Jimmy did not finish the rest of the toast. Isaac understood Jimmy's concern. Jimmy would not cheapen this occasion.

Kayleigh sipped the grog and added a pinch of sugar.

"Sometimes, miss, aboard ship we sweeten it with a bit of molasses, as molasses is all we have."

Kayleigh enjoyed her grog and enjoyed Jimmy Meehan. She wondered if Jimmy was comfortable living alone while Isaac was at sea. Kayleigh offered to help Jimmy clean up. Jimmy, however, would have nothing to do with it. He quickly and efficiently cleaned and restored the saloon to pristine condition.

"Captain, I'm heading ashore nigh. I left somethin' at th' Belle an' Maiden."

Griffin waited a few moments and then climbed the companionway ladder to make sure Jimmy had left. When he returned to the saloon, he and Kayleigh kissed, and then kissed again, hungry kisses, while embracing, with his good hand stroking the small of her back.

They were alone and free to talk. Like all new couples, they were perpetually starved for information about each other, for details of their lives and the troubles and joys of their souls. Both knew the course their lives had now taken. The two also knew their joint destination and the rocks and shoals of religion and separation they must navigate through.

Griffin was amazed with Kayleigh. She accepted her belief without question and found comfort in her church. She was one of the children He had suffered to come unto Him, and she had remained so even into her adult years. She told Griffin she could bear being alone knowing he would always return to her.

She thought of those things she wanted to do. When she imagined Griffin lying naked next to her, her heart froze and for a moment became a stone. *Did he notice?* She spoke impulsively to mask her reaction.

"Isaac, I want you to meet my family. Will you come to Mass with us tomorrow?"

Nine

O'Reilly's Daughter

For O'Reilly played on the big brass drum
O'Reilly had a mind for murder and slaughter,
O'Reilly had a bright red glittering eye,
And he kept an eye on his lovely daughter.

O'Reilly's Daughter
Traditional Irish Bawdy Song

Sunday, April 14, 1872
Back Bay, Home of Kayleigh's Parents

Mass had finished. The meal following communion had been eaten. Griffin was with Jim MacKenna, Kayleigh's father, as he and Kayleigh had planned. Kayleigh accompanied her mother to the garden.

Mary MacKenna spoke. "It's gonna to be so pretty this summer, Kayleigh. There'll be a path of zinnias leadin' t' the gazebo. There, under the shade, that's where the lilacs will grow, and over there, the lilies.

"Let's sit in the gazebo; 'tis not that chilly t'day. I suspect you've somethin' to say t' me. Peggy, would yer bring us some tea? Don't hurry with it."

Mother and daughter entered the gazebo. The daughter stood near the railing, looking off into the distance. The mother sat on the bench to Kayleigh's left.

"Sit by me, Kayleigh, here."

Kayleigh joined her mother on the bench. They turned to face each other, their knees nearly touching. Both assumed a pose of readiness, of anticipation to hold each other, to take each other's hands in hers.

"Ma, I love him. He's the man I want to marry."

Their hands joined.

"When did this come about?"

"I knew it when I met him, Ma."

"You're sure?" Her mother smiled.

"Yes, I've never felt anything so strongly. I love him and I know he loves me."

Kayleigh saw her mother's eyes redden as if to tear, then change suddenly, intensely. "Is your man Catholic?" Mary answered her own question, "Well, I know he's not. He's never been ter mass before. I could see that this morning."

Kayleigh stiffened. "What will Pa say?"

"He won't like it. It has nothing ter do with Isaac personally, just that he's Protestant. Would your man convert when it comes t' that?"

"I don't know, Ma. I don't understand what he believes in. There's something. He does feel something; I know that. Will you help me convince Pa?"

"This Griffin just can't refuse to do anythin' at all. Does your man love you that much?"

Kayleigh nodded. "Yes."

"Well, we'll see. I've always wanted you to be happy. Never have I seen you as happy as you are now. You're my sprog—always."

The two women embraced.

"Still, do you think I've not seen how you've behaved these years? What's been going on with you, Kayleigh?"

"Ma, please don't. I thought you promised to stop. Let the past stay buried. I only care about Isaac now."

Kayleigh continued, "We've come so close. We went to Hanna's house Friday. We were alone in the parlor. He built a fire for me in the fireplace; that was all the light. We had been talking about a painting of a girl, where she's setting the table for her mother?"

Mary then inquired, "What happened before Isaac? Why did you change so suddenly?"

Kayleigh pretended she had not understood her mother. "I sat on his lap. I wanted to and I did it. I guess I was thinking about how I used to sit in Pa's lap when I was a girl. I can't lie. I let my hair fall and then took his face in my hands and kissed him. I don't have to tell you, do I, Ma?"

"No."

"I think if he had pressed me, I could not have forced myself to stop him. Then when I felt him—"

Kayleigh paused to see if her mother understood. She was reluctant to speak that word. Her mother sat bolt erect on the bench, her hands lying palm down on her lap; she bent slightly forward at the waist.

"I was afraid, Ma. I wanted him but was afraid of him all at the same time."

"Would he hurt you? Would he force you?"

"Oh, no. He'd never hurt me. It was my fear, my memory."

"Memory! What memory? Tell me!" Her mother's face seemed to flush with anger.

The two women, mother and daughter, moved instinctively away from each other at the mention of the word "memory"—one in fear, the other in frustration. The daughter continued her story and ignored her mother's question, although she wanted to tell her mother what had happened. She wanted to be free of the fear possessing her.

"I let him hold me and kissed him again. That's when I told him to go. Then I said we could be together Saturday. I hoped he understood—"

Her mother interrupted her by suddenly taking hold of her shoulders as if she was about to scold her child. "Kayleigh, I have eyes in me head. Someone's hurt you. I knew it wasn't Isaac. You've tried ter hide somethin' these years. You're hiding it now. It has ter do with that college boy. I just know it does. It hurts me you won't tell me. Please—?"

Mary MacKenna stopped, obviously searching for the correct

words. Kayleigh realized her mother did not need words; her mother's face revealed deep unshakable love.

"Don't you think I heard you cryin'? Don't you think I know you took baths mornin' and night? What were you tryin' ter wash away and couldn't?"

Mary shook Kayleigh's shoulders gently, then stopped when it seemed she realized what she had done.

"There was the week you spent with the Dominicans at their convent, a cloistered convent. You can't imagine the sorrow that caused me. After that, there were no more men in your life. Those ugly dresses too, and the hospital. Tis plain ter me you were hurt badly. And—and all you ever say is 'Things happen.' What things? You let my imagination torture me."

Mary's face implored her daughter.

"Now you've hurt me, 'cause you won't tell me. Tell me now, please."

"Ma, things happen; that's all."

"No. No. No. Don't tell me that. Tell me what things." Mary released Kayleigh's shoulders to raise her hands near her own shoulders. Mary's hands seemed to shake in frustration and then dropped to her lap. Kayleigh imagined her mother's mind pleading with her but expecting silence. *Things happen, things happen, Ma.* Kayleigh could not restrain her own tears.

"Ma, I've never wanted to hurt you. I know what your brothers did in 'sixty-seven. I know they were transported. You don't need more—"

"Stop it. Remember who I am. I love you. I'm not made of plaster. The potatoes had turned black before your father and I left Ireland. There were corpses rotting, people begging t' get into the workhouses—I know evil. People were desperate then. They did anything t' stay alive. What d'yer think it was like fer us when we got here?"

"Ma—no."

"Trust me. I love you." Kayleigh felt her mother's hands on her shoulders again.

"Ma, I disobeyed you. I trusted him, and—and he raped me."

"It was that boy."

"It's my fault, Ma. It's all my fault."

"Oh. And I suppose the bastard had nothin' t' do with it?"

"That's what the priest said. It's the woman's fault, always the woman's. It started with Eve."

"What have celibate men ever known, but fear of us? Did they send you ter the Dominicans?"

"I couldn't accept holy orders. I felt so soiled, so guilty."

"You should have told me. Have you told him?"

"I'm afraid to."

"Why?"

"Men don't marry women who aren't virgins."

"Does he love you? Tell him. He needs to know."

"What if he says I've tricked him? What if he says I'm immoral?"

"You have t' trust him. Tell him, Kayleigh. You can't build a marriage on lies."

"But, Ma—that's not all, Ma. That boy, he was—I saw his—he forced himself into me—he beat me."

"So now you're afraid. That's not the way it is when a man loves you, nor you him."

Kayleigh saw her mother smile, a wonderful smile, a knowing smile, filled with assurance.

"No, not at all. Trust yourself. Trust your Isaac. Peggy is coming with the tea."

***

Isaac Griffin saw that Kayleigh's father, Jim MacKenna, was not a handsome man. He was aging, his features showed the remains of physical conflict, and his suits were from the best tailors but could never add dignity or grace to his stature. No, he might not be handsome, Griffin concluded, but he was as imposing as all hell. Kayleigh's father smiled and spoke in a velvet brogue. "Well, boyo, I'd say there's a lot to talk over. Come into me library."

Griffin had spent the entire night thinking about the words he was about to speak. He would ask the father for permission to court Kayleigh.

"You're not Catholic, are you, Griffin?"

"No, sir, I'm not. I know what Kayleigh's religion means to her. I'd never interfere."

"Come over t' me desk. There's something I want to show yer. See?"

Jim MacKenna handed Griffin a badly charred piece of oak.

"I don't understand. I'm sorry, you'll have to explain."

Jim continued, "I thought so. She's not told you about me, has she?" Jim MacKenna slipped increasingly into a brogue as he spoke.

"That wood came from County Sligo, in 'forty-six. 'Twas was a piece of the door ter me father's little cottage, our home. I saved that piece after the landlord threw us out and burned the cottage down. My father died in the fire. He tried to save my cradle. It was part of me mother's dowry. In her family, it went to the firstborn girl. The roof collapsed on me pa. The beadles made a sham of saving his life; the rent agent said he had it coming t' him, the tossing. The soldiers tried, but it was too late. Thatch and all."

Jim MacKenna opened a hidden compartment in the desk and removed a hand-forged butcher knife. "I killed him with that, the man who collected the rack rent and threw the torch. I was seventeen." There was a pause. "You're not goin' to ask how I killed him?"

"No."

"So you think ya know what happened. No, ya don't. Not all of it. I enjoyed it, the killin'. He wasn't the last either. I fled to Antrim. Made a livin' fightin' with me fists fer prizes. The killin' only stopped when Mary an' me immigrated to America. We came over in 'fifty."

"What's your point?"

"I don't want yer t' see Kayleigh again. I don't want a Protestant seeing my daughter. If she's t' marry, it'll be an Irish Catholic, Irish like me. Not a Yankee Protestant."

"So the wood and the knife are a threat?"

Jim MacKenna smiled, then answered, "Yes."

"Does Kayleigh have a say in this?"

"No. I'd rather see her die a spinster than marry the likes of yer."

"You don't know me. I love her. You won't stop us."

"Yer better leave now. Say good-bye t' Kayleigh and me wife and excuse yerself. I won't throw you out if yer'll do that."

Griffin saw him pick the heavy knife up from the desk again. He held the handle in his right hand with his thumb and forefinger where the blade and handle joined. He was poised to thrust it. His left forefinger tested the point.

"Do you think it's that easy? Has she told you about us? Has she told you anything about me at all?" There was no reaction on MacKenna's face. Griffin stepped closer. The point of the knife was now just inches from his chest. "I'd rather die than give her up."

"Go on, leave now. There's time fer that later."

***

That evening Mary MacKenna sat with her husband on their bed. She wore a loose cotton chemise that exposed her shoulders and revealed the shadow outline of her breasts in the gaslight by her nightstand.

"Jimmy, brush out me hair, fifty strokes."

Then Jim MacKenna spoke, ignoring his wife.

"She has to let him go. He's no good for her. I'll see ter it meself, Mary."

"Do you think it's that simple, Jimmy? Can't you see they're just like we were? Could me pa stop us with threats?"

"Didn't matter. We were Catholic."

"If they'd known, Jimmy, the church'd excommunicate yer for sure, for that night, fer that priest, th' traitor.

"Do yer think me parents approved? They knew. Every Catholic in Antrim knew who yer were. Didn't yer hear the whispers, 'Shhh, that's Jimmy MacKenna walkin' down the street'? My pa and ma let us marry because I told them. I told them we were making love. I told them I was pregnant."

Jim MacKenna rose to his feet. His face showed surprise.

Mary would not stop. "How long do you think Kayleigh and

Isaac can hold out? Lord, it burns in 'em, just as it burned in us, Jimmy. Remember? I don't give a damn about mortal sin. Did that stop us? Sooner or later Kayleigh and Griffin will do the deed. Do yer remember when we snuck off and did it the first time? I was so scared I'd have yer baby and you'd git yourself killed."

The anger returned to Jim MacKenna's face. "I'll kill him if I have ter. She can have her bastard in a convent. No one will know."

"Do you want Kayleigh hating you? Can't you understand that, Jimmy? My God, man."

"I don't care."

"No! That's your hate talkin.' Remember the little girl that once sat on your lap. She's a woman now, a woman. She was violated, raped, and I guess yer were too busy t' notice, brotherhood business and all, or was it just making money?"

"Griffin?"

"Jesus, Jimmy, not him."

"That college bastard from Beacon Hill!"

Jim MacKenna slammed his fist on the dressing table, knocking Mary's jewelry box onto the floor.

"Now look what yer did. What I'm trying t' tell yer is she's a woman, she's a woman, not a little girl saying, 'Yes, Pa. Yes, Pa.' She'll ignore you, Jimmy. She wants her man. Help her. Make her happy. Talk t' the bishop for her. Don't you want her t' hang round yer neck, t' thank you, ter kiss yer cheek and cry and say she loves you?"

"Damn it, Mary, I—"

"No, Jimmy, I'll not let yer. I'll not share my bed with a man who could do that ter his own daughter. Take your boots from under me bed an' go. I'll pick up the spilt jewelry."

Ten

Conspiracy

So the chief captain then let the young man depart, and charged him, see thou tell no man that thou hast shewed these things to me.

—Acts 23:22

Friday, April 19, 1872
Boston

It had been a good evening at the Harp and Plough. Eamon Kavanagh had finished cleaning the bar glasses and returning them to their shelves for use when men working nights were released and would come to the saloon. He hoped the two well-dressed men huddled in the corner had noticed and had decided to leave. They had not. So the muscular Irishman started to stack the chairs on their tables noisily. He spoke to gather the attention of the two men. "Damn chairs! A rayle paddy drinks 'is Guinness standin' on 'is legs."

One of the gentlemen turned toward Eamon and flashed a hand sign. John J. O'Corkerane had informed the barkeep that he was a member of the Clan na Gael. Had Eamon continued, O'Corkerane would have raised the walnut stock of his Colt pocket pistol out of the right-hand suit coat pocket. Jim MacKenna, the older of the two, the one with the broken nose and a build like a boxcar, rose from his seat and placed a five-dollar bill in Eamon's hand and said, "Quiet. We're almost finished."

Jim MacKenna returned, sat in his chair, and addressed his acquaintance. "I want yer t' do this fer me, Jack."

O'Corkerane replied, "Killin' a man's not exactly like askin' fer a match to light yer pipe."

"You know what I've done fer Clan na Gael, all that money, places fer people to hide. I'd do it meself, but you know the risk. If I'm caught, how will yer replace me? How would yer find a paddy that's done as well as me? That's out in the public eye like me. That's as connected as me."

A ridge formed on O'Corkerane's brow. "All I'm saying is that killin' a man t' revenge his daughter is hardly our line of work. We'll do it, though; he's Protestant. But after all these years?"

"All I care is he's done it. Besides me, you'd be revengin' a few Irish families too. This man has raped more than one man's daughter. He thinks our shame protects him. He thinks there's nobody that cares for these poor girls. Send a message, Jack. Once it's known, just watch the money pour in."

"What about this Isaac Griffin?"

"Ah, he's a thorn in me side. Mary's being hard on me. Won't even—damn women."

"So he's still seeing yer daughter?" No emotion showed on the Clan na Gael man's face.

"Yes, Mary knows it too. Says he's a good man, a sea captain, going to be a full partner in a shipping line. Damn women, heads hard as pig iron."

"Where does this line trade?"

"They ship grain from California to Liverpool, then back to Boston or else to Australia, general cargo."

"Have ya ever thought how helpful that could be to us, Jimmy? I mean, just think about the money we could smuggle in; arms, too. The Sassenach would never suspect it from Boston blue bloods. We could get a brither or two out of Australia too, maybe Mary's."

"Yer asking me to let me daughter wed a Protestant?"

"Hold yer horses, man. Ya'd kill yer daughter for us if ya had to—remember the oath ya took." He observed Jim MacKenna shudder.

71

"If ya wouldn't, we'd kill her and ya, too; that's the oath we both took. Soon or never, Jimmy lad, soon or never. Remember Cleary in East Boston? Ya'd not be the first. I'm just saying think this through. The blue blood's enough fer now.

"Do ya want to kill the Beacon Hill lad yerself, fer old times' sake? Ya know he didn't murder yer daughter. Ya could beat him. Maim him even. Better justice than we'd get."

Jim MacKenna smiled. "I want Mary— she has t' know how I feel about Kayleigh."

"Well, me boy, while yer waitin', just think about having a shippin' line in our hip pocket, a happy daughter, and a few grandchildren to carry around on those shoulders of yers. Wud yer Mary like that?

"What's the name of this line? Where's their office?"

"Christison and Son. Third floor of the India Wharf building."

Eamon Kavanagh made the sign of the cross as the two departed into an East Boston fog.

***

William Jr. looked up from his desk to see a man step from the shadows and stand at the bottom of his table. It was Saturday evening, nine p.m., the close of William Jr.'s business day. Jack O'Corkerane spoke, "Sorry to startle ya so, Mr. Christison. I won't be here but a minute. There's talk that yer firm is in trouble. I might be able t' help a bit if yer'll hear me out."

William Jr. soon gained control of his composure. "Who are you? You're Irish. Who let you in? There's no work for you here."

"The door was open. Maybe th' watchman fergot to latch it closed. I mean yer no harm. I'm here t' talk business, buyin' and tradin'. Ya do something for me and there's money in it fer yer."

"You're proposing something illegal. My family—"

"Yer family got what it's got by tradin' rum fer human flesh, African slaves, from the Gold Coast. It was yer grandfather Alva that made the money. Don't throw th' honor of yer family at me. Seeing how ya sold two ships fer what cash ya could get, I'd say yer honor is fast runnin' out on ya."

The Irishman smiled; his brogue grew soft.

"Now, what if I knew how ya could make some money? What if I could help ya ship yer crews? What if I could help ya with the docks?"

"You're Irish scum. I doubt—"

O'Corkerane ignored him and continued, "We raised two armies here and invaded Canada twice. Did ya ferget that? Have ya any idea th' money I collect? What if I could arrange a cargo fer ya t'day? What if ya got premium freight rates and a bonus if gets it to San Francisco quickly?"

"You?"

"Yes, me. The freight would be in railroad equipment for the Central Pacific, equipment they'd be willin t' pay a premium fer 'cause it's too much money t' drag over the Rockies."

"How?"

"Have ya heard of Jim MacKenna?"

"The blockade runner during the war?"

"Yes, Kayleigh MacKenna's father."

"I'll be damned. She never said so."

"All I'd be askin' of ya in return would be to ship some barrels fer me to Liverpool, machinery; that's all. Well, a dollar or two if it came t' that."

"I'd be smuggling!"

"What's smuggling but avoiding taxes and tariffs? D'ya think old Alva would refuse me? Everything would be cash."

"How much money are you talking about?"

Eleven

The Psalm of Solomon

If thou must love me, let it be for nought
Except for love's sake only.
—Elizabeth Barrett Browning

Saturday, April 27, 1872
Boston

Kayleigh watched Isaac build the fire in the parlor fireplace of the little house her father had bought for her near the hospital. It was still chilly in the evenings. She watched as he carefully layered the wood using only his left arm and hand. When the time came for the match, she produced the box, opened it, and handed the match to him. She held the box so he could strike the match. How she enjoyed such moments, the commonplace they shared. He stooped, lit the fire, and stood next to her. He placed his arm around her waist and said, "I have something for you." He kissed the top of her head, and with his left hand gave her a small jewelry box. "I can't open it. I don't want to leave you, to leave you with no bond between us except words. Will you marry me?"

The moment had come. It did not come as a storm as she had imagined it would, but gently, reflecting the man she loved. She looked at him, imagined his anticipation, saw the expectations he harbored in his smile. It was at that point the tears broke. She knew it was time to tell him. How angry would he become? What would he say? The anger would be justified, no matter how bitter. She wanted his love.

"I'm not a virgin..."

He replied, "Is that what you've been holding back?"

"Isaac, you don't deserve me. How could you ever trust me? Wouldn't you always wonder?"

Her hands started to tremble. Did he notice? She tried to hide them in the folds of her skirt.

Useless.

He replied, "Do you trust me? You're not some wanton woman; there's more. Tell me."

"I've been raped. It was my fault."

She grasped her hands in front of her. One hand grasped the other briefly as if each hand wanted to hide the other.

He noticed. His face. What will he say?

He replied, "What happened?"

She had no control of her guilt, no control of her fear, and the sobs came as tears welled in the bottoms of her eyes, then reddened them and left her lashes wet. They irritated her and she rubbed them with the backs of her hands. He offered her his handkerchief. She took it, wiped her eyes, and blew her nose into it, and when she realized what she had done, she felt embarrassment, foolish embarrassment. When she looked at his face, she saw that he smiled.

"I was in college. I met this boy who was so patient with me. He seemed to be tender, like you. I trusted him completely, just as I trust you now. Hanna warned me. My ma warned me. My pa forbade me to see him at all." She saw no hint of anger; his eyes remained soft and focused on hers, and she heard him tell her to go on.

"I met with him alone in his friend's house. He grabbed the hem of my skirt, lifted it, and touched my thigh, the inside, above my stocking. I brushed his hand away before—then he grabbed my breast. He tore my clothing, ripping my blouse open."

She pointed to her bosom.

"I told him no, to stop. I begged him.

"He called me a bitch, an Irish whore who should consider herself lucky to be taken by a man like him. He placed his hand up my skirt again, past my—I clawed at his face. It bled. He hit me with his fist, knocking me down. That's when he—I saw his manhood. Oh, Isaac. I couldn't fight him off and—"

He interrupted, "Who said you were at fault? Who?"

"My priest. It's what everyone knows."

He replied, "They're wrong. You're wrong. You fought."

"I'm afraid of—I don't know if I can share my bed—just the sight of it again—"

"Shhh, listen to you. How many times have you held my hand to your breast? How many times have we kissed? How many times have we been to the edge, our bodies demanding each other? Ask yourself why. Has it been only me?"She heard his words and struggled to reply. She opened her mouth. Pain, fear, sorrow, joy, each held it open; she gasped for words, but no words would come.

He spoke. "Why did you wait this long to tell me? Why couldn't you trust me? I knew it. I knew every time you remembered it. It came to you while we were—you sat on my lap. Don't you think I knew? Those words you'd say. Things happen. The coldness that followed."

She replied, "But you don't know—"

He replied, "I know about carrying a piece of hell with you. I know about dreams. Even making the fire—"

"It's not the same. It's not rape."

He replied, "No, it's not. The suffering has to stop. The bastard took your virginity, but he'll not take you from me. Come closer, please."

She looked into his eyes and stepped toward him. He held her.

"I'll not let you go, not me. It's up to you, Kayleigh. Marry me or leave me. I'll have a decision. Rest your head on my chest, just one more time; let me remember this."

She did.

He asked, "Are you afraid of me?"

No answer.

"I'm leaving for Bath tomorrow. Don't let me leave without something, even if it's no, that you'll not see me again, you'll not marry me. I still want you, rape or not, affair or not. I love you."

Kayleigh knew there was no retreat. The time had come.

"Isaac, undress me. Don't question me. Undress me, please; I can't by myself, the buttons on my blouse. I can't reach them in back. Isn't that silly?" She smiled.

He started to say, "I've only my—"

She would not let him finish his words. "Do it slowly. Please? I need you to undress me slowly. Start with the blouse, please."

Kayleigh wanted to feel the heat and tension of desire, to feel this need consume any fear she might have. She hoped his actions would be slow, kissing her body, caressing it, his passion leading hers. She hoped her arousal would triumph over her fear and free her from her past.

Griffin asked no questions.

He stood behind her and removed her blouse; he helped her from its sleeves and let the garment fall in front of her. Then he removed the pins holding her hair to the top of her head. He gathered her hair and placed it over her right shoulder, letting the hair fall to her front. He kissed the nape of her neck. She closed her eyes and leaned her head against his.

He resumed slowly removing her clothing; when her camisole fell, she wore nothing above her waist. He stood at her back. He placed his arms around her while making no contact and held his hands out with his palms toward her body, offering them to her. She hesitated, then placed her hands on his, whole and maimed, and brought them to her breasts. She remembered his hand. "Does it—"

"No, hold it there. Let me imagine."

He removed the remainder of her garments and knelt before her. She reached for him with her hands, bringing his face against her belly. His arms closed around her naked hips.

Kayleigh's emotions resembled an ingot of molten steel being drawn on a forge by a blacksmith's hammer. She felt the heat of passion and no fear. The forging continued hammer blow by hammer blow, drawing her ever stronger, ever more resolved. She thought of her soul; she thought of her innocence before God.

"Isaac, I want God to bless us. Pledge your love to me before Him."

Griffin responded, "If you were another woman, another time, I might simply tell you what I think you want to hear. I can't. I won't do that. We should marry. Were you taught the Bible, the Old Testament, and the Psalms of Solomon? Do you understand it?"

She whispered yes.

Then he said, "I am your husband and take you as my wife. My life is as much yours as mine. I will have no other. I will protect you always. I will be the father of your children. You are my beloved, my partner with whom I will share all of my life."

She felt joy, her face warmed, but she cried.

"We don't have to do this, not for me, Kayleigh."

"I want to do it, Isaac." She stopped talking. She raised her hand and gently touched his lips with her fingers.

"Then I am your wife, the mother of your children, your loving companion for the remainder of my days, and my life is as much yours as mine. I take you as my husband, my beloved. May God bless and witness our union."

She heard him reply, "Amen."

Kayleigh did undress Isaac; she wanted to. She touched him there beneath his linens and observed him close his eyes and draw breath in deeply and slowly. She was now Eve and every woman since time began.

Kayleigh's eyes had seen nakedness at the hospital. Yet Griffin's body astounded her, delighted her. It was pale where his clothes hid him from the sun. His back, shoulders, and arms were heavily muscled; there were tattoos, and there were scars. She had no fear of him because she knew he was hers, smiling gently and offering himself to her, kneeling before her in supplication.

They knew they would never forget this moment. They were to both give and receive their gifts of love and passion. It was apparent to her he had known women before, women who accepted their nature and his without shame, as he had told her. They'd taught him how to please. They'd taught him that patience and tenderness yielded to passion. This he gave to her. For this she thanked them without jealousy, for he was hers alone.

Now Kayleigh felt something entirely new. It exceeded whatever pleasure and urgency she had once enjoyed by her own hand so long ago. She wanted him within her. She wanted him to feel the tumult in her body, to enjoy it with her, for him to understand. She was his mate and he hers. She felt no shame and made wordless voice to the pleasure she felt.

Afterward, he had fallen into the slumber of Sampson, a still slumber. Was he aware of her?

She remained awake to look at him, to observe him sleep, to listen to his breathing, and to kiss his lips.

She withdrew her lips from his when he started suddenly. His body jerked to a sitting position. "What if you are pregnant? We're finding a judge. We can't wait. Come to Bath with me. We can have a few days more."

"We'll find a priest, Isaac, a priest."

Twelve

The Ship

An' Bill can have my sea-boots, Nigger Jim can
have my knife,
You can divvy up the dungarees an' bed,
An' the ship can have my blessing, an' the Lord can
have my life,
An' sails an' fish my body when I'm dead.
— John Masefield

Monday, April 29, 1872
Bath, Maine

The *Providence* had been towed from the William Rogers Shipyard and lay at anchorage with only the captain, his steward, and his second mate on board. Not too many days ago, the deck of the ship rang out with activity, the blows of caulkers' mauls, and the aromatic smell of Baltic tar and oakum being forced into the seams of her deck. Her top hamper became alive with activity. Riggers shouted while setting in place the miles of hemp line comprising her running rigging and crossing yards. These workers also had bent her white canvas sails and furled them on the yards they had crossed. Her sinew and muscle now adorned her towering wooden skeleton. The ship's repairs were now complete, and today, in the light of daybreak, the *Providence* rested silently at single anchor in the Kennebec River near Bath, Maine, as if to gather her courage for what lay ahead. She would round Cape Horn in Antarctic winter.

80

The purpose in Bath, now that her repairs were finished, would be to provision the ship with naval stores and rations, ship a skeleton crew, and await tow to New York. There she would load railway equipment for San Francisco and ship the remainder of her crew for the passage around the Horn.

Henry Lennon—the second mate and Scouser—Liverpool born—stood alone on the ship's deck holding a cup of coffee in his hand and watching the large dory approach from the starboard. His captain was ashore in Bath. Two old watermen quarreled as they rowed the boat. Henry Lennon could not hear their argument, but he knew why they squabbled: boredom. The scene appeared entirely mundane: a working boat being pulled by watermen on a river sided by sawmills and shipyards. A ferry sounded a long blast as it cleared its slip. Today would be a good day; the barometer remained both high and steady. Lennon heard the ensign snap occasionally in the cold wind. The second officer saw four boys in the dory and knew their names and the reason they would soon arrive aboard. The boys were why the second mate waited patiently on deck warming his arthritic thumbs with a steaming cup of coffee.

The boat approached and discharged the young men at the accommodation ladder. Since the apprentices, the brass bounders, were indentured to the shipping line and not the ship, they had been contracted for the entire voyage, to New York for cargo, to San Francisco for grain, to Liverpool to discharge grain, and to fill the ship's huge hold with general cargo for Boston. The voyage would, at the minimum, take the greater part of a year.

Edward Smallbridge, Nicholas Priest, and the Ernst brothers—Jeremy and Richard—climbed the accommodation ladder to begin their initiation into becoming deep-water sailors and square-rigged ship's officers. Had a full crew been aboard the ship, there would have been a timekeeper to ring the ship's bell eight times, marking the end of the watch: *ding, ding, ding, ding, ding, ding, ding, ding.*

A watch ended; theirs had begun.

Edward Smallbridge was the first of the boys to catch Lennon's attention because he dressed like a sailor and carried a worn sea chest on his shoulder as a seaman would. He was also short and wiry—a born captain of the topgallants. Lennon noted the sailor's neckerchief, sheath knife, and well-worn sea chest with its tight beckets and neat carving of a Grand Banks schooner.

Then there was Nicholas Priest. The second mate felt like swearing and did. "Damn that man! He's sent us a consumptive. This is no sanitarium." Lennon knew Priest had never worked a day in his life—a mouth to feed that would not earn its keep.

"Damn!"

The Ernst brothers presented an altogether different appearance, woodsmen and lumberjacks, tall and well-muscled, with tanned faces and confident strides, the picture of youth. Their sea chests were new.

Lennon knew the brothers would be a step behind at first. The two would need to watch the real seamen when an order was given. The younger boy—the boy with the wide eyes—would want to please the mates and the older seamen for a word of praise, and Richard Ernst would soon be anticipating orders and acting too quickly. Both brothers needed to learn to work in unison with the men of their watch. All these boys could be dangerous if not watched closely. The sailors would grind out their rough edges, and he and the first mate would hone them into men—hardworking seamen.

Henry thought of the work he and the first mate, when he arrived, would need to accomplish with these boys. He removed his weathered derby, scratched his head, and muttered, "Two rubes, a sailor, and one we'll surely bury at sea. Shit!" Then he demanded, "I'm Mr. Lennon, second mate. Who are you?" There was no hint of a welcome.

"Edward Smallbridge, sir. I'm from Boston."

Lennon remembered meeting a Smallbridge once before.

"Our last name is Ernst," the older of the brothers announced. "This is my younger brother, Richard. I'm Jeremy. Our home is here. If you look to your right, you can see our sawmill, the big one with three water runs and the biggest yard and dock on the river. Mr. Christison, Jr. was happy to sign us as apprentices for nothing. My father has shipped a lot of lumber on the Christison ships." Jeremy stood taller than his brother and clearly expected deference from the mate.

Henry Lennon replied, "Humility becomes yews. Does yer brother talk?"

Richard stuttered. "I speak, sir. Jeremy does things b-b-better than I do, so I let him t-t-talk."

"Oh." He looked directly at Priest. "What's yer name? Are yews sick?"

"I'm Nicholas Priest, sir. My father sent me here for my health. One of my father's legal associates, Mr. Dana, told me it might be the best thing I could do. My mother is a portrait artist. My father teaches law at Harvard and maintains his own practice in contract law. My father arranged this with Mr. Christison, Jr. I know my father paid to send me here; thirty dollars was the price."

Lennon thought: *Damn it all, bloody rich parents too! Who's going to tell them their son's dead and buried at sea? Old Kicking Billy would na' ship this lad. William Jr.'s been at work. He has to make a shilling any way he can.*

"Show me yer hands, lads. Turn them over. I don't care about yer nails; I ain't yer ma, Priest. Need ter see da bottoms." The mate studied each set of hands to see what they revealed about each boy.

Smallbridge had the remains of calluses on his hands; the Ernst brothers' hands were well callused. Priest's hands were soft. "Why on earth are yews here?"

"For my health, sir."

"Well, ain't that something.

"And yews, Smallbridge. Now, what's yer story?"

"I've been on schooners and brigs, sir, coasters mostly for two years now. I've been to sea with my father, too." He showed the mate an anchor tattooed on his right arm.

Smallbridge's unaffected pride triggered an instinctive reaction in Henry Lennon. He felt like showing the boy his own anchor tattoo, but he didn't because he was a mate.

"Do I know yer da'?"

"He's master of the *Natick*, sir, one of the Christison ships."

"And yews brothers, what story have yews to tell Mr. Lennon?"

The older boy again answered, "Since so much of our family business is with shipbuilders, Father thinks this is a good idea—to

83

know about ships. When we return, we'll work for Mr. Rogers's shipyard for a year."

Henry knew the Ernst brothers were accustomed to hard physical work; their calluses told him that. Their personalities differed. Jeremy was the more physical of the two and carried himself as someone who got his way. The younger of the brothers was obviously sea struck. He could barely keep his eyes away from the masts and rigging, hanging on to each word the mate spoke.

"All right, lads, follow me. I'll tell yews about da *Providence* and say it only once. Get used ter that. This ship is a downeaster, a medium clipper built ter carry a large cargo—bulk cargo—around Cape Horn and grain to Europe. A downeaster's got to earn her keep. She's fast—fourteen knots in topgallants and royals—has good manners and Thomaston-built of oak, pitch pine, and hackmatack." Lennon watched Nicholas Priest's face. He was curious about the reaction the face would display. It was filled with amazement.

The mate first showed the boys the quarterdeck. The quarterdeck was to be respected, he told them; it was captain's country. No one had any business being there except for duty or by invitation. He saw Nicholas Priest peer into the port window of the wheelhouse to see the wheel and binnacle inside. The wheelhouse was painted white and had a sliding scuttle over the helmsman's station behind the wheel. Lennon wondered if any of the boys standing there hoped to be a ship's master one day, as he had when he first went to sea.

Lennon herded the boys forward toward the crew's deckhouse. This deckhouse was more than forty feet long and had cradles on its roof for the ship's twenty-six-foot-long boat and twenty-four-foot whaleboat. He occasionally called this deckhouse the forecastle, confusing Priest and the Ernst brothers. Smallbridge saw the confusion and silently mouthed, "I'll explain. Be quiet."

Lennon named each mast and identified the fife-rails and pin-rails, explaining the function they performed and emphasizing that each pin held a specific line. He admonished the boys to memorize each line and each pin because no mistakes could be tolerated, no excuses accepted. He pointed out the cat-heads and their function and the bowsprit and its function. Except for Smallbridge, the boys were intimidated by the masses of running rigging coiled on their pins. They next walked aft of the deckhouse but not without a warning: "You, lads, never let your feet step over that coaming. Do you understand me?"

Then the second mate took them aft to apprentice berthing in the after cabin and explained why there were bunks on the port and starboard sides. "Pick a bunk, but don't get too attached to it until yew's assigned watches."

"Spill yer dunnage on the bunk; show me what's in there. We've no slop chest on board and won't until we reach New York."

Smallbridge had a sailor's dunnage and equipped himself to go to sea. Nicholas Priest did not. His clothing appeared more costume than anything else. The clothing mimicked the naval-type uniforms of a White Star Line steamer. When asked, Priest told Lennon his mother had crossed the Atlantic on an English liner. She obviously had no idea what deep-water sailors wore, what square-rig grain-ship sailors wore to sail from the Northern Hemisphere into the Southern Hemisphere and back. The most extraordinary thing tumbling from the carpetbag was a knife. The blade was long and heavy, for cutting line, and the top and bottom of the served hilt was held in place with expertly tied Turk's head knots. Priest explained, "Mr. Dana gave this to me. It was his own."

The clothing, though, wouldn't do. The boy would suffer. The Ernst boys had rugged new dungaree work clothes and new pea jackets in their new sea chests. The brothers also had new sheath knives. Their parents cared enough to send them to sea well prepared for what would come. Lennon's fierce eyes kept the other apprentices from laughing at Priest's dunnage.

"Smallbridge, take Priest ashore and make sure he has what he needs. Bring him back at least looking like a sailor. Sell them damn whistles and give him da money for new dunnage. Don't return until he's prepared to work and for da weather. Hop to it. Don't stand there. There's work here for yews lads, and I don't see it getting done."

Thirteen

La Belle

She found me roots of relish sweet,
And honey wild, and manna dew,
And sure in language strange she said—
"I love thee true."

She took me to her elfin grot,
And there she wept, and sigh'd full sore,
And there I shut her wild wild eyes
With kisses four

—John Keats

Tuesday, April 30, 1872
Bath, Maine

Smallbridge entered the Front Street pawnshop of Moses Hirsch and said, "Mr. Hirsch, my friend's come here to sell his belongings and get some dunnage for going to sea."

The sight of Nicholas Priest amazed Hirsch. He could not imagine a boy like that on the deck of a ship, but business was business. The pawnbroker called for his wife, who appeared from behind the curtains separating the shop from the Hirsch family's living quarters. She fussed over Priest, examining him as if he were poultry for their evening dinner and calling him *"bubala."* Priest blushed with embarrassment.

Priest saw a girl nearly as old as himself wearing a calico apron peering from behind the curtain. He saw blond hair and the bluest eyes he had ever seen. She giggled and hid in the shadows behind the curtains, still watching the thin boy.

"Spread the contents of your carpetbag out on the table, please. Let me see. Ah, the carpetbag's good for some money—you don't need that—your suit's good too, and I'll buy your derby and high-topped shoes—the leather's too flimsy for a ship. That's a good shirt. Yes, it's Egyptian long-strand cotton, Manchester looms. See, Sarah? You don't need all the rest. Don't know if I can sell it..."

His face formed a human question mark. "But seeing you're a good boy, how about a lot price? I can't let you leave my shop naked, can I? How about I throw in some work clothes too? What do you say? Fair deal?"

Priest left with the sum of thirty-five dollars, a serviceable pair of dungaree overalls, a dungaree jacket, a man's flannel work shirt a size too large, near-new sea-boots also a size too large, and a smiling shipmate. "Hell, Priest, he did right by you. Bet he'll sell all the junk to women, so they can cut it up and sew dresses."

The next stop was a chandlery. Priest liked the store. There were clothes, rope, blocks, tackle, casks of lamp oil, groceries, knives, charts, almanacs, tins of pilot biscuits, and old men sitting around a live stove telling stories of ships and dead shipmates from their pasts. It smelled of Baltic tar and pipe tobacco. When Priest left, he was wearing new tan cotton twill trousers held up with suspenders and a brown leather belt for Dana's sheath knife. Everything appeared to be a size too large. Smallbridge also dressed him in a blue woolen shirt, a longshoreman's hat, and a rolled black silk scarf tied around his neck with a reef knot. Smallbridge told Priest the scarf was worn loosely around the neck and everyone who saw it would know he was a sailor. Priest remembered details of the old men's stories and smiled. All the dead men seemed to be rascals, drunks, fighters, and clever cheats, but to a man, all were lovingly remembered.

Priest left with a navy canvas duffel bag stuffed with a pilot coat, woolen long johns, a Scotch hat, thick woolen socks, heavy wool felt slippers, and other things that absolutely baffled him. "What's that long thing, the fid? Why do I need needles and waxed thread? What's a donkey's breakfast?"

"Throw your duffel up on your shoulder, shipmate. You'll learn in good time. You have fourteen dollars left. I've got seven, and my stomach says eat."

Smallbridge asked the clerk where two sailors could get a good meal before going to sea. The clerk recommended three places, one known for its breakfasts—johnnycakes, Rhode Island–style—and said, "Now, keep clear of the Fouled Anchor, heeyuh. That place's no more than a saloon and is known for fights." Smallbridge turned to Priest and winked.

"Priest, shipmate, you're starting to look like a sailor now, so let's go see what victuals Bath has to offer. It'll be months before we see fresh meat again. Mr. Mate'll never know."

Priest's new friend ignored the warning and proceeded to the Fouled Anchor while promising a bewildered Nicholas Priest a damn good meal and an even better time.

Smallbridge took charge and ordered a beefsteak apiece and mugs of lager beer. Priest objected, "I've never in my life had a beer or as much meat on my plate as what you've pushed on me." Smallbridge just laughed.

"Eat your porterhouse and drink your beer, Priest. Two months from now you'll be dreamin' about a steak and cold beer. Besides, you look skinny; your flesh just hangs on your bones."

The beer tasted sour. Nicholas Priest's new acquaintance had said the cold lager would taste like horse piss at first and become better tasting with each swallow. Priest had never thought about the taste of horse urine before. Still, he took his first sip, and then by the third swallow, the beer had become deliciously bitter and sweet all at the same time. This made ample reason for quickly finishing his glass. Smallbridge said, "Tastes like another one, don't it?" Priest smiled in agreement. His mood was changing for the better.

Priest found a new appetite growing. As the beer seeped its way into Priest's mind, he began to notice the young girl who had served them their meal. The tavern maid had rich brown hair, a delightful nose just a little long, large brown eyes, and inviting, pink crowned lips. She wore a simple black skirt accented with a gray blouse with a small amount of white lace at the collar and cuffs. Priest unknowingly stared at the girl and failed to recognize her welcoming signs—a smile, movement of eyelids, a song being hummed.

Her full lips with their lush bow and maiden's teeth fascinated him, and he imagined himself kissing her. He tried to imagine the kiss, the taste and softness of her lips. Surely there had to be more than his mother's cheek. Still, he knew this girl, Lilith. It was she who came into his dreams. It was she whose face was never revealed. It was her body so close yet hidden in his ignorance. He imagined the soft warmth of her olive skin on the tips of his fingers.

Priest called for her to bring their second round of beer. He wanted her to come near him so he could see her more closely. The boy felt her belly momentarily brush against his arm as she took his money. He tried to enshrine the sensation in his memory while he watched the sway of her hips as she walked away.

"Why do they walk like that?"

Priest enjoyed himself, satisfying his appetite for food and, with the effect of his second beer, fueling an appetite he had known only while deep in sleep.

Women's faces tell a story. His imagination began inventing the young girl's tale—poor no doubt, but still adhering to her mother's high principles and soon to fall deeply in love with Nicholas Priest. How he would enjoy stroking the dark wisps of hair at her temples and feeling the sensation of her hands in his. He also imagined the touch of her fingers cradling his cheek and the sensation of her head resting upon his shoulder. Priest felt free to tell Smallbridge he had never before seen such beauty. Smallbridge laughed, but his smile held no hint of ridicule.

Then several sailors came in and asked the boys for their names and their ship. Priest immediately noticed the scarves around their necks and heavy knives on their hips. The sailors knew Priest was gullible the instant they saw him. They listened to Priest's question and answered that Captain Griffin was a hard but fair man and that he carried sail. Priest asked what carrying sail meant.

"Well, boy, your old man will bend sail to every yard in the face of a hurricane. Expect to be aloft as much as on deck and brace ship until your legs and arms are numb from hauling. Your watches will be called so often you will forget how to sleep. But, boys, the *Providence* is a feeder, you'll get a full measure of whack, and Captain Griffin pays a fair wage to good seamen. Now, you'll not hear the captain or mates swear often, but don't be confused. The mates will work you as hard as any bucko and on Sunday, too. These Yankees just ain't the Christian gentlemen you knew at home."

One of the sailors asked Priest if he would be kind to his shipmates. Priest replied, "Of course, sir." The boy did not realize he had unwittingly bought what appeared to be a gill of whiskey for all of the sailors as well as one for himself. Priest wondered why they watched him take his drink.

"Up spirits, mate!"

A Swede, one of the sailors, approached the pretty tavern maid. The two talked quietly, and the sailor discretely placed coin in her hand. She walked to the boys' table, positioned herself on the bench next to Priest, and made sure his hips and hers pressed each other. Priest felt the warmth of her body and found the long, soft legs beneath her skirt arousing. She lightly placed her right hand on his thigh and talked gently, almost silently, in his ear, occasionally looking directly into his eyes while smiling. The apprentice saw an expression he thought women reserved for children. He recognized that she whispered French in his ear, but became so excited that her words became more song than meaning. The girl's warm breath caressed him, and her moist tongue lapped the inside of his ear.

The Swede smiled; heads nodded in approval. She ignored them.

The whiskey had loosened Priest and made him happy indeed to be listening to the young woman. He became too thrilled by his good fortune to reexamine the story his imagination had made up for her and was now letting her write her own story. The story passing from her lips enthralled him. She asked Priest to follow her, saying, "I've something to show you. It's wonderful. I know you've had nothing so good in your life."

Without thinking, and leaving half his whiskey on the table, he followed her into a back room. She sat Priest on a small bed, placed her finger to his lips, kissed him on his forehead, and said in English, "I'll do everything." Her fingers undid the buttons of his fly. She raised her skirts and then sat down on him while still holding a finger to his astonished lips.

Priest reflexively closed his eyes in response to the sensation of entering her. She began to rock her hips forward. She kissed him on his lips. He did not know how to respond. She withdrew her lips and showed him how to kiss her, how to please her, to press, to hold, to part. All of this was accomplished without words. Their lips touched; their tongues touched. Priest's breath came in quick gasps; his eyes closed, then opened. She smiled.

"C'est bon?"

She carefully slowed the rocking of her hips to prolong his pleasure and her own. The girl brought Priest's right hand away from under her skirt to her breast. "We will speak French. You do understand? No one must know what we say. *Tu m'aimes? Tu peux m'aider? Tu peux m'aider?"* (Do you like me? Will you help me?)

Priest heard her words as she spoke simple French to him—well within his ability to understand—but in his excitement, the words passed barely recognized. He had never before felt such pleasure.

Priest moaned. The girl smiled again and kissed him with delight, pleased with what she had done. The moan carried out to the taproom, where the sailors burst into laughter. The sound of this amusement penetrated Priest's euphoria and robbed him of the moment's joy and his pride, made him feel shame, ignited his anger, and quenched his desire despite the pleasure she had just given him. Seeing this change, she kissed him, but he was lost to her.

When he could arrange himself, he left the room with her by his side. She grasped Priest's right hand and held it tightly, but the sensation of her hand was buried by the emotion overwhelming him. He now experienced yet another new feeling. He felt anger heat his face and straighten its features. He let loose her hand and unconsciously clenched his hands into fists. Had he the ability, Nicholas Priest would have enjoyed killing his mockers. The nail of the small finger of his right hand cut the soft flesh of his palm. Priest kept tightening his fist until the nail drew blood.

Smallbridge took Priest out to the alley and said he wanted to protect his new shipmate from himself. As they left, the young girl smiled at him. "*Je m'appelle Sophie. À demain?*" (My name is Sophie. Till tomorrow?)

Ignoring the girl's question, Priest cried, "I could kill them! I could kill them, Smallbridge. They tricked me; they made a fool of me. One day, one day..."

"One day what, Priest? The chances are you'll never see that girl or those men again in your life, but listen to you. I don't think you understand a damn thing about what happened."

Priest felt his chin drop and his mouth form a small circle; his eyebrows rose. He had expected Smallbridge to be sympathetic.

"The worst those sailors did was to laugh at you. Buying the girl for you was a gift. They saw you becoming all cow-eyed about her and were thankful you bought whiskey for them. You didn't carp about it either. Those men just wanted to show they liked you."

Smallbridge saw the amazement in Priest's eyes.

"They laughed because she did as they expected; that's all. Had it been the thin one or the Swede, they would've laughed just as hard."

Priest had never thought anyone could ever talk to him like that. His mother coddled his feelings. His father avoided them.

Smallbridge continued, "You ought to have been laughing with them and at yourself. She'd understand. She held your hand!"

Smallbridge still had not finished. "I talked to the big fair-headed Swede that bought her for you. He told me she had been sold to the tavern owner by her mother for a month's rent and is no older than you are. He brought her here from Quebec. Did you hear what she said to you? She's sweet on you."

Priest was drunk, but Smallbridge's words still penetrated the whiskey fog. A girl liked him. He stumbled, pissed in the alley to relieve himself, and fought nausea while stumbling with his duffel back to the wharf.

***

Smallbridge and a drunken Nicholas Priest left their hired dory and climbed *Providence*'s accommodation ladder. Henry Lennon saw them and muttered, "Enjoy yerselves, lads. Yews'll not take advantage of me again. I'll start making sailormen of yews tomorrow."

Later that evening Priest hurried to the side of the ship and violently emptied the contents of his stomach over the side. When he returned to his bunk, he found two silver dollars had slipped out of the watch pocket of his trousers; Sophie had given her price to him.

Fourteen

Ship's Work

Work! Work! Work!
While the cock is crowing aloof!
                              —Thomas Hood

Wednesday, May 1, 1872
Bath, Maine

At five in the morning—two bells of the morning watch—Lennon stuck his head in the apprentice cabin door and roared, "On deck now, there's work ter do. Bring yer cups and hop ter it." In five minutes' time, the boys were out of their bunks and through the cabin door, but a hungover Priest was the last to arrive. Lennon held a large enameled pot of steaming coffee and had a coat pocket stuffed with ship's biscuit. Lennon filled each boy's cup and said, "Drink this; it's all yews'll have 'til seven bells." Smallbridge and the Ernst brothers welcomed theirs, but it was a new thing to Priest—he drank only tea. However, the boy took the cup willingly so as not to offend the mate. The coffee was near boiling. His first attempt resulted in a flinch; the hot tin cup burned his lips. He blew across the rim of the cup a few times, sipped, and then winced; it was remarkably bitter as well as hot.

"Having trouble there, Priest?" Lennon remarked. "I've got just what it takes ter make yews like it." Lennon led the boys to the galley and poured a dollop of molasses into each of the cups. Nicholas Priest was not sure it tasted better, but the molasses did put

94

fuel in his empty belly, as did the hard ship's biscuits. The mate said, "Na hair of the dog ed this barky." He then handed each boy another ship's biscuit to eat.

"Come on, boys, finish up. On this ship, yews work from five in the morning until six at night and stand yer watches too."

The boys finished their coffee and Lennon led them forward to the passageway running between the port and starboard lockers in the forecastle. Lennon opened the door to one locker and handed each boy a stone the size of a paving stone, calling it a holystone. "Yews'll see why."

Smallbridge knew what was coming and rolled up his trouser legs and took off his boots. Nicholas Priest stared in confusion. The Ernst brothers also ignored Smallbridge's example and ended up with dungarees wet from the knee down as a result.

Lennon posted the boys at the hand pump, and they wet the deck with the fire hose.

"Now, lads, scrub it down, make it shine! This is the way the day begins at sea, every day at sea." Smallbridge showed the boys how holystoning was accomplished. Priest wondered why the decks were cleaned this way; it wore away the surface of the deck.

Priest's knees screeched in pain with each forward movement of the stone across the pine deck. As he continued, he began to feel small spasms in his lower back. The small twinges continued, growing in intensity, and soon joined each other in one unremitting wail for relief. He felt points of heat where his fingers joined his palms. Not only was the holystone wearing away the deck; it was also grinding and then burning blisters on his hands.

The effort required was not that much, but the repetition tested Priest's stamina. He quickly felt winded. He intuitively knew that it would do him no good to complain, and as a means of keeping his mind off his suffering, he attempted to keep pace with Smallbridge. It was a good strategy but not an adequate one, as the pain continued and spread to his arms and hands. Blisters began to form.

"Just push it, Priest. Let the stone's weight do the work." Smallbridge quickly saw his new friend's lack of practical knowledge and knew he was in pain. Their work had only progressed as far as the main-mast. He thought Priest suffered in silence, not from stoicism, but to avoid derision. Smallbridge asked if, before now, Priest had ever had a friend or worked a day in his whole life.

Jeremy Ernst was work-hardened like tool steel. He felt no pain or fatigue as Priest did but felt this work was beneath him. What had this to do with learning to be a mate? The older brother attempted to speak the word "mister," but as the *t* crossed his tongue, Lennon's boot impacted his butt and Jeremy found himself chest down on the wet deck. The diversion was enough for Smallbridge to catch Priest's attention and point to his own trouser knees and how he had rolled the material to form a cushion. Nicholas Priest rolled up his trousers. He silently thanked Smallbridge. His back screamed for relief, and the blisters on his hands soon started to bleed.

Lennon spoke in a matter-of-fact voice as he addressed the boys. His hard eyes and their contact with each of the boys' eyes produced fear. "Lads, I don't give a damn about yews ma or da, and I don't give a damn for why you're here. You'll learn by doing and keeping yer mouths shut. Understand this: I'm here to work yews, the other mate is here to work yews, and God forbid the captain ever sees yews na' working. All I want ter see is yer arses an' elbows an' this deck being cleaned. Why ain't those holystones scraping me bloody deck?"

The boys cleaned the deck in total silence, swept up the sand, and flogged the deck dry with swabs. At seven-thirty Lennon struck the ship's bell seven times and shouted, "It's time for brecky. Get below and shift canvas for going ashore." Priest threw his head back, closed his eyes, and breathed deeply. It was over, at least for now.

***

Lennon bought breakfast for the apprentices—oatmeal porridge with butter, molasses, and hot coffee. The boys bolted down their meal in silence, as their bodies were starving for food. Lennon gave them half an hour to eat and soon had them back on the ship and ready for work, but while at the table, he exhorted them, "Muck it in, mates, yews at yer granny's."

***

Back on the ship, Lennon inspected the deck and had the boys sweep it down. It did not pass—Lennon had no intention that it would—and soon they were busy sweeping again. The older of the two brothers shot an angry look at Lennon when he thought the mate was not looking.

"I saw dat, Ernst!"

Lennon knew three of the boys had worked hard and did not complain, but he knew Jeremy had not. "Ernsts, Smallbridge, and Priest, lay aloft ter de main topgallant yard." Smallbridge looked at Priest and Richard Ernst and said, "He wants us to climb the main-mast to there." He pointed to the main topgallant yard, nearly 125 feet in the air. "Smallbridge, bear a hand wi' this. Yews been aloft; they ain't."

Lennon saw fear in Priest's eyes and wild enthusiasm in Richard Ernst's. Lennon stopped the boys by the main-mast fife-rail and had them look up, then explained that the construction of the mast, which consisted of several units—the main-mast, top-mast, topgallant mast, and royal mast—together extended to nearly 145 feet above the deck.

The next topic was the wind: "It blows from windward and blows to leeward. Windward is called da weather side and leeward called da lee. Lads, everything here is da wind. This barky won't move unless we've got it, so learn its direction, learn ter judge its strength, make it part of yews. Always climb a mast on da windward shrouds. These and de stays are da standing rigging. You want da wind ter push yews into da shroud when a ratline parts beneath yews foot."

Lennon held the shroud in his hands and continued: "Yer hands go here and here only." He pointed to the ratlines and said their feet went there and there only. "Now, lads, while yer climbing, yews never, ever look down, and it's always one hand for yerself and one for da ship." Lennon laughed. "That's da one-hand business, da only fairy tale yews will hear aboard this barky."

97

Priest placed his right hand on the shroud. It was cold, and he could feel the taut wire rope beneath the serving. He then placed a foot on the ratline and it moved. The boy started to climb slowly. He felt his legs start to shake, but he kept climbing for fear that he would be called a coward. Despite this, he could not stop the trembling. For the first time in his life he contemplated death as real and not some imaginary revenge. Everyone knew he was afraid. No amount of will on his part could hide his fear. His legs betrayed him. Nicholas Priest reached the futtocks, which led to the main-top, despite his fear. The boy wanted to use the lubber's hole but the mate's sea-boot prevented him from using it.

"You'll use de futtocks, Priest; now, wait until da ship rolls ter leeward and then climb." Priest did as directed. With all the speed and power of adrenaline, he stepped onto the main-top as he was told to do. He felt a moment of intense pleasure.

When the three apprentices were comfortably on the main-top, Lennon explained the fittings on the yard and showed them the jackstay, where sails were bent; he explained the foot-ropes and stirrups, the blocks and braces, lifts and ties. The second mate watched the two boys carefully to see if they were over any initial fear. "Lay ter da top-mast cross-trees, lads."Priest was again the first to climb. The second officer was directly below him. The shrouds were narrower now, and he climbed placing his feet on the ratlines and hands on the shrouds. He kept his eyes aloft, looking to where he needed to place his hands and feet. Although his legs had stopped shaking, he still moved slowly. The boy thought he heard the mate encourage him. They reached the top-mast cross-tree. The mate swung out on the weather side of the yard and climbed on top of it, steadying himself with the lift. Smallbridge stepped out on the foot-rope of the lee yard. Richard Ernst's excitement grew, and fear still radiated from Priest's face. The boys climbed the even narrower shrouds to the topgallant mast cross-tree. Lennon pointed to the windward yard and said, "Lay out. Go on, now."

The younger Ernst boy started and then hesitated when he felt the foot-rope move. He slowly moved farther out on the yard. Nicholas

Priest carefully put a foot on the foot-rope and clinched his hands around the jackstay; he continued until both feet were on the rope and then, after several steps, realized he was outboard on the yard, one hundred feet over the deck.

Priest then felt momentary panic as the foot-rope moved beneath his feet from the actions of Richard Ernst, but he remained determined to lay out on the yard. His life depended on the line beneath his feet, and if it should fail, his hands must stop him. With that thought, he gripped the iron jackstay with enough force that he felt a forearm cramp. Still, he and Richard Ernst moved farther outboard on the yard to leave room for Smallbridge to join them.

When all were out on the yard, the mate spoke. "Take a look at da river, lads. Take a good look at da buildings on shore. Can yews feel da wind and hear da gulls? Don't yews look at da deck."

Priest spoke up. "Mr. Lennon, I can see how the wind moves the water; I bet I can see for miles."

Priest's mind outpaced his eyes, because he saw a sky not simply blue, but blue with tints of pink; he saw clouds floating upward in shades of white, gold, and orange; he saw yellow and white sunlight flecks dancing between the water's swells as it moved in rising crests downriver to lap on the shore. He was exultant; he was alive, as if he had just become immortal. He was euphoric. The pounding of his heart from the exhaustion of having climbed 100 feet and the consumption of air by his heavy breathing simply lent rhythm and pitch to his joy.

"Sure you can, lad. Don't yews sense something up here? Don't yews feel just a little bit free?" The younger Ernst blurted out, "Like a bird!"

"Nah, lad, like a sailorman. Yer a johnny now." Lennon chuckled. The young men joined him. Priest laughed for the first time since his father had told him he would go to sea.

Priest had not totally lost his fear, but he still reveled in a sense of accomplishment independent of his parents, his mind exulting in the sensations of a body exerting itself and responding to his will. There was something else too—he had dared himself to take the greatest risk of his life and had won. He experienced giddiness at seeing the mate happy with them, and he found himself thrilled with his own accomplishment. His mind raced and he silently repeated, *I did it. I did it. Me.*

"Now, lads, we're going back on deck, so da worst is not over. Look at da bowsprit; do you see it?"

The boys nodded.

"Sir, we're moving; we are swaying back and forth across the deck."

"That's right, Priest, like a bloody corkscrew."

"Now, look and see what yews need ter climb down."

The boys looked down, but their attention was drawn to the deck. Lennon took a risk, since he knew their minds were painting a picture of their broken bodies spilling out blood, but he also knew that bending and reefing sail required up-and-down movement on the foot-ropes and that the sight of the deck below could never, ever be completely avoided.

Lennon watched the untested boys for any sign of fear. He had seen fear many times before in the eyes and faces of men. Yes, the three boys were afraid, but they did not want to show it. They had felt the beginnings of acceptance by the mate, acceptance by one another, and satisfaction with themselves.

Now all the apprentices moved downward on the shrouds until they were once again on the main-top. Lennon called to Smallbridge, "Show them da quick way down." Smallbridge wrapped his legs around a backstay and used his arms and hands to control a rapid descent.

Lennon felt surprise to see Priest follow suit and then the younger Ernst. Lennon would have been even more astonished had he known that Priest considered his own death, a fall from the stay, but took the quick way down anyway. The mate slid down the backstay also.

The boys were beaming on deck and Priest's mind filled with music—a symphony, the wildly exultant cries of high and rapid violin and piccolo notes, and the swelling of a chorus of triumph led by emphatic tympani. Although it would draw attention, Nicholas

Priest remembered the chorale of the symphony and mustered his best impression of an operatic baritone and sang out, *"Freunde!"* It startled the mate momentarily.

Smallbridge looked at his friend and while laughing asked, "What the hell was that?" Lennon laughed so hard he was nearly out of breath. This mate was as much ursine as human but was consumed with hoots of laughter. Lennon performed what the boys would soon recognize as his ritual for regaining his composure. He first raised his derby, then scratched his bald scalp, and finished by taking a handkerchief from his hip pocket to blow his nose. Lennon's wrinkled blue eyes lit the beak nose and ruddy skin of his face. Priest thought, *He's a man like me, like the rest of us.* Mr. Lennon was the subject of much discussion in the apprentice cabin. Smallbridge explained how the port and starboard watches were to be selected by the mates and expressed hope that he be selected for the starboard watch. His new friend asked why, as did the Ernst brothers. "There are worse mates than Mr. Lennon, believe me."

A tired Nicholas Priest turned over on his back in his upper bunk. He looked around in the small cabin he shared with his young friend. The light from a single gimbaled oil lamp shed dim hues of white and yellow. Priest saw the whitewashed planks and heard the Ernst brothers snoring across the bulkhead. He stretched out on his straw mattress, his donkey's breakfast, and fell into a deep, satisfying sleep.

The second mate continued to work the apprentices and prepare them to learn from the seamen who would soon be shipped. There was no hesitation when the mate gave an order. There was no carping about the indignity of the work, and when criticism came—harsh criticism—the boys took it to heart. Within months, the boys could be rated as "ordinary seamen" instead of ship's boys, but the harshest tests were yet to come: Could they gain the respect of the crew? Could they withstand watch on watch and cold breaking seas? Lennon was pleased with them. He liked how quickly they learned and their attitudes also. Priest had caught his eye; he had worked as hard as he could despite the pain and never complained. "Good, lad!"

Nicholas Priest was proud of himself, a unique experience in his life. He had tasted beer and whiskey and liked them. He found a new appetite for plain food that he had never eaten before. Priest had lost his virginity and now had a girl who occupied his reveries. *Sophie likes me. Sophie likes me.* He had a face and name for his Lilith. Priest now had a friend in Smallbridge and had come to enjoy going aloft—the joy that comes with conquering fear. Smallbridge had said he had balls.

Maybe I do. I've got anchor watch at four this morning. I need to sleep.

Priest would not go ashore again until San Francisco. Soon, Sophie's fate wore at his conscience just as the holystone wore at his hands. His blisters, in time, would heal and harden into calluses, but not his conscience.

Fifteen

The First Mate

The King sets in Dumferling Town,
Drinking the blood-red wine:
O where will I get a good sailor,
To sail this ship of mine?

Child Ballad 58
Scotland, circa 1290

Friday, May 3, 1872
Bath, Maine

Peleg Carver was escorted to Isaac Griffin's office by Ezra, Griffin's steward. He then stood beside the steward waiting for his new captain to recognize his presence. Griffin was deeply absorbed in the receipts for the provisions for which he had just written a bank draft. As Carver waited, he pondered the uncertain future he would experience aboard *Providence* with a captain he knew only by hearsay. In the face of the unknown, he turned to what he did know—rumors—to reckon his future aboard this ship.

He thought: *He doesn't look odd—no spectacles, respectable beard. Been before the mast with that body.*

I've heard people say Griffin is an Ahab—questions the Almighty. Wouldn't do so if he was like me. He'd leave all that to the reverend doctors. A man should stick to what he knows and not trouble himself with what he don't.

See the books on the shelf? There's a King James Bible with a

103

concordance. There's Paradise Lost *and* Moby-Dick. *He has the* Book of Common Prayer. *At least that one's good for burying a man. Where's* The American Practical Navigator?

Guess I'll soon find out about him. Will he pick fights knowing a sailor can't stand up to a captain, just to humiliate the poor johnny? No one recalls him striking a man, but everyone accords him a temper. Will he flog a man because he wants to, to enjoy the man's suffering, and then weep over a pet dog swept overboard? You know men who have, Peleg. Yes, you do.

Will he belittle me before the foremast johnnies? You've seen it before, old man. Now you'll find out. He's so deep in those papers, ship's business.

Allows himself only anger and confidence. Aye, that's his reputation. Not one extra word ever spoken. Passes weeks without speaking at meals, they say. Sailors like him, though, if they do their duty, they like him. They like Peleg I. Carver too, if they avoid my fist.

A good fight is a good diversion. Keeps a man lively. Laugh, you old son of a bitch. You got them beaten before it begins. Pa taught me that.

Carver smiled and fingered the brass knuckleduster in his pants pocket and continued his thoughts.

This man gives you a lot to think about. People always find someone to talk—but Sally and I need the money; there'll be a baby for us in November. Please, God, let this one live. For Sally, Lord, if not for me.

Griffin could invite me to sit. Enough of this.

Carver grunted theatrically.

Griffin looked up from his papers, rose from his chair, and extended his left hand to the new first mate. "Isaac Griffin. I'm glad you are here. Sit, man, sit."

"Thankee, Captain, thankee. Peleg Carver, sir. Do you have any instructions for me, ayuh?"

"Do your job. You've been around the Horn?"

"Yes, sir. I did so in the golden times and seven times since. I shipped on *Great Republic*. Been a grain ship sailor too."

Griffin sat back from his desk. "Ah, set a record—*The Great Republic*—I remember, less than a hundred days. I understand you were in the navy during the war and that you were on the *Kearsarge*. Mr. Lennon served as a boatswain's mate on the Confederate raider *Shenandoah*. Is that a problem for you?"

Carver looked directly at his captain and said, "No, sir. As long as he knows I'm first mate."

Griffin laughed and replied, "He does. You'll want to get your dunnage stowed in the chief mate's stateroom and take a look at *Providence*. There's no one aboard now except us, Lennon, my steward, and the apprentices. Cup of coffee? No?

"I'll have four prime seamen, married men, able-bodied New Englanders, on board for the tow to New York, and we can start putting her in ship-like fashion. I mean the rigger work. I use first names aft and 'mister' on deck. Do you use your first name or is there another you prefer?"

"Sir, Peleg works fine."

"The patriarch—I've always thanked the Almighty my father named me Isaac instead of Nehemiah. It's easier to say and write out." Griffin laughed. "The name's fine. My father's a minister, you know. You've met my second mate? Henry Lennon and I have been together since 'sixty-seven so we've become a team—he knows his duty. He's from Liverpool. He's a Scouser from the docks. Just listen to him. He ought to be a first mate."

Ought to be a first mate!

"It doesn't matter, Captain. Seen 'em on both sides of that coin. I run things and he'll learn that if he wants to push it."

Griffin noticed Carver's hand tighten around what he thought was the bowl of a pipe in Carver's pocket.

"Peleg, don't anticipate a fight with Lennon. It's not what you'll do; it's what I do, and I won't abide my mates squabbling. My voice and my words are the only ones that matter on my ship, and both of you speak for me, not yourselves. Commodore Christison says you're ready to be a master. You've had a master's ticket some time now. The question's your judgment, not experience. I'm to see if you're ready. I know I'm blunt, but that's the case."

I'm glad he told me that raw.

Griffin's face settled. "Tonight, let me lay out how I've planned this voyage. I would appreciate your thoughts. I see a pipe there in your pocket, so we can have a smoke and talk about old shipmates. I'll ask Henry to show you the ship first."

The steward left the reception area. "Ezra's a good man, a Yankee. Don't say anything in front of him you might not want the crew to hear. Lennon knows that too. Ezra's going to tell the forecastle jacks you're a bucko mate now."

Griffin chuckled. "Make sure the saloon shines, Peleg. You, Lennon, and the apprentices, too. I'm bringing my wife on board this evening."

Sixteen

Father Must Be Told

'Tis sweet to win, no matter how, one's laurels
By blood or ink, 'tis sweet to put an end
To strife; 'tis sometimes sweet to have our quarrels,
Particularly with a tiresome friend:
Sweet is old wine in bottles, ale in barrels;
Dear is the helpless creature we defend...
—Lord Byron

Saturday, May 4, 1872
Boston

Kayleigh MacKenna sat quietly on the ferry carrying her from East Boston across the bay to Boston proper. She rose from her wooden seat and left the comfort of the cabin to feel the wind on her face and to watch the water in the bay and listen to it as the bow of the ferry cut its rippling path to Boston. The water was still gray from the overcast and calm because the wind was light. Then her mind returned to the purpose that brought her on deck—to feel wind and water and thus bring his voyage to mind. He was somewhere in the Bay of Maine now on his way to New York. She would meet him there and spend as much time as she could with him, sharing a bed with him.

As the ferry neared Boston, landmarks became more recognizable and brought her mind to the tasks she had appointed for herself. She needed to catch up with her work at the hospital and with the committee in Fall River. Work would carry her through the loneliness of an empty bed. It would exhaust her and let her sleep when concern for his safety kept her awake. Work would compress time.

The wind changed and briefly carried smoke from the ferry's stack in her direction. She thought of his hand. She thought of his courage and determination.

Her mind turned to the problems she must face. The first of these was her father, his prejudice toward Griffin for being Protestant, and his association of Protestantism with the trouble in Ireland. She feared that in his mind, Griffin had become a symbol for what he had suffered at English hands.

What would her father say when he learned? He could disown her, banish her from his life and her home. She shuddered.

Then Kayleigh thought of her mother and the joy the news of her marriage would bring her. Until Kayleigh revealed the rape to her mother, she never knew how strong her mother really was, nor the depth of the bond between them.

Kayleigh was Mrs. Isaac Griffin now, in a marriage performed and sanctified by her church. Her husband submitted to baptism for her and understood his obligation to her and their children. What caused her the greatest hope was his presence with her at Mass and his words, "I feel a presence, Kayleigh, being here with you, listening to your responses to the priest, hearing you sing."

She thought of what she must do. There must be no more deception in her life. She was the wife of Isaac Griffin and the world must know that and respect it, father or not.

The ferry would land; then, after a horsecar ride, she would walk to the three-story brownstone off Marlborough Avenue, her parents' home.

Kayleigh smiled. She had worn her wedding ring on the train ride from Maine and remembered how the conductor treated her with courtesy and seemed to hover near her, a brusque guardian angel with a deep down east accent: "Fall Rivah, Fall Rivah, next stop, Fall Rivah."

She sat alone in the coach, free to doze off or watch scenery. The conductor moved near her when men came near. In the conductor's presence they seemed to pass without comment, forbidden to imagine and wonder those things men do about the women they pass on the street. Only women spoke to her. Kayleigh wondered how they knew. Could it be true an aura surrounded her? Did she glow as they said a woman would? Did these passing women share her joy? Did they remember? "Good afternoon, missus, a good day t' you."

She knocked upon the door. The family butler greeted her and reminded her that dinner would soon be served. He let her know that her mother was concerned about how thin she had become. Kayleigh then rushed to the second floor, to her old bedroom, washed her face in the washbasin, and changed her blouse and chemise. She saw no change in her mirror and wondered how that could be. What had those women seen? The fresh blouse and chemise would have to do. She unpinned, then brushed out her hair and repinned it. A chime sounded. It was time; dinner was being served and her father would sit at the head of the table.

"Kayleigh, you've been gone more than a week. You weren't at the hospital. Where were you?"

Mary MacKenna bristled. "Jim, she's a grown woman."

"As long as she's my daughter, she'll answer my questions."

Kayleigh's mother was quick to remind her husband, "She is a woman."

Mary MacKenna emphasized the word "is."

Kayleigh placed her left hand on top of the table. Her mother immediately saw the rings, then gasped, relaxed, and smiled. Jim MacKenna did not see the rings.

Kayleigh knew a confrontation would occur, but she refused to think about it. She knew this was the time to assert herself.

She announced in a firm contralto, "I'm married. Isaac Griffin is my husband. A priest married us in Bath, Maine, after Isaac was baptized." She smiled. There was pride in what she had done, and this smile heralded the invulnerability she felt.

Jim MacKenna quickly raised his napkin to his mouth and spit what he was chewing into it. His eyes turned to Kayleigh, but she heard no words. She thought he would be angry, that he would threaten and curse her or Griffin, but he said nothing, just stared for a moment, then averted his eyes. His face was as gray as wood ashes from a cookstove. She watched him turn to his wife.

Mary MacKenna spoke. "Jimmy. Our daughter has married a good man who loves her and will provide for her and our grandchildren."

Jim MacKenna remained seemingly dumb. Although Kayleigh could see only his profile, she was sure his eyes were reddening.

Her mother looked at her and smiled. "Kayleigh, please be patient; please forgive us. I need t' speak alone with yer father. He's so upset, the shock, you know. It was so sudden."

Jim MacKenna and his wife left the table and went to the parlor, leaving Kayleigh alone with her meal.

***

In the parlor, Mary watched as flashes of emotion lit her husband's eyes. An internal battle raged. She knew he was silently fighting with himself, afraid to speak lest his words might be remembered. He once told her that he feared words, words that could never be withdrawn or forgotten.

"Mary, I—I want..."

"I know, Jimmy. Don't be angry with yerself. She loves you, and so do I."

***

Mary MacKenna sat alone before the mirror behind her dressing table. She wore a white cotton sleeping gown embroidered in lace, Irish lace. The last time she'd worn this gown was the last time she and Jim shared a bed. The cotton was so fine, so soft, and draped so beautifully.

There it was, the quiet rap on her bedroom door. "Come in, Jimmy." She unbuttoned two buttons in the front and let the garment drape from her shoulders. She was proud of her breasts and her smooth skin, something her daughter had inherited.

Jim MacKenna opened the door slowly and peered within. She

saw the tears in his eyes.

"Mary, she was listening for me to come up the stairs. She rushed out of her bedroom and kissed me just like she did when—she called me Pa—she said she loved me and always would."

"Sit here on the bed next to me, Jimmy."

He sat by her and bent his head down on his chest and he cried.

"She's my pride. I know I spoiled her. I know I did. She's always been my delight."

Mary moved closer to her husband; their hips and legs touched. She placed her left arm around his shoulders and with her right hand gently brought his head up from his chest, then to her.

She kissed his cheek.

"Give her your love, Jimmy. Have a mass said to celebrate her marriage. If people ask, say yer proud; she's independent and strong like you are."

"That's not why I'm crying. You don't know what I've done. I never thought he would ever threaten her."

"Who? Who threatened Kayleigh?"

"Not yet. Not now. It'll come, though. He'll use her as blackmail."

"Who, Jimmy?"

"O'Corkerane. The Clan na Gael wants to use Griffin's shipping line to smuggle men, arms, and money into Ireland. They wanted Kayleigh to marry him. For me to force her if it came to that."

"Well, she's in no danger now, Jimmy. How could she be? She married him."

"You don't understand, Mary. They'll use her to blackmail Griffin if they have to. They're rabid dogs. They'll never let loose of her. They threatened me, and then Kayleigh, with death if I opposed their marriage. Said I knew the oath. Reminded me of poor Terrence Cleary."

She felt his body stiffen and thought he might pull away from her. "Can't you do something?"

"No. Nothing. I've taken the oath; they'll never let loose now. Did you know that it was me that arranged for the cargo of railroad equipment? It was me that contacted the Rallis? It's all part of a scheme to see that Christison ships regularly ship grain to England and Europe from California. Every crew he ships will have Clan na Gael men smuggled aboard. Every cargo will have money hidden in a sack or two of grain. There'll be rifles too. After they get to know Griffin, God knows what they'll expect him to do. They won't trust the Christisons—bought the son, they did. Said it was too easy. Did you know they're talking about getting your brothers out of Australia? That's how they plan to keep me in line, as if Kayleigh ain't enough."

"Jimmy—I—O'Corkerane seems such a good man. He seems so gentle when he speaks in Gaelic."

"No, Mary. That's what he wants people to believe. That the cause is just—is sacred even. That's not what he is, though. He's filled with hate and revenge, and he's come to love it. It's revenge that drives him. They killed his brother. Ireland's how he justifies it, how he settles his soul with the killing. Mary, I know revenge."

"Don't tell her, Jimmy. You've got to protect her. Can't you see how happy she is? The rape is behind her. Let her be happy. Don't spoil it, please."

"Mary, I love—She's me daughter."

"I know that. Why do you think I've not raised my voice at you? There's no anger here in my heart. They deceived and used you. It had to be that. I trusted him as much as you. You've frightened me, though."

"I'm going to my bedroom, Mary. That's where I belong. I don't deserve—"

"This is your bedroom, Jimmy. This is our bed. Will you stay and brush out my hair? Just fifty strokes are all it needs. It's not the same when I do it myself. Sit closer. Sit behind me on the bed. It feels good when you're near me."

***

It was exactly as O'Corkerane promised, the East Boston saloon, the street, the three men who stood hidden in the shadows with Jim MacKenna as they waited for Kayleigh's violator to leave. Every time the doors opened and a man left, Jim MacKenna tensed, every muscle strained in anticipation, the veins on his neck swelled. The three men, Irish immigrants, Clan na Gael men, were calm. This was nothing new to them; murder was their trade.

Then it finally happened; he emerged with a friend and a girl on his arm, a housemaid or seamstress, Irish, who had had a little too much of his cheap champagne and compliments—perhaps a poor man's wife.

Jim MacKenna stopped the Clan na Gael men with his arm. "I'll do it."

He then addressed the girl. "Go home, girl! You don't know what this man has in store for yer. Go on, now."

The rapist grabbed her arm and restrained her. "Just who in hell are you? Her father?"

The big man replied, his brogue thickening with anger, "Let her go and I'll make it quick for yer. That's all I'll promise yer. Girl, get along, now. You'll not want t' see what I'm about t' do."

Jim MacKenna watched the girl leave. When he felt she was out of eyesight and hearing, Jim MacKenna brought his face to within inches of the rapist's. "I'm calling you out. I'm here to beat you, you bastard." The rapist's companion heard the words and stared into MacKenna's face. The companion muttered, "I've got to leave."

"Who are you?" the rapist pleaded.

Jim MacKenna replied, "D' yer remember me daughter, Kayleigh, or has there been so many you've forgotten? How could yer forget her? I see the scar she left on yer face."

Urine ran down the rapist's leg and pooled by his left shoe.

"Please, Mr. MacKenna, I didn't know. You know how it is with women. That was years ago. Jesus—so long. Don't, I'm married now."

Two Irishmen stepped into the saloon while one remained as a lookout. The two then stood before the saloon door, blocking entry to the street. One of O'Corkerane's men shouted, "Piano man, make some music, some O'Carolan, the 'Ode to Whiskey,' if you would, an' since we're buyin' it fer th' house."

At the first note from the piano, Jim MacKenna launched a boxer's jab that broke the rapist's nose. Another jab struck the man's right eye. As it landed, Jim MacKenna gave his left fist a quick twist to open the skin and produce bleeding. Then his right hand crossed viciously through the space separating him from his victim. When it landed, MacKenna knew he had dislodged teeth. The man staggered, leaned up against the brick wall of the saloon, and pleaded for his life. Jim MacKenna coldly, methodically beat the man until he fell to the pavement and convulsed. Blood ran from his mouth and ears, and then the convulsing stopped.

Jim MacKenna knew he had beaten the man to death.

MacKenna then rapped on the saloon door. "It's over. Get rid of the bastard. If you lads see Jack O'Corkerane before I do, tell him what I've done this evening. Tell him this is what waits anyone that ever harms me daughter."

Seventeen

Farewell, New England

Good Gossip, let us draw near.
And let us drink ere we depart,
For oftentimes we have done so;
For at a draught thou drink'st a quart,
And so will I do, ere I go.

—Anonymous

Monday, May 6, 1872
Kennebec River

The dove gray and silver loom of the sun heralded daybreak by painting the cirrus clouds the morning of May 6, 1872. Sam Duder's heavy wool vest provided a degree of comfort from the chill, as did standing in the heat of the lee of the deck cabin door as the oceangoing tug *E.M. Smith* made steam in her boilers. A column of thick black smoke swirled upward from her stack, then bent horizontally with the wind before settling on the surface of the Kennebec River. The tug smelled of sulfur and fresh roasted peanuts from the expended effort of the burning coal. Hot cinders fell occasionally from the dense smoke. The pungent odor of lubricating oil also passed upward and through the engine room hatch, while the scrape of the coal heavers' shovels could be heard from below. The tug's idle deckhands stood nearby, warming themselves with the escaping heat, waiting for the order to bring in the lines holding the tug to the shore. In a few minutes the engineman would crack the tug's throttle to set the engine to turning over slowly, giving motion to the propeller shaft to heat the brass bearings and lead babbitting in the stuffing box, thereby sealing off the seep of river water trickling into her iron bilge.

The pilot arrived wearing a suit, a poplin overcoat, and a derby, and carrying his papers in a brown leather satchel with a shoulder strap. He smiled at the sailors and joined the tug's captain on the bridge. Each man addressed the other as Captain. The pilot was offered a cup of coffee.

The pilot would guide the tug and tow downriver into the Bay of Maine. He imagined the anxiety of the *Providence*'s captain to get under way with the tide. The river pilot, however, preferred to take Fiddler's Reach, the most worrisome leg of the journey, at as near slack water as possible when going downstream.

Seven men were on board with their dunnage for the short trip out to where the *Providence* lay anchored. They stood on the fantail shuffling foot to foot and side to side to stay warm. Llewellyn James offered a small bottle of rye whiskey to the other men. "You might want to try a swig, boys; there won't be another chance till New York. I know you, Sam Duder. We sailed together once. Said you'd buy a farm, and here you are, shipped and bound to go."

"We shipped together for San Francisco, Lew, in the golden days when the pay was good. I did buy a farm and married too. You went to the gold fields, I remember. Well, I ain't a farmer, and that's why I shipped. Made no lasting money off the cod bank either. Don't look like you struck a gold vein."

Albert Crother took a generous sip of the whiskey and passed it on to John Stedwin, who asked where the raw liquor came from as Maine was a dry state—a fact regularly overlooked on the riverfront. Two men smoked pipes, but most chewed tobacco for convenience. The small talk continued when the engine began to turn, churning up white water at the tug's stern. Several of the deep-water sailors huddled beneath the collars of their jackets while suffering the remnants of the night before. Most took a taste of the whiskey and said, "Thank you," in quiet, defeated voices.

Eoghan Gabriel, the boatswain, stood away from the men. If

they were to obey his orders, he need not be drinking and chewing tobacco with them. He feigned interest in the Sampson post and hemp fenders with one of the deckhands, who pretended similar interest in explaining them. Gabriel agreed the work was good marlinspike seamanship and a rarity these days. The deckhand replied, "Thankee, Mr. Gabriel."

The crew of the *E.M. Smith* brought the tug's bow and stern lines aboard and stood by the remaining spring line to warp the tug out. The engine telegraph rang and signaled she would be backing slowly, walking her stern to port. The gangplank was pulled ashore with a thud and the final spring line was brought aboard. The tug pulled away from the pier, and soon the order came to put the engine ahead and take the tug the short distance to the *Providence*. For a moment the smoke from the stack swept the deck, then rose and pointed away as the tug gained speed. Sam Duder asked the name of the tug's captain. Maybe he would be hiring in a year or so.

The tug was made fast on *Providence*'s starboard side by its deckhands and the ship's apprentices. The deckhands and the newly shipped men took heavers into hand and inched the ship's anchor cable aboard pawl click by click. *E.M. Smith* assisted the ship by nudging her gently upwind toward her anchor. Peleg Carver missed hearing "Blood Red Roses" sung out. The shantey would have helped the men leave the beach behind them and accept being at sea again.

Sam Duder shouted, "Up and down, Mr. Carver." The next shout was, "Anchor's aweigh." With the anchor at the cat-head, the apprentices strained at the task of cleaning and faking the anchor chain. Carver watched to make sure their work was flawless, as it was a reflection of the first mate's authority. The ship would use the anchor soon off the Battery.

Once the anchor had been raised, the pilot looked to Captain Griffin for the go-ahead to move the ship down the river. At Griffin's nod, the pilot gave the commands to start the voyage. He pointed in the direction he wanted the tug to go and said, "Slow."

As the tug put her shoulder to her work, the tug's smoke thickened and left the tall black stack above the red band at its top. The pistons thudded side to side and the Kennebec churned white and brown at the tug's stern. The *Providence* moved downriver.

Tug and tow floated past Hospital Point, keeping to the center of the river to avoid the shallows above the entrance to Winnegance Creek. They turned nearly ninety degrees into the narrow waters of Fiddler's Reach, laboring against its strong currents and eddies. The tug forced its way to the right of the channel. She dodged a submerged log lost from one of the lumber camps upriver from Bath. The twelve-foot log had been caught in an eddy and moved more rapidly than the tug.

The next turn was almost due east at Doubling Point. Tug and tow followed the river's channel to Bluff Head. Past the Sasanoa River, the Kennebec opened up. After a few miles, the pilot directed the tug to take a course toward Seguin Island with its lighthouse. The pilot would be picked up by a pilot boat near Seguin Island to wait for the opportunity to take a vessel up the Kennebec to Bath, his job finished with *E.M. Smith* and her tow, *Providence*. This was not a leisurely cruise; the *Providence*'s deck was holystoned down and swept dry before breakfast was served. Carver watched the men work while muttering, "Filthy coal smoke."

Peleg Carver and Henry Lennon divided the shipped men into watches using the traditional method: The first mate picked his man first and directed him to the port side. Then the second mate made his choice, directing him to the starboard side. Soon there were no men left to choose. As the men walked to where the mates stood, the port and starboard watches were established. Carver chose his three picks and the Ernst brothers. Henry Lennon got his wish to have Smallbridge and Priest on the starboard watch. He chose Sam Duder also. Both mates were pleased, but for different reasons. The Ernst boys were good strong Maine lads. Priest and Smallbridge were friends and would work and learn well together. Duder was a shantey man.

After much thought, Carver decided to let Lennon bury Priest at sea if need be. Besides, the Ernst brothers knew how to work.

***

The Downeaster

Blunt's American Coast Pilot states that the Bay of Maine is a demanding place to navigate a ship. The tug's master and Captain Griffin had agreed to a general plan to use Cape Elizabeth as the departure, then to steer SW by S for fifty-five miles to Cape Ann, and from there to steer south by east by one-half east for seventy-two miles to Cape Cod. This would permit verification of their dead reckoning by use of navigational aids and soundings in the likely event of fog.

Because of the Nantucket shoals, their planned course would be to steer eastward of Martha's Vineyard, then through the Vineyard Sound. From there they would steer to the westward side of Long Island, past Sandy Hook and into the lower bay to anchor off the Battery, as had been arranged.

Cape Cod came up and was rounded. The tug and tow turned into Pollock Rip Channel and stood for Vineyard Sound. On leaving the sound, they passed Block Island and left Montauk light to starboard, taking the Atlantic side of Long Island to avoid the chance of being fogbound in Long Island Sound, to avoid a piloting fee, and to avoid Hell Gate.

The weather broke for the short trip past Sandy Hook with its anchored ships, and continued clear for the trip up the Narrows to the Battery. Peleg Carver made absolutely sure *Providence* appeared in Bristol fashion for this trip because every sailorman, every master, mate, and lowly ship's boy would pass a comment about the *Providence* as she entered New York Harbor.

The *Providence* was special because she flew a long-pointed emerald green burgee directly below her house flag and above her signal. There was a large Irish harp at the head of the burgee. The harp stood alone with no English crown above it. This was the silent partner's special request, to fly the harp burgee, a Fenian symbol, when entering and leaving U.S. harbors. The partner's name was known to William Christison Jr., who had assured Griffin the partner merely wanted anonymity and profit.

Eighteen

Bound to Go

*Our advance note's in our pocket, boys, it sure will
take us far,
Heave away, me johnnies, heave away-away
An' now a cruise down Lime Street, boys, an' to the
American bar
Heave away, me bully boys
We're all bound to go!*

Brake Windlass Shantey

Sunday, May 26, 1872
New York

"*The Several Persons whose names are hereto
subscribed, and whose descriptions are contained on
the other side or sides and of whom 20 are engaged as
sailors hereby agree to serve on board said ship, in the
several capacities expressed against their respective
Names, on a voyage from the harbor of the City of
New York, in the state of New York in these United
States of America, to San Francisco, California in
these United States of America, and to any other port
so deemed necessary by the Master of said vessel
for reasons of safety, repairs or those required by
maritime law and which are not foreseen or a matter
of due plan for this voyage as set forth herein.*

120

The Downeaster

"And the crew agree to conduct themselves in an orderly, faithful, honest, and sober manner, and to be at all times diligent in their respective duties, and to be obedient to the lawful commands of the said Master...and it is also agreed That if Any member of the Crew considers himself aggrieved by any breach of this Agreement or otherwise, he shall represent the same to the Master or Officer in charge in a quiet and orderly manner, who shall thereupon take such steps as the case may require."

And thus sixteen men at the Port of New York, drunk and sober, did so agree by signing their names or making their mark before witness to the shipping agreement. The maritime commissioner witnessed the agreement and had each attest in the presence of the shipping master that no debts were owed for room and board. Most were foreign, coming from the Scandinavian countries, Ireland, or Germany. Each attested to his competency as seaman, ordinary seaman, or landsman. They were all bound to go. Of the sixteen men shipped in New York, only one raised concerns beyond those normally expected.

Men who have long experience working with other men often sense trouble well before any sign or real reason for suspicion arises. Samuel Craig, shipped by way of boarding master in New York, raised suspicions. He shipped as an ordinary seaman, meaning that he could hand, reef, and steer, but lacked the skills and experience, particularly experience, needed to do advanced repairs to the rigging and sails. Samuel was from Kentucky, an unusual birthplace for a man making a living at sea. He was young, barely into his thirties, and had several missing teeth and the white and pink complexion of an alcoholic. He was lean, sinewy, with dark black hair and high cheekbones; perhaps Cherokee blood was somewhere in his ancestry.

Samuel was a thin five feet six inches tall and seemed to defer to the other men. He spoke quietly, with a soft Appalachian brogue, but you could sense in his eyes a mind busy at work, taking in everything around him, every word spoken, and mulling deeply on everything seen and heard. This mind, this dark and angry organ, was indeed busy, as it felt the world and men owed him more than he had, far more than he earned by work or initiative. This mind was confident in its ability to manipulate other men. This mind convinced its owner of his superiority as a predator. Here also was a mind with little esteem, a mind ashamed of its owner but deeply committed to avenging this shame by obeying his walking boss. Henry Lennon was correct to think that when refusals to do duty, complaints, and fights would occur, this man would always be somewhere hidden in the root causes and prospering from the occurrence of trouble, but seamen were always in short supply, and persuading men to work was the core of a mate's trade.

Samuel Craig, last hand chosen by the mates, was assigned to the starboard watch, the second mate's watch. Henry Lennon, by tradition and by default, had drawn a losing card.

***

That evening after supper in the saloon, Isaac Griffin took his officers to the chart room to lay out his plans for Friday. "Peleg, the tug will tow us out at four p.m. tomorrow. Have the ship ready. Once past Sandy Point, make sail and set the watch."

"Aye. Anything special?"

"No. You'll have the ship taking her out. We'll receive our fresh provisions, pigs, chickens, and potable water before four. I'll be busy with the bill of lading and with the consignee's agent. We've checked blocking and bracing of the cargo. I think you know what to do."

Carver smiled. "I'll make sure the hands know the stationing bill and the fire bill. She'll be set to go."

***

In the forecastle that evening, Samuel Craig complained about the food, his first meal aboard the ship, a beef stew of fresh beef and vegetables, and soft bread and tea. He started taking the steps needed to raise his standing with the crew.

Craig fostered discontent to get men to listen to him, to fear what he might say about them. He had chosen his victim, Nicholas Priest, his object of ridicule, and began the process of instilling fear among the forecastle hands. "That brass bounder, Priest, is a nancy-boy, an abomination. I'll bet he'll suck me off within a week."

Paul Thomas Fuhrman

PART TWO

Paul Thomas Fuhrman

Nineteen

Departure from New York

Oh, gallant was our galley from her carven
Steering-wheel
To her figurehead of silver and her beak of
Hammered steel
The leg-bar chafed the ankle, and we gasped for cooler air
But no galley on the water with our galley
Could compare

—Rudyard Kipling

Monday, May 27, 1872
Lat 40°30′29″ N, Long 73°58′15″W

Nicholas Priest needed little encouragement to be on deck this morning; his adventure was to begin today. Smallbridge remained in his bunk, his blanket drawn tightly over his head. Priest was dressed and waiting at the galley door well before the boatswain called all hands on deck. Old Bishop gave him a cup of coffee from the officer's pot and a ship's biscuit fifteen minutes before the others were even on deck. The loom of the yet-to-rise sun had already begun to light up the city. Priest took his cup and hardtack to the starboard bulwark to watch Manhattan go to work. He saw tugs, ferries, and small coastal passenger steamers ply the waters of the Hudson and East Rivers. He watched as they extinguished their navigational lights. Weeks ago, he thought the voyage would be his death, but today the prospect of a sixteen-thousand-mile voyage spanning two hemispheres excited him.

"Good morning, Mr. Gabriel."

"The mate'll cure ya of risen' before the others, lad. Ya'll learn the value of sleep soon enough." Eoghan Gabriel smiled at Priest, who wondered how the boatswain felt on the day of his first voyage.

Priest watched as the boatswain walked forward to the deck cabin and shouted, "Heave out there, johnnies, on deck with yers. The sun's above the horizon. On deck now."

Priest watched as the men slowly emerged on deck. Most had bloodshot eyes and the mild confusion of too little sleep and too much whiskey the night before. The apprentices made their way on deck for their coffee and ship's biscuit. Only Smallbridge smoked, and his implement was a small, short-stemmed pipe that stubbornly refused to stay lit. When Mr. Carver and Mr. Lennon emerged from the cabin, Priest laughed. "Time to work."

The scrape of the holystone had become a familiar sound to Priest, as had the feel of wet sand, seawater, and the drag of the swabs used to flail the deck dry. He knelt now, his knees cushioned by his rolled-up trousers, and he pushed and pulled the holystone rhythmically in front of him. His body no longer complained. A smudge from someone's sea-boots disappeared beneath his stone with a moment's extra labor. Priest glimpsed upward at the gray, overcast sky filling with the gradual pale light of daybreak. He wondered if he would hear the morning gun on Governor's Island. His mind wandered; he had been watching the building of the Brooklyn Bridge and thought of the men in the cofferdams.

I'm lucky.

Scrape, scrape. "More water." The seawater pumped up from the harbor was cold and a little greasy. The salt stung an open abrasion on his right hand. He felt a sense of peace and comfort in routine work, work that required little thought. This thoughtless peace was soon replaced with reverie, the feel of Sophie's naked hips on his fingers, the orbs of her breasts in his palms.

128

The Downeaster

Priest saw Jeremy Ernst glance quickly over his shoulder to see where the mates and the boatswain were, if they were out of earshot. Ernst's expression was familiar to Priest—all too familiar.

"Priest. What was all that moaning about last night? Haven't you learned to be quiet when you're pulling the pudding? Oh, oh, *ooooh*, Sophie."

"Who in hell is Sophie? She's not that young whore up in Maine. Everyone's had a poke or two with her. That's what my dad's foreman says. Sooophie, Sooophie, I'm gonna, I'm goonna..."

Smallbridge had had enough. "Shut the hell up, Jeremy. Ain't no business of yours what Priest did."

"Don't spoil the fun, Smallbridge. I bet he's a virgin. The only screwing he's ever done is choking his chicken." Ernst laughed. "Soophie."

Priest shouted, "Go to hell, Ernst."

Sam Duder, who, by virtue of being an able-bodied, observed but did not holystone, knowing that if the elder Ernst kept up his verbal assault, a fight would break out and Peleg Carver would be happy to end it on the spot with his fists or his massive boots. "Pipe down, damn it. Ernst, shut your mouth. Priest, get that hand back on your holystone and your knees back on deck."

Smallbridge fired the last volley. "Priest's no virgin, I'll swear to it."

***

Sam Duder's voice was the sort of rough tenor that cut through fogs and relieved swollen sinuses of their contents. Peleg Carver heard the "damn it" and saw Nicholas Priest standing, enraged. Carver turned to Henry Lennon and said in a voice that showed humor as well as irritation. "Hear that, Mr. Lennon?"

"Aye, I did. Priest and da elder Ernst. Wondered when that was ter start."

Carver smiled. "Both watches involved, Lennon. Starboard watch and it would be your problem. Both watches makes it my business, don't it?"

Lennon chuckled. "Not that I care a jot."

129

Carver smiled and then bellowed, "Elder Ernst! Priest! Lay here."
Sam Duder looked at the two boys. "You're in for it now."

***

Isaac Griffin had spent the night aboard ship, as Kayleigh had departed for Boston the previous morning. Today was the day; the charter party's agent would arrive shortly before noon to sign the bill of lading.

Griffin knew from experience that the bill of lading was the foremost protection given to the shipper, the ship's master, and the consignee also. He very carefully read the bill of lading word by word and sentence by sentence—

It is mutually agreed and so forth.

Although Griffin was not a lawyer, ship's masters must understand certain legal fundamentals such as in rem, general averages and particular averages, barratry, and bottomry bond, subjects he knew well. Griffin read the negligence clause and others pertaining to the specifics of this voyage, a passage from New York to San Francisco. He also read where the consignee specified that the cargo be delivered in no more than 160 days from the day of departure, with exceptions being made for exigencies such as rescue at sea and the towing of distressed vessels.

The bill of lading appeared to have been taken from a standard Brown Brothers, Ferguson form.

> *General Averages payable according the proportion of interest, and as to matters not therein provided for, according to the usages of the Port of New York, or at port of destination in owner's option, adjusters to be named by Owners or their agents, and average bond to be signed with values declared therein...the owner of the ship shall have exercised due diligence to make said ship in all respects seaworthy and properly manned...*

Of particular interest to Griffin was an agreement for the

consignee to pay the shipper a five percent bonus for delivery in 110 days or less.

***

Peleg Carver stood with his left shoulder angled toward the boys, his hands by his hips folded in fists. "Well, well, well. Mr. Ernst and you there, Mr. Priest—what's the shouting about?"

Sam Duder had warned both boys that Peleg Carver had a reputation for the administration of immediate justice even though that justice was not always appropriate to the offense. Tempting a Yankee mate was a fool's business.

Priest was first to respond to the mate's question. "Nothing, sir. We're not angry at each other. It was no more than a joke, a prank, sir." Priest saw the surprise on Jeremy's face. Jeremy had not expected Priest to say what he had said and take the risk of offending the mate.

"And you agree with Mr. Priest there?"

"Yes, sir. We were just joking with each other. We're not angry at all."

Peleg Carver looked first to Priest and then to Jeremy Ernst. A smile formed on his face. "Since the two of you are having so much fun with each other, you can't be working hard enough. I have something in mind that you'll enjoy. You'll be laughing and smiling like young monkeys in heat."

A few moments later, Priest found himself climbing the fore-mast with a brush in his rear pants pocket and a slush bucket in his left hand. He was on his way to the topsail yards to grease the parral for the upper topsail. Jeremy Ernst, similarly equipped, made a voyage up the main-mast.

Carver's voice carried upward. "Clean it off first! Where's your rags?"

Priest and Ernst descended to the main deck, buckets in hand, and walked with Peleg Carver to the boatswain's locker. Suitably equipped to rub the old grease off the iron parrals, the boys climbed their masts again, but not quickly enough to stem Carver's comments

131

about their energy. "What are you, old women?"

A drop of grease fell on the deck with a gentle splat. The boys were called to the deck, shown the spot. "What's this? What the hell is this? Did one of you spit tobacco on my deck? What kind of fool do ye take me for? Stick your nose in it and tell me what that is. Both of you!"

Priest answered the mate. "Sir, that's grease from our buckets. Nobody spit."

"Well, why are you looking at me? Do you need an invitation or something? Get a stone and a bucket of water and get it up. Move! This barky's getting under way today."

***

Isaac Griffin stood amidships, starboard side, watching two squat lighters approach under tow with potable water for his forward and main steel water tanks. By now the sun had been up for nearly two hours and the sound of New York had reached a vigorous note. Smoke and steam curled upward from the roofs of buildings to disappear in swirling confusion from the wind twisting and spilling around the buildings. The sound of horses' shoes clattered, and teamsters' voices rose sharply above the low hum of those going to and from work.

Griffin was having a busy day. He had reviewed the bill of lading and the principle clauses of the charter party, the voyage, freight, lay days, negligence clause, ice clause, penalties for nonperformance, canceling date, liberty to tow and assist vessels, as near the port as she could safely get, and other clauses reflecting a voyage doubling Cape Horn.

He would see the water put aboard and sign a draft for Christison and Son to pay for it. He would hear the ship's bell ring out the hours of the watch, and supper would be served by watch. Unconsciously, he examined the hatch gratings and the canvas applied to make them waterproof using both hands, although only his left palm and fingers felt the taut, rough canvas. If the cargo was damaged or rusted beyond repair from his negligence, he and Billy would be liable, not the underwriters.

A small steam launch approached with a telegram for Captain Griffin. He opened it to find it was from Kayleigh:

"I love you. Don't worry. My prayers are for you and the *Providence*."

He had hoped for a letter, a letter having the faint trace of her scent, nutmeg and flowers, as well as the flow of her script across the page.

An hour later, another steam launch approached, carrying the agent for the consignee, Westinghouse. His cargo was the new Westinghouse railway air brakes and knuckle couplers and the tools for their installation and repair. This cargo promised to revolutionize railroading by making it far safer for passenger, train crews, and freight. The Central Pacific Railroad was willing to pay a premium to get it.

The agent was led to Griffin's reception area and office. There was a rap on his door and his steward announced, "Mr. Sean McWhorter, sir."

The agent was in his mid-forties and had probably read hundreds of bills of lading. He sat across from Griffin and nodded his head and said, "Uh-haw," as he finished each paragraph. He reached for his pen and signed for the consignees and remarked, "Guess you'll carry a bit of sail to get the bonus. Be careful with the cargo."

***

At three in the afternoon, the New York Harbor tug *John H. Dialogue* hailed the *Providence* and asked if she was ready for the tow. Peleg Carver answered aye and requested the tug to heave over a messenger so the towing hawser could be hauled aboard and made fast. Once the hawser was made fast, Carver shouted, "All hands, up anchor!"

Lennon then ordered, "Man the capstan." Heavers were inserted and made fast with steel pins. The boatswain assembled the cat and fish gear and made it ready.

"Heave round!"

Sam Duder had wanted to sing out, "Away Santy Ano," but several of the Irish hands asked him to sing, "Holy Ground Once More."

Fourteen barebacked and barefooted men began the labor of raising anchor. Duder sang the verse and the capstan gang sang the chorus. Feet and voices thumped out a rhythm on the forecastle deck. The hardest work was gathering the first coil around the capstan. Several of the landsmen broke sweat. The ship moved upwind toward the anchor and the work became gradually easier as the ship gained momentum. Feet pounded, the pawls clicked, and the anchor cable rose through the hawse-pipe to the controllers and round the capstan. Priest and Jeremy Ernst, still under instruction from the mate, tailed off each length of anchor chain, unshackled it with a maul and spike, and faked it out on deck for stowage.

Despite their hangovers, the capstan gang sang out:

Fare thee well, my lovely Dinah, A thousand times adieu. We are bound away from the Holy Ground And the girls we love so true. We'll sail the salt seas over And we'll return once more, And still I live in hope to see the Holy Ground once more.

Chorus:
You're the girl that I adore, And still I live in hope to see The Holy Ground once more. Now when we're out a-sailing And you are far behind Fine letters will I write to you With the secrets of my mind, The secrets of my mind, my girl,

Oh now the storm is raging And we are far from shore; The poor old ship she's sinking fast And the riggings they are tore. The night is dark and dreary, We can scarcely see the moon, But still I live in hope to see The Holy Ground once more. It's now the storm is over And we are safe on shore We'll drink a toast to the Holy Ground And the girls that we adore. We'll drink strong ale and porter And we'll make the taproom roar, And when our money is all spent We'll go to sea once more.

Lennon shouted, "Long stay." The chain moved round and was tailed off. "Short stay, Mr. Carver."

Eoghan Gabriel shouted out, "Bust her, boys, bust her. You're the boys to bust her." By this time, Duder sang out "Away Santy Ano," a shantey that foretold the voyage ahead and described the ship and its captain.

From New York Town we're bound away, Heave aweigh (Heave aweigh!) Santy Ano. Around Cape Horn to Frisco Bay, We're bound for Californi-o.

So Heave her up and away we'll go, Heave aweigh (Heave aweigh!) Santy Ano. Heave her up and away we'll go, We're bound for Californi-o.

She's a fast clipper ship and a bully crew, Heave aweigh (Heave aweigh!) Santy Ano. A down-east Yankee for her captain, too. We're bound for Californi-o.

Henry Lennon soon shouted, "Up and down," as the anchor was about to break from the mud.

The boatswain added his encouragement, "Heave now. Heave. Two more turns."

At last, Henry Lennon shouted, "Anchor's aweigh."

The tug strained on her towing line and the *Providence* turned downriver. She was soon past Bedloe Island and moving toward the Narrows. The anchor was raised to the cat-head and fished and stowed for sea. Jackasses were placed in the hawse-pipes. It was six in the afternoon.

A quiet Isaac Griffin chuckled under his breath. He peered through his watch glasses and saw a young lieutenant of artillery in his red kepi watching the *Providence* from on top of a rampart on Governor's Island. She had put on a show.

By seven-thirty in the evening, the pilot had departed on the tug and Carver gave the order to make sail: "Let fall the upper and lower topsails." Then the spanker and forward staysails were unfurled and soon drawing wind. Carver thought he felt the bow of the ship rise and cut the water better. Then her two courses and all topgallants were let fall; Sandy Hook light bore WSW at three miles. All sails were trimmed and *Providence* continued eastward. By eight that evening, the light ship bore due north. The port watch was fed supper, then sent on deck; the starboard watch was then fed. Watch on watch had begun and would not end until the ship was safely moored in San Francisco.

At twenty minutes before midnight, Priest and the elder Ernst finished chipping and stowing the anchor cable. Priest, a member of the starboard watch, stood his watch when called on deck despite having worked nearly continuously since seven that morning. Jeremy Ernst gladly fell asleep in his bunk, too exhausted to care about what he had started with Priest.

While departing from New York, the ship experienced hard gales and cloudy weather. Several men were seasick. No observations of the navigational stars, the moon, or the planets were made. One careful observation had been made having nothing to do with navigation; Samuel Craig had overheard the exchange between Priest and the elder Ernst.

At four-thirty that morning, Priest had not yet gone to sleep after being relieved by the port watch. He tossed noisily beneath his blanket. Smallbridge reached up and shook him in his bunk. "Christ sakes, Priest. Get some sleep or at least allow me to."

Priest then asked Smallbridge the question that burned in his mind: "Sophie—she didn't just want to use me, did she?"

Smallbridge thought for a moment and replied, "Why does that matter now? Get some sleep, Priest."

Twenty

First Sunday at Sea

Grasshopper sitting on a sweet potato vine
Along comes a chicken and says you're mine
The Soldier's Joy

Sunday, June 2, 1872
Lat 35°57′00″N, Long 54°22′00″W

Griffin stood at the chart table and prepared to write his daily entry into the ship's log. He had Peleg Carver's sailings calculations before him and the deck log recording, watch by watch, the ship's tack, sails carried, wind direction and strength, and the courses steered and speeds attained since noon Saturday. The ship's position had been calculated by dead reckoning. Griffin always accepted the necessity of using an estimated position but never liked it. He muttered something to himself about Columbus's reliance on dead reckoning and laughed. Having had his spell of humor, he opened the page of the logbook and entered the latitude and longitude—leaving the seconds at zero—distance sailed, and wind direction. Then the following:

> *"It remained very nearly calm all the first part till*
> *nearly 2 am and then the wind increased some and*
> *we set the royals. Toward noon it increased again*
> *and hauled more easterly and the sea day ends with*

a brisk breeze from about SSE and very pleasant Sunday weather. We came in sight of a ship-rigged vessel at daylight and noon..."

He stopped writing in frustration. No matter how much effort or attention he gave it, his script was barely legible and the letters had a pronounced list to port, the sure mark of left-handed penmanship. He set the pencil down. By now, he refused to think of the ease and facility he'd had with his right hand prior to the accident. He spoke to himself. "Damn it. Pick the pencil up. Concentrate."

"She was about 2 miles off on our lee quarters and steering rather more southerly than we are. I think she's bound from Boston to Australia. (If she were bound for San Francisco, I could compare logs with her on my arrival there.) We are steering E by S to make our sails full off the wind. Sometimes we cannot lie up better than east."

Compare logs. Chitchat about this tack or topsails and topgallants. Hell, he wanted to race. He wanted to see that ship up close enough to speak to her. He wanted to challenge her master to a wager. He wanted his crew to feel the rush of a race as he drove them to squeeze all the speed he could from wind, sail, and his knowledge of the seas he sailed upon. He wanted to see that ship steadily fall behind him and disappear beneath the horizon. "Beat her, boys, and we'll splice the main brace with fine Kentucky bourbon, my bourbon. 'Whiskey for My Johnnies.' " That's what he imagined saying.

The image of Kayleigh's face and the money to pay off *San Matias*'s mortgage crossed his mind. He slammed his left hand palm-down on the chart table and relished his imaginary triumph and its delicious reward. He then went on deck, checked sail trim, and used the patent log to calculate the ship's speed. Finished and satisfied, he joined the mates and apprentices for dinner in the saloon.

***

The Downeaster

Sam Duder spoke with both his hands and his mouth. "Anybody that can play or sing a tune's welcome to. Don't be shy. Bring out your instruments, now. C'mon, Priest, Smallbridge says you got a fiddle; wouldn't pawn it for ten dollars is what he says. Craig, I saw that mandolin. Go on, bring 'em out. Let's have some fun before Mr. Carver finds us another lesson from the Philadelphia Catechism."

Those were Sam Duder's words introducing Nicholas Priest and the Ernst brothers to a Sunday at sea during the dogwatches. "Boys, a johnny's got Sunday to clean, mend, and play, and we ain't done none of the playing yet. There's men here want to stamp their feet and sing."

"I reckon I'll play and sing if you do too. I got a good ear for music and I'll tetch you a tune or two if you'll tetch me." Priest was pleased to hear Craig's offer.

"I'll go get my violin, Craig. Do you think there's something we both could play?"

Craig turned his head away from Priest to look at the men sitting aft of the forecastle. He winked to remind them of his boast. Turning back to Priest, he smiled and stated, "Reckon so."

As Priest returned from the apprentice cabin with his violin and joined Craig on the forecastle deck, heads turned to see what would happen. The ship's carpenter paused while giving a haircut. Needles stopped mid-stitch while mending worn oilskins, and pipes were extracted from the lips of idle men. Only the landsmen, exhausted from watch on watch and sleeping on faked coils of line, failed to notice the musicians step out on their stage. Silence and expectation took the deck. Duder laughed. "Violin. We'll show you how to turn that thing into a fiddle."

Samuel Craig said, "You go first Priest. Seein' as you're the young 'un."

Priest opened his mouth and started to say, "I've only played for myself and in school," when a sailor shouted out, "Give us a show!"

Surprised, Priest continued, "My mother insisted I learn. I think you'll like this one, though. It's by my favorite composer—"

"Don't need a blathering sermon; just get on with it," one of the Irish boys bellowed.

Priest realized what he had been doing and laughed, "Okay. Okay. It has no words but goes da-da-de-da-da...

Priest saw a man point to Mr. Carver and immediately started the third movement of Beethoven's Violin Concerto. He was a little nervous at first, but when he heard a strong *"Ja, gute"* and saw men break into a sailor's reel, he became very comfortable. In truth, he was really pleased with himself. He had never, never in his life experienced the thrill of being the focus of attention, of providing so much joy. He finished and was surprised to be asked to play it again. When it was complete for the second time, he was greeted with, *"Hoch soll er leben!"*

He could not have felt better. He bowed formally while making a dramatic sweep with his bow hand and said, "Thank you. *Danke.*"

The laughter roared and two Germans shouted, *"Hals und beinbruch!"* and, *"Tausend dank!"* The sleeping landsmen were now sitting on the cargo hatch wide-awake and clapping. One Irishman rubbed his eyes and shouted, "Play us a jig."

Samuel Craig was next. He sat on top of the capstan, tapped the dead tobacco from his pipe on the cast iron, then took up his mandolin and addressed his audience.

"Boys, I reckon that was good, but you better loosen up them knees, 'cause here comes one you can jig to. D'ya know it?"

> *Love somebody, yes I do.*
> *Love somebody, yes I do.*
> *Love somebody, yes I do.*
> *Love somebody, but it ain't you.*

One man shouted, "That's a sesh song; heard it at Petersburg." He stood and pumped his fist in the air to call for more.

> *I am my mama's darling boy*
> *I am my mama's darling boy*
> *I am my mama's darling boy*
> *Sing a little song called "Soldier's Joy"*

"That's it, that's it. That's what I thought it was." The veterans, Yank and Rebel, reveled together, no longer separated by fortifications, muskets, officers, or causes.

> *Fifteen cents for the morphine, twenty-five cents for the beer*
> *Fifteen cents for the morphine, gonna carry me 'way from here*
> *Oh, my Soldier's Joy.*

As Craig sang and played his mandolin, he gradually increased the tempo with each verse. The forecastle gang quickly picked up on the chorus, and two of the men did jigs. Their legs blazed beneath them but their backs were straight and their arms hung by their sides—no smiles, but legs moving and crossing and kicking out the rhythm in unison. One man shouted enthusiastically, "Soon or never."

The lyrics were grim, yet these men wrung every ounce of enjoyment they could from each note. Even old Bishop stepped out of the galley door and smiled.

"Hey, Priest, do you have an ear for it?"

"I'll try."

Priest's violin scratched a few notes while Craig plucked a single note on his mandolin. When the scratching stopped and both instruments resonated together, Priest nodded to Craig. "Got the chord."

"Now slowly, Craig, the dadle-dadle-dadle-dadle-daw-daw-dee..." The music emerged from Priest's violin and soon the boy felt comfortable enough to let Craig carry the song while he played harmony.

"Let's go, Maestro Craig. From the beginning."

Both played. Craig's eyes closed and it was obvious he was smiling while he sang. No beer. No morphine. But for a moment Craig and eighteen men were in a hollow somewhere in the Southern Appalachian Mountains dancing and singing.

"Priest, short bow strokes, strong strokes!"

"Like this?"

"That's it!"

I am my mama's darling child
I am my mama's darling child
I am my mama's darling child
And I don't care for you.

Eoghan Gabriel approached and quietly reminded them the watch was soon to change. The starboard watch was to be on deck. Both nodded, and the music continued as sweetly as before. When it was finished and after bows were taken, applause rendered, and several appreciative slaps placed on Priest's back, Craig put his arm over Priest's shoulder. "Pretty good fiddlin', boy. Let me tell you what that song's all about. I'm a Johnny Reb. I've been wounded. We'll need to make you a new bridge for your fiddle, and next Sunday rosin that bow more. I'll tetch you another 'un after our watch."

"I've this pocket knife. We can use it to carve the bridge."

Craig laughed. "That old thing won't cut butter. I reckon I'll show you the cure."

The port watch timekeeper walked forward and pulled the lanyard on the ship's bell four times. He looked to both Craig and Priest and said, "Sorry, you're on deck now."

Priest went aloft to his watch station on the foremast. He was there for the entire dogwatch, two hours, to be the lookout and to overhaul the running rigging and make it ready to brace to the wind if needed. Craig remained in the waist. Under the eye of the boatswain, he went from pin to pin to make sure that tacks and sheets were ready when needed, when the wind hauled. After his trick aloft, Priest joined Craig, who was sitting on the capstan again, smoking his pipe.

"Heard that Ernst boy make fun of you. Pay him no mind. You and me's friends. Don't doubt one bit you fucked that girl. Felt real good too, didn't it?"

Priest blushed and lowered his eyes.

"Ah, I'm making you red-faced. Meant no harm. You can tell me about it if you want to. Just saying that once you done it, you'll always want more." Craig chuckled at Priest's reaction and relit his pipe. "I understand. After supper, I'll tech you a new song we can play, 'The Sourwood Mountain Song.' "

***

Griffin opened the weather door of *Providence*'s wheelhouse and motioned for Peleg Carver to join him by the taffrail. "What did you think about that show—Craig and Priest?"

Carver replied, "It was entertaining, I suppose."

"What do you know about Craig?"

Carver replied, "This ain't about passing the time of day, is it?"

"It ain't. I promised that boy's father I'd keep him safe."

Twenty-One

Nursing—Doctor Marie Zakrzewska

Some three, or five, or seven, and thirty years;
A Roman nose; a dimpling double-chin;
Dark eyes and shy that, ignorant of sin,
Are yet acquainted, it would seem, with tears;
A comely shape; a slim, high-coloured hand,
Graced, rather oddly, with a signet ring;
A bashful air, becoming everything;
A well-bred silence always at command.
Her plain print gown, prim cap, and bright steel chain
Look out of place on her, and I remain
Absorbed in her, as in a pleasant mystery.
Quick, skillful, quiet, soft in speech and touch...
"Do you like nursing?" "Yes, Sir, very much."
Somehow, I rather think she has a history.
                              —William Ernest Henley

Monday, June 3, 1872
Boston

Kayleigh lowered her head and shook it slightly from left to right once, then smiled, relieved, as she rose from the gynecological examination table adjacent to Dr. Marie Zakrzewska's office in the New England Hospital for Women and Children. Kayleigh could still feel the coldness of the speculum although it had been removed for more than a few minutes. She stepped behind a screen, undid her examination gown, and started to dress herself. As she picked up her undergarments, she remembered the spotting, why she had hurriedly arranged the examination with Dr. Zakrzewska, who was both a friend and now her physician. She expected Dr. Zakrzewska to either confirm her suspicions or set her mind at ease.

Once dressed, she paced nervously in front of a window opening on Warrenton Street. Kayleigh could see the dome of the Bullfinch Building in the distance. She thought of all that was accomplished there, including her own efforts. As she did so, the corners of her lips unconsciously curved upward in a small bow.

As she paced, the door to Dr. Zakrzewska's office opened and the doctor entered. "So we both think you are pregnant. You and your husband wasted no time, did you? Did you as much as discuss the possibility before he rushed off to sea?"

Dr. Marie Zakrzewska's smile set Kayleigh at ease as she invited Kayleigh to take a seat across the desk from her.

"It is early in your pregnancy. I do believe you are pregnant. Women often know when conception occurs and they are correct. My examination told me your breasts are unusually sensitive and your areolae are darker than I expected for your fair complexion. Then, too, you say you have been spotting, virtually a sure sign. I wish you had come to see me when this first occurred so I could examine the blood under a microscope. But it is too early for you to have missed a cycle."

"I'm so glad you agreed to see me, Doctor. I did not want to be seen by a male physician."

"Kayleigh, I will have no talk about gender and the ability to practice medicine."

"I just wanted to avoid someone telling me I suffer from nervous exhaustion or telling me I'm just being female."

Kayleigh and Dr. Zakrzewska both laughed, but it took Kayleigh a moment to realize the humor in what she had just said.

"In my medical practice, I've noticed that being pregnant is peculiar to the female, yes?"

Dr. Zakrzewska smiled warmly and assumed a relaxed position, settling back in her chair while tucking the curled index finger of her right hand under her chin. Her right elbow rested on the arm of her chair.

"I will assume you are happy? I say that because you lose so much when you marry, your wealth, and what you may wish to do with your life. Having a child is such a responsibility. I'm sorry, Kayleigh; those are my thoughts. I should not have been so direct."

Kayleigh smiled. "I've never been as happy. Griffin is an unusual man, Doctor. What brought us together was physical attraction at first. I did nothing to discourage it. I surprised him as well as myself the first time we were alone.

"That's not enough, of course, but it is important." Kayleigh laughed. "And so enjoyable. We found we could reveal ourselves to each other, our strengths, weaknesses, and even our wounds."

The doctor relaxed further into her seat. "I understand. What future do you see for yourself? What future does he see?"

Kayleigh smoothed the folds of her skirt and moved slightly toward the edge of her seat. "We've discussed children—we both want them. He wants to be financially secure, but that's not what drives him. He's religious although he's reluctant to admit it. He says there is no need for God to interfere in our lives, yet he feels God's presence in the terrible storms of Cape Horn."

"Unusual. Has he read Emerson, perhaps Locke?"

"I think he has. He has read Huxley and Darwin. I don't think he's unusual as much as honest with himself; a willingness to admit that he has questions. I don't think he will ever be complete until he has his answers."

"Aren't you afraid of where this may lead?"

"He loves me. It's so obvious that he cares more for me than he does for himself. I have nothing to fear. We will face the future together, his, mine, whatever happens."

"Let's talk about your future. I know how you feel about women. You've sacrificed so much of your time and refused to hide your opinions. Why do you work so hard, this nursing? I need to know as your physician, you understand?"

"As my physician and not a friend?"

"Yes."

"I volunteered as a nurse at first because I had been raped. I hid this from everyone. I tried to hide it from myself. I was afraid of men. I was ashamed. The hours and the work isolated me from my fears and from myself. Now nursing speeds time until I'm reunited with my husband."

Dr. Zakrzewska leaned forward in her seat, bringing her face closer to Kayleigh's. "I never knew about the rape. I should have been more perceptive. Are you still ashamed?"

Kayleigh took a deep breath. "It's not an issue now. When I finally told what had happened to my mother and to Isaac, telling about it freed me from fear and shame also." Kayleigh laughed. "I do enjoy sex."

"Good. You should, and so should he. But is it necessary to continue to work so hard?"

"One reason is financial independence for women. Unless they—"

Dr. Zakrzewska became impatient, sitting bolt straight in her seat. "I know. I know. But you?"

Kayleigh's posture stiffened. "Nursing suffers because it is women's work, an extension of nurture. Because it is women's work it is drudgery. It's work too menial for men. It will never pay a living wage as it is. That's why Florence Nightingale is so important. She proves nursing is important to healing."

"Her ideas are too limited, Kayleigh." Dr. Zakrzewska drummed the fingers of her right hand on her desk and then took hold of the fingers with her left hand and pressed them into the wood to stop the drumming. "And," she continued, "Nightingale mentioned gender, competition with men. Here's what you must know. You will not like this, so I might as well be blunt."

Now Kayleigh sat bolt upright.

"You waste your time and ability nursing as you do. I also believe the stress of hard labor will place your health and your baby's at risk. Think of yourself as an egg and a hen in one. It's so easy to injure your uterus, and pregnancy can be painful. You must stop. It's devastating to lose a baby. I've seen it too often, the guilt."

Although Kayleigh knew such a warning would come, her mind still refused to accept the limitations of her pregnancy. "Do I need to stop now?"

"Yes, no more twelve-hour days and whole weeks spent in your ward."

"But I'm setting a positive example."

"No, that's not so. Florence Nightingale came from a titled English family. Your Dorothea Dix had money as you do. Don't you think ordinary women know they will never be given the respect or opportunity these women were given? Have the women you work with ever revealed what they think of you?"

Kayleigh was not prepared for that question. "No. I never thought it mattered."

Dr. Zakrzewska pointed a finger as if to scold Kayleigh. "What matters is what women see as an opportunity. Not just to make money, but to be respected, to feel pride in themselves."

"But don't you teach the students in your nursing school what Florence Nightingale teaches?"

"*Klein Wissenschaft*. Do you know that phrase?"

Dr. Zakrzewska did not wait for a reply.

"It means 'little science,' and it was used by Dr. Schmidt, my mentor in Berlin, to describe what a professional, a licensed midwife, should be taught. This is my model for nursing. When I first became familiar with that term, it meant all science other than the science needed for discovery. It meant clinical and not laboratory science, but I'm not sure *klein Wissenschaft* is all a nurse should know. I'm very concerned about limitations. I'm already seeing shortcomings with the experience my hospital provides women physicians, but I don't know the answer yet."

Kayleigh could not hide the puzzled look on her face.

"I believe, Kayleigh, that the emphasis of a nurse's work is clinical. But the nurse must understand what she sees, what her hands, her ears, her nose tell her. She must understand pathology and the process of healing. It is so much more than cleanliness, fresh air, and good food. The nurse is an extension of the doctor's mind and hands. A nurse's mind must also have scientific acuity and absolute impartiality." She then relaxed again, placing her index finger under her chin.

Kayleigh asked, "Don't you think the directors at Massachusetts General might balk at such a school? Most oppose even the school we've proposed."

Dr. Zakrzewska smiled. "It is how I've organized my nursing school. Watch, you will come to me for instructors one day."

The smile disappeared from the doctor's face and her face grew stern. "I go on too much. I want to see you again when your menses fail to come, but in no more than a month. I want you to keep a record of your temperature. I'll lend you a thermometer. You must see me sooner if you think it's needed. You will be a healthy mother, and your child will be healthy too. That is our goal, you and I. First, a healthy baby and a healthy mother; then I will introduce you to a few of my friends."

The stern expression changed to that of a mother instructing a child. "We will help you discover the ability you've been given and the opportunity you have. We will talk more about nursing and your ambitions."

The dispassionate medical expression appeared again. "Here is what you must do now." Kayleigh accepted the pamphlet Dr. Zakrzewska handed her.

"This tells you what you must expect; your body is changing by the minute."

Dr. Zakrzewska stood at her desk and extended her hand to Kayleigh. Before Kayleigh could take her hand and say, "Thank you," Dr. Zakrzewska made one last point. "Kayleigh, not every woman can or should be a nurse."

Thursday, June 6, 1872
Massachusetts General Hospital

Two days had passed and 5:30 a.m. had arrived in the Bullfinch Building, in the postoperative ward. Kayleigh MacKenna awoke in the fold-up bed she shared with another nurse, Rachael, in a little room in the middle of the ward that was used during the day as a sitting room for patients and their visitors. Kayleigh and Rachael were not alone. Two feet away, against the opposite wall, two additional nurses, Clara, and the physically formidable and older Kazia, occupied another fold-up bed.

Kayleigh awoke from restlessness and from sharing a bed with a partner who tossed and turned and whose breath emitted the sweetly rancid odor of whiskey. She shook her partner. "Come on, Rachael, get up. We've fifteen minutes to get dressed and leave the room."

Rachael stirred, groaned, propped her body up on one elbow, and stared at Kayleigh through an open eye. "All right, Miss Prissy. I hear you."

With that, Rachael moved her legs so that her feet were dangling over the side of the bed. She then plunged them over the edge, until they struck the wooden floor with a soft thud before seeking her felt slippers.

"There, Miss Prissy, don't that make you happy now? Daylight, girls! If I can get up, so can you. Get up!"

The four women shook off their sleeping gowns and took their day clothes off makeshift racks hanging off the backs of two spartan chairs. When dressed, the four nurses went directly to the common lavatory shared by the nurses and patients. Faces were splashed, hands washed, as they waited in turn for the toilet.

"Go fetch the breakfast for the patients and us too. It's your turn, Kayleigh; you too, Rachael," Kazia demanded.

Kayleigh and Rachael walked to the kitchen, loaded twelve breakfasts on wooden trays, and carried them back from the main kitchen to their ward using a cart with racks stacked on top of each other. Only after the breakfast had been distributed to the ward's patients would the nurses eat.

After finishing her meal, Kayleigh spoke to the other nurses.

"We'll need to start washing the linen. It's not right to be told what to do. The directors are coming here Friday."

Kazia looked at Kayleigh through squinted eyes. "It can wait until you get back from the kitchen. Don't want Miss Rich Lady missing any of the fun, now, do we?"

Kayleigh replied, "Why do you always say things like that to me? Why?"

"Well, what's true is true. You can work or not work as suits your whim. Take whole weeks off without a worry."

"I'm here now, though. I do the same work as you do. I'm not too good for that."

"Just you and Rachael get them things back to the kitchen and watch your tongue."

Kazia puffed herself up like a grackle and threatened Kayleigh with her eyes.

Rachael put a forefinger to her lips. "Shh. Stop it. The matron's just outside. C'mon, Kayleigh, I don't want to be here when the matron sticks her head through that door."

Kayleigh and Rachael quickly gathered the dirty earthenware and utensils from the patients and left. Rachael smiled and did something like a curtsy on passing the matron of nurses.

"Good morning, mum."

"Good morning, Rachael, Mrs. Griffin."

After a pleasant, unburdened, and silent walk from the kitchen scullery back to her ward, Kayleigh found the pile of dressings and linens untouched. Kazia had found some pretext to accompany the matron to the next visit ward while Clara waited idly, standing by the hamper that contained the dirty linen.

Rachael became agitated. "You let the matron near that? With it just standing there? Did you? We are going to catch all hell now. Nothing can hide that smell. Where's that fat bitch? Shirking work as usual?"

The nurses' job was to prepare the dirty linen for the hospital laundry. This meant separating the linen by use and type, scraping off

151

the excess filth of human waste, blood, and poultices, then washing the linen in a mixture of hot water and strong lye soap, wringing it in wooden rollers until it was damp-dry, then moving the linen to the hospital laundry for boiling, bluing, and pressing with mangles.

Kayleigh found herself at her usual job, standing, waist bent over a laundry tub, using a scrub board and a stiff-bristle brush to remove as much of the staining as she could. Her hands had turned red from chapping. She felt her belly pressing against the wooden tub as she worked her brush downward across the corrugated board. She continued her labor until as much dirt as possible dissolved into the hot gray water in the tub. Rachael took the washed linen from Kayleigh and rinsed it vigorously on her own scrubbing board in a tub of fresh water. When Rachael's tub became saturated with soap, she and Kayleigh lifted it and poured the contents down the drain. Clara then refilled it with hot water from a stove. When the laundry was rinsed, Clara ran the linen through a wooden wringer and then sorted and stacked it in a canvas hamper fitted with wheels. The weight of the damp linen would require three women to push it up the hill to the laundry.

Late in the afternoon, Kayleigh made rounds with her assigned patients. She cleaned wounds, examined stitches, and dressed the incisions with fresh linen. She then gave them the doses of medicines the physicians had prescribed. It pleased Kayleigh that the ward was bright with sunlight and aired out daily. It also pleased her to see the reactions to her smile. The frescoes in the Bullfinch Building added an intentional sense of cheer. To complete the homelike atmosphere, each patient had a small wool rug by his or her white metal bed to add color to the white paint and gray wainscoting covering the ward's walls. Once a week, the nurses took the rugs outside and beat the dust from them.

As Rachael made her rounds, she sat on the edge of a bed and flirted with a law student who had been injured in a horsecar accident. She seemed to take unusual care and time with changing his dressings, bathing him, and joking with him. His student friends snuck her whiskey and complimented her for her jet-black hair and buxom figure.

Dr. Zakrzewska's pamphlet was proving itself to be true. Kayleigh's lower back began to hurt; her uterus was growing with new life inside and pushing her internal organs to unaccustomed places. She felt nauseous. There was a sharp pain followed by the resumption of a now familiar rumbling ache. The sharp ache brought tears to the edges of her eyes. As evening approached and the final meal was served and taken away, Kayleigh told Rachael that she would have the bed to herself. Kayleigh was in pain and exhausted.

Kazia overheard. "Sneaking off again to leave all the dirty work for us poor girls. You're no better than we are, Irish trash—just got money; that's all."

Kayleigh felt Rachael's hand on her shoulder. "Pay her no attention. She's just jealous."

Twenty-Two

The Northeast Trades

With mast, and helm, and pennon fair,
That well had borne their part,
But the noblest thing which perish'd there
Was that young faithful heart!
                    —Felicia Dorothea Hemans

Sunday, June 4, 1872
Lat 33°52′29″N, Long 44°20′15″W
The North Atlantic, 272 Miles Logged

Providence averaged eight and a half knots on Friday, ten knots on Saturday, and, if the winds held, ought to average eleven knots today. The wind had been steady and brisk from southwest and south. Large waves crested with white foam rolled atop sides carved rough with gouges. These made *Providence* behave like a young stallion racing, absorbed and satisfied by the joy of its own physicality. It was such a beautiful sky with those cumulus clouds, and shirtsleeve temperatures in the warm sunlight. These thoughts came to Peleg Carver as he extended his dead reckoning track in the chart room. He was pleased; she was prancing and snorting along with sweat on her chest. All sails to royals muscled her forward, starboard tack, running free, the bow wake singing, the standing rigging strained like swollen sinews. This was perfect had the spanker not required constant attention to balance a heavy weather helm.

154

Peleg Carver returned to the quarterdeck to see that Griffin was still there, calculating speed from his Bliss patent log, squinting at the topsail leeches, choking off his words until Lennon and Gabriel directed the watch to trim sail to take out the offending shake or flatten the weather leeches with the bowlines. Griffin had refused to let the helm luff or come down unless the wind hauled. He would not suffer even a half-knot loss of speed. The only thing occasionally distracting Griffin was the barometer. Thus he stood, absorbed and on deck for the last thirty-six hours, unaware of all the eyes watching him, but sublimely aware of the ship's speed, feeling his identity and the ship's as one. Only one thought repeated itself in Griffin's mind: *faster.*

"Mr. Carver, fix our position and show me where we are."

Peleg Carver gritted his teeth; barely an hour had passed since noon. Still, he went to his stateroom to get his sextant, compared his hack watch to the chronometer in the chart house, and stepped back on deck. "Priest, you need to record the time and altitude, upper limb this time of day."

Carver was a Yankee and former navy officer as well; he used Priest as a quartermaster's mate because the boy was good with numbers and neat. Peleg had assigned him to help the captain navigate whenever the captain had the urge to do the first mate's duty. Carver had made sure the boy knew how, but habitually repeated, "Get ready, time first. Altitude's on the sextant."

He then went amidships and used the main-mast fife-rail to brace himself for using his sextant. When Carver felt himself move in complete harmony with the ship, he selected a reliable combination of smoked lenses to observe the sun through the sextant's low-power telescope.

"Look at the watch and listen to me; be ready to write."

The mate used his arms to steady his heavy brass sextant. He brought the sun down to the horizon, then rocked his sextant slowly to set the upper limb precisely on the horizon.

Peleg Carver barked the word "mark," then read the vernier scale for degrees, minutes, and tenths of seconds. He then asked for the recorded time.

Priest read back the elevation and time he had recorded.

Peleg Carver was an experienced navigator. He knew the ship's approximate latitude from his dead reckonings and the sextant's recorded altitude.

Carver waited an hour and repeated the process; he would use a running fix to locate the ship's position. Carver took Priest with him to the chart room.

"Do you think you can work it on your own, Priest? You've seen me and the captain do it enough to know how yourself if you've been alert."

"Aye, sir. I can do it. Watch."

Carter observed Priest step up to the chart table, then stand on his toes to reach the almanac and bring it down from its shelf. The boy took a blank piece of paper and set out a sheet to record the data needed to work the two sun sights. Bowditch was at his left elbow.

Priest asked, "What was our height above the water, sir?"

Priest then used what he had recorded, the sextant altitudes and times, the almanac data, the logarithmic tables, and other tables from Bowditch to calculate the two lines of position. When finished, he showed his work to Carver.

"You plot it on the chart." Carver admired the way the boy handled the parallel rulers and drew light, precise pencil lines.

Priest drew the two lines of position and carefully advanced the earlier line to intersect with the later one. He used the latitude scale to measure distance and calculated speed mentally. He smiled toward Carver. "The ship really is rolling along, sir!"

Carver smiled toward Priest and said, "Go see Bishop and get yourself some coffee. Tell him I would like biscuits for breakfast tomorrow."

As Priest left the chart room, Isaac Griffin entered and asked Carver, "Current? Set? Drift? Look at the pilot charts."

***

At three bells of the forenoon watch, Mr. Lennon called for the apprentices to report to him. "Lads, de captain wants ter see yews now. He's standing outside de wheelhouse. Make it smart."

Smallbridge knew the captain would be standing on the weather side of the wheelhouse and led the way. Priest was close behind him, swaying from side to side, catching his balance with every footfall, and doing so absolutely without conscious thought of the difficulty of walking on a deck in a seaway.

Smallbridge spoke. "Sir, Mr. Lennon told us you wanted to see us."

"Yes. Mr. Carver tells me there's reasonable hope you might become seamen. Smallbridge, you and Priest are going to start helming. You'll stand tricks with Stedwin and Duder, lee helm.

"Now that you can box the compass and tie a reef knot, thought you might like learning officer's work. I've carried sail to take advantage of the trades. What's the ship doing, Jeremy?"

"Mr. Carver says ten knots or better."

Griffin frowned. "That's not what I wanted to hear. You know, Smallbridge, don't you?"

"Yes, sir. She's—"

Griffin interrupted, "You tell me, Priest."

"She's started to heel hard on her lee, sir. She's nearly got her deck in it at times. Started heeling hard over before two bells."

"What do you think that does to her, Richard?"

"Ca-ca-capsize? He-heel too much?"

Griffin smiled toward Richard Ernst and said, "Good answer, but you're missing something. She's slowing down, too much sail, too much rudder. That's right, too much. Causes weather helm. We're going to furl the royals to right her up a bit and see how much faster she'll go."

Jeremy Ernst started to frown at the word "furl." He drew a rebuke from his captain.

"Don't ever let me see that again, Ernst.

"Officer's work: the rules for managing sails. Remember them." Griffin peered down his nose at each boy to measure his level of attention.

"First, always make the wind help you by blowing the sail to ease the hauling. If you're taking in sail, get the balloon out of it as soon as possible. No sense working the men on the yards harder than you have to. If the lee sheet is let go, a sail always shakes. If the weather sheet is let go, the wind stays in the sail and steadies it. Remember, a sail will always split if you allow it to shake in a gale.

"Think about that when Mr. Carver takes in the royals. On deck."
The apprentices returned to their stations.

***

Priest was excited. "He's going to let us helm."

Smallbridge replied, "Yeah. Don't smile until you've done it awhile. You saw Carver kick Craig out of the wheelhouse and swear so loud at him it startled the captain."

"Yeah, I saw that. Do you think Craig had it coming?"

When Carver gave the preparatory command for furling sail, Priest was careful to observe and commit to memory everything Mr. Carver and the boatswain did. He watched how the running rigging was prepared. How the helm and sheets were used to spill the wind from the sails, when the bunt and clewlines were bowsed. When he and the other top-men were allowed to go aloft, he made note of what gear he overhauled prior to furling and how close to the yard it was brought with clewlines and buntlines.

Although Priest was stationed on the weather side of the sail's bunt, he impulsively shouted out, "No, that's no way to make a skin. Watch me, Craig. Watch me. I'll show you." All Priest wanted to do was save Craig from a tongue-lashing. He was shocked with the anger on Craig's face.

When the top-men were permitted to leave the yard and go back on deck, Priest attempted to talk to Craig, but Craig rebuffed him and walked away while swearing that the bastards never let him be.

***

A tired Nicholas Priest felt the tension ease as Stedwin and Smallbridge took the helm and repeated the course steered and the spokes. His first trick had ended with no reprimands. Duder just smiled.

Feeling released from tension, Priest walked to the galley door and took a piece of ship's biscuit from the bread kid, poured himself a cup of coffee, and sat on the deck. He had by now become used to drinking coffee at all hours of the day and night in order to maintain alertness despite his body's desire for sleep. He had barely walked to the galley door when he heard the timekeeper strike eight bells of the afternoon watch on *Providence*'s large ship's bell. The dogwatches had begun. Ship's work stopped. Men squatted on deck with their backs to bulwarks or the deck cabin, their eyes barely open, their hands moving slowly, almost wandering about their personal tasks.

The men were tired and spent and would use what leisure time they had for cleaning and mending clothes. With Mr. Carver's permission, men went aloft to string clotheslines in the standing rigging, which soon filled with flapping white and checkered calico shirts and faded dungaree trousers. Priest imagined East Boston on Mondays, the day wives and daughters did laundry. He was relieved that Duder had not asked him or Craig to play their instruments and was surprised when he saw Craig approach him. Craig's gait was slow and doglike, not making a straight line but keeping a shoulder turned toward Priest, using the shoulder to hide his face.

Priest placed his ship's biscuit between his upper and lower teeth, using his jaws as pliers, and between biting and bending separated a chewable piece of the hard bread. Coffee and saliva softened the hardtack, releasing the flavor in his mouth. Priest thought of a cold glass of sweet milk and the hard bread. It was Craig's words that drew Priest's mind away from milk, East Boston, flapping clothes, and the numbing desire for sleep.

"Priest, d'you reckon I can have a word with you?"

Priest smiled and said, "Sure." He hoped he and Craig were still friends and would again play their mandolin and fiddle together. Priest was learning "Jenny on the Railroad." He eagerly listened to Craig's words.

"I got a temper and lots of sorrowful memories. Things happen that brings them up, and sometimes I just don't act right. I'm sorry I got mad. I reckon you just meant to help me. I'm sorry the way I acted."

Paul Thomas Fuhrman

Priest pressed his back against the warm galley bulwark and moved his shoulders forward to stretch his back muscles. This was a simple thing, but a satisfying moment's delight as the muscles lost their tension. Priest was happy to hear Craig's apology and told him he accepted it while anticipating another of Craig's stories about Kentucky and the Civil War. Appalachian music had come to delight the boy, and he too had begun to sing in the high lonesome mountain style, ending each phrase with a brief rising note as if crying.

Craig continued to hang his head low. "Priest, this here world's a cruel one. Always been so to me, always. My pa said that wars and rumors of wars was a sign the end was coming. I believe that. Jesus's gonna call the final muster soon, and I ain't agonna be found lacking."

Priest motioned for Craig to sit down with him near the galley door. Priest anticipated another of Craig's tales of privation and suffering and the strength of human endurance.

"You bed that gal, Sophie. I know what that's like and what you're yearnin' for. I had a girl, Perlie, back in Kentucky. We was hitched in this little church and she was sweet. We went at it like rabbits in the spring. Weren't even twenty. I reckon I know all about the delight there is between a girl's legs. Praise Jesus, but I miss it. I understand."

Craig stopped, let his head rise, and observed Priest's reaction. Priest observed this, and it surprised him. Sympathy? Curiosity?

"It was a cold January day. Snow was on the ground and the smell of blue wood smoke filled the hollow where we lived. My Perlie died trying to give birth; baby died too. A breech birth; the baby tried to enter this world backward. It was too much for my wife, despite all that Aunt May did to help her. The labor was pitiful hard and more than—she was just barely a woman, so tiny."

Priest thought he saw Craig's eyes start to water.

"Aunt May said it was the fever that took her. Robbed her strength from her body. Came at the wrong time, her giving birth."

Priest looked at Craig and words spilled from his mouth. "I'm sorry. I'm not sure what I would do if that happened to me. I didn't

160

really get to know Sophie much, but she asked me to help her. I can't forget that. I feel guilty and can't stop wondering what happened to her. Was that how you felt about your wife? I mean you can't stop thinking about her?"

Craig nodded his head while answering Priest's question. "I reckon so. There was nothing I could do. Aunt May said so, and she had helped nearly all the women in Lynn Camp with their birthing. I felt alone without my wife, Priest. Nothing ever again would fill me with such joy as she did. But I made up my mind. I would never again marry or do anything to bring an innocent baby into this evil world. There's no justice in it, just war, sickness, and death."

Priest felt Craig's eyes staring into his own.

"You do what you think you have to, Sophie and all, but I swore off women forever. I hoped a bullet would catch me during the war and end it, but I'm still here. I'm here and I yearn for my wife. I want to feel her body, the warmth, the softness of her thighs, even the way she smelt after she washed herself Saturdays. That won't go away, and it torments me."

"But you said you gave women up."

"I had to do something, never again. No children born into this wickedness. Still, you just can't wish you didn't feel them. You can't stop remembering. That's why I go to sea, to forget her, get away from women."

Priest saw Craig's eyes lower and look at the boy's crotch. He thought of his mother, the story she told of sailors staring at her and talking behind her back when she crossed the Atlantic.

"There's something you ken do to relieve the pain."

"What's that?"

"A man can give another man pleasure. Think on it. A man knows a man's body far better'n any woman."

Priest instinctively raised his hands to his waist, palms toward Craig, fingers spread. "I don't—"

"There ain't any harm to it. There's no babies. It ain't like marriage. You do it, then walk away. Two people doin' a favor to help each other."

"It's not right."

"Just think on it. Bible says to not let your seed fall on the ground. I'll be there if you want me. Won't tell a soul neither. We's friends, Priest."

Priest went aft to the main-mast. He hoped Mr. Lennon would send him aloft. He needed to be alone.

Craig went forward to the boatswain's lockers.

Jonathon Bishop, the cook, came through the galley door. He had overheard Samuel Craig attempt to seduce Priest, and rage showed on his broad black face. He had come to enjoy the early morning talks and the deep respect he and Priest shared.

Twenty-Three

The Garden of Eden According to Duder

The Mind is its own place, and in itself
Can make a Heaven of Hell, a Hell
Of Heaven.

—John Milton

Monday, June 5, 1872
Lat 32°38′11″N, Long 39°46′50″W
The North Atlantic in Pleasant Weather, 143 Miles Covered

It was Monday and the beginning of the dogwatches. Samuel Craig played his mandolin and sang in the high lonesome pitch of his native Kentucky hills.

Ye gentlemen and ladies fair,
Who grace this famous city,
Just listen if you've time to spare
While I rehearse a ditty,
And for the opportunity
Conceive yourself quite lucky,
For 'tis not often here you see
A hunter from Kentucky.

Craig's music and stories still excited Priest's imagination. He still wanted to believe that he and Craig were friends despite what had happened—never in his lifetime had something like that happened. Craig had not tried to threaten him, force him. Priest was confused, so he spoke to Smallbridge and Duder.

"Listen to that man sing. You know, he's lived a lot of what he sings. He's told me about life in the mountains, hunting to eat, and working in the mines. He served Lee's army and was wounded at Petersburg. He can't be bad."

Smallbridge replied first. "I'd be damned careful, Priest. He's a liar. He doesn't do his share of the work and never stops bitching. He talks about people behind their backs. Now he wants to be your sea daddy. Ask yourself why."

Priest saw Duder's face twist in anger as he spoke. "Every word out of that man's mouth is a damned lie. What you did in Bath was your business. Craig has no right t' stick his nose in it."

Priest next saw Duder's face relax and his eyes twinkle. By now Priest had learned that no one enjoyed Duder's long-winded stories more than Sam Duder himself. A story was coming, there was the smile, the silent laugh that looked like a quick swallow.

Smallbridge knew it too. "He's gonna reveal some wisdom to you, shipmate."

Duder took a breath and began, "You had yourself some tail in Bath. Ain't no use denying it. We all did that one time or another. I mean a Judy. So now you want more. That's just the way it is, wantin' more. A sailor can get his fair share of tail ashore, but remember, all the whores want money for it. The best of it comes from a wife."

Priest blurted out, "She gave me..."

Sam had heard that before and interrupted him. "Hell, boy, I been married nearly twenty-five years, and every time it's different. She knows what pleases me and I know what pleases her. Just listen and learn."

Priest winced. "Sam!"

"I'm not trying to make fun of you. Maybe you need to sow some more wild oats. I don't know. Won't hurt any to listen."

Priest took a deep breath; this story would be long.

"I can tell your parents never talked to you like I'm going to. I bet they let you think women is saints, like your mother, right? They ain't saints; they're just human like you and me. Sophie had her needs. That's why she was sweet on you.

"Let me tell you the story about how man and woman got parts down there." He pointed to his crotch. "Then you'll understand women and the way it's supposed to be.

"When God invented man and put him in the Garden of Eden, God saw that he was lonely and created woman. That's in the Bible. Now, what you don't know is Adam and Eve could never agree on anything! He said, 'I want to do this,' and she said, 'You can't do that; it'll displease God.' Now, when she wanted something, most often for Adam to do something for her, he would say no. But instead of bringing in the Higher Authority, he'd just say it was stupid, and, of course, she always would remember that and bring it up again and again. That was despite the fact that he admitted his wrongdoing and professed great buckets of sorrow at ever saying it at all. Remember, Priest, what's once said can never be called back, particularly to a sweetheart.

"Adam and Eve argued, and that made God angry because He likes things to be orderly. So God waited until they were asleep and gave Adam a cock and Eve a cunt down there."

Sam's gesture, sticking both thumbs in his trouser just above his fly, and pointing downward with his two index fingers, left no doubt as to his meaning.

"Now, they had nothing down there before because they didn't need nothin'. With these new parts came desire. You know what that is, now, don't you?

"They woke up; Eve looks over and says to Adam, 'It's long.' Adam looks over and says, 'Yours ain't. Can I touch it?'

Smallbridge muttered, "Oh, God. I can't believe—" But Duder continued.

"It doesn't take them more than three crows of a rooster to figure out what the whole man-woman short haul is and to have done it and to be thinking about doing it again."

Sam's hand gestures left little to the imagination about what a short haul was all about.

"They still argue, only not as much and not as loud. What's different now is that they got something the other wants. Oh, yes, they do.

"So they learn to make up, particularly in time for bed. God knew they would find out they needed each other and had to cooperate. Sophie knew that; all women are born knowin' it. You know about the tree of good and evil and the serpent? Well, Adam's appetite for Eve persuaded Adam to bite that apple.

"So God appears, they gets all ashamed of being naked, and they begin learning all about what good and evil is, by the sweat on thy brow and all. So cleaning up baby poop, workin' for a living, money, death, and all that came after God evicted them and us from Eden forever."

Sam briefly glanced upward, making the serious face he remembered a preacher once making while looking at Priest and Smallbridge through the corner of his left eye.

"Now, God's both wise and kind; He left one thing from the Garden of Eden for both men and women to enjoy to this very day. Getting a good fucking with your old lady is all that's left of paradise on this earth. Forget what Craig says. Now you know the true story. Man and woman are to go forth and multiply."

Sam Duder walked to the leeward side and spit tobacco juice loudly to emphasize his point, then returned.

By this time, Smallbridge was rolling with laughter while Priest was blushing from ear to ear. Smallbridge slapped Priest on the back. "Now, wasn't that some sermon?"

Jonathon Bishop had heard the conversation, particularly the laughter, and stuck his head out the galley door. "There's some truth to what Duder says, Priest. Men and women both have the urge. Damn Craig told you the devil's own chapter and verse."

The other Sam, Samuel Craig, stopped his singing long enough to see that Priest, Smallbridge, and the two old sailors were enjoying themselves. He knew that Duder disliked him. In Samuel Craig's mind, Duder and Bishop were making fun of him, ridiculing him in front of the apprentices. He thought, *Why else spit with such contempt? I can't do anything about you, Duder, but I won't take that from a nigger.*

He looked at Jonathon Bishop through the slits of his eyes and sang a song he calculated would bring fear to the black man standing in the galley door.

Oh, I'm a good old Rebel,
Now that's just what I am;
For this "fair land of Freedom"
I do not care a damn.
I'm glad I fit against it—
I only wish we'd won.
And I don't want no pardon
For anything I've done.

Wish I could take up my musket
And shoot em now yes, suh',
Sure ain't a-goin' to love 'em,
Now that is sartin sho';

And I don't want no pardon
For what I was and am;
And I won't be reconstructed,
I'm riding with the Klan.

Old Bishop turned, walked to where Craig was standing, brought his emotionless face within inches of Craig's, and laughed a low laugh from deep within his chest. He then turned his back to Craig and walked slowly, deliberately, away.

***

It had been a long day for Priest. His mind was spinning. He liked Craig, or at least he wanted to. He stopped in the galley, asked for a cup of coffee, thanked Bishop, and left before the man could speak to him. Priest wanted to clear his mind, to understand for himself what had happened with Craig. He walked aft and sat between the weather bulwark and a deck capstan and attempted to drink his coffee and relax. He listened to the sea and the sound of *Providence* making way. A voice shook him.

"Priest, I need to talk to you. You ain't heard my side. Duder and Bishop don't know. They cain't. They don't know me, why I do things."

Priest shut his eyes to close out Craig's words. He did not want to talk to Craig, Smallbridge, Duder, or even old Bishop. He wanted to be alone.

His head slumped on his chest. There was no escape. His mind kept asking why and hoping there was a way he could avoid Craig and the situation he had caused. He couldn't get up and walk away. If he went to his bunk, Smallbridge would bring Craig up again.

Priest laughed to himself; the irony of his situation came to him. All his life, he'd wanted friends, people who liked and cared for him.

"Go ahead, Craig. I am tired, though. I was just about ready to turn in."

"Perlie was true. I didn't lie to you. I just wanted to let you know I knew how you felt. I wanted to help you. As Jesus is my witness, that's all it was. If I've made you scared, jest fergit it. I didn't know no better. You're my friend, Priest, jest about the only one I have on this damned ship. I hope you and me—I ain't about to lie to you. That's all I got to say."

Twenty-Four

Twenty-Two Days from Sandy Hook

*When, in disgrace with fortune and in men's eyes,
I all alone beweep my outcast state, and trouble deaf
heaven with my bootless cries...*

—William Shakespeare

Tuesday, June 18, 1872
Lat 0°03′36″N, Long 28°34′00″W
Crossing the Line

The ship's bell rang seven times in the forenoon watch. Priest finished his meal and prepared to go on watch early before the rest of the starboard watch. He would have the first trick at the helm, and this excited him. Priest's ability to helm had been tested with large seas from the east during the middle watch. He had not drawn a rebuke from Mr. Lennon and appreciated Sam Duder's steady but quiet encouragement.

The watch was relieved. This, for Priest, meant the second mate relieved the first mate and the helm was relieved. The information passed was course steered, any expected evolution ordered by the captain, and time and any other captain's order. Peleg Carver and Henry Lennon did this with more ritual than most, as they were former navy men and understood full well that the words, "I relieve you, sir," meant an assumption of responsibility.

169

The helmsman also had his ceremony. It consisted of relaying the course steered and the relieving helmsman placing his hands on the spokes of the ship's wheel, assuming management of the helm and using words such as, "I have the helm, steering southeast by south. Two spokes a weather."

As it approached noon, the officers shot the meridian passage of the sun, which gave them both the ship's position and exact noon for the latitude on which they were located. Griffin compared Carver and Lennon's altitude with his own. At the command "Make it noon," Priest struck the small binnacle bell eight times while the mate adjusted the ship's clock to the exact minute as revealed by the sun, sextant, and almanac. The timekeeper forward struck the large ship's bell eight times and a new day at sea had begun.

Priest could say nothing during his two-hour trick except repeat the mate's orders to him. The helm demanded his full attention. Steering was physically tiring in the heavy sea because he had to work against a weather helm. It was mentally exhausting, a far greater cause for fatigue, because it demanded his total concentration and he was determined to not make a mistake.

Providence was a mannerly vessel and steered with a slight weather helm when balanced. She was long and heavy and slow to turn, but when she started to turn, beyond a point or so, she would continue to do so. You could not saw at the helm. It cost the ship speed and drew a rebuke from the mate. Priest gave his attention to the compass, found a cloud, and looked to the weather leeches of the topsails and moved the wheel in growing confidence that he understood how to helm.

"Do you have her, Priest?" It was a routine question from Henry Lennon, who intended to focus his own attention to sail trim. Priest replied, "Aye, sir. Southeast by south. Two spokes a weather."

Carver and the boatswain supervised ship's work with the port watch.

As Priest seemed in firm control of the helm, Lennon felt he could risk Duder being away from the helm. "Duder, have Craig lay aft and report ter me." Priest realized he stood alone at the helm.

The Downeaster

The glass started to slowly drop overnight. Both mates knew it had dropped, and it was of concern to them. Mare's tails and mackerel scales had been observed the previous day.

Sam Duder approached Craig and told him to lay aft and report to the second mate.

Craig spit. "What's that lime-juicer want with me, Duder?"

"Lay aft and find out for yourself, Craig." Duder thought to himself how much he would enjoy crossing the line with Craig and welcoming him to Neptune's brotherhood, but Mr. Carver said that would have to wait until past Cape Stiff and the Pacific line.

Craig muttered to himself something about how he reckoned the second mate had no right to put him to work since there were other men in the waist.

Lennon spoke before a single word left Craig's mouth. "Get up da main-mast and be lookout. I want warning if da wind shifts or gusts, do yews understand?"

This was a reasonable precaution on Henry Lennon's part, to post an additional lookout aloft, with an apprentice at the helm. It was also the first duty that Craig had been tasked to do that was his responsibility alone. Anyone who could hand, reef, and steer could do it. This was not a difficult task for anyone who claimed to have spent three years under sail.

"Aye, sir." Craig went forward and climbed up to the fore topgallant yard. He did so slowly, keeping his eyes from Lennon. Craig was an additional lookout, the only one aloft. He had hoped to go forward to sing and play his mandolin for the crew.

Priest struck the small bell one time to indicate the first half hour of the watch had passed. As the large ship's bell struck the half hour, the lookout on deck reported, "All's well."

Craig shouted, "All's well," from the top hamper. The bell had caught him by surprise, as the solitude and inactivity had let his mind drift. A proper report would have indicated wind direction by point and speed: "By the starboard beam, fresh breeze."

Lennon walked closer to Priest and quietly said, "Bring 'er up just a bit, thus, thus. We'll see how she's doing, keep the rudder still.

Save yer sawin' for yews fiddle."

Lennon then left the wheelhouse through the weather door.

Another half hour passed, the bell was rung two strokes, and Eoghan Gabriel recorded distance run and computed the ship's speed. "Five and a half knots, Mr. Lennon."

Priest smiled because he felt a sense of accomplishment, for it was his skill in light winds and heading seas that had her moving along.

The wind began to come in gusts, enough that the ship would lean further to lee and her sails would shudder as the gust hauled forward, then eased. "Priest, bring her up when it hauls. Keep da sails full. Don't wait fer me to give a helm order. Watch da leeches. Steer full and by."

"Craig!" he shouted. "Stay alert there!" He also spoke quietly to Duder. "Watch Priest."

Priest beamed and repeated, "Steer full and by, aye, sir!"

Duder stood behind Priest and said nothing.

Three bells were struck. Henry Lennon walked to the leeward side of the quarterdeck and watched the bow wave and wake as an indication of the ship's speed. Every gust produced a little acceleration and the water moved more sharply past the ship's hull. Lennon saw that the gusts were occurring more frequently and growing stronger. The sky had clouded over and a squall line could be seen a point and a half off the starboard bow. "Mr. Gabriel, what's da glass doing?"

Eoghan Gabriel stuck his head through the door to the wheelhouse and read the barometer. "It's falling, Mr. Lennon, three-tenths in the last hour. Have it on the slate."

"Mr. Gabriel, ask da captain to come on deck; tell him da glass is falling quickly and there's a storm forming off da port bow. Tell him wind's ahead of it and getting fresher by da minute."

"Aye, aye, sir!"

Isaac Griffin had been taking his meal alone in his cabin. Griffin knew Henry Lennon took no chances with weather. He was a cautious man; he would recommend reefing sail or taking it in if needed. Griffin went on deck and left the remainder of his meal to grow cold.

"Captain, da glass is starting to fall and I think that cloud line to port is a storm. We may need ter reef soon. That's no bloody squall." He pointed to the waves. "The wind's gonna haul—"

At that point the wind gusted at full gale force from southwest to due south, setting the sails nearly aback and shaking against the yards. The force was enough to cause the bow to pitch up and settle down in a spray of white and green water. The wind working against the masts, yards, and sails was a heavy strain for a ship with wood spars.

"Hard a starboard!" Henry Lennon bellowed. Priest began to turn the wheel sharply with all his strength in a counterclockwise direction as ordered, and the ship began to turn to port, forcing the wind aft. The ship was turning by the force of her forward momentum; had she not turned, the wind would hit her full aback, asking her standing rigging and yards to take the full brunt of the wind and the ship's forward momentum. Now another gust, another blow, would be a glancing and not set her sails aback.

Henry shouted, "Meet her. Keep her close-hauled!" Priest used all of his strength to reverse the rudder to check the turn. The sails filled. Lennon's action prevented a catastrophe.

Priest repeated, "Steering close-hauled, sir, and southing."

Griffin knew that his second mate's orders had caused the ship to turn and avoided potential damage to the ship's spars and rigging, perhaps even springing a mast. The ship was now gaining headway on a southerly course with her sails drawing but shaking from the wind's rapid backing and hauling forward. Gradually the wind steadied as it drew nearer and permitted her to resume sailing in a southeasterly direction on her long board toward Rio de Janeiro.

"Mr. Lennon, you had no warning? No one saw it coming?"

"Craig's aloft. Useless son of a bitch."

"Have Craig report to me when the watch is relieved. Bring him and Duder with you to the cabin."

"Aye, Captain."

"Keep a sharp eye on the glass. Keep all sails on. Call me when the glass drops another tenth or when that storm starts to close in. By the way, Mr. Lennon, well done. If you would, Mr. Lennon, bring Priest back to the saloon after I've finished with Craig. You and Mr. Carver are to bring her back to SE by S and keep her there! When that gale is on us, we will need to furl the royals and put a single reef in the topgallants, but not one thing more until I say so. You may call both watches to shorten sail. I want to be on deck."

"Aye, Captain."

Griffin smiled broadly and patted Henry Lennon on the shoulder. He wanted no doubt to exist in any of the crew's minds of his trust and confidence in his second mate.

***

The starboard watch was relieved; the dogwatch started for the port watch; the glass was falling. Carver called both watches on deck. Henry Lennon, Samuel Craig, and Samuel Duder reported to Isaac Griffin in his reception room; now their supper was growing cold.

"What's your name?"

"Samuel Craig, sir."

Isaac Griffin ran his eyes down the shipping articles and found Samuel Craig's name.

"It says here that you shipped as an ordinary seaman?"

"Yes, sir."

"That means you have at least two years at sea."

"Three, sir, in all. I've crossed the line and been around the Horn," he lied.

"What were your duties as lookout?"

"Mr. Lennon wanted me to report any change in wind."

"And did you?"

"I could not see it coming, Captain; the sun had me blinded."

"Oh, were you asleep? That wind gusted to gale force. You had to see it coming. Why do you think it clouded over? If he was looking, Duder, what would he have seen?"

"Captain, the water's color darkens if the winds are on a cloud and the water between waves is all crinkly and disturbed. The waves are blown higher and longer too. You can see white horses when it's fresh or more."

Griffin's anger grew hotter. "We could have had the courses set aback, broke a spar, or even sprung a mast. You've either been negligent in your duty or lied when you shipped. Now, what do you think I ought to do, Craig?"

"I reckon I need to say I'm sorry, Captain."

"And you think I ought to accept your apology and ask if you'll make the mistake again?"

Craig smiled a weak smile while saying he agreed and that it would never happen again.

Griffin did his best to mimic the father in the return of the prodigal son. He let his eyes soften. A smile warmed his face.

Craig took Griffin's expression as sincere and laughed silently, thinking his captain was softhearted. Then Griffin spoke.

"Sorry—sorry! Call the damn boatswain! Do it now, Ezra!"

Craig shuddered. *The boatswain. I'm going to be flogged.*

When Eoghan Gabriel entered the reception area, Griffin suddenly turned around, took Craig's shirt in his left hand, and brought Craig's face to within inches of his own.

"I'm tempted to trice you up but I won't. But damn it, I want to. I'm going to do worse. Incompetence! You're a landsman. It's going into the log. Mr. Lennon and Duder will witness it. Get his ass out of here, Mr. Gabriel, before I change my mind. Lay forward, Craig. Get out of here! On deck!"

The boatswain followed a retreating Samuel Craig out of the door. Both could hear Griffin shouting, "Damned Paddy West sailor!"

Samuel Craig went forward to the forecastle. "The Captain knocked me down to landsman, fifteen dollars a month! Wouldn't hear a word I'd say, and me with three years before the mast. Damn mate just stood there too, not a word, not a single true word for me. You'll not see me past 'Frisco. I don't care. It's Virginia City for me, boys. It was that nancy-boy Priest's fault. Daydreaming at the helm, and that know-nothing mate let him."

Griffin next saw Nicholas Priest. He smiled warmly, genuinely warmly, as Priest entered.

"Priest, I asked that you come here because I know what you did. You remained calm at the helm. Well done. That's all, Priest, thank you."

Priest left his captain and the second mate in the cabin and rejoined his watch. The boy could hardly restrain his joy; he had been noticed and complimented by the captain himself.

***

"Henry, don't take your eye off that liar."

"Aye, sir. It was me what sent Craig aloft."

Griffin shook his head, indicating that Lennon's decision didn't matter to him.

Lennon raised the knuckle of his right hand to his forehead. "Thanks, Captain."

Griffin laughed at the old navy gesture. "We're shy a man-o'-war by two hundred or so hands. I have a book for you to give to Priest. I read it when I first went to sea, *Two Years Before the Mast*. I'll bet he doesn't know who Dana really is. When Priest sees who the author is, let me know how he reacts. I'm tempted to call him back and give it to him now, just to watch his face."

"It'll be a story Priest'll tell his gran'kids."

***

Smallbridge spoke to Priest in the apprentice cabin. "Priest, watch out for Craig. Duder was there in the cabin, and what he missed, he got from Ezra in the forecastle. Craig blamed the whole thing on you and bad-mouthed the captain and Mr. Lennon to the starboard watch. Be careful!"

Priest looked confused.

"He's phony money. You just can't tell people you're a great hero in Lee's army and act like that. The captain and Henry Lennon know their business. Badmouthing the captain is trouble. It always gets back to the old man."

"I don't understand, Smallbridge. Craig's had a hard life. Says everyone is out for him."

"He told the starboard watch that you were a queer, an abomination, a little Mary, Nick."

"No! You have to be wrong. He couldn't. I told him—why would he?"

Smallbridge replied, "I won't lie. Now he's got it in for you. He's bragged about buggering you. Said he'd do it and then it would be the whole watch's turn. He bragged himself in a corner. He's gonna come after you. He has to."

"He called me a queer?"

"Watch your back. Craig was the last man picked when the watches were chosen. Craig's scum. Duder tried to warn you. So did I."

Priest just shook his head. "Why? Why would Craig say that?"

***

Eight bells rang and the starboard watch took the deck. The glass began to drop rapidly; the ship took a hard roll, and white and green water rose over the bow.

The watch below was called on deck to single reef the topsails and topgallants, but that was all. The royals had been furled earlier. The night was spent reefing and then taking out the reefs as the wind rose and fell. The ship maintained a southeasterly course, giving her master every knot of speed the wind could give her.

The squall became a storm and lasted several hours. A tired, wet Nicholas Priest and the rest of the crew welcomed the large steaming cups of molasses-laced coffee at five that morning and used the coffee to soften their hardtack between long draws of the warm brew and the calming effect of tobacco.

Griffin never left the deck. At one point, she gave him nine knots. Griffin turned to Carver and said, "She's stiff, ain't she?"

Paul Thomas Fuhrman

Paddy West's (Traditional Shantey)

As I was walkin' down London Road,
I come to Paddy West's house,
He gave me a dish of American hash;
he called it Liverpool scouse,
He said, "There's a ship and she's wantin' hands,
and on her you must sign,
The mate's a bastard, the captain's worse,
but she will suit you fine."

Chorus:
Take off yer dungaree jacket,
and give yerself a rest,
And we'll think on them cold nor'westers
that we had at Paddy West's.

When we had finished our dinner, boys,
the wind began to blow.
Paddy sent me to the attic,
the main-royal for to stow,
But when I got to the attic,
no main-royal could I find,
So I turned myself 'round to the window,
and I furled the window blind.

Now Paddy he pipes all hands on deck,
their stations for to man.
His wife she stood in the doorway,
a bucket in her hand;
And Paddy he cries, "Now let 'er rip!"
and she throws the water our way,
Cryin', "Clew in the fore t'gan'sl, boys,
she's takin' on the spray!"

Now seein' she's bound for the south'ard,
to Frisco she was bound;
Paddy he takes a length of rope,

178

The Downeaster

and he lays it on the ground,
We all steps over, and back again,
and he says to me, "That's fine,
And if ever they ask were you ever at sea
you can say you crossed the line."

To every two men that graduates,
I'll give one outfit free,
For two good men on watch at once,
ye never need to see,
Oilskins, me boys, ye'll never want,
or carpet slippers made of felt,
But, I'll dish out to the pair o' you,
a rope yarn for a belt.

Paddy says, "Now pay attention,
these lessons you will learn.
The starboard is where the ship she points,
the right is called the stern,
So look ye aft, to yer starboard port
and you will find northwest."
And that's the way they teach you
at the school of Paddy West.

There's just one thing for you to do
before you sail away,
Just step around the table,
where the bullock's horn do lay
And if ever they ask, "Were you ever at sea?"
you can say, "Ten times 'round the Horn,"
And bejesus but you're an old sailor man
from the day that you were born.

Put on yer dungaree jacket,
And walk out lookin' yer best,
And tell 'em that you're an old sailor man
That's come from Paddy West's.

179

Twenty-Five

Justice before the Bar

They hurled upon an army
The bellowing heart of hell,
We saw but the meadows
Torn with their shot and shell.

—Henry Sidgwick

Thursday, June 20, 1872
Lat 05°38′45″S, Long 31°22′15″W
The South Atlantic

Port watch had eaten first, and then relieved the starboard watch, who were now seated on their sea chests in the forecastle, ready to eat their supper following a day of heavy squalls, gales, and rain. The air inside the forward deck cabin smelled of sweat and wet oilskins. Sam Duder grinned from ear to ear. John Stedwin closed his eyes briefly, shook his head, and announced, "Sam feels like telling us one."

Amidst the groans and "not agains," Sam began his tale.

"Did I ever tell you boys about the time I spent in Hawaii? Well, you remember that they did things like the English, King Kamehameha and all. Now, I'm talking about the Old Bailey in London; that's how the king wanted his courts to be. Seems they got themselves a wicked good nor'easter of a trial going, a murder trial."

Sam paused enough to see that three men were listening to him and the rest were somewhere between annoyance and complete boredom. Some men contented themselves with simply doing nothing, legs sprawled, heads lowered, and eyes nearly shut. Others could not sit still, talking with one another, comparing knives, a piece of scrimshaw, or simply enjoying the plug tobacco from the slop chest, and completely ignoring Sam. But Sam did not care.

"Now, the judge sets up on high throne-like affair, decked out in a scarlet robe and wearing a long, curly wig. His bare legs and feet were poking from beneath that robe. The mace of justice hung on the wall in back of him. The lawyers—barristers, they call them— had black robes and short wigs; they were all regal too. The accused was brought in and set in a box below the judge. He was a big man, almost wider than tall, and tattooed from head to toe. Copied one of his tattoos, see?"

Mention of tattoos always worked. Sam saw two heads turn his way.

"The jury, twelve Hawaii men, set on one side of the court, and on the other side sat the bailiff, the lawyers, and a bare-breasted maiden with perky rosebuds as pretty as any man could dream of."

Sam could not show his joy; he must remain calm, emotionless, but he knew he had them with the word "rosebud." Yes, getting a man's imagination was the secret of a good story.

"Now, lads," John Stedwin spoke. "Old Sam ain't one to stretch things a little, is he?" They all laughed, including Samuel Craig, who sat alone on his sea chest away from the others.

Sam winked at his friend John Stedwin. "Soon the trial started with the bailiff reading the charges, all proper legal words too. At this point, the bare-breasted maiden rose up, grabbed a short-handled broom-like thing covered in scarlet baize and all made up with bird feathers secured at one end by a Turk's head knot. The maiden walks around in the crowd tickling those people on the nose, under the armpits, and on the women's rosebuds too, 'cause that crowd doesn't believe much in clothes. The maiden gets the crowd all going and then as if on a cue goes back and sits down again. The

181

judge raps his gavel a couple times, gives us a fine harrumph, and there's order in the court."

One younger sailor asked, "What do you call those?" His hands mimicked holding a woman's breasts in his palms.

Sam ignored his question but was pleased with the curiosity. Now was the time for the story to get better.

"The prosecutor gets up, addresses the judge as, 'My lord, gentlemen of the jury, and my learned adversary,' and starts his case. He just gets into the most interesting parts, all the rage and ranting, this big dagger and a dead body on the beach, and then the maiden gets up again—feather broom and all—and the crowd is all roaring as they gets their rosebuds tickled.

"My barrister is sitting by my side and says to me, 'See, my man, you'll get a fair trial here 'cause we do everything English fashion, all right and proper.' I look at him a bit strange, and he says, 'Oh, yes, most proper.'"

The Irishmen laughed.

"The trial goes on, the defense makes its case, the maiden is running all over, and she is dusting every Johnny and Judy in the crowd. I begin to notice something. This maiden seems to wait until it gets juicy, and I notice the bailiff giving her cues from a book he's got in his hand.

"The trial ends with the crowd all shouting, the maiden running from one end of the pews to another just shaking that feather duster like a palm tree in a typhoon. It was a grand sight! They find the bastard guilty and the judge puts a black rag over his head and orders him to be hung on Thursday at high noon.

"Being next, I go up for my turn. I was drunk and disorderly. The barristers start all over."

Sam stops for a dramatic pause and continues.

"Now, boys, I ain't a learned man or have I spent much time in courts for being drunk—"

The sailors laugh and wink at one another.

"But I felt like they had rehearsed the whole thing. Had it all down to memory. The maiden gets up, does some dusting, sits down, but to tell you the truth, lads, I had fun in that saloon, but not that much fun.

"I gets a week in jail, five days set aside for time served and two days waived because of my young and tender age. It helps having a sweet, innocent face like mine."

The watch all laughed again.

"Since I paid my barrister three dollars, I figure I can ask him a question. 'Sir, I say, my trial; I didn't break up the furniture, I didn't bust a man's nose open, and you said nothing about that. In fact, you said nothing at all! And what was that bare-breasted maiden about?'

"Then the barrister says to me, 'See here, my man, everything was done proper.' He takes a sheaf of papers from his satchel and shows them to me. My trial is there, all word for word and taken from a London law book. I begin to see some things real clear.

"*Where is she?* I says to myself.

"Then I says to my lawyer, 'I just can't get up and go unless I know. I still don't understand the bare-breasted maiden.' I can't see her in the papers he has either. My barrister tells me it's all proper, done every day in the Old Bailey, and turns the page and reads to me, 'Upon a remark from the accused, a titter ran through the crowd.' "

There were one or two chortles, several pairs of eyes rolled back, and one Finn looked confused; despite the best efforts of a countryman, it wasn't a pun in Finnish. Billy Kauwe, an able-bodied, rose, pointed to his trousers and shirt, and muttered, "Asshole."

John Stedwin, however, made sense out of the situation. "Craig, Jacobson, it's up to you two to bring back the mess kids." With that, the watch got out their tin pans, tin cups, and what flatware they owned—for some only a spoon.

The two landsmen returned with the meal, black-eyed pea soup with large chunks of smoked ham and onions, boiled rice, hot biscuits, hardtack, hot tea, molasses, and lemon juice. The mess kids were set in the center of their cabin and the men used their spoons and sheaf knives to fill their tin pans. The molasses and lemon were used to sweeten the steaming tea, steeped in a rather inelegant metal pot with a bail handle and spout.

Almost immediately Craig began to complain. This had gotten to be a routine, and it had already begun to irritate the experienced seamen, who normally tolerated a fair amount of complaint as a sailor's right to bitch.

"Look at this here shit; I wouldn't use it as pig slop back home!"

John Stedwin spit out a plug into the oak bucket that served as a spittoon and growled, "Speaking of shit, Craig, you don't know the difference between a turd and a pint of apple butter! You just like to stir up trouble and watch what happens. This ship feeds good and we're lucky to have that black man, Bishop, for our cook. We got no right by law to have hot biscuits here or doughnuts some days with coffee, but he does it and the Captain knows it too. The steward even said we get the same rations as what the captain and mates get."

Craig began to start something between a snarl and whine, to have it greeted by a heavily accented German voice telling him to shut up while there was food to eat. The German had shipped on lime-juicers and knew what poor rations could be in hard times.

John Stedwin usually didn't say much, as was his right, given the time he'd spent at sea and the tattoos he had. But today, Craig inspired him to lecture, "Now, what did you read when you signed the articles, or didn't you care to even ask? I bet you don't even know your letters! Well, today is Thursday. That means you get a pound and a half of salt meat, a third pint of chickpeas, tea or coffee, sugar and water for your whack. That's the law!

"What do we have here? Smoked ham, black-eyed pea soup, biscuits, tea, boiled rice, and hardtack, and nothing's been short-weighed. You ain't got a right to bitch like that. You did it this morning too, and the man fed us buckwheat pancakes and bacon! Did you notice that every time when both watches are called, we get a duff? The *Providence* feeds as good as it gets, and that Yankee captain wants it that way! For all I care, Craig, you can go ask that black cook for a lemon to suck on!"

Craig went to his sea chest, sat, and ate by himself. No one spoke to him.

The sailors also ate in silence, and quickly, because they were hungry men. One of the Finns split a biscuit, poured a little molasses on a half, and ate it while smiling in Craig's direction.

These men could eat. Some scooped the soup over the rice; some did not. All took lemon with their tea because they were cautious and concerned about scurvy. When they had finished their meal, Craig and Jacobson returned the mess kids to the galley and cleaned them with coarse salt and boiling water. Craig kept his distance from the cook. Most people, and that included Craig, who never favored a frontal assault, were cautious about attempting to intimidate a man who stood six inches taller, weighed fifty pounds more, and had a meat cleaver near his left hand.

Craig also noticed that Bishop had a tattoo on his right biceps. It was crossed Enfield rifles with fixed bayonets. He could not make out the number tattooed between the rifle muzzles and bayonets. The number was fifty-four. It represented the Fifty-Fourth Massachusetts Colored Infantry.

***

By the time the two landsmen returned, the starboard watch sailors were in their bunks and the air was cut with snores and seasoned farts. Jacobson turned in and Craig returned to his sea chest. He took his knife from the sheaf and reached for a hard black Arkansas stone from his pocket. He spit on the stone to wet it and began honing his knife, a sharply pointed double-edged dagger, his Arkansas toothpick. The weapon made little snick-like noises as he carefully moved an edge over the stone's surface, maintaining a precise angle.

It took time to treat both sides of the knife, four edges in all. When he was finished honing, he lightly touched one edge of the knife to the top of his left thumbnail. It effortlessly shaved a sliver from the nail, and Samuel Craig was pleased with his work. Had someone been awake, he would have spit on his forearm to shave a few hairs to show all who watched that the knife was razor sharp.

Craig thought, *I reckon you bastards had best treat this Kentucky boy with a little respect. Walkin' boss is speakin' to me.*

185

He then laughed to himself, a quiet laugh that sounded almost like a small girl lost amid her toys. His thoughts then turned to Nicholas Priest. The laughter stopped.

You'll learn 'em I'm not to be trifled with, rich boy. You'll show 'em what I am.

He turned in.

Twenty-Six

The Mechanics Mill Girls

Work—work—work!
From weary chime to chime,
Work—work—work,
As prisoners work for crime!
Band, and gusset, and seam,
Seam, and gusset, and band,
Till the heart is sick, and the brain benumbed,
As well as the weary hand.

—Thomas Hood

Sunday, June 23, 1872
Fall River, Massachusetts

As Kayleigh waited to board the Fall River Line train to take her and Jennie Collins, Dr. Zakrzewska's friend, and founder of Boffin's Bower, to Fall River, the fireman in the cab of the train's locomotive threw a shovelful of coal into the firebox to build steam. A few seconds later, a fresh black column of smoke rose from the engine's smokestack and drew her attention. Now, or so it seemed to her, she was haunted by a spirit, a sidhe, that announced itself in the scent of burning coal. This spirit came to her mind with her husband and foretold events to come. These events were fearsome and caused

Kayleigh to shudder. She knew something would occur but not what shape or form it would take.

During her trip, Kayleigh looked out the window of the train and saw the images of a muscular Massachusetts. Great factories and mills grew in the small towns as well as the Boston suburbs. These sights drew her mind to Fall River itself, massive four- and five-story mills built of granite and brick with tall bell towers rising stories above the mills. Towers summoning workers to their looms and sending them home after twelve-hour workdays. Some mills were still water-driven, but more and more used the abundant water of Fall River to generate steam for huge stationary steam engines driving the looms and spinning jennies. Tall smokestacks provided the draft for huge, coal-fired steam boilers. Mill, tower, and stack were all the property of investors, men isolated by their wealth from want or toil, invincible men of industry. As these images passed beyond her window, she thought of herself and Jennie Collins, her companion—two seemingly insignificant women, one pregnant, who would soon discuss challenging the authority of the mill owners while being overshadowed by the granite and brick manifestation of the owners' authority over the lives of those working within.

Jennie Collins was surprised to see that the tenement house of Bridget Guiney, the mill girl seeking Kayleigh's help, was a new three-story frame structure, and though it was made without much embellishment, it appeared comfortable. It stood in a neighborhood of tenements similar to itself and was within walking distance of the Mechanics Mill on Davol Street.

Jennie was concerned as they approached the doorway to the central hallway and stairs that led to the home of Bridget Guiney, her brother Terrence, and his wife, Mary.

"Kayleigh, it's on the third floor. Will that be too much for you? Dr. Zakrzewska worries about you overexerting yourself."

"I'm not to that point, Jennie. Not quite yet."

The hallway was wainscoted in pine painted in dark brown enamel; the walls above and the ceiling were plaster and white; a gaslight lit each hallway. The stairs were plain also but with oak treads, rails, and banisters. The doors to the apartments were varnished oak, six-paneled, and fitted with brass and cast-iron hardware. Everything was well made, sturdy, and plain, but the work reflected the pride of the carpenters, jointers, plasterers, and other craftsmen who had built the tenement for the Mechanics Mill.

Kayleigh took a deep breath, looked upward at the landing, and started to climb. It was her intention to climb briskly if not bound up the stairs, but at the fourth step, her intentions changed. She was pregnant barely a month, if that, but still, she was pregnant. The bounding display of energy slowed.

Jennie noticed. "Kayleigh, let's stop a minute when we reach the second-floor landing."

Kayleigh happily placed both feet on the varnished hardwood floor of the landing and leaned against a wall. "Dr. Zakrzewska scolded me for gaining too much weight and predicted this would happen. I don't know how she resisted wagging a finger at me and telling me it's forbidden. 'You mustn't work too hard.' "

Jennie replied, "She can be very direct, can't she?"

They laughed. Jennie then continued, "We'll stop a moment or two; there's plenty of time and we won't be late."

Kayleigh smiled. "I need to walk more, to work harder."

Both women took in what their senses told them of life in the tenement on Sundays, the smells of Sunday supper, the cry of new life, and the smell of soda bread from ovens.

"One more flight." Kayleigh smiled and placed her left foot on the stairs as she gripped the oak handrail. This time, her pace was more deliberate.

"The stairs don't squeak like they do in Boston. These tenements are new." Jennie Collins had seen much of the hard life Boston afforded workingwomen and had talked with many of the first mill girls from Lowell. Sometimes, these women married well and led comfortable lives; some educated themselves and remained comfortably independent; but all too often others found themselves in domestic service or sewing for a meager living, only to be pushed aside in favor of wave after wave of younger immigrant women willing to work harder for even less. These, the destitute, were Jennie's charges. This was why Jennie accompanied Kayleigh.

Jennie was the first to reach the third-floor landing. Kayleigh was two steps behind and labored with the last step.

Jennie smiled. "Catch your breath. There's time enough. It's not yet three."

When Kayleigh told Jennie she was rested, Jennie walked to one of the two doors facing into the hallway. "The one closest to the front is the parlor door, Kayleigh."

Jennie and Kayleigh stood before the parlor door and by habit smiled as Jennie knocked. The Guiney family—Bridget, the sister who had invited them, and Terrence and his wife, Mary—greeted them. Bridget invited them in. "Mrs. Griffin, Miss Collins, we are so happy you came to talk with us. All the girls are here and Mary has made tea for us."

Kayleigh observed that the parlor was bright with light from the three bay windows at its front. A couch, two upholstered chairs, and various small marble-topped tables covered with crochet table covers dressed the room, and a wool rug covered the hardwood floor. The large bay front windows were also framed in handmade crochet curtains. The walls were covered in figured pale green wallpaper and decorated with a mixture of prints reflecting the culture and pride of the apartment's occupants. There was a framed print of the Sacred Heart of Jesus occupying the focal point of interest of the room behind the couch, a print of President Abraham Lincoln, a photograph of an elderly couple posed rigidly in a studio setting, and a crucifix that housed the articles needed for administering last rites. In additions to the Guineys, five other women were seated around the parlor on chairs brought from the kitchen. Everyone there smiled and seemed genuinely pleased to see the two Boston visitors.

Bridget invited her guests to take their seats. "Please take a seat on the sofa. The tea's ready and you can still smell the scones hot from the oven. You'll not be needing supper with Mary's scones."

Kayleigh turned her head in the direction Bridget pointed and saw that the family had brought the kitchen table into the parlor and set it against the rear wall. The table was covered with a machine-made tablecloth upon which sat sultana scones, Irish shortbread, herb scones, a potato cake, jams, curds, butter, cream, and a pot of strong Irish tea. Kayleigh was delighted because her mother had set such a table for tea on Sundays. The train ride had been long, and she no longer ate for just herself.

Bridget invited her guests to serve themselves, Kayleigh and Jennie first, and to take a seat in the parlor. Everyone knew the couch had been reserved for Kayleigh and Jennie.

Kayleigh asked, "Where did you find this butter? It's so fresh," as she took another bite of her scone and helped herself to the potato cake.

A beaming Mary Guiney replied, "We get it from Rhode Island. There's a farmers' market we go to Sundays after Mass. It's in Tiverton."

After everyone was seated, Bridget addressed Kayleigh, as they had been in correspondence with each other. "Mrs. Griffin, we want to do something on the Fourth of July that draws some attention to us. We want it to be respectable, but you have to know all the agents and supervisors from the mills will be there to see if we're behaving ourselves. People have been snooping around and asking questions in the weaving room where my looms are."

Jennie Collins was quick to reply, "I'm with the New England Labor Reform League—"

Bridget cut her off. "Miss, we don't care much if t' money comes from banks or the government as long as stores take it for bread and potatoes and give it full value. Most of us here have husbands too or hope to get one."

Jennie laughed and shot back, "I'm the practical one in the league. Those things, free money, and free love are interesting. I've started Boffin's Bower, and I see women unable to find work and living on the street. Marriage didn't help these women; neither has age, dear."

Kayleigh realized that without intervention, Bridget and Jennie would become adversaries and the meeting would end in heated arguments and not much else.

"I'm just married and my husband is a sea captain." Kayleigh patted her belly to emphasize her pregnancy. "I understand, but what do you hope to accomplish? What do you think is the most important thing that needs to be done?"

Jennie asked, "Is it wages? Is it working conditions? Is it hours? I'm told that looms like the ones you operate make eight hundred dollars a day for the investors."

"Ah now, you got to be fair," Terrence Guiney interjected. "I'm a millwright. It took ten years here and in Manchester, England, for me to rise to that. One day, I may be a hand. Some of these girls came from Canada, off farms. Some of us are Irish. Some Polish. All live better here than at home. Don't you think it fair that the investors, particularly the Mechanics Mill investors, earn a fair return?"

Terrence stood up and looked at each of the mill girls to see if anyone disagreed with him. "Those Boston papers ignore the fact that cotton's got to be purchased from the Mississippi delta, shipped here, sorted, carded, spun, and woven into fabric. All that ignored. All that costs money and wages too before a single cent is made on a bolt of cloth coming off a loom."

Kayleigh replied, "The issue is fairness. Is what they pay you fair?"

Bridget replied, "Fair? Terry, tell her how they threatened you when you had the speed-up."

Terrence looked first to his wife and then to the Boston visitors before speaking. "Once—not at this mill—they added another loom to the four I was operating. I asked, all politely too, if that meant I'd be takin' home more money. Well, the supervisor's face got all red and he says to me, 'We can take your job to South Carolina and find someone there who'll work for a third less than what you're getting now. They would be happy to have the work.' You see, I don't know what's fair. If they're not making money, I have no job. Even if they're not making enough money, I could be on the street. That's the power they have. You can be comfortable, a good home, food on the table, and a sense that there's a job for you tomorrow, and they can take it all away just to make more money. You're no more to them than a claw hammer. Use it until it breaks and buy a new one."

Bridget added, "There's other issues; a woman can go from the carding room to spinning, and then from spinning to the looms, but there it stops. A woman's wages are kept low because it's so hard for us if you're not married. There's good reason to be afraid."

As the Guineys spoke, Kayleigh's mind paused at the word "afraid." She knew she'd told her mother about the rape in frustration. She knew she'd had to tell Isaac, but she'd feared what his reaction could be. What if her mother had screamed and pointed a finger and said, "You've shamed us"? What if Isaac had rejected her and called her a deceitful slut? As these thoughts passed through her mind, freezing her heart, she looked at Bridget and said in a clear, firm contralto, "Fear is a powerful thing. It's even more powerful than chains and shackles because your mind clasps them on your wrists and ankles. You're afraid to say something or do something that might provoke the agents to fire you, aren't you?"

Jennie Collins shook her head. "It's a terrible thing for a woman to grow old and have no family, no job. I see it every day. I try to help these women, but once a woman can no longer have children or work, she's of no use to anyone, not even her family."

Kayleigh looked at Jennie and whispered, "Easy." Then she addressed Bridget and the other mill girls. "You have to confront fear. You have to expect the worst and be willing to risk it. You can't overcome fear by hiding from it. You can't be free, have dignity and respect for yourself, unless you are willing to accept the consequences."

Bridget responded first to Kayleigh, then turned toward Jennie, "But what if they sack us?"

Kayleigh spoke before Jennie could speak. "At least they would respect you, maybe even fear you. They would realize others would follow your example. If enough women were involved, they would hesitate to provoke trouble, women's anger with them."

Bridget laughed. "I'd disguise myself as a man and go to sea, maybe become a lobsterman." The girls voiced their approval.

Bridget continued, "We all want the vote. We all want decent wages too. But I understand what Kayleigh is telling us. What we want and need will only come from respect, and we must be willing to lose everything we have to gain it. Those men have to see that. They have to see there will be consequences to treating us without respect."

Terrence spoke next. "Think about it. Think. They're building new mills here. You read about it every day. They have to recruit in Canada and in Europe too. If we all stopped working, the investors would lose money and the agents would lose face, maybe get fired. Fear ain't on us alone."

Bridget stood by her brother and spoke. "But we'd lose nothing that's ours. We'd only lose what those men give us. And, Terrence, they could take it all away, march or not, if it suits them. So let's march."

Jennie interjected, "We don't believe in strikes—"

Terrence interrupted her. "We're not talking about striking. We're talking about fear, their fear of us."

***

Kayleigh and Jennie Collins sat facing each other in a coach on the Boston train. Jennie spoke first. "Kayleigh, I'm tired. As soon as they squeeze all the money out of those mills, out of Fall River, out of those girls, they'll shut the mills down and abandon them. Those big granite buildings will stand like tombstones in a poor parish graveyard. They'll say, 'Tsk, tsk, we had to do it, kept the mills going as long as we could. Just had to do it; the stockholders expect it of us."

Kayleigh replied, "And one day we'll die too. I'd rather die a respected old woman than a poor little thing."

Twenty-Seven

Duty

A prince can make a belted knight,
A marquise, duke, an' a' that;
But an honest man's aboon his might,
Guid faith, he mauna fa that!
For a' that, an' a that,
The pith o' sense, an pride o' worth,
Are higher rank than a' that.

—Robert Burns

Friday, June 28, 1872
Lat 26°18′55″N, Long 45°05′30″W

Henry Lennon's warning about Griffin remaining on deck too long had proven to be true. On Wednesday, Griffin spent the entire afternoon and evening on deck battling calms. He stayed on deck through the mid-watch and forenoon watch. A hard squall flooded the decks Thursday evening and brought him again on deck. The wind blew from the southeast, a port tack close-hauled. Griffin was on deck to brace sails and furl the royals through all of this and remained there, refusing himself sleep. At two bells of the morning watch Thursday, the wind died to a light breeze and the royals were set again. Thereafter, the barometer started to drop and movement of the clouds slowed. Griffin stood on deck watching the clouds against the moon and frequently asking for the barometric pressure. *Providence*'s sails dropped motionless from eleven in the morning until one in the afternoon on the twenty-seventh. Then the weather turned fine—a moderate breeze, a steady breeze again from the south-southeast. Griffin smiled to see the sails shake, snap loudly with wind, and then fill. Once again he fussed with the weather bowlines, getting the last ounce of power from his sails. His joy with the wind sustained his vigil. This wind lasted until nearly eight in the evening. She gave him six and seven knots speed southward while it blew. Then it rained again, killing off the wind, becalming the ship. Griffin was still on deck. He had ignored the chance to sleep.

Dogwatches or not, the captain was still on deck. The men sat to the lee of the deckhouse, out of sight of the captain as he paced on the weather side of the quarterdeck. They knew how long their captain had been awake; a sailor's an odd creature, has more ears than two, and more eyes than those in his head.

Griffin was absorbed only with speed and direction. Carver let the crew hide near the deckhouse. The captain was his business, not theirs. He would absorb Griffin's anger and fatigue.

To most masters, recording a 177-mile day despite hours of calms would have meant satisfaction. By now, however, nothing pleased Griffin because there had been no wind since eight that evening despite the return of rain squalls. His mind was focused only on the ship's speed and direction at the moment. He had even lost recognition of why this was important.

The first watch Thursday, Lennon's watch, was spent in a windless drizzle with Griffin pacing the quarterdeck and insisting the wheelhouse scuttle be kept open. Both mates wondered why he had bothered to have an enclosed wheelhouse constructed in Bath at all. However, Griffin did go below—finally—at one in the morning. Carver, now on watch, saw the gimbaled oil lamps glowing through the window of the chart room and knew exactly what Griffin was doing. He wasn't resting, but struggling with plotting an extended dead reckoning track and reading his pilot charts. The first mate would see Griffin again, and soon; it was the easiest of prophesies. Carver prepared himself for an angry captain who had not slept in nearly forty hours.

The ship's bell was struck four times to indicate half the midwatch had passed. It was two in the morning. Time passed slowly in the chart room when charts reveal what you do not want to admit and your dividers and parallel rulers do not cooperate with your one good hand.

Carver, as did most experienced mariners, found the midwatch to be a relaxing experience when left alone. Then, too, most captains were content to check their telltale and listen, consciously or unconsciously, for what their ship told them while they were lying in their bunks. The whole point of port and starboard watches, of first and second mates, was to permit the master to be on deck only when needed. It was intended to keep at least one person aboard clearheaded: the captain.

At 2:15 in the morning, the barometer stood at a low 29.8 inches of mercury and the wind came coyly at five knots from east by east-southeast, in cat's-paws. Griffin saw *Providence* brace her yards. The waves were running from nine to twelve feet high and the lightning put on a spectacular show, illuminating the sky with a copper hue. *Providence* was on the port tack, carrying every ounce of canvas she could carry, and steering full and by and southing. When the chip log was tossed to check her speed against the Bliss log, both recorded a bare three knots; still, this was southing.

"Damn it." Isaac Griffin wanted to pound his chart table to find some relief from his frustration. He had spent nearly a week on deck watching the sky and watching the barometer. He projected his dead reckoning track through noon of the twenty-eighth and measured the day's run at just fifty miles. His mind, his imagination, saw the heat smiling and sucking up the ocean's moisture, storing it in great vertical columns of immobile clouds, only to let it fall back down on him, on his helpless ship. The clouds laughed at his helplessness.

When will I see the clouds move? They're supposed to! I'm south. I'm south.

197

There were no mirrors in the chart room to reveal to Griffin the extent of his fatigue. He did not see the dark bags under his eyes, the bloodshot whites, the slump of his posture, or the deterioration of his mental acuity. No mirror could reveal the conflict waging within his mind—his desire for sleep contested by the will to drive his ship. He had always imagined himself as a Titan.

"Damn you, Carver!" His pencil flew across the chart room. For a moment Griffin realized how ridiculous it was to vent his anger on a pencil. "Why can't that man push her harder?" He left the chart room, turned left through the saloon, entered his parlor, and then climbed his companionway ladder. He was on deck again. The rain seemed to boil off him in wisps of steam as he stood again on the quarterdeck peering into the wheelhouse through the open port door.

"Where's Mr. Carver? I want you—"

"When's the last time you've slept, Captain? Why are you still on deck? All we can do is keep her pointing south and take what the wind and ocean give us. No, sir, this ship will not run into Cape Saint Rogue or move a quarter knot faster than what the wind allows."

Griffin saw Carver's anger and realized he had pushed himself and his mates too hard. He attempted light conversation.

"You know, this watch was my favorite when I was a mate. It's nearly always peaceful. We should be sighting a homeward bound sail or two the closer we get to Rio. I've got a letter for Boston."

Damn it, Captain, why are you here? Don't you think I'd call for you if you were needed? Look at you, man! Any fool can tell you're exhausted. Go below and let me stand my watch!

"I'm concerned about Thomsen, Captain. He has a fever and can't work. Mr. Lennon will need to send Craig aloft again."

"It's too early to tell on Thomsen," Griffin replied. "We'll need to wait and see what type of fever he has."

"What if we need to set Thomsen off in Rio, to the hospital, Captain?"

"No. Not now. Damn it, man, we cannot afford the time! Why even consider that when we don't know if it's serious or not!" Griffin began to simmer. "I hate losing time! We won't make fifty miles today!" He realized he had just vented his anger. He stopped abruptly and changed subjects. "What did I tell you about crossing the doldrums? The farther east you cross, the less chance of wind. You can really cost yourself time by hunting for it." He knew Carver was aware of this. It was common knowledge. They'd seen three other ships near the line and had exchanged signals with the *Arlie* bound for Liverpool.

Isaac Griffin walked forward on the windward side past the whaleboat. He was tired from being on deck and he knew he was not treating Peleg Carver evenly. His mind drifted a moment to remind itself that it needed sleep. He brought himself back by focusing ahead to the Southeast Trades. There the ship would quickly gain latitude.

Rise, rise, let the damn air pressure rise and bring back the trades.
He forced himself awake and returned to the quarterdeck.

"Mr. Carver, once past Rio, I want you to be in heavy canvas by the fifties."

Peleg Carter knew that. Some mates would take offense at a captain telling them something so obvious, but he knew his captain had to be straining to keep awake.

"Heavy canvas, sir."

Peleg Carver made a mental note to have the lifelines made ready to rig on a moment's notice and to have the beckets made up for the yards. It would not be a bad idea to check every purchase also and once again overhaul each block and check each line for chafing. He'd waste no man's life. He would intensify the men's work.

"When's your wife due?"

"November, Captain, early November."

"So you'll have no word until we reach Liverpool."

"Sally's a strong woman, Captain. It will be our first, though, and I'm looking forward to a son." *Please, God, bless us this time, no miscarriage. Thy will be done.*

Griffin saw what he thought was a smile on Carver's face and mumbled Kayleigh's name aloud. *I can't concentrate. Stay awake.*

Peleg Carver pretended he did not hear and ordered, "Come up, there, thus, thus, so." The helmsman came closer to the wind and the slight shake in the topsails stopped. The wheel moved no more than a spoke.

"Keep those sails as full as possible, Mr. Carver."

He did not need to say that to me.

Peleg Carver had seen fatigue before. He had seen captains lose so much sleep that they were consumed by blind rage and insensitive to their surroundings. This captain was stronger, but still he kept the deck too long. *Irresponsible.*

"Captain, Priest appreciated Dana's book. Said he understands why Dana did what he did." *Go below!*

Before Griffin replied, his first mate bellowed deliberately, "Lookout! What do you see?"

The lookout gave his report: "All's clear, sir, lights bright and burning."

"Thankee, Elder," Carver answered, and then said, "Younger, relieve your brother aloft at six bells."

"Aye, Mr. C-Carver."

"Mr. Carver, you call the Ernst brothers Elder and Younger?"

"Whole watch does, Captain. All of the port watch to a man likes the two of them. I could have a lot worse for apprentices." *Griffin's mind's gone now. His mind focuses where I point him. He'd talk to a bollard if I wanted him to.*

Cinnamon and nutmeg escaped from Griffin's mind and became spoken words. These and the faint hint of lilacs were Kayleigh's scent.

He regained his train of thought. "Watch the barometer. We should see pressure start to rise in the next hundred miles. You and Mr. Lennon both need to watch it carefully." He hoped Peleg Carver had not heard the words or at least thought he had said something else. *I can't stay alert.*

"Captain, you just said 'cinnamon and nutmeg' right out of the blue. I think you need to turn in. Mr. Lennon and I will take care of your ship. Even a couple hours of sleep will help you." *Next he'll start seeing things and getting suspicious.*

Griffin tried to laugh, but it was not convincing. "I don't know where that came from, Mr. Carver." He lied. It came from the first evening he and Kayleigh had spent together, when she had rested her head on his shoulder. It was her scent.

Carver moved close enough to the captain that he could smell coffee on Griffin's breath. Carver took control of his voice, and in a whispered, carefully measured cadence, "Captain, I really think you should turn in. Your eyes are bloodshot. You must feel like you've got sand in them. We'll need you for what lies ahead. Something's driving this sea. Mr. Lennon and I will keep *Providence* safe and on course. We'll call you on deck. Will you please turn in, sir?"

Griffin felt his anger rise and focus on the first mate, and he choked off his reply. The thought that he had spoken those words, "cinnamon and nutmeg," rattled his confidence. Griffin's left eyelid twitched with a spasm and he rubbed it to stop the irritation. This caused the eye to water. A gray film clouded the vision from his left eye. He rubbed it again but this made the eye worse. He was sure he had rubbed an eyelash under the lid.

"You're right. Thank you, Mr. Carver."

"Good night, Captain. Get some sleep. Mr. Lennon and I'll tend to the ship."

Griffin did not really want to leave the deck, but he did. He'd let the words escape. He should never tell the first mate his business. Carver was a good mate, a damned good mate. An officer of the watch should never be addressed by his given name, and Griffin had done so. He knew he needed to get below and sleep. Coffee was no longer enough, not even Bishop's coffee. He thought he would sit in his easy chair and let sleep take him. He washed his eyes out with potable water from his pitcher and then sat in the leather chair. He hoped he would dream of Kayleigh, a pleasant dream, but he could not find a comfortable position for his legs. Griffin then focused and committed himself to awaken again at eight bells. *I'll listen. I'll hear.*

His efforts failed him. Even dreams eluded him. He passed quickly into a deep sleep.

Providence stood on slowly and steadily in a heading sea, her masts and spars emitting low creaks, her chain sheets rattling between clew and sheave. She accepted an occasional spray of white water across her bow to splash her own eyes while her master slept. The morning watch came on deck. Lennon stopped Ezra from waking the captain. Lightning lit the sky in a copper glow.

Twenty-Eight

South of Rio de Janeiro

The sun came up upon the left,
Out of the sea came he!
And shone bright and on the right
Went down into the sea.
                            —Samuel Taylor Coleridge

Saturday, June 29, 1872
Lat 28°11′07″S, Long 47°07′30″W

Eight bells, four in the morning. The starboard watch came on deck to relieve the port watch. Jonathon Bishop gathered himself from his bunk to prepare for another day at sea. The first order of business was to start the fire in the wood cook-stove, which could be an easy task or not, depending on the weather and the chance of a back draft. Today, all it took was some kindling, a flame, and patience. The second order of business was to meet the second mate and captain's steward forward by the forecastle food lockers to draw the day's allotment of rations.

It was Friday and the allotment would be forty-eight pounds of salt meat, thirty-two pounds of ship's bread, eleven pounds of navy beans, sixty-four ounces of molasses, four pounds of tea, sixteen pounds of coffee, and ninety-six quarts of fresh water for cooking and drinking. The captain also had issued sixteen pounds of oatmeal and eight pounds of butter, and three five-pound airtights of tomatoes. Since everyone's rations were the same, the day's catch of bonito would be shared equally between aft and forward and would not be substituted for the meat ration. That is, if any were caught.

The immediate order of business after the fire was making coffee for issue at two bells, and then boiling the beans. It was also common practice for both officers and hands to bring delicacies aboard for their own use and to be traded or shared with messmates. Having married seamen aboard meant that there would be home-canned marmalade for the ship's biscuits forward and Sally Carver's peaches aft. Breakfast would be served at seven bells first to the relieving port watch, then to the relieved starboard watch.

Henry Lennon took his balance scales from their place near the food lockers and used the mess kids to weigh out and distribute the rations. "Bishop," said Lennon, "it's a good idea to make the whack good. Da men are tetchy."

Bishop replied, "Mr. Lennon, it would help to have some raisins for the porridge if the captain would let us. Dinner's going to be bean soup with pork and stewed tomatoes. Now, for supper it's more of the same, but if the captain gave us about ten pounds of dried apples and a few pounds of white flour, all hands could have dried apple pie for supper. If he wants to save the apples, then I could make soft molasses cookies. All I would need is some sugar and vinegar and flour. I got all the spices and baking soda in the galley."

"Let's save the apples for the Horn. Now, tell me what you need for the molasses cookies."

***

Two bells sounded and all hands were on deck for coffee and a smoke. Although the coffee was served in a low tin bucket-like affair to avoid spillage, it was made two gallons at a time in an old and much-cherished blue porcelain-coated pot. This pot had never in its life seen soap and was seasoned with the essence of coffee. It was filled with water and brought to a boil. The coffee was added and stirred with a wooden cooking paddle, and a whole crushed egg was added to settle the grounds. After the coffee was poured out, the pot was cleaned by rinsing it overboard to get rid of the grounds and add a little salt seasoning. That was *Providence* coffee, and you could never see the bottom of the pot.

"Your sea daddy let you drink coffee, Priestie?" This was the first time Samuel Craig had addressed Priest in this manner.

"I don't understand you, Craig, and why are you calling me 'Priestie?' " The boy's mind carried him back to boarding school and the hazing he had endured. Here, though, the sailors and the apprentices had treated him well, accepting him and, as Smallbridge once said, according him a set of balls. Priest understood why Craig asked the question; he was once again to be the butt of crude jokes. Priest understood but was surprised; he had not expected this to happen.

"I'll call you what I want to, Priestie. I asked if Duder let you drink coffee."

"Sea daddy?"

"A sea daddy is the man who buggers you, Priestie, and don't tell me old Duder hasn't been up your bunghole, just like me. After all, Priestie-boy, ain't old Duder your very special friend?" Craig's voice mimicked an effeminate lisp. "I heard tell he takes care of you."

"I don't like your accusation, Craig." Priest's temper began to grow.

"Now, Priestie-boy, I just told the gospel truth, didn't I?"

"No, not a single word is true. Why'd you come up with these lies?"

"What you going to do about it, Priestie-boy?" Craig slapped Priest on his cheek like a cat. "Now, you ain't man enough to fight me, are you, Priestie? You ain't man enough to call me a liar, are you, faggot?"

Fear was no longer a stranger to Priest, but fighting was. He had no idea how to go about fighting, even something as simple as making a fist and delivering a blow. He was not afraid of pain, but he took a rational approach.

"The captain will have us in irons for fighting, Craig!"

Craig looked around, saw that the mates were not looking forward, and spit on Priest. "Go run to the mate, you little Mary. You're too afraid, ain't you, Priestie?"

Priest's boarding schools were religious to the extent that divine services and Sunday school were mandatory, and these memories served to remind him of the suffering and crucifixion of Christ. The Romans scourged and spat on Christ. Was this to be Priest's role? Priest did not feel the burden of mankind's sins, and his own father had barely begun to know him when he sent him to sea. His suffering at Craig's hands did nothing for anyone but Craig, and Priest would not have it.

Smallbridge had heard his friend being called "Priestie." He saw Craig standing almost in Priest's face and quickly came to join his shipmate. He saw the same anger rise in Priest that he'd seen in the tavern in Bath. Craig, seeing Smallbridge approach, went forward and started to joke with two hands, making up the end of a jib sheet.

"Priest, what's going on?"

"Craig called me a queer and said Sam Duder has been buggering me. What's wrong with me? Why do people do this to me? I'm— I'm tired of it!"

Smallbridge pointed to the open galley door. "Come into the galley. I don't want any of the hands to hear what I've got to say." They stepped over the galley hatch coming in and talked with their backs to the small galley pantry and woodbin.

"Priest, he wants to fight you. He wants to fight you because he knows he can beat you because he weighs twenty-five pounds more than you do and has been in fights all his life. He wants to fight you because he needs someone to ridicule, someone to take his place as the ship's dog. If he wins, he'll say every lie he's told about you is true. Everyone hates him. The starboard watch is fed up with him, his bitching, shirking his work, and talking about people behind their backs. It's all over the ship that you sucked him off, lie or not."

"I'll fight him."

"No, you won't, not now. He'll hurt you badly. You're not ready to fight. That's why he's bullying you. That dagger he carries ain't a sailor's knife. You have to stay clear of that bastard, Priest."

Jonathon Bishop stepped over the coming and into the galley. "What are you boys doing here? I don't like hands in my galley making a mess for me to clean up. Get the hell out!"

"Craig just called Priest a queer and said Sam Duder was buggering him. He tried to force Priest into a fight."

Jonathon Bishop made a small guttural noise like a hen's clucking and said, "Well, well. Thought so."

"Why can't I fight him now and get it over with?"

Bishop answered, "Because he'd win and then there would be people who'd listen to him. He wants you to be an outcast. He'd not be through with you either. He's got you in a knot. First thing he's doing is telling anyone who'll listen that you are a Nancy-boy and a coward. I've seen it before. He won't leave you alone now. You'll be fair game for anyone. He's going to do his best to force you to fight him, and if you do, that's just what he wants. You'd best get ready to whip him."

"I still can't understand why, Bishop."

An exasperated Jonathon Bishop replied, "He's a bastard, a son of a bitch who enjoys making people suffer! Can't you see that? He wants to fight you because you said no to him, embarrassed him."

Bishop made sure Priest looked him directly in the eye.

"Don't get out of sight of the mates. He won't do anything if the mate's looking. You keep away from him, and if he pushes you in front of the watch, just tell him you are no fool. Say it straight out too: 'I'm not a fool, Craig.' You can't let him convince the hands that you're a coward. Can you fight?"

"My mother always told me that violence was wrong. She said it's better to suffer than to hurt anyone."

"What did your pa say?"

"He never said anything."

"Are you a Quaker?"

"No, I just believe it's foolish to fight."

"It is, boy, but sometimes you have to fight whether you like it or not. The whole crew will know what's going on between the two of you before the dogwatches tonight. They'll be watching you and looking to see any sign of fear. Hell, Priest, it's still a long way from San Francisco. You don't want that man rubbing your nose in his shit for the next two months. If you were just fifteen or twenty pounds heavier and a little tougher, you could fight. Craig's got no backbone; you'd beat him in a fair fight."

Bishop then settled his eyes on Priest's and said, "You're right, Priest. You will fight him, but you need to beat the shit out of him when you do, or else, if you decide to take the beating, you got to stand tall and take it without a whimper. You're risking your life to let him beat on you. You got to hope someone stops it before he kills you."

"Do I have any other choices?" Priest's face asked the question as well as his words.

Bishop placed both of his hands on the boy's shoulders to make his point. "Not if you expect to stay alive and keep half the crew out of your drawers."

Priest shut his eyes, opened them, then looked at the deck and then to Jonathon Bishop. "I've never been—are you sure?"

Bishop gripped Priest's shoulder harder and shook the boy once, a very gentle shake. "I know. It's coming, and you can't run. You got to accept that and get yourself ready. You got to."

Priest let his arms drop to his sides and slumped his shoulders. "What can I do?"

Bishop put his big right hand under Priest's jaw, raised it, and said, "Would you let me help you? Would you do what a nigger tells you to do?"

Priest asked, "Can you help?"

"I can try, but you got to do the fighting."

"What do I have to do?"

Bishop made sure Priest listened carefully to him. "I'll teach you bare-knuckle boxing. I'll feed you extra beef too. Captain and mates won't say anything either. Priest, learning to fight ain't going to be fun. It's going to hurt. That's how you toughen yourself up."

Priest was surprised. "You'd do this for me? Why?"

"Because I've seen too many like him. Because I've had to help black men, just boys like you, line up and be killed, no difference. Maybe I'd like to see you hurt him. I ain't ashamed to admit that. Are you willing? Will you listen to me?"

Bishop extended his right hand for Priest to shake it.

Priest reached for Bishop's hand and shook it firmly. "Okay."

Bishop smiled. "It's a deal."

Priest's mind raced. He saw himself fighting, bleeding. He couldn't run. He remembered Bishop calling himself a nigger. He imagined young black men in blue army uniforms standing in line. He imagined the rattle of musket fire, the flash of muzzles aimed toward him, and saw these same black men die. Perhaps he was among the dead or injured. He imagined their thoughts, his thoughts: *I must show them I'm a man. God, what if I had been born black?*

***

"Damn good porridge today! Raisins, butter, and molasses and *Providence* coffee; now, that's the style. Peleg, finish up. I want to show you my charts." A much-refreshed Griffin felt expansive. He knew amends needed to be made.

"Captain, can the steward pour us another cup of coffee to take to the chart room?"

"You're not going to spill it all over my charts, are you? Ezra, pour us some coffee, please."

They took their cups and walked to the chart room, where Isaac Griffin had spread out his navigation and pilot charts.

"We're going to transit Le Maire Strait. Right now, I want to make the most of the trade winds and make a long board to Rio."

Carver saw where Griffin had made erasures Thursday night.

"There's risks to Le Maire, Captain. You have to transit with low tide." Carver then used the fingers of his right hand as a divider to point out how narrow the strait really was. "See the rocks off Cabo San Diego? Now look across to Staten Island—more rocks. All you

209

got is six miles to tack or wear. Now include an offing from the rocks. Only two miles left, ayuh?"

Griffin did not appreciate Carver's caution. He didn't care about anything other than the bonus. He knew the alternative was to go around Staten Island to enter the Drake Passage. Five added days or even more. He also knew the westerlies and graybeards of Drake's Passage had defeated many ships, including HMS *Beagle*.

"Have you been through the strait?"

"I have, Captain, several times."

Griffin smiled and placed his good left hand on Carver's shoulder. "Well, you'll go through it one more time with me."

***

"Mr. Lennon, can I talk with you after you finish your watch?" Bishop spoke to the second mate near the main hatch.

"What's going on?"

"It's Craig and Priest. Craig's picking a fight and I won't put up with it."

Twenty-Nine

Fever

I see Lily on thy brow
With anguish moist and fever dew
And on thy cheeks a fading rose
Fast withereth too.

—John Keats

Sunday, June 30, 1872
Lat 31°50′24″S, Long 47°48′00″W

"Captain, Captain! Come alive, there. Wake up, Captain, you've a noon site to shoot! I have ya' some coffee. Priest's waitin' to help you. Wake up, Captain."

Isaac tottered for a moment between sleep and consciousness and finally began to hear the words Ezra was shouting at him. He also felt Ezra shake him gently as his eyes opened and he returned once more to the *Providence* at sea. He jerked his head and straightened himself in his easy chair. He raised his left hand and rubbed his cheeks and lower neck. These features were not covered by his beard, but he had a day's stubble.

"Let me have the coffee, please. I'll need a bowl of hot water to shave. Okay, I see the teakettle. Thankee, Ezra. What time is it?"

"They've just rung seven bells of the morning watch, Mr. Carver's watch, sir."

211

"Damn, I'm embarrassed! That man will cut me no slack."

Griffin hurriedly shaved, threw water on his face, and saw that his eyes were clear.

He took his hack watch, set it to the chronometers, strapped his sextant to his right arm, and walked on deck. Both Carver and Lennon were there, similarly armed with their sextants and watches.

Peleg Carver, being the senior mate, was first to speak.

"Good morning, Captain. Mr. Lennon and I did not run her aground or put her masts in the water this morning, ayuh?"

Griffin attempted to smile. He knew what he looked like even without seeing himself in a mirror. While he could never know the thoughts of Carver and Lennon, it took little imagination to hear Carver's mind—*foolish man, foolish man*—while Lennon's mind cautioned him not to tempt his captain.

Lennon added, "Da moon was still up early this morning, 'n' Mr. Carver 'n' me fixed da ship's position. Carver's teaching me lunars. He says it's a blind bit antwackie but it never hurts anyone ter know da correct time of day."

Griffin asked, "Did you or Carver look at the almanac first?"

Lennon replied, "And just who do yews think is first mate on this barky?"

Carver smiled.

Griffin then brought his sextant to his eye and pointed it in the general direction of the sun. He brought the sextant down to waist level and lowered two dark shade lenses to protect his eyes and allow him to observe the orb of the sun distinctly and set it down precisely on the horizon.

Carver looked slyly at Lennon and passed a quick wink. "You know why navigators have patches on their right eyes, ayuh?"

The two mates knew it made no sense to further bait the bear. At least the captain seemed in a decent mood, and Priest stood by, ready to record the time and their observed altitudes.

The sights were taken, all sextant readings and time all near identical to the hundredth. The ship's clock on the binnacle was adjusted for exact noon; the big ship's bell was struck eight times, ending Carver's watch while beginning Lennon's. A new day at sea had begun.

Griffin gathered the deck log and prepared to draft his daily entry into the ship's log. He put together his notes and had Priest plot the ship's position on his chart. The day's run had been spectacular and was evidence enough of the validity of Maury's routes.

Twelve straight hours on deck, the bracing sails at every change of the wind. The bonus from the Central Pacific and the recognition due him from the Rallis grain dealers were a step closer. It was still no occasion to relax, because the Horn was ahead of them, and the River Plate and the south fifties were never without a challenge. Still, Griffin was consumed with optimism.

***

June 30, 1872

Dear Kayleigh,

I am happy with the last day's run. We made good 92 miles despite losing the wind by noon. The sea is large, though, being pushed around the Cape, and it's from the east by southeast, perhaps pushing us along with the Brazil current. The bonus money and you are—

"Captain, Mr. Carver needs you on deck now. Thomsen's sick. He's puking up yellow!"

At Ezra's words, Griffin put down his pen, picked up his medical guide, and went back on deck. He would have to finish his letter another time.

Griffin, Carver, and Ezra stood by Thomsen's bunk in the port watch compartment of the forward deckhouse. Griffin spoke to the sick man.

"Does your head hurt, Thomsen?"

The Dane raised a hand and held it to his forehead.

"I need to feel your pulse. Give me your arm there." Griffin found the man's pulse on his wrist and asked Carver to time it for him.

213

"Mr. Carver, come here and feel his pulse and tell me what you feel. Use my hack watch if you want."

"There, sir, I found it. It's a hard pulse and I count ninety-two beats."

"That's exactly what I felt. The book tells us that seventy-two is about normal for a healthy man. Do you feel how hot he is and how dry his skin has become?'"

"Thankee, Captain. I do."

"Have you thrown up before, man?" Thomsen nodded yes.

"Do you feel like you have to or are going to vomit now?"

Thomsen answered his captain's question by clutching a wooden pail and attempting to heave out the contents of his empty stomach into it. The vomiting consisted of violent dry heaving followed by bringing up yellow bile. The man's pain was intense, and he remained doubled over after the vomiting stopped.

"Lay back, man. Rest. You ache, don't you? I mean even before this." Griffin pointed to the bucket.

Griffin picked up the bucket Thomsen had thrown up in. "What do you see in there?"

Carver replied, "He's thrown up bile and it's yellow."

"Take a look at the whites of his eyes, Mr. Carver. Do you see how they are yellowing?"

"Aye, sir. I do."

"Good. As near as I can make out, he has bilious fever. His symptoms fit what the guide describes.

"Thomsen, I'm going to be looking after you for the next few days, and Mr. Carver and Mr. Lennon will be looking in on you also. We'll get you well, man. Don't you worry; this ship has a good medicine chest and I've seen this before. All you need to do now is rest and take your medicine."

"Mr. Carver, come back aft with me and ask Mr. Lennon if he can leave the deck and come with you."

Fifteen minutes later, both mates joined their captain in his reception area.

"Peleg, Henry, you're going to have the ship pretty much to

yourselves the next few days. I'm going to be spending my time with Thomsen. I've seen this before. He's been to Africa or South America, hasn't he?"

"He's one of the New York men, Captain, and he'd been in the Caribbean for some time before shipping in New York. It's been within six months." Carver knew each man's history.

"I thought so. There's a good chance we'll not have to set him ashore. Matter of fact, he'll get as good treatment on this ship as what he would on shore anyway. A hospital can't do much more than we can."

Griffin pulled a small brown book from his shelf and opened it to its index, and then to page thirty-seven.

"Peleg, read this to page thirty-nine, where it says Bilious, or Remittent Fever."

Both men read the pages and turned toward Griffin. Henry Lennon was the first to speak.

"Da book says it might be two weeks before remission takes place."

Carver added, "Captain, someone's goin' to be seein' him every few hours, ayuh?"

"We've got a problem, Peleg. He's near a full-time job all on his own. I'm going to take care of him. I have to do it, to see to him and what medicine is needed. I want one man from each of your watches, the timekeeper, to check on him and report any change in his condition whenever I can't be with him. In the meantime, I'm not slowing this ship down, nor am I going into port. I've seen this before. The fever will break."

Both mates exchanged a wry smile and thought, *He'll not slow down or lose time.* Carver even thought that Griffin would rather bury Thomsen than stop at Rio. Lennon knew Griffin took risks and was gambling that Thomsen's fever would break. He looked at Carver's facial expression, then muttered, "Not that," and shook his head to say, *Yer'll never change his mind once it's set.*

After the mates left, Griffin prepared a mixture of thirty grains of calomel and jalap and made another mixture of six grains of fever

215

powder. Bishop and Ezra would take care of Thomsen's food—gruel, barley water, rice water, and vegetable soup stock. Griffin asked Bishop to come aft. Thomsen would also need ley water to help reduce the fever.

***

Well, Kayleigh, fortunes change quickly at sea. Thomsen has bilious fever. We will be shorthanded until this is in remission and I will be working even harder. His care falls to me.

Providence did speak with a homeward-bound Yankee steamer. Griffin, Carver, and several of the married men entrusted letters to the captain of the steamer for posting in New York.

When Kayleigh read her husband's letter three weeks later, she spoke two words: "*Mal aria.*"

Thirty

Off Argentina

Her mirth the world required;
She bathed it in smiles of glee.
But her heart was tired, tired,
And now they let her be.

—Mathew Arnold

Thursday, July 4, 1872
Lat 43°16′00″S, Long 49°416′00″W

July 4, 1872

My Dearest Kayleigh,

The weather fights me. All this day it has been a steady rainstorm in which we've managed only 100 miles. The wind came on severe and in squalls since 8 this morning. My poor, wet, tired sailors furled the upper topsails, close reefed the lower and by 9 this morning furled the mains. As noon approached the wind came from the northeast in a gale and in long regular seas. All jibs save for the inner jib are in and everything attached below the bowsprit is now mostly underwater.

Peleg Carver is preparing the ship for the south fifties latitudes. There are lifelines in place and

217

everything aloft that protects a sailor's life in wind and storm has been overhauled, wire standing rigging strengthens the ship and adds to our ability to tack and wear despite the weather. I have great confidence in Carver's seamanship and loyalty. He stood his ground and sent me below to sleep. Not every first mate would brave the wrath of his captain and do that. It's so easy to ignore what is right to do and think, let the old man cook his own goose. What do I care?

An hour later, Griffin again sat at his desk and resumed writing.

Trouble visits the Providence. We shipped one man while in New York who I have had to lower from ordinary seaman to landsman. He lied about his qualifications and I demoted him for incompetence and failure to do his duty. He is from Kentucky and I suspect a fugitive. Men have sought escape from their crimes at sea since Jonah. This is not the worst of our troubles, though. The man is a bully and attempted to intimidate one of my apprentices, Nicholas Priest. Craig wants to cruelly humiliate this boy to gain influence with the crew and because he is sadistic. Henry Lennon, Peleg Carver, and Jonathon Bishop, our cook, a courageous man, all engaged in a secret plot to prepare this boy to fight. Priest showed exceptional progress since coming aboard and impresses everyone with his courage. The issue must be settled without our apparent interference so he can further gain respect and standing with the hands.

I have also written a letter to the police in Boston describing the bully in detail and relating to them my suspicions of the man being a fugitive. If my suspicions are true, he will be arrested in San Francisco.

How I miss you! Kicking Billy was so fortunate to have a wife who went to sea with him. My mind was so addled by fatigue the words cinnamon and nutmeg left my mouth in the presence of Peleg Carver. I had no control, apparently. These are your scent and they delight me.

When this letter reaches you—what, in September?—please give my kindest regards to your mother. I hope your father has found it in his heart to forgive me for taking you from him. Tell Jimmy Meehan to stay out of trouble while I am away. He hates crimps as much as I do, but unlike me has no one to love. He was pressed into the Royal Navy and shanghaied in Liverpool. He's fortunate to be alive.

How I love you and always will.
Isaac

Independence Day in Fall River

July 4, 1872

Dearest Isaac,

I am pregnant! We will be parents in late March or April. How I wish you could be home! I know you will be at sea. Has it always been this way for mariners' wives?

I marched today with the mill girls from Fall River. It was the most liberating experience of my life, as you shall see.

The girls were wonderful. We all wore our very best summer white dresses and white hats with large brims to protect us from the sun. So many of the girls made their own dresses from cloth that had been made here in Fall River. There is a sense of pride with these women that lifts my spirits. We hugged each other and laughed before the parade because we did not know how people would react to young women marching proudly for the entire world to see and demanding the vote. We knew the mill agents and supervisors would see the parade, and if they were not there, their informers would surely be. There would be no anonymity, nothing to stop reprisals. That's why we all tried to be cheerful and encouraging so we could keep our courage and proclaim what we all believe to be our right, equality with men and the right to vote.

The parade was very large, with a band from the state militia, Civil War veterans marching in their uniforms, the police marched, and the fire department paraded with a pumper and a ladder wagon. Every one of them in their best parade uniforms. There were also men's groups from the Catholic churches and a small group of Freemasons—many of the second hands and supervisors are Masons.

Our route was to take us down Anawan Street past the mill yards and to eventually end at the cemetery, where speeches were to be made and people could decorate the graves of fallen veterans and patriots.

We were cheered as we marched along by people who lived in the mill tenements because we were their own. It didn't matter that we were women. As the parade neared the cemetery, we passed by a group of young toughs, all Irish, men who didn't work at the mills, and none of the girls seemed to recognize them.

I worry that my belly is becoming large with our child. Several of these toughs saw me and began to ridicule me. I don't know why this happens, but it seems that once people start acting terribly, one will try to outdo the other. One man, I'm sure he was drunk, he had to be, shouted swear words to me. They were the same words the rapist used, those terrible words; I started to tremble with fear. Mary Ryan, the girl to my right, held my hand tightly and told me to not be afraid. We were all together. The man kept shouting out that I was an Irish whore and then worse—those cruel words reducing me to an animal and making my sex all I am. He threw rotten vegetables at us and laughed when he hit one girl in the face. They laughed and I heard one shout out to me, just to me, "Soon or never."

Words, threats, and fear are the tools of enslavement for women—they keep us in the place men keep for us. They force us to cower, but only if we allow it. Then I realized, these men must fear us because they know in their hearts that we are their equals, if not betters, in courage and ability. Those words set me free. I have confronted my worst fear and am willing to suffer the worst it could bring.

What we share, our love, our bed, our future, our child, we share because we give to each other freely of our own will. Yes, I yearn for your comfort while I am alone in my bed. I want you. I want you but could never give myself to you unless my body, my soul was truly mine to give. I give you so much more. Freedom is the knowledge sure and strong that everyone, man or woman, has the right to love and to be loved.

Your wife,
Kayleigh

Thirty-One

A Reminder

*I seed him rise in the white o' the wake, I seed him
lift a hand ('N' him in his oilskins suit 'n' all), I heard
him lift a cry; 'N' there was his place on the yard 'n'
all, 'n' the stirrup's busted strand.*

—John Masefield

Saturday, July 6, 1872
Lat 48°20′00″S, Long 58°54′00″W
The Roaring Forties

Priest's mind was focused only on climbing to his station aloft.
He lifted his body to the top of the windward bulwark under the
foremast shrouds and swung past the sheer-pole to ascend the
shrouds. He could see the storm-darkened sky and hear the wind
blow over the water and through the rigging. Smallbridge was ahead
of him, near the futtock shrouds of the foremast. Two other top-men
were waiting for him to start his climb. As his back stuck overboard,
facing the water, he began his climb, one ratline, then another, and
then it happened.

Green water slapped Priest into the shrouds with sufficient force
to knock the wind from his lungs. In that odd sensibility that life
bestows on us when we are in peril, Priest grimaced as the cold
water spilled past the collar of his oilskins and trickled down his

back between his shoulders. In the same instant, he realized that the ratlines beneath his feet were broken. The cold water teasing his back was forgotten. No boat could be lowered into this sea. A life ring could be thrown, but he might be unconscious, unable to use the ring to float himself, unable to hold on as it was hauled back to the hull and onto the deck. Death froze his mind in terror while it birthed strength he never knew he had.

Death would be an end. It would end an incomplete life just starting to find itself, the coffee in the mornings, obscene jokes meant to embarrass him, kisses, the feel of Sophie's breasts, her nipples in his fingers, her lips. Sunday sermons provided answers to what would happen beyond death, but Priest had his doubts. His hands gripped the shroud lines tightly; later they would pain him, but for now they held fast, supporting his weight while his feet danced to find a ratline. Justice was of no concern now; regret and anger flashed with the thoughts of what would never again happen, a spring, the emergence of green, the warmth of the sun.

Then he felt something grab hold of his left ankle. "Here, stop that kicking! Stand here." Peleg Carver placed his foot on a ratline. "Damn it, Mr. Lennon told you to be careful. What were you thinking? Are you all right? Then get up to where you belong: we're carrying too much sail."

Making a Point
The Harp and Plough, Boston

Eamon Kavanagh knew them. They were back, drinking whiskey and talking so low the noise of their voices could be heard, but not the words spoken. Suddenly the big man, the man built like a boxcar, jumped to his feet and grabbed the other man by his lapels, the man with the Colt pistol, the Clan na Gael man, and shoved him to the floor.

"Don't you ever again send your men t' threaten me daughter!"

Eamon watched the big man sprint around the table to the man on the floor and step on the man's right hand before it could reach his pocket.

"This is between you and me. Leave my family alone. Damn you, sending men to Fall River to threaten a pregnant woman. If I think just a tiny thought about you harmin' Kayleigh, just a tiny one, I'll kill yer."

Eamon Kavanagh watched the big man pick the other up from the floor as easily as a sack of potatoes and shove him out the door. Eamon went to the bar and took a bottle of Jameson's from the top shelf. He poured himself a generous drink and then another in an additional glass. He carried the drinks to the big man.

Eamon raised his glass and said, "To our children."

Thirty-Two

Two Miles Southwest of Stanley

Six days shalt thou labor and do all thou art able,
And on the seventh—holystone the decks and scrape
the cable.

—Philadelphia Catechism

Sunday, July 7, 1872
Lat 48°52′00″S, Long 59°57′00″W

"Duder, Stedwin, put two men on cat-head lookout and one up the rigging. Relieve them every hour. Yews helm; use Priest as your lee helm. Open the scuttle; we're steering full and by. I'm taking no chance with the helm. Keep the starboard watch on deck, but let them rest."

"Aye, aye, Mr. Lennon."

"Duder," Priest asked, "I thought the south fifties were the hardest, worse than the roaring forties."

"We ain't there yet. Besides, this won't last, Priest. You'll see what the fifties are like soon enough."

Duder suddenly changed the subject. "You going back to Bath, to see that girl? I could ask about her for you when I get home and let you know what happened to her."

Priest replied, "Sophie's all you and Smallbridge want to talk about, rub it in about me leaving."

Duder shrugged. "Hell, boy! She's all you think about! Held your hand too, right in front of them johnnies. When I was your age, I could get sweet on someone if they just smiled at me." Duder turned toward Priest and flashed a toothy smile. "That's okay." He laughed. "Everybody goes through it. She's a whore and that don't bother you? It's a rare gift to see things all faired and true, women in particular." He laughed. "She had you standing proud, now, didn't she?"

Duder's smile told Priest there was no sense of ridicule in what was said.

"That don't stand for true love, but"—Duder was chuckling—"it does make the girls interesting, don't it?" He broke into a full laugh. "Caught you by surprise, too."

Priest replied, "Smallbridge told me about her being sold. I'm not letting my cock do the thinking. Being a whore wasn't her choice. She didn't laugh at me and she didn't act hard either. She slipped the money the Swede paid her into my pocket. She didn't whore me. When we walked back into the tavern, she did hold my hand. I shouldn't have let it go or got drunk."

Duder smiled.

"She stood by me, held my hand, right there for everyone to see. They did stop laughing, but I was too angry to know what was going on. Then I was drunk. Smallbridge said I would probably never see her again. She spoke to me in French. She wanted me to help her, Duder. That's what's on my mind. She was alone with no one to help her and she needed me."

"Smallbridge told you the truth; you'll likely never see that girl again. There'll be others. But nothing's ever for sure, I mean, not seeing her."

Duder made certain Priest looked him in the eye. "That girl's got a will; she don't want to be there, to be a whore, she'll escape and set her life right. She'd make a good wife if she gets free before she's all used up."

Priest replied, "Smallbridge said she had a knife and some money."

"The tavern keeper beats her, Priest. Didn't get naked for you, did she? The girl didn't want you to see her bruises. That's why she's got the knife. She saw something in you. Maybe she just wanted someone to care for or to care for her. She's human all the same. She hoped you'd want to help. She'll get free. Did you tell her anything?"

"Before she did it, I said she was pretty and asked her to tell me her name."

Duder thought out loud. "Maybe that was enough—asking for a name says you like her, maybe that you'd not walk away from her.

"Your folks live in Back Bay, don't they? You ain't ready for a wife now. It takes time, more girls, happiness and sorrow. It ain't easy as it seems to love a woman."

"Why isn't it easy?"

"Because no one's perfect. She'll let you down one day. You'll do the same to her."

"I don't understand—"

"Son, you'll know you're ready when you know how much you can forgive her."

Priest was puzzled.

"It'll come to you."

Priest thought on what Duder had told him, and the word "forgive" kept turning and turning over in his mind and not settling anywhere he recognized.

Duder continued, "If you're lucky, you'll remember all the girls you've known for the rest of your life because they taught you about being a man, just like you'll help teach them to be women. It's cruel to leave them, but that's the way life is. Our trick will be at two bells, so start thinking on being at the helm. Why do you think Mr. Lennon wants you to be lee helm, Priest?"

"I don't know. There's hardly a wind."

"I'll tell you. Pay attention. Have you noticed the sea's been picking up? Wind pushes the sea around to make waves. Officers call it fetch. Just wait until we get into Drake's Passage. The wind's got the whole bottom of the world to blow the water around, and it pushes it between the Antarctic and Cape Horn. What we're feeling now is its ripples. The wind could come on us hard without any warning. It could set the main course aback or spring our rudder. I've seen it hit the rudder so hard it flung a man into the air. Mr. Lennon doesn't want the ship to broach. That's why you're lee helm."

Priest nodded his understanding.

"We'll be steering full and bye. If we handle these cat's-paws real wicked-like, there'll be no need to brace the yards. He wants me and Old John to teach you and Smallbridge how that's done, which sails to watch and what to look for, and it ain't on the mizzen! The captain and the mates on this ship don't do things for the hell of it.

"We'd better relieve the helm now. It's our trick."

The day passed slowly. The wind, when it came, was from all quarters and in whispers. There was no pattern to it. Henry Lennon avoided calling both watches on deck. There was not enough wind to warrant it. Priest saw the men go to the weather side and watch to see if a bow wake formed when it blew at least fair. *Providence* was inching forward.

Griffin appeared on deck with the changing of the watches. He was less concerned with the calm than overjoyed to be able to use his sextant. The wind picked up for a second. Griffin went forward and joined the hands to see if a bow wake formed.

"See there, johnnies, she's a good girl, *Providence*. She won't waste a thing."

The trick over, Priest asked Duder another question. "What's a clean upper limb, Sam?"

"I think you need to ask Mr. Lennon or Mr. Carver. Don't bother them on watch, and wait until they have time to give you an answer. Navigation is the sailor's science. It takes calculations and an almanac. Those sextants and chronometer clocks are the pride of a ship's master. He owns them, not the ship. If I had more education, I might be a mate. Speaking of education, what's the most important sail on a ship?"

"I don't know, Duder."

"Here's your schoolwork. Recollect the first sail we bend. Watch when we get in heavy weather and see which ones the captain leaves up. When you know that answer, tell me and I'll tell you why.

"You also need to think about how the sails work together, like the jibs and spanker. You see, Captain Griffin and his mates were all before the mast when they started. They learned the sailor's trade, then day men's, particularly the boatswain's. Then they became mates and finally ship's masters. They take tests and have to certify they've spent time at sea and have a good record. They belong to associations now that issue them papers that tell ship owners that they are masters and mates. You'll do that too. Hell, boy! The lime-juicers will certify a mate at seventeen if he's got the time at sea."

Shortly after four in the afternoon, just as the watch was relieved, the weather shut in again with cold, drizzling rain. The wind was loud, and you could hear the rigging sing and the spars moan. The landsmen were assigned to operate the ship's foghorn, and it blew continually throughout the day and night. There were no forecastle songs sung that Sunday. They had all they could do to stay warm and dry when they came off deck. Lines were kept strung in the galley so men could try to dry their wet clothes when not on watch. This helped, but the clothes would never again completely dry until the ship turned north and entered the Pacific trade winds. Salt sores started to form on the men's hands. The evening came, and finally Priest was able to rest.

Priest was exhausted when the starboard watch was relieved. Every muscle in his body begged for rest. He looked forward to climbing into his bunk and wrapping himself in his blankets. He wondered why his feet were the last to feel warm and why just when they were warm and he could completely give in to sleep, his watch would be called on deck. Heaving out was not easy. He knew of no greater comfort, no greater relief now than to sleep and be warm, but he forced himself up and out on the cold, dangerous deck.

When he first went aloft, he felt triumphant. Now he felt cold and exhausted. But still he felt both satisfaction with himself and an obligation not to let his fellow seamen down. He would be there with them and working. He would drink his coffee at five in the morning with the other men, huddled in the lee of the forward cabin, and respond that he was okay when asked and then smile. These men, Priest's watch, huddled in their worn oilskins, holding their tin cups in both hands to warm their fingers and thumbs, chewing plugs of rough-cut tobacco and swearing through stained teeth, were his shipmates, and he a shipmate to them. He occasionally looked at their faces; he did not want time to rob them from his memory.

While Priest and the rest had their coffee and tobacco, Griffin turned to Carver and said, "Eighteen days from Saint Rogue to this latitude. Wonder how many days it will take for Cape Horn?"

Thirty-Three

Bare Knuckles

The government is not best which secures mere life and property—there is a more valuable thing—manhood.

—Mark Twain

Monday, July 8, 1872
Lat 50°28'13"S, Long 63°32'45"W
South of the Falkland Islands

The ship was becalmed, the water as still as a Connecticut millpond, and the sea shimmered like silk in the predawn light. The Falkland Islands now lay astern on the port side. The sails hung from their yards like curtains in a theater, limp and lifeless. The moon shone bright and the sea was full of lengths of kelp. Cape pigeons flew overhead. The barometer showed 30.9 inches of mercury and had been falling progressively as *Providence* neared Cape Horn. They had as near perfect conditions for boxing as Tierra del Fuego would allow in winter. When the sparring began, there would be no need for heavy pilot coats. Priest and Bishop were on the cargo deck by the barrels of salt beef and pork and numerous ten-gallon airtights of meat and vegetables. The cargo lamps were burning while the starboard watch slept.

"What did I tell you, Priest, about a right-handed man? You move

231

away from his right hand when he hits! That's so there's never any power behind the punch. Take your stance, now, and move left when you see me start to cock my right arm. That's it, boy! Now, jab, jab, keep moving left."

Bishop threw a right cross at Priest. The boy's left arm blocked the blow and Priest quickly threw his right into Bishop as his coach dropped his left hand with the punch.

"No, Priest! You're off balance! You got to throw that right using your whole body! The arm ain't enough. Use the waist. Use the legs! What are you doing? Trying to knock a piece of oakum off my chin? Let's do it again. Jab, jab, and here it comes! Damn, that's a good one, Priest! Anybody ever tell you that you're quick? What do you do when you hit him good?"

"I hit him again!"

"Okay, let's try that again. Jab, jab, jab!" The punch was thrown. Priest counterpunched. Bishop stepped away, dropped his right arm slightly, and with lightning speed, Priest threw a left hook, then a right uppercut.

"Oh, you're a sweet young man! Damn but that stung! Didn't pull any of those punches. We're friends here, ain't we? Keep your feet moving; don't you dare stop. I'm coming in now. Show me what I taught you. That's right! Keep your arms above mine! Punch the kidneys! If you got to head butt, head butt the damn eyes! Boy, the forecastle hands will know you are one sweet son of a bitch now. All right, that's enough for now. I got to start the fire and make coffee."

"How am I coming along? Am I ready?"

"I'd like to see five more pounds, but that speed you've got is so sweet. Damned if I don't have me a natural lightweight! Tell me what you do with that jab? Why do I keep telling you jab, jab, jab?"

"You want me to keep him off balance. You want me to cut his eyes and break his nose."

"Why, Priest?"

"If he can't see, he can't punch. If he can't breathe, he can't fight. Why so bloody? Why do I have to be an animal?"

"Because he is! His mind is made up to harm you. He doesn't

give a damn. You got to have your mind made up to fight, to take the fight to him. There's no time to make up your mind in a fight. It's all reaction. No thinking, just punch, counterpunch. Things happen too quickly. You got to be an animal. No thinking, just cunning. It's nature! It's in you, I know it is, and it's there for a reason.

"When I was a prizefighter, every time they said, 'Hit the nigger; hit the nigger!' it made me madder than hell, but I kept my wits. I waited. I was patient. When the time came to throw my punch, I remembered them yelling out, 'Hit that damn nigger.' They did me a favor. Oh, that's when I stoked up the hate and let it loose. I hit a man so hard you could hear the crowd gasp. Don't know if it was the money they lost or seeing that man's head snap and spin so suddenly and then watching him stagger and fall.

" 'Nigger' hurts because I am a man. You're a man, Priest. You can't let anyone or anything rob you of your manhood. I guess they didn't teach you that at all those schools. As long as you believe you're a man, nobody can beat you. They might whip you, but you'll still be a man.

"I'll ask Mr. Lennon to send you to me to help after breakfast, so you can get some sleep. Oh, Priest, you are one sweet lightweight. Got to get the fire started. That bastard Craig's going to think he tried to screw a wildcat!"

***

The morning routine called for Henry Lennon and Jonathon Bishop to meet after coffee had been provided to the crew at five in the morning, time to draw the day's rations. Five in the morning was also the time the two men had come to talk. Usually the talk was just to pass the time and for each the sort of mutual respect that passes between friends.

"How's da lad coming, Bishop?"

"He's a natural lightweight, Mr. Lennon. Look how his eyes are set back and protected by his forehead? Do you see the size of his hands? He knows how to deliver a punch now—well, mostly; he'll be all right. I'd like to see five more pounds, but if he gets cornered,

Craig will be the one who regrets being there.

"He's toughened up his stomach and has been soaking his hands and face in brine. When he makes a fist, it's like a stone."

"What did you say to da lad, though? He stands up to Craig and says, 'I'm na fool; you'll know when I'm ready.' What did yews tell that lad?"

"That's between him and me."

"Black magic, I take it."

"Ha! Maybe. I like that boy, Mr. Lennon. I'm training him hard. He's a good boy. I'm having some fun with him."

"Fun?"

"Sure. We can joke all the time, even when he's hurting. He don't take himself too serious. He's getting his body toughened up. I've seen him lie there on the deck, holding his legs up, and pound on his stomach until his gut is beet red. He'll wince with pain, but he never complains. You've seen how he's filled out. He'll not be the same boy once he gets home."

"Do yews think he'll go ter sea for a livin'?"

Bishop laughed. "How in hell do you expect me to know that? Priest and Smallbridge are planning to get Cape Horn tattoos in San Francisco."

"Jon, why are yew helpin' da lad?"

"Why not? He comes to me for coffee and hardtack before the others are on deck. We've been talking. You know he asked me about the war, how anyone could just stand there in a line of battle and see the faces of people trying to kill you, see them aim their rifles right at you. He asked how I could stand there and fight while the man next to me got shot. He's not wanting war stories neither."

"What'd yews tell him—why?"

"Told him we stood there, got wounded, and died because of our friends, our brothers, our company and platoon, no one would let a brother down, no one wanted to be known as a coward. I told him about the hate. You know, Mr. Lennon. You been there. Then he asks me if living is worth it if you think you're a coward."

Boston

July 8, 1872

Dearest Isaac,

I am so excited to write to you because I feel a celebration is needed after last week's events. It seems the Boston Training School for Nurses will soon be in existence and join the New England Hospital for Women and Children in training women for this profession. Father helped with the money and even the poorest of people gave us their pennies. Jimmy Meehan organized what he has named the New England Brotherhood of Merchant Seamen and Steamship Clerks. They too helped raise money by passing the hat at the Seamen's Bethel and at all the taverns on the waterfront. He raised 173 dollars from the sailors!

Jimmy is now living in the small apartment above my parents' carriage house. San Matias is in a shipyard in South Boston and out of the water. He checks her every day. Mother says he is sweet on her Irish cook. You should hear them talk, two cooks who love to complain about each other's dishes. Jimmy no longer is confined to boiling and frying and is now baking pastries! I think Jimmy is sweet on several women. I will always be sweet on you, Isaac.

I recruited two young women doctors from the Women's Medical School to help with the curricula for the new school. We agree on instruction based on Florence Nightingale's example. We will teach our students to dress blisters, sores, burns, and make poultices as well as minor dressings. They will learn to give enemas to men, women, and children. We also believe in teaching them how to physically handle the helpless and bedridden. The rest is sanitation, which is simply housekeeping.

Nurses need to know how to dose patients and enough about diseases and bodily functions to keep a valuable record for the physicians' use. Since medicine can now measure things such as body temperature, blood pressure, and actually listen to organs like the heart, nurses need to acquire these skills too. So I stress the need for a foundation in the eclectic school of medicine and modern thinking. Science must be part of nursing and we must break the concept of the household as the model of our care. Until we do, nurses will never be justly compensated for the care they give.

Florence Nightingale wrote a letter encouraging me to see my ideas through. I also wrote to the Institution of Protestant Deaconesses at Kaiserswerth for their advice, particularly for curriculum matters and how single women who enter nursing are treated in Germany. Some of the younger doctors at Massachusetts General are also helping me form a curriculum together with my young women doctors.

Each day, my mother has drawn closer to me since we have become married. In so many things, she is much stronger than my father. This surprises me. I believe mother convinced my father to persuade you and the Christisons to fly the Irish harp beneath the American flag.

I do not look as forward to going home after a day's work now. I cannot share my parlor with you and my bed is a lonely place for me. Do you feel as I do?

Sadly, I must tell you Hanna and William Jr. are having problems. He is much more involved in business than before and ignores her most simple and intimate needs. He explains this neglect as chronic nervous exhaustion. She wants a child and he is so inattentive.

The Downeaster

His disease seems to be a fashion these days. I know women who are constantly complaining and visiting their physicians, claiming they too suffer from nervous exhaustion. These women are proud because their ailment is a sign of their place in society.

Hanna is so beautiful. Her face would please Botticelli. Her body must be all that any man could desire. Yet William barely seems to notice Hanna's existence. I am so happy to have you as my husband and lover. It seems silly; Hanna could excite the beast in any man. I found an old "The Ancient Wisdom of Aristotle." It provides the most delicious examples of how to have a happy, fruitful marriage. I will teach Hanna to be as patient with William as you were with me. You and I will read Aristotle together when we are reunited. There's so much wisdom to try.

Captain Christison tells me you and your ship should rapidly approach Cape Horn now. You've never expressed fear of this awful place to me or even Jimmy Meehan, but I pray you navigate Cape Horn with skill and courage. The Commodore says you are a fighter at heart and Cape Horn and the Southern Ocean strengthen you. How can such a thing be? I do not understand, but I know in my heart that is true and you, your ship, and crew will triumph over the cold and raging seas and soon be in San Francisco. I've asked Saint Christopher and the apostle Peter to be at your side.

How I love you and how I know you love me. These letters lead my mind to imagining us speaking together, of walking hand in hand and when our lips touch. I shall write and write so you are in my every thought.

Your most loving friend and Life's partner forever,

Kayleigh

Thirty-Four

The Fight

And to myself I boasting said,
Now I a conqu'ror sure shall be.
                              —Anne Kingsmill Finch

Wednesday, July 10, 1872
Lat 53°24′00″S, Long 63°55′00″W
Off Punta Arenas

July 10, 1872

My Dearest Kayleigh,
    We are becalmed. We are forced to estimate our position at sea and, in this calm, moving only where the current takes us. So we are blind and lost save for soundings. While we are not in danger, I believe we are drifting to the northwest along the coast of Isla Grande de la Tierra del Fuego. We will be delayed entering the Le Maire Strait as I had planned. Overcast, squalls, calms!
    The Le Maire Strait will save us 5 or more days as compared to sailing eastward around Staten Island to enter the Drake Passage. However, the strait is difficult if the weather is against you, as it has been these past days. Its sides are lined with rocks and it has treacherous tides capable of setting a ship

238

aground on its shores. Although there is deep water in the strait, safe offings must be kept off Cabo San Diego at the strait's entrance and off Cabo Setabense at its exit.

I've not slept and am growing increasingly impatient. It means so much to me to gain the bonus the Central Pacific Railroad has promised and to secure regular cargoes from the Rallis. If all of this comes to pass, I can pay off the mortgage on San Matias, *sell her, and look to purchasing a home for us.*

Are you pregnant? I don't know if I should dread the answer or look forward to a child of our own. So much depends on how you are being treated, if your family still welcomes you as their daughter. Yet another reason to reach San Francisco quickly.

Life aboard Providence *is not without interest. Peleg Carver decided that the calm weather was as good an occasion as we might find to do a thorough inspection of our rigging. We changed our sails to heavy Cape Horn canvas after reaching the River Plate. Since men will soon, within days, be aloft in freezing weather with high winds, snow, and ice, Peleg is determined to risk no life unnecessarily. Caution is cheap insurance.*

Peleg took Samuel Craig, the fugitive from Kentucky, aloft with him because Thomsen is still not well. Peleg Carver can be a stern man when he needs to be and the crew respects him for it. I suspect this sternness is why he chose Craig to accompany him.

Once aloft, Craig was asked to attach a jigger tackle to part of the running rigging so a block could be removed and overhauled. This meant he attached a small purchase or, what most people say, a block and tackle, on the running rigging to maintain tension while he removed the block and the hemp rope running through it. Peleg Carver had to show him how this was to be accomplished, as Craig is a poor sailor. When we overhaul a block, we make sure the wood and strapping are sound and the sheave is working freely. Then we recoat it with varnish to protect it from the weather or if we need it immediately, coat it with linseed oil. This is all routine work.

Nicholas Priest was on deck under the mizzen where Craig was working. Just as soon as Craig was able to distract Peleg, he attempted to drop the block on Nicholas Priest. Smallbridge, Priest's friend, shouted, and Henry Lennon dove in to tackle Priest and kept the block from hitting him. As it was, the block hit the deck hard enough to put a large dent in the yellow pine. If it hit Priest in the head, it may have killed him. It certainly would have fractured his skull.

Peleg Carver nearly kicked Craig out of the rigging and literally forced him back down on deck. I had Peleg bring Craig and Priest into my reception area. You should have heard the excuses Craig offered, all lies. "It was oily, Captain, and slipped from my hand!" I told Craig that I knew he had told the starboard watch that he would vilely assault Priest and that it was common knowledge he had been bullying Priest. I gave Craig a choice: He could box Priest according to the London Prize Ring Rules, if Priest was willing, or he would spend the rest of the voyage in irons until we reached San Francisco. Once there, I would make the charge of attempted murder. Well, Priest was only too happy to fight, which surprised a sigh out of Craig.

I should have simply put Craig in irons, but I let the fight occur for Priest's benefit. I think you may disagree with me, but Priest needed to fight. He needed to discover he had the sand within him to face another man who might harm him.

Priest will surprise everyone who ever knew him once this voyage is over. Peleg Carver seems to be the person Priest is patterning himself after. Perhaps you could say you watch a woman bloom as in a flower. For Priest it is more like a sturdy oak growing.

The London rules are not the same as the boxing matches fought in leather gloves. It is fought bareknuckled and there is a fair amount of grappling allowed. It is fought until either one of the fighters concedes the match or one can no longer toe the scratch mark. I appointed Henry Lennon to be Priest's second and Eoghan Gabriel, the boatswain, to be Craig's second. Peleg Carver was to be the referee.

The crew was mustered to watch the fight, which took place on the main cargo hatch. Both fighters were warned that it must be a good clean fight. Craig was given the warning that this must end his hostility toward Priest or I would end it on my own terms.

The crew had long suspected a fight would occur, and there were substantial wagers on its outcome.

***

Jonathon Bishop had finished greasing Priest's face and gave him his last-minute instructions and encouragement before the first round began. "What have I taught you? You have to go in there and finish him. You can't leave him standing. The longer you let him stand, the greater the chance he will do something dirty. Are you ready? Are you going to knock him out?"

"I'm ready."

"But will you knock the bastard out, Priest?"

"C'mon, Smallbridge, you don't have to say that."

Bishop exclaimed, "Damn it, Priest! This ain't a joke. This is what I've trained you for. You can get hurt in there, even killed. Make up your mind! Forget your ma and pa; you got to get angry. You got to see red; you got to want to hurt him."

The bell sounded, the combatants stripped off their heavy coats, and the fight began.

Craig began the fight with a wild flurry of blows delivered during a charge into Priest. The apprentice easily deflected the blows with his arms and circled to his left. Craig repeated his attack again and again, only to see it fail.

After ten minutes into the first round, Smallbridge turned to Bishop. "What in hell is he doing?"

"He's playing with him, Smallbridge. He doesn't want to hit him."

Craig charged in again, and Priest repeated his defense but this time threw a jab to Craig's face, which ripped open his upper lip, drawing first blood. Craig in turn went into a blind rage and attempted to lock Priest up in his arms, but to no avail. Priest kept his arms above Craig's and delivered a head butt, a loud thud, which brought a puffy purple bruise to Craig's left eye.

"That's sweet, boy, that's sweet. Stop playing with him!"

Priest heard Bishop and launched an offensive. He still was not trying to finish Craig by knocking him out. He struck two quick jabs into Craig's face, and when Craig attempted to punch back with a wild right, Priest instinctively counterpunched with a well-delivered left uppercut, catching Craig in the upper rib cage. He would later find that he had broken Craig's rib.

"Damn it, Sweets, finish him, finish him, he can't fight you!"

This time Craig was seized with pain and fear. He could not hurt Priest. In fact, he could not even land a blow to Priest's body or head. He attempted to back away from Priest but was shoved back into the center of the ring by the big German in the starboard watch, the crew all chanting now, "Fight him, fight him, coward!"

Priest once again began to jab until Craig was backing away and off balance. The bully wanted to run. Then Priest threw a right-left combination to Craig's face, smashing his nose and sending him to the canvas.

Panic set in for Craig. He looked around with his one good eye, crawled rapidly into his corner, and reached out and grabbed a knife from one of the sailor's belts. He stood and began to charge at Priest with the knife held at waist level with the intent of delivering a fatal thrust to Priest's body.

Nicholas Priest screamed in rage. Griffin fired his pistol in the air.

In the flash of a single second, Nicholas Priest had considered the worth of his life and determined he would not die this day at Craig's hand. Unlike before in Virginia, he was not helpless; he did not have to accept death.

The boy's rage was so startling and violent that several sailors stepped back and the younger of the Ernst brothers instinctively turned toward his brother. Bishop yelled out, "Sweets! Sweets! The knife!" Priest heard nothing, not even the pistol shot.

Priest grabbed Craig by the biceps of his knife arm and by his crotch, lifted his would-be killer overhead, and threw him from the cargo hatch into the main fife-rail. Craig dropped the knife on impact and yelped, then screamed in pain. By this time Priest was on the fallen man in berserk fury, kicking him and screaming until Bishop and Lennon could restrain him.

"It's over, Priest, its over!"

Priest had released years of pent-up rage, and with its sudden departure he went nearly limp. It was as if every ounce of emotion had been drained and replaced with lead, causing his body to slump in Bishop's arms.

Jonathon Bishop placed his huge black arm around Priest's back and under his armpit, steadying his fighter. "Damn it, Sweets, I told you to knock him out, not try to kill him." He laughed. Smallbridge wiped the grease and sweat from his shipmate's face and upper body.

By this time Priest began to hear the cheering of the forecastle hands and heard them calling him "Sweets." He felt pats on his back and heard one man say, "He deserved it, Sweets. No shame on your part. I would have killed him had he drawn a knife on me."

"You made me a rich johnny, Sweets. I'll buy you a whiskey in the Cobweb Palace, shipmate."

The blood returned to Priest's face and he began to realize triumph. He began to realize that the crew admired him for what he had accomplished, holding his ground until ready and then fighting with great skill and berserk fury. The story would be told and retold in taprooms and ginhouses ashore for years. Priest had earned a reputation now and gained standing among his fellow mariners.

Priest said he just wanted a cold beer and a large beefsteak. Smallbridge just smiled.

***

And so it ended in only one round. I've applied lint and plaster to Craig's ribs. Broken as he is, he should not be a threat to anyone. I did remove him from the forecastle and placed him in a small cabin in the forward deckhouse. He's a pariah. I will make charges for attempted murder against him when we reach San Francisco. Until then and when he is able, he will rejoin his watch and work. We are shorthanded. I have no other choice.

I will post this letter to you in San Francisco if we do not speak to an eastbound American ship in Drake's Passage. With luck, I'll be in San Francisco before any Atlantic-bound ship reaches New York or Boston from here.

I live to see you again. You occupy my dreams.

Isaac

***

That evening, Peleg Carver and Henry Lennon asked to meet with the captain alone in his reception area. Eoghan Gabriel had the deck.

Henry Lennon spoke. "Captain, I broke da point off that bastard's sticker. Did you know it's a double-edged and has an eight-inch blade? Put him in chains before he kills someone. I tinnie do without him on da starboard watch. The bastard's too dangerous."

"No, he'll work. No free passage!"

"Damn it, Captain, listen to him. Lennon's right. If this were the navy, he would have been flogged, and by God, I'd use the cat. He's going to kill somebody if he's not locked up and in chains. I wish you had shot him."

"I've made up my mind. I'll have no deadweight on my ship! I expect you two to make sure there's no trouble. Let the law take him in San Francisco, but until then he works and earns his whack!"

"If that's your decision, put him on port watch. I can keep him under my heel. Henry, I'll give you my landsman for him to make it fair."

"There's na need, Peleg. Nothing's fair about that feller. He'll cost you more than he's worth."

Griffin had heard enough. "That's it; I've heard all I'm willing to listen to. Peleg, you've got Craig now. Gentlemen, one of you is on watch."

Thirty-Five

Cabo San Diego

Black it blows and bad, and it howls like slaughter,
And the ship she shudders as she takes the water,
Hissing flies the spindrift like a wind-blown smoke.
                                        —John Masefield

Monday, July 10, 1872
Lat 53°24′00″S, Long 63°55′00″W

The ship's bell sounded eight bells for midnight; the starboard watch was in the process of being relieved. Peleg Carver greeted his relief.

"Good morning, Mr. Lennon. No change since your last watch, hard gale, wind S by SE and snow and thick weather. We're steering south-southwest by one-quarter west under the forestaysail, reefed upper topsails, and the spanker. We're in 170 fathoms of water and I am certain with this sea we're not making much southing. I don't think we're making much more than two knots headway. The captain's concerned about leeway in this gale, and so am I."

"Captain's night orders, Mr. Carver?"

"Call him for any break in the clouds, change of wind, change of weather, and any sudden loss of water under her hull. He's concerned that we've had no reliable observation in the last—what is it, now?—twenty-four hours or so."

"Steering south-southwest by one-quarter west. I relieve you."

"Mr. Lennon has the deck!"

"Da old feller's concerned that she's riding low in the water, Mr. Carver. Are we shipping any water forward? When's de last time we checked da cargo? Been any shifting?"

Carver was too exhausted to take offense about Lennon's asking him about his responsibility. After a moment, he realized the second mate actually might be seeking some direction from him about the work for his watch.

"I know, Mr. Lennon. I checked the cargo for shifting during the dogwatches with Chips. Everything is exactly as it was when we left New York. We have to be heavy by the bow from ice. That's got to be why. You might have the hands see how much of the snow and ice we can get overboard. You also might want to send someone aloft to break the ice on the foot-ropes."

The ship's bell sounded at the half hours of the watch. The men were kept hard at work attempting to remove ice as quickly as it accumulated. Henry Lennon formed a party of top-men and went aloft to attempt to get the ice off the foot-ropes and make sure the beckets were firmly attached to the jackstays and that they were sound. It was dangerous work laying out on the icy yard, but it was work that needed to be done if the ship was to be able to tack or wear or, for that matter, reef or make sail. The apprentices were sent aloft with the top-men.

At eight bells, the weather started to moderate. Coffee was brought on deck at five. Breakfast was delayed in order to make sail. Bishop made fresh drop biscuits in addition to the pancakes and ham. The new refined white flour was wonderful; it didn't spoil quickly. Bishop hoped to bake fresh soft bread later. The aroma would cheer the hands and provide him some relief from the smell of drying clothes hanging in his galley.

***

Isaac Griffin had been on deck since about four in the morning. He knew that once the gale had passed, the sky might clear and an observation of the sun could be made to fix his position. If the clouds did not break, daylight might reveal landfall. *Providence* proceeded slowly southward under topgallants and topsails in light wind. The hours passed until five bells in the morning watch. It was pitch-black, but the moon began to shine through. At seven bells of the forenoon watch—

"Land ho! Land ho! Dead ahead!"

Griffin took his watch glasses to his eyes, observed the land on the horizon for a few moments, and then turned to Henry Lennon and said, "Cabo San Diego. Take a look. Staten Island should come into view soon and we can fix our position by two bearings. I recognize the outline from the coast pilot. We're northwest of the strait."

At six bells Staten Island came into view. Griffin took bearings, Cabo San Diego due south, Staten Island to the southeast. "Tack her, Mr. Lennon. Tack ENE. When you're steady on that heading, I'll calculate how far we need to go to be ready to enter the strait." Griffin knew the ship was set WSW at the rate of one and a half knots each hour. The result was that the ship had drifted west on the coast of Argentina and away from the Le Maire Strait. Griffin's distance calculation was futile because the ship was becalmed near noon and cloud cover set in anew, dead reckoning again, but from a known position far less than two days old.

Griffin knew he would have to wait until the wind favored passage through the strait and an ebbing tide would help in the transit. "It's just as well we're here. We wouldn't make headway in the countercurrent in the strait. Secure the lead; I know where we are now. It could have been much worse. Damn, more lost time."

Thirty-Six

Estrecho de Le Maire

She came two shakes of turning top
Or stripping all her shroud-screws, that first quiff.
Now fish those wash-deck buckets out of the slop.
Here's Dauber says he doesn't like Cape Stiff.
This isn't wind, man, this is only a whiff.
"Hold on, all hands, hold on!" a sea half seen,
Paused, mounted, burst, and filled the main-deck green.
                                    —John Masefield

Thursday, July 11, 1872
Lat 54°10′00″S, Long 64°50′00″W

"With respect to this part of the voyage, whether to pass through the Strait le Maire, or round Staten Island, much difference of opinion exists. Prudence, I think, suggests the latter; yet I should very reluctantly give up the opportunity that might offer of clearing the strait, and therefore of being so much more to windward. With southerly wind, it would not be advisable to attempt the strait; for, with a weather tide, the sea runs very cross and deep, and might severely injure and endanger the safety of a small vessel, and to a large one do much damage."
                                    —Admiralty South American Pilot

Paul Thomas Fuhrman

Wednesday, July 10, 1872
Three Bells, First Dogwatch (5:30 p.m.)

Isaac Griffin and Peleg Carver were huddled beneath an overhead oil lamp over the chart for Le Maire Strait in *Providence*'s chart room. Scattered around the chart table were several coast pilots as well an older Maury's *Explanations* for his wind and current charts. Peleg Carver was first to speak.

"All these"—Carver pointed to Maury's *Explanations* and the coast pilots—"do is tell you the strait is dangerous, ayuh? It's your decision, Captain. Go now or go later, the damn weather can change three times before you leave Le Maire."

Griffin, irritated from days of calms since the Falkland Islands, replied, "I know all that. What I don't know is your recommendation. Tell me."

Carver looked at his captain and said in as calm a voice as he could muster, "Any choice we make will likely be wrong. Accept it and go when we have wind; just expect a fight to get through."

Griffin attempted to mollify Carver with a forced smile. "Show me."

"Nothing too bold or daring, Captain." Peleg bent over the chart and with his finger laid out his plan. "Here's the danger, these rocks off Cabo San Diego and the rocks here from Galeano to Peninsula Lopez. Now"—using the thumb and little finger of his right hand as dividers—"we keep a three-mile offing from the rocks on both sides, and when Cabo San Diego bears about ninety degrees off the starboard, about where my finger is pointing, we come to south-southwest by one-quarter west and make at least six knots or better through the water." Peleg Carver stopped speaking and looked Griffin in the eye.

"Here's the beauty of it. The drop-off past Buen Suceso tells us when we're in the southern half of the strait—low visibility—and on a south-southwest by one-quarter west course, we've room to wear in the southern half of the strait and make for Buen Suceso if we have to."

Griffin did not immediately reply; instead he traced out what Carver had shown him on the chart. "It's going to snow, be a gale,

250

The Downeaster

maybe a bad one. The glass is dropping."

Carver laughed. "Well, we both got master's tickets and eyes and ears. God willing, we'll make it."

Griffin replied, "God willing—do you really believe that?"

Eight Bells, First Watch (Midnight)

Griffin had his wind and gave the deck to Peleg Carver. The barometer registered 29.8 inches and was dropping rapidly, and the tide was flowing into the strait. Yes, it would come, a storm and snow. It would be difficult to maintain steerageway until slack water and an ebbing tide. Eventually they would be blind and dependent upon Duder and Stedwin's ability to hold to a course.

Griffin had made this transit before, as had Carver. Both understood the tides; high water at Bahia Buen Suceso meant slack in the strait. But Griffin had lost days with the calm, and the current did set him westward of Cabo San Diego, causing the need to tack and lose ground. No more delay; he had waited on deck since noon of the tenth of July and he could wait no more. He felt the bonus money slipping through his fingers.

"Captain, I'll use distance off to confirm our offing from San Diego, then Cook's Road to see where we are in the channel. Make use of visibility while we got it."

The ship's master smiled and replied, "Use your eyes if you have to. Put us in single-reefed topgallants on the fore and main. Both watches and idlers on deck." Then Griffin placed his injured right hand inside his coat, beneath his belt by the watch pocket, and held the hand against his belly. The cold caused intense pain in the hand, and the risk he was taking had tied knots in his colon.

***

At fifteen minutes before midnight, Priest felt Richard Ernst shake his shoulder. "On deck, P-Priest."

Priest quickly climbed into his wool trousers, wool shirt, sea-boots, pilot coat, and Scotch hat in the pitch black of the apprentice stateroom. He marveled at how cold it was and how the warmth of

251

his heavy trousers seemed to climb up his legs as he raised them to his waist.

"Thanks, Richard. What's going on?" Priest rubbed his eyes.

"We're sailing into the strait."

The weather was overcast, but the waning moon was nearly full and filled the stratus clouds in gray light. All Priest could think about was snow. The cold, the humidity, and the chill penetrated the layers of his clothing, reminding him of a New England winter. Ice had formed again on the lower parts of the standing rigging.

There was no time for coffee or ship's biscuits. As soon as the upper topsail yard had been raised, Priest and the other top-men assigned to the foremast were aloft, overhauling the tackle needed to let fall sail. With the yard raised to the cap and ready, Priest and the other top-men loosened the sail from its gaskets and let it fall upon command. Minutes later, the upper and lower topsails on the fore and main-masts were braced and filled. Priest smiled to himself; these sails, the flying jib, the fore and main topsails, the main topgallant staysail, and the spanker would propel her forward into the strait while lifting her bow. He was learning and pleased with himself. So pleased, he momentarily forgot the pain caused by the saltwater boils on his legs and the salt sores on the bottoms of his hands.

The visibility was good from Priest's lookout station high aloft the foremast. He could see the promontory of Cabo San Diego pass astern and could see the rocks guarding it. The rocks were small island peaks surrounded by black kelp beds. As the ship moved south through the strait, the moon illuminated the surf breaking against the shore. The line of luminescent white lapped powerfully, making a roar, but by Priest's estimation, the ship's offing was at least three miles. Although the evergreen trees of Tierra del Fuego appeared black in the overcast moonlight, the undulating surf line and the snow in the highlands stood out white and provided depth of vision.

Staten Island was all chiseled mountain rock, white, tall, and wildly beautiful, with the muscular beauty of large predator cats. Their stillness reminded him of a lion's eyes, deep set, with an expressionless stare that hid the danger within. Priest's emotions, still accustomed to open horizons, told him both sides of the strait seemed to be near enough to touch, and the anxiety encroached on his comfort. It seemed that as soon as the rocks around the perimeter of Cabo San Diego passed astern to starboard, more rocks appeared to port off the Staten Islands, the snow tiger's teeth and claws. Priest thought the tide must be flowing into the strait from the south, as the surf was violent and filled the cold air with its roar. The waning moon, virtually full, meant the tide would still be high and powerful. The ship crept forward against the tide's flow.

Four Bells, Middle Watch (2 a.m.)

Griffin stood outside the open starboard door of the wheelhouse. His face must show no emotion. He knew Carver must believe he had total confidence in him. He knew the men watched him for any sign that he might be afraid. He and his officers were not the only men aboard who had experience with the Le Maire Strait. Despite his demeanor, his mind weighed his decision.

Twenty-nine point six inches of mercury! Should I have waited? We're offshore from Bahia Buen Suceso, past Caleta San Mauricio. Two reasonably good positions using distance off calculations. Carver likes this, the tables, measuring distance, right triangles. The man loves piloting. He's estimating the current's drift, what? Two knots is reasonable, maybe as much as three? Yes, Peleg, three is better. Four? Eyeballing it? You must see to tell distance over ground.

Steer south-southwest by one-quarter west. The tide is ebbing now. Winds southwest. We'll go faster in slack water; she'll steer better too. Peleg trim—we'll be in the passage sooner.

Griffin's stomach felt better; Carver balanced the helm with the spanker even as he thought of the need.

Gale! Twenty-nine point five inches on the glass, the mercury steadily dropping. Driven snow. I can barely see the bowsprit. Topsails, reefed topgallants, spanker and main topgallant staysail, flying jib. She pitches fiercely. Who has the helm? Duder and Priest. The boy will get a lesson today. Port tack. Excellent. Wind's from the southeast. How much leeway?

"Mr. Carver, brace fore and main yards to the wind. How does she steer? How much weather helm?"

Carver's bracing to the wind. What's he thinking? Brace to the wind. Keep headway, momentum. South-southwest by one-quarter west. I can see no landmarks. Twelve miles to the Drake Passage? It's got to be less. What if I have to wear? How will we know? We can't see. Leeway?

"Duder, south-southwest by one-quarter west. Mr. Carver, the outer jib and double-reefed fore topgallant—if you please, sir."

An ebbing tide. How much weather helm? Watch, don't ask. That's Carver's business. We'll move southward.

"Wind's hauled forward. Green water! Head seas!"

The bottom drops past Bahia Buen Suceso. She'll ride better now. Smoother water. Spill the wind from the main. Brace square. Soundings. Sixty fathoms on the Tanner machine. Are we past Buen Suceso? Sixty fathoms, I'm in the southern part of the channel. Leeway? Are we between the Ensenada and Peninsula Lopez? Plenty room for a wear. Steer south-southwest by one-quarter west.

***

Priest did not expect Mr. Lennon to place his arm suddenly across the wheelhouse door.

"Listen to me. Priest, I know yews want ter help da old man and Mr. Carver navigate, but that ain't yew's lesson today. She's steering south-southwest by one-quarter west. We're blind in this snow. Can't see a bloody quarter-mile. She's has ter keep her course. Tide's changing. Do yews understand me? We're dead reckoning, and we're blind."

Lennon lowered his arm and let Priest enter the wheelhouse. When Priest passed, Lennon placed an arm on Duder's shoulder. "Watch him. He's got ter learn."

The helmsman, John Stedwin, saw Duder approach to relieve him. "Sam, it's blowing mostly west-southwest but wanders a bit to the south. Mate said to watch the current; it's ebbing due south now. Watch how she steers. Be careful. The old man's on deck. She's steering south-southwest by one-quarter west. Careful when the wind wanders; she'll loosen up by two spokes then."

Duder firmly repeated the course steered and turned to Priest. "Are you ready?"

Priest replied, "Yes."

Duder placed his hands over the helmsman's and assumed management of the wheel. "I've got her, south-southwest by one-quarter west." Carver carefully observed the wheel being relieved.

Priest relieved Smallbridge at the lee helm. John Stedwin and Smallbridge left the wheelhouse and became part of the on-deck watch. Smallbridge went aloft and Stedwin stood with his back against the wall of the deck cabin and in the shelter of its lee and his oilskins. Mr. Carver and the old man had gone to the chart room, giving the con to Lennon.

It came on suddenly, sweeping northward from the Drake Passage. *Providence* was fighting, clawing her way to the top of the wave, only to have it pass beneath her, slamming her bow down amidst a crash and spray of cold water. Water rose in fat green columns from the sides of the bow and filled the ship's main deck. One man was knocked from his feet and carried by the rushing water into a bulwark. Another man pulled him to his feet. Smallbridge was pitched up off the foot-rope, and then struck violently in the stomach by the yard as the bow plummeted into the wave's trough. He was held to the yard by the jackstay beckets ordered by the first mate. The wind was pushing wall after wall of foam-crested black water and spindrift before them, in an effort to prevent the ship's forward movement, to trap her in a broach. The sails would shake but remained filled. She had steerage way.

Priest heard Lennon give orders to brace the yards to the wind. He then ordered Duder to bring her up. Carver entered the wheelhouse and shouted, "Christ Almighty, Sam, careful, can't let her broach!" *Providence* now met the head seas obliquely off her port bow. The force of wind and water still caused her bow to pitch upward, clear of the water. Duder told Priest to count the waves; every seventh was the big one. Water rushed past and under the hull, hitting the rudder with force. The wheel went slack, then suddenly started to turn hard to starboard, seemingly of its own volition. A spoke caught Priest's right arm, raising a nasty bruise, but Priest held on and with the strength of both his arms turned the spoke upward. Duder shouted, "Hold fast. More. Hold it there." As the rudder swung amidships, the wheel became taut with a weather helm and the ship was under control again close-hauled. Lennon, at Carver's direction, trimmed sail for balance and to reduce the pitching.

For two hours, Duder and Priest battled to keep management of the helm. After Lennon braced to the wind, the work eased but never ceased being demanding. An exhausted Nicholas Priest was euphoric to hear Duder's relief repeat steering south-southwest by one-quarter west and assume the helm. He was ecstatic to see another pair of hands replace his own on the spokes. He had learned another lesson; you must watch the bow to see how the compass will move. Anticipate the wave's effect and have the rudder in place before the wave hits; the faster the water, the more sensitive the rudder. All of this seemed so natural to Duder.

As Priest left the wheelhouse, both Mr. Carver and Mr. Lennon were waiting for him. As Duder was behind him, he did not see Sam look in his direction, smile, and then nod to the mates. He did hear Mr. Lennon say, "Good lad. Yews understand da lesson?" He felt Mr. Carver's massive hand fold over his right shoulder, then pat his back once. Nothing more was said, and Priest assumed his duty station aloft in the foremast. Both watches were still on deck. Mr. Carver still had the deck. The wind headed up to the southeast, still blowing fierce gales and snow squalls. It was time to relieve the watch, but both remained on deck.

Eight Bells, Middle Watch (4 a.m.)

Griffin was intensely involved but silent. His mind must be aware of everything happening to the ship.

Fresh gale wind pushing water against an ebbing tide. South-southwest by one-quarter west. Seventy fathoms beneath us. Near out of the strait; the head seas are slacking.

"This is nothing, boys. See, I ain't worried. Tell 'em you heard the old man say it."

Should we have waited? No. How far can I sail to the west in Drake's Passage? Look at the barometer. Holding, bad weather. I'll warm my hand near the binnacle lamp.

***

Priest was back aloft, on the twisting foremast, holding fast to the jackstay with bleeding hands. He could see nothing in the snow beyond the bowsprit. The running lights colored the airborne snow in arcs of gentle red and green.

Priest felt a difference in the sea; they had to be through the strait. The head seas gave way to a gale, and it did not beat them so badly. He had changed into oilskins and secured them around his waist with a rope. He was wet around his collar and the cold wind robbed him of his breath, his boils had broken, and there were cracks beneath his knuckles. He bled, but this did not concern him. Only staying out on the foot-ropes, aloft and not plummeting to his death, occupied his mind.

Two Bells, Forenoon Watch (9 a.m.)

Griffin ordered, "Mr. Carver, wear ship, bring her west. Set the courses, single-reef the topsail, set the jib and spanker."

At noon of the next day, Cape Horn bore true north and astern of the ship. She was forty-seven days, sixteen hours from New York. But she had still not completed her windward passage around Cape Horn.

Griffin remarked to Carver, "The strait, the Horn, ain't for the timid. They'll push them back, even a man like Bligh."

Providence continued southing by inches and, when possible, sailing to westward. When her captain was alone in his cabin, the ship's medicine chest was sitting on his desk and open. He held a bottle of laudanum in his left hand, moved it to his lips to remove the cork with his teeth. As he felt the cork in his teeth, he stopped, replaced the bottle in its slot, and then closed the chest's lid. He spoke aloud, "No, Kayleigh, I won't."

Thirty-Seven

The Drake Passage Southing

*I would hasten my escape from the windy storm
and tempest.*

—Psalm 55:8

Thursday, July 25, 1872
Lat 56°40′00″S, Long 67°25′00″W

July 25, 1872

Dear Mother,

*I am so sorry there have been so few letters. I am
writing this letter now when I should be sleeping.
I wish I could talk to you and father. The work on
this ship continues day and night and I often think
of doing only one thing and that is to sleep. Also, I
do not know when this letter will reach you. Hearing
you and Father argue about me was the most painful
experience I've ever had. I was the cause. By now, I
know pain, cold, hunger, and have an almost insane
desire to be warm and to sleep. I feel so guilty.*

*We are at the bottom of the world, the Southern
Ocean sailing south by southwest. We want to sail
west but that is where the winds blow from and a
sailing ship cannot sail directly into the wind. So we
find ourselves sailing toward Antarctica and inching*

ever westward against the wind to round Cape Horn and to finally turn north to complete our voyage to San Francisco.

My ribs ache from being seasick. My hands have salt sores and I've grown something of a beard. Smallbridge, my best friend, says it looks like a small rat's nest. Sometimes the beard is caked with ice as are my eyebrows. That is not at all uncommon among my fellow sailors, my brothers.

Today at 4 P M we reefed the courses and the lower topsails to protect them from ripping apart. I will try to explain. To reef a sail is pulling it up from its bottom, folding the part that will not be used, and lashing the shortened sail to its yard. Imagine pulling up your skirt to show the tops of your shoes to another lady.

Peleg Carver, the first mate, taught me to estimate wind by observing the sea. The waves are over 20 feet high and the wind has to be 40 knots or more. The sea might have been beautiful had I not been suffering from its fury. The tops of the waves spill over and cover the waves in white foam. The wind picks up the foam and fills the air with spindrift making it difficult to see. The ship takes white and green water over its side, the starboard side. Anything not lashed down or secured would be carried over the side. The sea crashes, the wind howls, and the ship moans.

We also would be in danger of being swept overboard were it not for the lifelines that are rigged so we can hold on to them. This morning I had to check the lashings we use to hold down our longboat and our whaleboat on their cradles. I walked the deck clutching the lifeline and moved in water up to my waist. The water was so cold it hurt like being stabbed with a knife.

There are only 24 of us to work the ship. When the order was given to reef the lower topsails, the captain turned the ship away from the wind to keep her steady in the water so we could safely go aloft. The first sail we reefed was the fore lower topsail. Some work such as spilling the wind from the sail and raising it to the reefing points is done on deck using the running rigging.

When all the work that can be done on deck is finished, men have to climb aloft and lay out on the yard to stretch the sail and lash it to the yardarms. We were forty feet above the deck and out over the sea. When the ends of the sails are lashed to the yardarms, we let loose of the jackstay, crouch below the yard, and balance ourselves on the footropes, and wrap our arms around the sail to tie the excess sail to the yard with the reefing points.

All the time my hands were very stiff and it hurt to close them. Since my boots were wet inside, my feet were cold and almost numb. I climbed though. When we let go of the jackstays, Jeremy Ernst, another apprentice, froze from fear and started to fall. I grabbed his right arm with my left and held on to the reefing point with my right hand. I do not know where the strength or the quickness to do this came from? I guess I saved a man's life, mother. That is who your son has become.

The work aloft is very hard to do. The topsails and courses are the largest sails on the ship and made of thick, heavy canvas. These sails weigh hundreds and hundreds of pounds dry. Our sails are soaked from rain, snow, and ice. They are also very stiff. That's why 12 of us had to go aloft. My hands are now calloused and no longer look like a Boston gentleman's hands. There's dirt under my fingernails.

I've not washed for days now. No one has.

It took more than a half hour to reef the lower fore topsail. We were exhausted; we could not have our supper on time. We are the only men there are to do the reefing work. There's no one else. We had two more topsails to reef, and the fore and main courses, nearly three hours more work. Where does our strength and endurance come from?

When finished, we had more work to do on deck. We braced the sails and the ship resumed sailing south by southwest. I heard Mr. Carver bellow out my name above the roar of the wind and sea. I reported to him on the quarterdeck. He said, "Say nothing to Elder about freezing up. Let him keep his pride. Do you understand me?" Mr. Carver's face was fearsome. Then, suddenly, a smile broke out on his face and he punched my shoulder briskly. "Well done, son. Well done, indeed."

My body feels leaden. My joints and back ache without relief. The veins on my arms now rise clearly above skin. For the first time in my life I like the person I've become. I'm happy. I hope you and father are happy now that I am away.

I am now and always will be your loving son.

Nicholas Priest

Thirty-Eight

Around Cape Horn

"Wear ship!"

—Joseph Conrad

Saturday, July 27, 1872
Lat 57°00′00″S, Long 73°35′00″W

At two p.m. Friday, *Providence* found herself in an angry gale, forcing her weary crew aloft to reef the topsails. Both watches remained on deck until eight p.m., when the gale and wind moderated and the ship was once again in a cold calm with fifteen-foot seas running. By midnight the sails hung lifeless from their yards and the ship was filled with the sterile groans and cracks of her yards and rigging working under the strain of nothing but their own weight. The downeaster moved only where the Cape Horn current and seas pushed her. Griffin used every wisp, every breath to keep her southing, piling on sail, furling sail, reefing, and then taking the reefs out, bracing to the wind, and flattening the weather bowlines.

The men below lay on their straw mattresses in damp blankets and wet wool work clothes, nursing the salt sores on their hands. These sores had opened up wounds on the palms of their hands and in the cracks below the joints of their fingers. The men's fingers bled when worked and, at their worst, showed bone beneath their knuckles. They slept fully clothed, knowing they could be called upon at a moment's notice to work, breaking into their allotted four hours of rest. Most were too exhausted to remove their clothing. The stench of sweat, wet oilcloth, wet wool, and wet men was as bad as that of cattle shut up for long periods in a closed barn.

The men were given little relief from their pain by sleep, as a ship becalmed moves uneasily to every whim of the waves striking its hull, a movement opposite to the rhythm of having way on; and besides, the seas were high and long. All knew they were not making any further distance westward, the calm once again delaying progress and holding the ship in the Drake Passage. All who had rounded Cape Horn from east to west knew that the delay, the struggle to move westward, could take days more, weeks more, or even months more, and still end in failure.

It was six a.m. now, and it was breath-sucking cold; the calm had ended and the wind came on mild from the south, clearing the overcast from the morning sky. Henry Lennon sent for his captain and the first mate. The moon was crisply visible in the sky, and so was the horizon.

Isaac Griffin was delighted. He obtained good sextant observations of the moon at last. From these sights, he calculated his position, calculated lunars to check his trusted Negus chronometers, and concluded that he was not only west of Cape Horn, but into the Pacific. Cape Horn had been rounded! He showed his calculations to Peleg Carver, who compared them to his own. Both men smiled at the realization they were in agreement—no further southing was needed! Both men in turn showed their calculations to the second mate, barely containing their joy. They had found the right conditions to move them away from the Antarctic ice northward, up the west coast of South America.

Griffin spoke to his officers: "We've had five to fifteen hours of calm every day since we reached the Falkland Islands. We lived in darkness without sun or moon. But all we needed was a fair wind and we could steer north, and we have that wind now. Mr. Lennon, wear ship."

It was forty-three minutes past six in the morning when the command to wear was given.

***

Sam Duder beamed. "Can you feel it, Priest, Smallbridge? Even you ought to be smiling, John Stedwin! He's gonna wear ship! We're going north. You boys have earned your ink. We're round Cape Stiff!"

***

Had Griffin just given Henry Lennon one hundred dollars, more than twice a month's pay, the money could not have brought the joy of knowing his captain trusted him to execute a wear. It meant his captain had confidence in his ability to be a first mate and his promotion would be forthcoming when the ship finally reached Boston. Lennon, an experienced second mate, knew the captain took her out and the first mate brought her in, knew that captains almost always directed course changes requiring tacks and wears. Lennon gave the order to wear ship and to bring the ship to NNW, to steer up the West Coast of South America and toward *Providence*'s destination, San Francisco.

***

The boatswain, Eoghan Gabriel, knew what he was doing. Duder and Stedwin, the two senior seamen of the starboard watch, also knew their trade and immediately set themselves and the other hands to taking the lee braces off their pins, flaking them out on the deck in preparation for hauling. The other watch began dousing the spanker and preparing a preventer for the new tack. The apprentices were sent aloft with the staysails, shifting their sheets and preparing the sails for setting. This was no man-o'-war; there were no shrill boatswain calls, no repeated orders, no crowds of men scurrying to their stations, because this ship was a downeaster manned by twenty-eight now deep water sailors and three seasoned officers.

Despite their pain, the men before the mast moved quickly in the bitter cold and with the efficiency of determined men.

"Smartly, boys, smartly. Step lively, now, before we lose our wind! This is what we've waited for," Eoghan Gabriel encouraged them on because he too was happy, and the men gained excitement from his exhortations and the grin on his face.

The boatswain moved from mast to mast, progressing from aft to forward, checking each mast and seeing that the men and gear were prepared to respond to the next command. When satisfied with the readiness of each line to be used, and seeing the men properly stationed, he turned and shouted, "Ready to wear, Mr. Lennon." All the men turned to Lennon and watched and waited to hear his command. Lennon bellowed, "Stand by to wear ship. Hard a starboard! Brace main and mizzen yards to the wind!"

Duder bellowed out the shantey "Eliza Lee" as the men hauled sail, *"and the bulgine ran free."*

By bracing the main and mizzen yards parallel to the wind, the men emptied the sails on those masts of their wind, leaving the wind to fill only on the foremast's sails and jibs. The foremast sails and jibs now pushed the bow as it fell off the wind and started the wear. As the wear continued, each mast was progressively braced to the wind in order to let its sails fill and continue the wear. As the wear neared completion, the jibs were progressively shifted to the opposite tack. At the completion of the wear, all yards were braced sharp to the wind, the spanker shifted and raised, while the ship proceeded to the northwest.

Wearing ship required a high degree of seamanship on the part of the watch officer who had the deck, and the boatswain to prevent the sails from backing, and to ease the burden of the men as they hauled against the force of the wind. If the wear was not executed with great skill by the conning officer, the boatswain, and the helmsman, the wear could take hours to complete and occupy a great amount of sea space. This was sure to displease the ship's captain—indeed, any ship's captain.

Isaac Griffin had watched the full hour involved in wearing ship without speaking a single word or so much as furrowing his brow, choking off all display of emotion, fully realizing the pressure his presence placed on the second mate. Lennon performed as well as anyone could expect of a ship's master, let alone a second mate. Lennon had been careful to use the helm to ease the men's work, and his timing with the wind bordered on perfection. Eoghan Gabriel was exceptional also.

When yards are braced, the higher, lighter yards such as the topgallant tend to get ahead of the lower yards, and he was alert to avoiding this, thus saving the men the additional work of pulling against the wind to correct them. Griffin also saw that his men performed with a heart and with minimal direction from the second mate and boatswain. He also saw occasional traces of blood on the braces from the men's salt-sore hands. They had given him and their ship everything expected of square-rigged seamen. Neither the men nor their officers expected anything less or—if need be—would accept anything less.

Nineteen crewmen, four day-men, four apprentices, and the second mate, all exhausted, now sitting huddled against the protection of the weather bulwark, had brought the stern of *Providence* through the eye of the wind. The crew forced leaden arms and legs to set courses and topsails, topgallants, and royals. *Providence* was now sailing NNW in fourteen knots of wind under all common sail. The starboard watch was relieved, and both watches turned to with routine ship's work and approached the day as bloodied, but unbroken and unconquered men. They ignored their hands, the salt-sores, and their bodies, the boils, and their staggering lack of sleep, and fueled an appetite for their daily rations. Snow and ice were removed, the running rigging checked and overhauled where needed, and chafing gear put in place or moved as required. Hot coffee and a cold hardtack breakfast had been served late because of the wear.

Isaac Griffin once again looked forward to writing to Kayleigh, telling her that they were sailing north, away from the bottom of the world and toward San Francisco. There was joy to share. He actually could tell her that a bonus from the Central Pacific was still possible. He could tell her that he, his officers, his crew, and his ship were soon to be safe from the terrible Southern Ocean. He was in such a good mood, he gave the order—yes, that order seldom heard aboard a Yankee sailing ship—"Mr. Lennon, tell the hands we'll splice the main brace at noon."

266

The Downeaster

***

O, whiskey is the life of man,
Whiskey, Johnny!
I drink whiskey when I can
Whiskey for my Johnny!

Whiskey from an old tin can,
Whiskey, Johnny!
I'll drink whiskey when I can.
Whiskey for my Johnny!

I drink it hot, I drink it cold,
Whiskey, Johnny!
I drink it new, I drink it old.
Whiskey for my Johnny!

Whiskey makes me feel so sad,
Whiskey, Johnny!
Whiskey killed my poor old dad.
Whiskey for my Johnny!

I thought I heard the old man say,
Whiskey, Johnny!
I'll treat my crew in a decent way.
Whiskey for my Johnny!

Whiskey made the skipper say,
Whiskey, Johnny!
"Another pull and then belay."
Whiskey for my Johnny!

Oh whiskey here and whiskey there
Whiskey, Johnny!
Oh I'd have whiskey everywhere
Whiskey for my Johnny!

Paul Thomas Fuhrman

Now if ye ever go to Frisco town,
Whiskey, Johnny!
Mind ye steer clear of Shanghai Brown.
Whiskey for my Johnny!

A tot of grog for each man,
Whiskey, Johnny!
An' a bloody big bottle for the shanteyman.
Whiskey for my Johnny!

PART THREE

Paul Thomas Fuhrman

Thirty-Nine

Let Us Unite

Then let us pray that come it may, (As come it will for a' that,) That Sense and Worth, o'er a' the earth, Shall bear the gree, an' a' that. For a' that, an' a' that, It's coming yet for a' that, That Man to Man, the world o'er, Shall brothers be for a' that.

—Robert Burns

Monday, July 29, 1872
Boston

Jimmy Meehan had gathered his newly formed Brotherhood of New England Merchant Seamen and Steamship Clerks into the chapel of the Seamen's Bethel. Twenty-three men were there, of whom seventeen spoke English to one degree or another.

"I tell you johnnies it's nathin' to demand the New York wage if yer can't keep it in yer pockets. How many of you have been fleeced clean by some crimp? How many have yer been shipped aboard some hell ship naked and drunk because she could not ship good men?"

"We've got to put the fear of Jaysus into these boarding masters. They've got to learn to trate a sailor fair. I ain't saying yer should have no fun ashore. I'm saying it's wrong to rob a johnny of his wages and his freedom."

Father Joe, the Methodist minister at the chapel, next spoke. "You can't mean violence, Jimmy!"

271

"And wasn't it Jaysus himself who drove de nicker changers from the steps of the temple, Father Joe? Isn't it true these merchants, politicians, and judges all let the crimps shanghai good men because it's grand for their business? How many of yer know of a johnny, a grand shipmate, to a come up a floater or just drop off the face o' the earth?"

Jimmy saw many heads shake and heard mutterings of anger.

"I can't let you kill men, Jimmy. I can't have this bethel support savagery as bad as those the crimps practice!"

Jimmy was disappointed in the minister's lack of confidence in him. "And who is blathering about killing? I'm talking about keeping good men from being shipped out against their will. All I'm saying is to rescue our lads, our brothers, and have a little fun. Father Joe, yer can stay and that would please us, or yer can go if yer wish to; these men want to do something about it, and if they don't, nigh, who will? You can open your Bible to Good Friday and I'll swear on the chapter and verse that I intend no lasting harm to no man!"

Father Joe placed a hand on Jimmy's shoulder. "You're going to plan something I think I would be better off not knowing about. I'm going to forget I ever saw you all gathered in this chapel for anything other than to say 'praise Jesus.' I'm going to pray that men are rescued too and that I see all of you here again on your knees and asking for God's forgiveness. In the meantime—should you need me—I'll be in my room on my knees praying for your salvation by faith, as deeds are doubtful for the likes of you." Father Joe laughed at his own joke.

"I call that yer blessing."

"You can call it what you want to, Jimmy. Just remember the Lord loves all of you and so do I." Father Joe removed his right hand from Jimmy's shoulder and looked him square in the eye. "Never forget His loving Son. May He keep all of you in his grace." He turned and left.

Seeing that he was gone, Jimmy laid out his plan.

"That crimp Lard Ass Jesse's taking some men to the *Natick* ternight. The ship's old man, Nate Smallbridge, was forced into it by that young whelp William Jr. She's gonna put them aboard her express wagon and have her runners cart them to the ship at midnight. Now, those thugs and gurriers will have knives, slung shots, knuckle-dusters, and pistols as sure as all of us are standing here. Can't count on the men in the wagon to help neither. If we stop that wagon and stand tall and call out, 'Stand and deliver!' some of us ain't coming back to a snug berth here. Some of you won't be breathing. So here's how we'll chucker the deed."

***

Blue-Eyed Tommy Nangle was sitting atop Lard Ass Jesse's express wagon with his assistant, Fred, and a dozen helpless men. Tommy was touched by a sharp pang of desire to be doing something else. Something he thought of as the fun of his ignoble calling. He knew delivery of drugged and intoxicated sailors to ships was the only way the blood money could change hands, but there was another challenge he enjoyed, something involving guile, trickery, and the occasional use of leather-wrapped lead. And here the challenge was before him. Stumbling down the street were three drunken sailors and a shapely young adventuress with her ample breasts nearly out of her bodice. Oh, and they were singing too, "The Parting Glass," which meant they were really drunk. They were easy pickings, but tonight, the wagon and its cargo of drugged men were on their way to the *Natick*. Tommy fidgeted in his seat like a cat ready to pounce while his mind raced and delighted with the temptation.

As the drunks approached near enough to the wagon for Tommy to stare into the strumpet's cleavage and smell the stale whiskey, the runner instinctively reached for the bottle of opium- laced rum he regularly carried. "You johnnies care for a drink? It's good to see men having a little fun." *There's ninety dollars for me pocket and Lard Butt will never know. His helper would keep his mouth shut for a cut, no more than ten bucks. Hell, if I wrap the whore in a blanket, I can ship her too!*

"Shhh...keep them men down under the sides, Fred, and keep them still. That's a lad. There's room for one or two more. You, girl,

273

off with you now. I'll show these lads someone with bigger paps than yours and legs spread wide open!"

Tommy could almost imagine them taking his drink and passing out on the spot. Even from where he sat high in the wagon he could smell their evening on their breath and clothing. "Come here, fellows, and I'll have one with you."

When the sailors were close to the wagon, Tommy offered his bottle to the first man who stepped up. The man took the bottle, only to have it snatched from his unsteady hand by the strumpet, who giggled and shrieked with laughter while she hid the bottle between her breasts. "Who'll take the bottle now?" she called out, while lowering the top of her bodice to tempt her companions.

Tommy's eyes were instantly drawn to the girl in the hope of seeing her nipples, when an iron belaying pin struck him and his helper across the back of their skulls, sending them into an unconscious blackness.

As if by miracle, the three sailors in the street regained sobriety and Jimmy Meehan appeared from a side street with six more men bearing axe handles. Jimmy climbed into the wagon and poured the runner and his helper onto the cobblestones of the street.

"Strip the sons of bitches naked, boys. Gag their mouths. Tie them up and throw them into the wagon's bed. We'll take them back to Jesse's boarding house after we get these poor lads to the bethel.

"Bathsheba, me grand doll, Delilah, me lassie, put those pistols and knives in yer husband's satchel and hand it here. I'll keep the slung shot and blackjack in me pocket. Nigh, don't yer be looking at their private parts, me good flower. Yer someone's wife now."

When the wagon and its victims arrived at the Seamen's Bethel, Jimmy knocked on the door of Father Joe's bedroom. "Get up, Father Joe. Here's a wagon full of heathen sailors for you to convert if you can get them out of their stupor."

The next event in Jimmy's evening was to deliver the naked runner and helper to the porch of the boarding house and stretch out their still-unconscious bodies lengthwise before the door like a proud cat displaying its night's catch of mice. Jimmy hung a sign around Tommy's neck. The sign was crudely lettered, but Jimmy was sure Lard Ass Jesse would understand the meaning. It read, "Stop fucking over sailors. Someone's watching you."

And thus, The Brotherhood of New England Merchant Seamen and Steamship Clerks made a name for itself on the Boston waterfront. No one was killed, which pleased Father Joe, although the two runners would have a severe headache for a day or so, and every sailor at every tavern and boarding house in Boston looked to his fellow sailors and said, "Did you hear what happened to Blue-Eyed Tommy Nangle?"

Forty

The South Pacific

I, the albatross that awaits for you at the end of the world.

I, the forgotten soul of the sailors lost that crossed Cape Horn from all the seas of the world.

But die they did not in the fierce waves, for today towards eternity in my wings they soar in the last crevice of the Antarctic winds

—Sara Vial
Poem from the Cape Horn Memorial

Thursday, August 1, 1872
Lat 33°06′15″S, Long 94°12′45″W

It was four bells into the morning watch of August second. The sun broke clear of the red clouds.

By now holystoning a deck was so natural to Priest, he found it almost relaxing. Just push the stone forward, move it back, push, pull, bear down for a stubborn stain, push, pull, and soon you were finished and would go to other work, sailorizing. It was by far preferable to cleaning paint or polishing brass. You could talk without drawing a rebuke from a mate as long as the stone kept moving. The mates understood. They came from before the mast.

"Duder, why do those big birds follow us? They've been there since we rounded the Horn. I've seen them every day. It's almost like they want coffee with us."

276

"Priest, they do. They long for coffee and tobacco, but they want something else."

Lennon overheard them. It was a conversation he'd hoped would not occur. He knew the legend. "It's just an old sailor's tale. Priest, they're birds—albatross. Big birds, for sure, but just birds."

"Mr. Lennon, the boy needs to know."

"Do yews believe everything yews hear, Priest? God gave you something between yer ears besides a nose. It's all superstition, just a good sea story some people believe because they've told it so often. Just believin' their own bloody lies, they do."

"All due respect, Mr. Lennon, that just ain't so. Some things you need to believe in. Some things you need to fear. The birds are here for souls. There'll be two deaths aboard this barky, yes, sir."

Priest was amazed. "That's pretty fantastic, Duder. How do you know Mr. Lennon's wrong?"

"It ain't 'cause I say so. I've seen it before; so's Stedwin; so's Mr. Carver."

Lennon scoffed, "Go ahead, Duder, tell da boy. Now when yews hear it, Sweets, you'll know it's far-fetched, just nonsense, old sailors' tales, and a good ghost story."

Duder shook his head to contradict the mate. "Those big albatrosses spend their lives flying. They're the souls of men who've perished at the Horn. Mostly, you'll see a big flock of them sail down a mountain wind to look at a ship. See how they glide. They're hoping, just hoping, another man dies and takes their place. Once a soul is released, it could go to heaven or hell—I can't say. But those two are special. They ain't hoping; they know. They're just waiting 'cause they know two deaths will happen."

"They got bird brains, Priest, pea-sized bird brains."

"No, Mr. Lennon, they are souls, souls crying out to be set free. Bird brains, shit!"

Lennon stiffened. "Careful there, Sam."

"So they are following us, waiting for two of us to die?"

"Bloody dewlolly!"

Duder spoke. "Only those birds are special. They want atonement

277

for sin. There's a Jonah aboard. He'll pay for his sins, he'll draw his penance, and two men will die. If not, the sea'll take us." Sam Duder shuddered.

Priest saw fear on Duder's face. "You believe that, don't you, Sam? You're shaking. You believe it."

Lennon's face showed disgust. "He does, Sweets, but that don't make it so."

Harvard Law School, Boston

The female detective sat in front of George Priest's desk and began her report. "He hired me because I work cheap. But I do see the books. It's all there, where the money went."

George nodded. "Are you sure?"

"Oh, yes, sir. He's not trying to steal, but he's just not been very forthcoming to his father. It's an abuse of trust, not larceny."

"I understand. What happened to the money?"

"He lost it at the Mercantile Exchange. That's not to say he's made no money; he has. He seems desperate to make a killing and invests in high-risk ventures. That's where Griffin's bottomry money went."

"Are any of these investments liquid?"

"Some. I'd say at least half from the sale of the two ships is still there in bonds that are drawing interest."

"How much is that?"

"Nearly fifty thousand. Am I through there? Do you want me to keep working for him?"

"You said he's not trying to take advantage of you?"

"Oh, God, no. He's the coldest man I've ever known. He thinks he's the pinnacle of evolution, the modern man. I've never heard him even speak of his wife. It's either all money or some new illness that comes from his high position in society, the anxiety of evolution's noblest product. He brags about what he spends on doctors, on electrical treatments."

George Priest scratched his head and nodded. "It's going to be some time before I can even get a telegraph to Griffin. Stay there.

Keep working. We need to know where the money is at all times."

"Oh, Mr. Priest, he's been seeing this Irishman, a Mr. O'Corkerane. There's money involved that's not on the books. O'Corkerane is Clan na Gael."

"Will you be safe, Brannagh?"

"Oh, yes. I'm a woman. William Jr. doesn't think I've enough sense to sneeze when I've got a cold."

The New England Hospital for Women and Children

It was late in Kayleigh's first trimester. Her menses had stopped ten weeks before. Her mother laughed gently at the size her breasts had grown to and told her to expect a big baby. She was once again in Dr. Marie Zakrzewska's office. She had been spread open, poked, measured, and asked a hundred questions, and now was being scolded.

"Why do you continue with this nursing? I've done everything I can to convince you that your talent for raising money, your talent for persuading important people, is far more important than washing soiled dressings. And those women, those nurses—your example is tossing pearls before swine."

Kayleigh angrily shoved her chair back from the doctor's desk, stood, and walked to the window to stare at the dome of the Bullfinch Building. When she brought her arms straight down by her sides and clenched her fists, Dr. Zakrzewska spoke with anxiety in her voice. "Kayleigh, there's no need. Why are you so upset with me? What I say is true."

Kayleigh's head dropped down to her chest, her fists became unclenched, but she still stared at the Bullfinch Building and fought back tears. Each day of her pregnancy seemed to bring her emotions closer and closer to the surface. She knew that if Dr. Zakrzewska saw her tears, she would discount anything she had to say and attribute it to the mind of a distraught pregnant woman.

"You're wrong, Doctor. I don't think you understand. In Berlin, you had a path to take, a mentor to guide you and promote your welfare. These women, particularly Rachael, have none of that. They all believe that marriage to an income will be their only salvation. They see themselves as society paints them, common, fit only for nurture and common drudgery. The fact that I work with them, share stories, laugh and cry with them, helps show them I see their worth. You are right; nursing must be a profession. But you don't realize that these women do not believe in themselves or realize their own potential."

Kayleigh turned and faced Dr. Zakrzewska. "You'd find Kazia repulsive. She's huge, strong, and a bully. I had enough of her one day and stood up to her. I got in her face. She started to cry because I punctured the wall she used to protect herself, the bullying. She could barely read English and was afraid if the matron knew, the hospital would fire her. Her husband died; she has no one to care for her except herself."

Dr. Zakrzewska seemed surprised as Kayleigh sat down across from her. "I held her, Doctor. I held her in my arms, a woman at least fifteen years older than I am. I talked to Jennie and sent Kazia to Boffin's Bower. Jennie will help her read and write better. But Kazia makes my point. Who tells women like Kazia that they are worthwhile? Who sees the potential they have but never see in themselves?"

"I never considered this, Kayleigh."

"You, all of us, are held captive by the prejudices we hold. I'm not promoting nursing or the school to these women; I'm just showing them how wonderful they are if only they could believe in themselves."

"I see."

"Do you, Doctor? The story you told me, about the apprenticeships you arranged for women. You said none would take them because they took six years to complete. Those women may have told you that six years was too long, and I know you believed them. But did you ask if they could afford to support themselves for six years? Were they convinced they would fail, as everyone they knew said they would?"

Forty-One

Beating North

*'Twas cold and dark when I fetched the deck, dirty
'n' cold 'n' thick, 'n' there was a feel in the way she
rode as fairly turned me sick...*

—John Masefield

Tuesday, August 6, 1872
Lat 44°40′03″S, Long 86°55′49″W

Providence fought the heavy head seas as best she could. The wind had been fierce and blowing steadily from the northwest, imposing a wall of head seas and wind coming from exactly the direction the ship needed to go. The *Providence* was a good ship— she rewarded fine seamanship—but in this weather she could not give her master what he wanted; no sailing vessel could. To sail the path laid out in Maury, on Griffin's charts, and in his mind, he must sail to the left and to the right of northwest. He must sail in a series of zigzags, beating close-hauled.

Griffin's goal was ever present in his mind: one hundred days. His strategy was always to make the best he could of what nature gave him. He beat in long boards and sailed close-hauled to the wind, pinching the wind as much as fine helming could hold. This minimized time lost in wearing; it also minimized the work of the crew, who, like Griffin and his mates, must live and sail in the near hurricane weather.

Each day, each hour, the waves grew in height. The waves' fetch extended for more than a hundred miles, and the waves themselves were a mile or more in length, with great hollows separating them. At first foam was blown in dense streaks; gradually the waves became high and had overhanging crests and large patches of foam. Strong gale became whole gale; then, when only topsails and higher could be seen because of the troughs, they were in a storm with winds of sixty knots or more.

No one slept. No one was dry. The meals were cold. The decks were swept with running white and green water. She was heavy laden, her hull low in the water. Her bow was held high by her fore and main topsails and a storm jib. A more timid master might have heaved-to and rested on the tops of the waves in the comparative calm of the ship's lee. *Providence* did not have a timid master.

Griffin and Carver were in the main saloon; Lennon had the deck as Griffin handed Carver a dry lucifer to relight his pipe. Griffin was upset; the weather again held him back, jeopardizing his goal.

"Captain, this weather will break; six more degrees latitude and we're in the trades."

"That's not the issue. The issue's when. When will it break? How much time do we lose?" Griffin then indicated to Ezra to refill his and Carver's coffee cups. They were not using the ship's good china in weather like this, but then neither Griffin nor Carver would have even noticed.

Carver replied, "The barometer started to fall yesterday at ten in the morning and is still falling, everything is furled from the topgallants upward, and she's still pitching. The wind's been coming in half-hour intervals, hard then light. At least she's going quickly to west; we're not standing still, ayuh?"

"Henry's rotating Duder and Priest, then Stedwin and Smallbridge at the helm, one-hour tricks. You should put an apprentice on the weather helm every other trick and keep the regular helmsmen halfway rested. Are the Ernst boys up to it?"

As the word "rested" left Carver's mouth, the ship pitched its bow upward, then slammed it down nearly twenty feet in the trough of a thirty-six foot wave, the child of this precipitous sea. The mates and master heard the crash of tons of water hitting the bow, pouring straight down on the decks, and rushing aft in fast-moving streams of a foot or more depth. Glass shattered in the butterfly hatches, letting water pour into the saloon. Had something been stove in? Griffin waited for a report, anticipated Ezra letting a wet seaman in oilskins inside his reception area to stand before them and tell them the damage. No one came. *Providence* was a downeaster, a New Englander as much as the men who built and sailed her; she endured hard weather as a mere fact of life. The carpenter and sailmaker nailed canvas over the broken skylight and Ezra mopped up the water. Carver and the carpenter surveyed the ship for damages.

In this weather, Griffin could not sleep because he needed to be seen on deck by each successive watch, once or twice every four hours.

I must stand here and let them see me. They want to see me. They only follow because they want to, for whatever reason. They must see I'm not afraid, although fear grips my stomach as well as theirs. Fold your arms, man; there, look down the side, smile a bit, look that johnny in the eyes. He returns your smile, happy to be noticed.

Griffin stood on the weather side with his arms folded over each other while beaming confidence in plain sight of his crew.

They want me. They'll not ask, but their eyes tell me they need me. Go, man! Go down to the lee of the forward deckhouse, where you can seek shelter from wind and spray. They need me to joke, to feel my confidence and joke. I need them.

"Enjoying this weather, boys? Well, johnnies, you're earning your pay now, ain't ya?"

They still could laugh. And going aft, I heard the helmsman say, "Add one now, pull down, lad. Hold her tight, the old man's looking."

"Helmsmen, have you got her? How's she steer? Any stretch in the cables? How many spokes to take her off the wind?"

***

Carver could not sleep either. When he was not on watch, he or the carpenter checked the hull every hour. He worried; the pounding had started movement in one of the upper planks forward on the weather side. It moved in slight flexes, letting in a little water now, but Carver and Chips both knew each flex was weakening the plank. One bell, two bells, and three bells, until eight bells, watch by watch, they alternated checking the plank. Lennon relieved Carver when not on watch. The pumps were manned as a precaution.

If that was not enough, Carver and Eoghan Gabriel were constantly checking the rigging for strain, to see if the standing rigging stretched, to place pudding where the running rigging chafed on the yards or sails. A block failed and men went aloft to replace it; Priest and Smallbridge did the high work.

Each boy, tired but still working, knew the ship and its crew depended on them to go aloft and balance on the yards attached to the corkscrewing masts. They would lay forward over the yards, pushing their feet and the foot-ropes out for balance. Both hands were needed for the ship. Sometimes it was the quickness of youth that kept them alive.

Eight bells rang; the port watch relieved the starboard. The noon meal was served, hardtack, coffee, raw salt meat, and peaches—canned peaches from the hold.

The afternoon watch continued. The ship's bell reported the passage of each half hour. The sun, what they could see of it, dipped below the horizon.

Providence and her crew labored on. Craig complained of his ribs and did not go aloft. Jeremy and Richard Ernst took up the slack. Craig argued that the captain was mad. "That idiot ought to heave-to and ride it out. He's risking our damned lives."

The ship lent her voice to the matter. She groaned, creaked, and popped, and her rigging moaned, yet she kept on going and providing what shelter she could to the men who worked her. If she could have spoken, her voice would have said, "They are my sons and I will see them ashore."

The Pacific Ocean roared, spewed foam, and formed long ridges of curling white water at the crests of the towering waves. The tops curled and broke forward, sending foam downward on the flanks of the waves. Spindrift filled the air. The ocean did not know or care. Caress or kill, there was no difference. It roared but did not speak. The men at the pumps sang:

> *We was made to pump all night an' day,*
> *Leave her, Johnny, leave her!*
> *An' we half-dead had beggar-all to say,*
> *An' it's time for us to leave her!*
>
> *Oh, leave her, Johnny, and we'll work no more,*
> *Leave her, Johnny, leave her!*
> *Of pump or drown we've had full store.*
> *An' it's time for us to leave her!*

***

Sam Duder was not known for silent brooding, "Drink your coffee, Sweets. Try dunking your biscuit in it, softens it up and warms it too." Priest smiled. He would never dunk the corner of his toast or a roll in his teacup in front of his parents. It did warm and soften the hard ship's biscuit, though.

Nicholas Priest was drenched in his own sweat beneath his oilskins and southwester. His body still burned from exertion from having the weather helm for an hour. "Old Bishop snuck me some dried apple slices. Here, Duder."

Priest gave Duder three of the largest pieces of dehydrated apple, saving the smaller pieces for himself.

"Thankee, Sweets. I'll make a regular pie out of it, hardtack 'n' apple, lean back and think I'm at home in the kitchen with my darling Betsy, all snug and warm."

Sam chuckled; it would take more than this weather to test his humor. He bit off a chunk of apple, took a swig of coffee, and chewed. "It's good, Sweets. Keep eating, anything you can get in this weather; you need to keep your strength up. The waves have got to get bigger if this wind holds."

"Are you counting them? They come in sevens; last one's the biggest. Do you see the trough under the front of the big one? It's sucking all that water up and piling it on top of the wave. Can't ever let the ship get sideways. That water dropping from the top of the wave can capsize her, knock her down. Are you anticipating her? Use just enough rudder to keep her straight. Don't have the wheel hard to any side going down; that's inviting a broach. Did you notice how the steering cable stretches? Only one up and two or three to feel her come off?"

"That's the reason she's fast coming off the wind?"

"Yes, you understand it, boy. The mate's got to check the cables. Can't afford to have one part. Spoke to Mr. Carver about the stretch. He'll look. The man's no one's fool and a seaman too. He's a Yankee like you and me. Ease her when she pitches."

***

Peleg Carver was a good listener. Men like Sam Duder didn't tell mates how to do their business unless they were concerned about something out of the ordinary. Anyone who could hand, reef, and steer knew about cable stretch and a weather helm. Duder had to think the stretch was excessive.

"Mr. Gabriel, Chips, come with me. We need to look at the tiller arm and steering gear; grab a lantern." The boatswain examined the steering cables. They had stretched. He then supervised the installation of relieving tackle so the stretched cable could be repaired by splicing in fresh cable.

Gabriel raised his right hand to behind his neck and seemed to coax words from his mouth, "Mr. Carver, it's not a bad idea to leave the relieving tackle in place."

***

Sleep visited no one. Clothes were soaked through and left on when turning in. The straw mattresses were damp. The smell of wet sea salt on wool and cotton mixed with the barnlike smell of men, the smell of sweat and filthy clothing. The work did not stop. The sea provided no respite. This was how the sea baptized and confirmed deep-water square-rig seamen. Their watch was called; they rose

286

from their squalid bunks and risked lives and injury, and worked their ship. If they didn't, she would founder.

Ship's Song

My sons curse me but love me above all other women.
I am only born of the minds of men and gifts of the
forest, fields and Pits of the earth.

They curse me for what I require of them and boast of
me while drinking porter and playing cards.
They forget me for other women.

I must take them to their shore and hear them sing,
"It's time for us to leave her."

Forty-Two

The Roaring Forties

This sea that bares her bosom to the moon;
The winds that will be howling at all hours,
And are up-gathered now like sleeping flowers;
For this, for everything, we are out of tune;
It moves us not.

— William Wordsworth

Thursday, August 8, 1872
Lat 43°00′00″S, Long 87°30′00″W

August 8, 1872

My Dearest Isaac,
    I shall report the news to you. How I wish we could be together to parse some meaning to what I have to say.
    Father has regularly been seeing John J. O'Corkerane of the Clan na Gael. I have no idea why, except I am certain that my mother is somehow involved. Mr. O'Corkerane has twice been to dinner and tells us he and his friends are quickly bringing the Fenian Brotherhood together again in America. The money is flowing in and, he says, it is little problem to smuggle it into Ireland. He is concerned about spies, though, and the efforts of some Irish to

seek relief through the British Parliament. He has no faith in England whatsoever.

Mother seems to have grown cold to Mr. O'Corkerane. They used to sing the old songs in Gaelic together, but she refuses to do so now. I've seen Father hold her hand beneath the tablecloth, and his lips seemed to mouth silent words telling Mother to be polite.

On a happier note, Hanna is going to have a baby! She told me that Kicking Billy and William had a huge argument over Jimmy Meehan and his union. Kicking Billy saw that William appeared unable to control his emotions and that his health was on the verge of failing. He forced William Jr. to stop work and to spend time with Hanna. I now know why you call him Kicking Billy.

Hanna told me that after three solid days of rest, the William Jr. she had come to love started to rise again. It was so wonderful for her. I had lunch with them one day and I can tell you that it is a joy to see him smile and laugh again. Hanna and I left the restaurant singing "Barbara Allen." William seemed beside himself with merriment, I cannot fathom why. The ballad is so sweet. Hanna calls William "Sweet William" from the ballad.

Jimmy seems to have succeeded in forming a sailors' union. They have been fighting the waterfront crimps but the violence appears to be restrained. Instead of intercepting crimps' wagons, they have taken to picketing ships known to use the crimps. This has not been entirely successful, but Jimmy seems content with the practice. The union is growing and the police have no cause to interfere.

Kicking Billy supports Jimmy's efforts. He likes the union hiring hall and the fact that when the union certifies the sailors' skills, that certification is true. He told me this means so much aboard ship, that men are capable of doing what they are paid for. I heard him tell William he doesn't give a damn if the union charges a fee; so do shipping masters, only more.

I am sorry to tell you that the strain of running the shipping line without William's help seems to be aging Billy more quickly than just nature and time. He is using a cane now to climb stairs and complains that his sleep is disturbed and fitful.

Hanna says he is approaching eighty years of age. It is wonderful that he maintains his old attitude despite it all. Has it ever struck you as odd that so many captains and mates seem like terrible tyrants but are really sentimental men? One of Billy's old friends has a small white Maltese dog. It seems to have charmed its owner and Kicking Billy too. He calls the dog his little girlfriend and lets the dog lick his nose.

Father has approached me about taking Mother and me to San Francisco on the railroad. He will use his private car, cook, maid, and butler to take care of our needs. He also intends to hire the Pinkertons to see to our safety.

My life goes on with nursing. The schools are progressing well, and—can you believe this?— Harvard will require medical students to take exams and have practical experience before giving them a medical doctor degree. The medical college and Massachusetts General Hospital are cooperating. I understand the Europeans do this and that Austrian and German medical schools may well be the world's best. I really believe this is a great step forward for American medicine! And it will be medicine based on science and not tradition or someone's notions.

Enough! I prattle on and on. How I wish we were

together again. I doubt we would spend too much time with the news and even gossip. There are so many better things for our lips and hearts to do.

Oh, Hanna has returned the book I found in a used bookstore. The title is "The Ancient Wisdom of Aristotle." She says it really inspired William Jr. to new heights of accomplishment. I love to read certain passages before sleeping. When I read them, I imagine being with you again.

I will love you always.
Kayleigh

***

Dear Kayleigh,
We continue with yet another day of head seas. The longer we have winds from the northwest, the larger the sea becomes. My chief concern for the moment is the heavy pitching of the ship. Our cargo is ponderous and we ride low in the water. This forces me to be concerned about the water we take over our decks and the pounding of our hull. The shear of the ship has kept us reasonably dry, but as the sea continues to build and the ship continues to pitch, the pounding increases. We are close-hauled, beating, and covered a respectable 120 miles noon the sixth to noon the seventh. Yesterday, we had a little excitement as we replaced the plank that started to move. Men were over the side. Since we are caulked on both sides of the ship's ribs, the water that has come into the ship must remain there.

At two in the afternoon of the seventh, the overcast cleared, but it brought on calm. Soon the sun came out and with it another north by northwest wind. We wore ship to the westward but there was not enough wind to stay her against the continuing head sea.

I was called again on deck at midnight. The sky turned hazy and the wind began to blow hard while the barometer began to fall. This is typical of the forties. By noon today, I ordered the topsails double-reefed and furled our courses and spanker. As I sit at my desk I can hear the wind howling and the sea pounding our bow. Reefing the topsails did help reduce the pitching, and the ship is riding much better. Worse weather is coming, the barometer tells us that.

My spirits are high. I had nearly 6 hours sleep and my log shows we made 138 miles between yesterday at noon and today. My spirits are high because I am nearer to San Francisco, a step closer to achieving our goals, and closer to receiving your letters. We've left so much undone, so much to be resolved. I wonder if anyone has ever built a future on such haste as we have?

Your husband and friend,
Isaac

***

"Bring the wind off our port side, abeam, reef topsails, and dowse the spanker, Mr. Lennon."

"Aye, sir."

"Helmsman, take her off the wind and spill the topsails. Mr. Gabriel, reef topsails. Stay alert, there! Keep the yards steady!"

Eoghan Gabriel shouted for the men to reef topsails. The able-bodied seamen quickly organized their men, stationing them at the topsail clewlines, buntlines, and weather braces of the main-mast. Gabriel then shouted out the order to clear away the bowlines and round in the weather braces. This brought the main topsail yard at right angles to the keel, clearing the upper yard for dropping to the mast-cap below it.

"Haul out the reef tackles. Haul up the buntlines." The fore upper topsail now rose upward toward its yard as the men hauled away.

The Downeaster

The ship luffed to spill the wind from the sail. The top-men including the apprentices ascended the rigging and lay out to windward on the yard. Gabriel had the men on deck haul taut the lee braces and halyards to steady the yard so as not to throw men from it. The men then gathered the sail in folds, bringing it up to and forward of the yard. The weather and lee reef cringles were drawn taut to their respective earrings, the reef band now stretched taut in a neat line against its yard, holding the folds of sail up. The top-men then passed the reef lines over the folds, crossing them and bringing them under the jackstays, where they were secured with a reef knot. When finished, they laid in to the cross-tree and returned to the deck.

Gabriel then gave the order to ease the halyards. After that, the rigging was overhauled, and the buntlines, clewlines, and reef tackles were cleared away. The lee brace was let go and the weather braces manned. The order was then given to hoist the upper topsail yard until the leeches were taut. The bowlines were steadied out and the halyards belayed to their pins. This operation was then repeated on the other masts in succession, and the spanker furled. One hour later, at noon, the upper topsails were double-reefed. The pitching was relieved and the important function of the foretopsails continued, driving the ship forward and lifting the bow.

Reefing required the top-men, including Nicholas Priest, to use both arms and hands to pass the reef points over the mast. They placed their lives in the hands of the helmsman and boatswain to keep the yard steady so as to not throw them off. Nicholas Priest understood this trust. He was to benefit again and again from it and returned the trust in kind for his shipmates.

293

Forty-Three

Monster

The "Loch Achray" was a clipper tall
With seven-and-twenty hands in all.
Twenty to hand and reef and haul,
A skipper to sail and mates to bawl
"Tally on to the tackle fall,
Heave now 'n' start her, heave and pawl!"
Hear the yarn of a sailor,
An old yarn learned at sea.

—John Masefield

Sunday, July 28, 1872
Lat 42°00′00″S, Long 90°05′00″W

"Wind increased all the afternoon & sea rising all the time. Hauled up the courses at 6pm. About 4pm the sun came out & I got an altitude 5 high, making D.R. Longitude about right. At 10pm wind hauled to WSW suddenly & we wore ship to NNW & soon after shipped a tremendous sea over the bow, tearing away main-rail & doing other damage & obliging us to haul to the wind & lay by till we got the place covered over with sheet copper. Kept her on her course & made all sail at 10am. Ends moderating sea, large sea on."

Ship's Log

Four Bells, First Watch (10 p.m.)

Nicholas Priest was curled on his side beneath his heavy blankets attempting to sleep. The back of his right leg was dotted with boils, and he knew he could no longer avoid seeing his captain to have them cut open. His hands were held beneath his armpits for warmth and the hope that this act would help the salt sores on his palms and fingers heal. He could not sleep in his upper bunk; Sophie would not come in his dreams. She had not visited him since the Le Maire Strait. All he could do was watch the overhead kerosene lamp sway and burn, shedding its yellow-orange light about the small cabin.

As he closed his eyes, he suddenly heard a great crash of tons of water pounding onto the deck, forcing the ship first into a precipitous pitch, then into a deep roll to port. The sound mixed with the noise of wood being smashed and he saw the overhead kerosene lamp dent its broad reflector against the overhead. He felt the wind enter the apprentice cabin through a hole torn in the outboard cabin wall. As he jumped from his bunk to the deck, his stocking feet sank into six inches of frigid water. He heard Smallbridge shout, "Shit! Shit!" The next voice he heard was that of Eoghan Gabriel, shouting, "On deck. Get the hell on deck now!"

***

Issac Griffin struggled to reach the quarterdeck. He saw dazed men clutching the overhead lifelines with both hands, a seven-foot breach of the forward bulkhead where the wave had struck, a stove-in whale boat, and doors and bulkheads in the forward deckhouse breached, with water draining from them. The first words spoken to Griffin came from Peleg Carver, "Heave-to?"

"Heave-to. Get them moving. Get canvas across that breach. Get the topsails down and furled."

It was then that Griffin realized his ship was heeled over at a thirty-five-degree angle, but as the water rushed overboard through the scuppers, he saw that she was righting herself slowly. He feared she had shipped water into her hold. In the background, the two pigs caged on the foredeck screamed in terror over a roaring sea and the rigging's moan. Stunned men, screaming pigs, a damaged ship, and only Peleg Carver seemed unmoved. Griffin saw Carver kick a seaman and shout, "Pray later; lay aloft."

Carver soon had her hove-to, with her bow to the winds and riding the tops of the waves in comparative comfort. As soon as heaving-to was completed, he held a quick muster and reported to Griffin, "A few broken noses, scrapes and bruises, thank God, but no one lost." Griffin smiled; he had indeed a Yankee mate.

Spare copper sheet was brought up and nailed into a rough bulkhead and main-rail where the breach occurred, men were at the Liverpool pump, and others were bailing out the deck cabins. The carpenter and Peleg Carver asked Griffin for permission to use a spare yard to fashion the lumber needed to repair the damage. The carpenter stated, "I need them Maine boys, the Ernsts, to do the sawin' and adze work."

Griffin did not turn in until the ship had righted herself and the crew had emptied her of shipped water. Chips then split the spare yard with a maul and wedges while muttering about the waste of good wood. As Griffin sat in his chair in his cabin, beneath his blankets, he could hear the sounds of wood being sawed, the blows of the carpenter's maul, and the curses of Peleg Carver, Henry Lennon, and Eoghan Gabriel. The men at the pumps sang,

The mate was a bucko and the Old Man a Turk,
Leave her, Johnny, leave her!
The bosun was a beggar with the middle name of work.
And it's time for us to leave her.

The wind was foul and the sea ran high,
Leave her, Johnny, leave her!
She shipped it green and none went by.
And it's time for us to leave her.

Oh, leave her, Johnny, and we'll work no more,
Leave her, Johnny, leave her!
Of pump or drown we've had full store.
And it's time for us to leave her.

The Downeaster
***

Griffin's mind churned. It was over now; he was sitting in his cabin in his easy chair, exhausted, but still could not sleep. It was the fourth day of winds from the northwest generally, the direction the ship needed to go. But they did vary from calm, WSW, then NNW, the only constant being a large head sea. 73 miles run one day, 120 the next, then 138. The ship pitched heavily and took large quantities of green water over the bow. It would have been quite a show except for the exhaustion of the men and the constant wet they endured. The upper topsails and courses were furled to reduce the pitching, then the spanker. She still pitched and took water over her decks.

He wanted to drive his ship to the northwest, but wind and head seas opposed her. It blew too strong to tack, then not at all, but what little distance made good that had been sailed came through beating against the wind in long, carefully planned boards, plotted out on the charts and recorded by dead reckoning. The sun came out and the dead reckoning proved to be good; his estimated position and calculated position differed by five minutes. But each wear took an hour and set the ship back by a mile. His long boards close-hauled to the left of the wind lasted eight to twelve hours; his boards to the right of the wind six to eight hours. Each wear required both watches, and wear after wear exhausted his cold, wet crew.

Griffin had a tremendous knowledge of the sea and weather. There were more than four thousand miles of water over which the wind might blow. NNW meant it came from the direction of Japan. The wind's persistence and growing strength made its origin a matter of speculation. *Providence* had no way of knowing the weather except by observation and the barometer, which dropped slowly, day by day. The increasing height and length of the waves did not surprise him; they were the servants of the laws of nature as Griffin reckoned those laws to be. He knew the weather had to change. He knew the trade winds were just beyond the roaring forties. Two or more degrees of latitude and the ship would be free.

Griffin sat in his leather chair, fully clothed under two twelve-pound blankets, and attempted to sleep, to let his exhaustion lull him into unconsciousness. His mind would not permit it. These thoughts kept repeating themselves.

A clockwork set in motion, then left to unwind since the beginning of time. We understand more, gradients, the law of storms, spring detent escapements, no mystery left. No awe, but occasional surprise, knowing appreciation. Our new deity, mathematical laws to which all must conform or not exist. Ha! Yet, I hear Him speak to me, He says, "Love her." He will always be there, just beyond our laws of mathematics, quietly whispering, "Love as I do. Forgive as I do."

Peleg said no one saw it coming until it was upon us. He ordered the men aloft to keep them from being swept overboard. Sixty feet tall and moving faster than any clipper, any steamer could move. Who would believe us? Thank God we took it by the bow. Pure chance, the spanker? We didn't breach and capsize.

It could not happen. Waves do not grow that high, yet we, the mariners, know they do, graybeards, three sisters. Peleg said it turned everything white with cascading water as it approached. It was dying, the wave subsiding back into the sea, returning to its womb, as it hit us. If it had hit us at full height, we would be dead. Heave-to a week to overhaul the damage? No, damn it. I'll check the cargo again with daylight.

She rolled twenty-three degrees and paused for a terrible moment to make up her mind. Would she put her masts in the water? No, she fought, then slowly rolled back, only listing until all the water spilled through the scuppers and the deck cabins were emptied.

These last days no one has slept. Held to our bunks by lee curtains and wrapped in our wet clothes, the stench of vomit now assaulting our nostrils, tempting others to retch. Now this.

He asked himself these questions: *Have I seen God this night? Have I felt his rod? What if Kayleigh knew what had happened? He has not slipped through my hands.*

Forty-Four

Horned Shellbacks

Of Neptune's empire let us sing,
At whose command the waves obey;
To whom the rivers tribute pay,
Down the high mountains sliding:
To whom the scaly nation yields
Homage for the crystal fields
Wherein they dwell:
And every sea-dog pays a gem
Yearly out of his wat'ry cell
To deck great Neptune's diadem.

—Thomas Campion

Monday, August 12, 1872
Lat 0°23′00″S, Long 117°30′00″W

The Sunday supper had just been eaten and the starboard watch took the deck. Isaac Griffin sat in his chart room and smiled because he had traveled 1,725 miles in the last week and was preparing to cross the equator on Monday in just seventy-seven days since leaving New York. He referred for a moment to his plans for the ship for a tidbit of information to pass to Kayleigh in a letter. *Yes; there it is—total yardage. We're carrying 9,850 square feet of sail! Magnificent!*

Isaac heard a knock on his door and saw his steward stick his head inside. "Captain, there's a dignitary to see you. Come to your

299

parlor, as this man ain't one to be kept waiting, sir." Griffin chuckled to himself. He had been expecting guests, and these visitors were welcome indeed. He had met them many times before.

"Ahoy and hail to Captain Griffin. I am a royal Triton and herald of his most briny majesty, Neptune Rex, king and master of the raging seas. His Majesty has sent me to tell you that tomorrow you are to heave-to at the line for there are among your children slimy pollywogs which ain't been tested for worthiness to enter into the beloved brotherhood of the sea, trusty shellbacks, and the subjects of King Neptune Rex.

"Now, sir, you must direct the boatswain to pipe all hands to assemble amidships, 'cause Neptune himself is wantin' me to speak to them."

"I most humbly will comply in respect of the wrath of King Neptune, sir, and the blue stars you have tattooed on your earlobes, and your neck. Twenty-five thousand miles? No sailor defies the ruler of the seas except to risk mortal danger. Ezra, tell Mr. Gabriel to call the hands amidships and knock off all ship's and personal work."

The before-the-mast crew assembled near the cargo hatch in the lee of the forward deck cabin. The Triton, herald of King Neptune, climbed to its roof and spoke. "Shellbacks, rejoice! Your king and master, Neptune Rex, will visit this good ship tomorrow as she passes the line, for among you are certain slimy creatures of the land who are known as pollywogs, slimy miserable pollywogs.

"His Majesty, his queen, Davy Jones, and other royal personages of the watery court will make their presence known to you. Now, hear me, pollywogs, and hear me well, for your weak and slimy hearts should be seized by fear. You have been accused of crimes against your shipmates, disrespect to Davy Jones, and are to be tried by Neptune himself. There'll be gnashing of your teeth, wogs.

"No man, even a pollywog, should be tried without knowing the charges against him or the severity of the punishment he will endure. So you wogs may question any trusty shellback as to what shall befall you, but the questioning ends on the eighth stroke of the ship's bell at midnight."

A bloody shriek of pain sounded suddenly, aft of the officers' deckhouse, which caused all assembled to turn their heads momentarily. When they turned again to see the Triton, he had disappeared.

And then, on the starboard side, the sailmaker pointed and shouted, "It's the fiery car of Neptune come to take his herald home." The brightly burning object quickly fell astern of *Providence*.

***

"I don't think I've ever seen it done better!" Griffin laughed. "I mean, letting that fired barrel drift alongside the ship. The shriek and disappearance were as clever as I've seen it done too. We've got men-o'-war's men amongst our trusty shellbacks. It explains why there was no appearance of Neptune in the Atlantic. They've waited to initiate the wogs as trusty horned shellbacks."

Isaac Griffin had good reason to be pleased. It's seldom you have a crew as clever as the men he had aboard *Providence*. They were in good spirits too. "Proves my point about the four married men. I'll have no one hurt and tradition observed all the same. What pollywogs do we have besides the apprentices?"

"There are four landsmen, apprentices, and Craig, Captain, but he don't matter." Peleg Carver, as usual, was ahead of the game because he was indeed the shellback's secret benefactor. Henry Lennon, though, had seen crossing ceremonies on English ships and had deep reservations about their worth, particularly if they got out of hand. "We'll see, Captain, Mr. Carver, we'll see."

***

"What's going on? Tell me, Smallbridge."

"It's called the night of the pollywogs, Sweets. We get the run of the ship and can ask the shellbacks about what to expect. I mean, we can tie them up, lather up their hair, and threaten to throw them overboard or drink a pint of castor oil. Haze them pretty much any way we want except cause them real harm. Then tomorrow, King

Neptune comes aboard and it's their turn to get us."

"Let's get Duder!"

***

Peleg Carver had an imagination and a sense that anything worth doing was worth doing well. He had been conniving with Sam Duder, Jonathon Bishop, and Eoghan Gabriel in planning for this line-crossing ceremony; it was he who persuaded the most salty of the trusty shellbacks to wait until the Horn had been crossed in order to initiate the apprentices as horned shellbacks. Peleg had one regret: There were not enough hands on board for a real ceremony in the navy tradition, but, "By God, Duder, we'll try, ayuh? No one's to be hurt, though."

At eight bells of the morning watch, John Stedwin called all hands to muster amidships as the American flag was slowly lowered and the Jolly Roger rose to the monkey gaff. The captain, looking at his crew, his eyebrows lowered, said, "Men, the Triton informed me that today, at noon while on the equator, his most seaworthy majesty Neptune Rex will appear together with Davy Jones. You pollywogs are accused of high crimes against the traditions of the eternal sea and must submit to his judgment or, God forbid, we might just as well scuttle her and go to our watery graves. Prepare for your justice as men, pollywogs!"

Peleg Carver made sure no apprentice could see him, as his face just barely concealed a broad Yankee grin as his brown eyes turned upward to the heavens. "Mr. Gabriel, bring the brass line throwing gun up on deck and have her charged and ready, blank shot."

"Aye, aye, Mr. Carver."

Peleg Carver had *Providence* lie-to at precisely one hour before noon. Both he and his captain took careful sun sights and calculated their position. The ship was as close to the equator as expert navigators could place her.

"We'll announce that we are on the equator at noon, Mr. Carver. I like your idea of firing a salute charge instead of ringing eight bells. I had forgotten we had the gun aboard. How's the powder?"

"I wouldn't expect to hit anything with it since the stuff is blasting powder, but it's dry and has no sign of deterioration. Stedwin served in the navy, and both he and I see no problem with it."

"It's the younger Christison's idea to carry the powder, Peleg. I'm supposed to sell it in San Francisco.

"Let's start the noon sight. Ask Mr. Lennon to join us. He'll enjoy being hove-to. It will be enjoyable to see how close our calculations are to each other. The captain's calculations are always right, ahem."

It took only ten or so minutes for the three men to determine the sun was at its zenith, and with the calm sea, it was exceptionally easy to set the lower limb precisely on the horizon. They all acknowledged their sight by saying "now," and they were virtually simultaneous. The meridian passage and Polaris sights are relatively easy celestial calculations; both Griffin and Carver could do them without benefit of paper or pencil as long as they had the almanac data. Peleg Carver, having the deck, gave the order, "Make it noon." The timekeeper struck the bell solemnly, ringing out eight chimes.

The old brass gun went off with relatively mild recoil, a great thunderous report, and—much to the pleasure of the trusty shellbacks—a great deal of sulfuric gray smoke, which nearly enveloped the forward deckhouse. When the smoke cleared, the Triton herald stood before the deckhouse and bellowed, "Gangway, you pollywogs, for mighty King Neptune and his Royal Court!"

"All bow now as the Royal Barber comes aft.

"All salute as the Royal Constables take their places.

"All bow as the Royal Baby, the darling delight of Queen Aphrodite, shows his preponderance to you.

"All bow to Her Royal Majesty, the most beautiful woman to ever ride the oceans' waves, Queen Aphrodite.

"Now quake in fear, you miserable creatures, you lubberly pollywogs, as Davy Jones shows himself to you.

"Now gangway, make a hole there, and bow low for His Majesty, Neptune Rex!"

The Royal Barber appeared dressed as a Moor, with soot-blackened face and a costume of painted canvas. In one hand, he held the Royal Razor, which had been forged from two feet of barrel hoop. A Triton bearing the Royal Shaving Cup and strop stood by his side. The Royal Shaving Soap was a mixture of oakum, bleached white, parral slush, and Baltic tar. The strop was made from heavy canvas sewn in layers and was obviously meant to be used as a schoolhouse paddle.

Queen Aphrodite was adorned with a great mop head flowing down to her shoulders; her carved wooden breasts were adorned with two scallop shells and tied around her hairy chest by small stuff. Her eyes were large and watery and made up with heavy eyebrows darkened from shoe blacking. Her lips were painted red. She held a golden painted goblet in one hand to catch her tobacco spittings. She had not shaved for a day or two.

The Royal Baby was a tall black man naked from the waist up with the ponderous belly of a cook. He wore a grass skirt made from shredded canvas held to his waist by cummerbund made from canvas painted to resemble a tiger's stripes. His upper body appeared to be covered in shiny grease, but in truth it was slush, the grease skimmed off water used for boiling salt beef and pork. The slush was rancid too.

Davy Jones wore a canvas mask painted to portray the hideous face of a cannibal, or pirate, or some other creature of its owner's imagination, perhaps a Humboldt squid. His eyes were surrounded by dark circles, making his orbs appear to be enormous. He was crowned with an old-fashioned tricorn hat adorned with a yard-long cat-o'-nine-tails, a toy made of small stuff. He wore short broad sailors' slops held to his waist by a thick leather belt that passed around the hilt of an enormous broad-bladed wooden cutlass.

King Neptune was the most glorious of all, with his magnificent head of golden hair fashioned from a mop head, a seashell crown, and a trident spear. He wore a canvas cape and a canvas loincloth decorated with compass roses and anchors. He had a magnificent beard of braided small stuff like King Nebuchadnezzar. King Neptune spoke in a powerful tenor voice eerily similar to the shantey voice of Sam Duder.

The Downeaster

"Captain Griffin, there, your children have not prepared for me. Have that mate take these wogs and rig the Royal Bath here amidships."

One of the ship's awnings was rigged from the stays and held up at its sides by jigger tackle. The mate set the four apprentices to the pump and filled the Royal Bath with bilgewater.

"Now bring the wogs before me. Kneel, you slimy creatures, and bow to the master of the ocean waves, the mighty breath of the Southern Ocean, and he that keeps the deep within its bounds. Constables, blindfold these miserable creatures.

"Now, Davy Jones, my son, what is the charge for that pollywog, there, the old one that's on his first voyage?"

"Your Majesty, this wog's name is O'Brien and he is charged by the port watch of not being able to carry a tune in a bucket or bring the mess kids quick enough and him from Ireland and all."

"How do you plead, wog?"

The trusty shellbacks of the port watch roared in rough unison, "Guilty, guilty, guilty!"

King Neptune spoke. "No mortal has ever said Neptune Rex was anything but fair. You wog, sing out a song, a sad Irish song to make my queen weep, and you'll be spared."

As the man started to sing, the queen let out a sharp scream in her best falsetto voice. "Constable, constable, shut that man up! Barber, shave off his hair."

The man's hair was lathered from the Royal Shaving Cup and the Royal Barber ran the Royal Razor through his hair. The edge of the Royal Razor had been sharpened to feel like a rasp.

It was the Royal Baby's turn to speak. "Oh, Father Neptune, baptize him and wash his guilt away in the Royal Bath."

The Royal Constable observed Neptune's signal and walked the man to the edge of the Royal Bath, stood him there with his back to the awning, and pushed him into the bilgewater.

The ceremony continued as before until all of the pollywogs had been tried and sentenced. The apprentices were the last to appear before Neptune Rex, and of these the last was Nicholas Priest.

Jeremy Ernst was accused of impersonating a figurehead; Richard Ernst was accused of working too hard; Smallbridge was accused of impersonating a seaman. Each charge was read; each asked for his plea, only to be ignored in the bellowing of the trusty shellbacks. The Ernst boys were told their sentence was to kiss the queen. This turned out to be the kissing of the garlic-laden mouth of a dead fish.

"And you, wog, Priest, is it? What's his charge, Davy?"

"His charges, great Neptune, were to steal a young girl's affection and then go to sea the next day. He's also attempted to fool the hands to thinking the cook's food is actually good by eating huge quantities of the whack!"

"I forgive him the first as that's traditional with sailormen, but the last is the most hideous I've heard all day. He must kiss the Royal Baby's belly and kiss the queen three times. Is this wog guilty? All knowing the truth of the matter say, 'Aye!'"

The crew roared their approval, and Priest was brought forward to kiss the Royal Baby's belly. Bishop wrapped his massive arms around Priest's head and buried it in the folds of his belly.

Neptune turned to his queen. "Has he atoned?"

The queen began to sop huge crocodile boo-hoo tears and moaned in her falsetto voice, "But that poor girl, the victim of this young Lothario."

Davy Jones yelled, "Shave him!"

The Royal Barber applied lather roughly to Priest's head and slowly ran the razor through his hair. At the end of each stroke, the shellbacks roared their approval. The razor was brought across all of Priest's crown and his cheeks and chin. The Royal Barber sprinkled oakum down his neck and onto his shoulders.

They're really shaving me; I'm bald!

Davy Jones turned to the Royal Barber and said, "Bald! Looks like a chicken's ass that's ready for the stew pot."

The queen yelled, "Baptize him, wash his sins away in the Royal Bath," and Priest fell over backward into the odorous bilgewater.

Only one remained, and this man claimed to have crossed the line and been around the Horn before. The Royal Triton shouted out the name. "Samuel Craig, kneel before His Majesty and prepare yourself for your fate, for you are charged with lying to the forecastle gang, shirking your duties, spreading slander, and losing a fair fight to a mere boy."

Craig protested, "I've crossed the line! I'm no pollywog!"

Neptune's court screamed in unison, "Liar!"

As punishment for his sins, Craig was given twelve good ones with Davey Jones's cat-o'-nine tails across his naked ass, and his mouth washed clean with soap and oakum. The men cheered wildly. Griffin was taken by surprise that Craig was accused by the men, but it was rough justice and not permanently harmful, so the captain let the judgment stand.

Griffin did not know what had been set in motion. The crew thought the punishment only just and good warning. For them, their anger would end, if Craig would change his behavior.

King Neptune now turned to Captain Griffin. "I have tried these wogs and washed away the guilt of their sins. This is damned dry work, sir, and a libation of grog would go well for me and the Royal Court. Do that for the sake of smooth seas and fair winds. Do it and I shall give your children back to you as trusty horned shellbacks and true deep-water salts."

Griffin turned to his steward. "Ezra, tradition is tradition. Serve His Majesty and his court with my best whiskey, ahem, grog."

The newly initiated trusty horned shellbacks were brought before His Majesty Neptune Rex and his court. Their blindfolds were removed and hands untied. Almost immediately they began rubbing the tops of their heads to find all of the hair was still there, albeit deep in oakum, tar, and grease.

"Let all who fare upon the seas know by my royal decree that these men are henceforth to be given all customary rights and privileges of mariners, of dwellers on the roaring main, of those souls brave enough to have rounded Cape Horn from the great Atlantic Ocean to the Pacific. Henceforth, these men shall be called horned shellbacks and enjoy my personal protection from all that would accuse them of being lubbers. So be it!"

Only Craig's face showed no smile.

The shellbacks cheered the newly initiated and individually shook the hand of each new shellback, even Craig. King Neptune shook Nicholas Priest's hand and said, "There, Sweets, you've earned two tattoos, and damned if I'm not proud of you. I'll show you where to get your tattoos in Frisco."

Peleg Carver turned to his captain and said, "See, Captain, no blood, no broken bones, and Neptune Rex and Davy Jones are appeased again."

Forty-Five

Man's Justice

"And whatten penance will ye drie for that?
Edward, Edward,
And whatten penance will ye drie for that?
My deir son, now tell me O"

"Ile set my feit in yonder boat,
mither, mither,
Ile set my feit in yonder boat,
And fare ovir the sea O."

A Child Ballad

Friday, August 23, 1872
Lat 26°11′48″N, Long 121°29′00″W
The Pacific Trades

With the second stroke of the ship's bell, the port watch came on deck for morning coffee, tobacco, and fresh biscuits from the cook's oven. It was a cold, foggy dawn. They also came to see what work the first mate would have them do: holystoning, painting the long boat, overhauling the running rigging, painting the forward deckhouse, repairing sails, putting up chafing gear, getting *Providence* ready for her grand entrance into San Francisco Bay and repairing the damage from rounding Cape Horn. The port watch had had less than one hour's sleep today. Tomorrow, the starboard watch would stand the mid-watch.

Samuel Craig had stood the midnight to four with the rest of the port watch. He spent his time thinking about the line crossing, running his fingers through his hair, and remembering being bent over the hatch, naked from the waist down, and flogged with that ridiculous cat-o'-nine tails. He thought of the laughter, derision, and humiliation. Why? It was because of Nicholas Priest. He had tried to kill Priest before and would do so now if the opportunity came, but even if it did not, he lusted for blood on his hands, to relish the terror of murder. Anyone would do—anyone—but Priest especially.

The voice was there, whispering in Craig's ear again, calling him to obey. He must abide by his walking boss when he spoke, when the walking boss had crossed a continent and an ocean to be with him and tell him what he must do. The boss had spoken to Craig before; he remembered hearing him speak to him as he fled from Lee's army in Virginia. He remembered the farmer, his wife, and children, but he did not mourn for them. He longed to see the instant of death again, life then lifelessness at his hands, and enjoy his work, his calling, and his service to the walking boss.

Craig smelled the hot coffee steaming and the aroma of the fresh biscuits coming from the galley. Perlie made biscuits with fresh buttermilk in a Dutch oven in an open hearth. Death and hot biscuits were familiar to him. He enjoyed both.

Craig looked to find the apprentices. They were with Duder and Stedwin on the weather side with the rest of the crew, sitting beneath the bulwark drinking coffee and eating their warm biscuits. Bishop stood in the galley door and smiled. One of the apprentices stood, braced himself against the forward deck cabin, and made his way to the port head. Craig saw that his wrists were longer than the sleeves of his pea jacket. Craig laughed at the boy's modesty, after months at sea; he would use the lee head so no one would hear him, as if by now anyone cared. His lust for blood—the feelings of heart and loin—built hope, then anticipation; the pea jacket, it was Priest!

Craig followed him. He stood forward of the privy, hidden by the deckhouse, waiting for the apprentice to open the door. It opened. The boy emerged carrying the cedar bucket in hand to throw his waste overboard. As the boy extended the bucket over the side, Craig plunged a knife through the boy's ribs, causing the apprentice to straighten as the tip of the blade punctured his heart. The bucket hit the water. The dead body fell to the deck, and only when Craig turned the body on its back did he discover he had killed Elder. He had murdered the older of the two Ernst brothers, Jeremy, by mistake. But he had killed again as the walking boss had told him to do. His soul filled with joy. *You made me happy again, boss.* He then whined, "Priestie."

The forward lookout yelled murder from his station aloft on the foremast topsail yard. It was Smitty. He had seen it all. Craig fled, seeking a hiding place in the forecastle.

"Mr. Carver, I saw him do it. I'll swear to it. Craig was just standing there like nothing at all; then his face got twisted and red and he jabs that thing with his left hand straight into the boy's ribs and kills him, from behind. Not a word out of him. It was so quick, like he knew what he was doing. Then he stops, looks at the dead body, and smiles. Said something to himself, but I couldn't hear it."

"Thankee, Smitty. You'll swear on a Bible to that?"

"Yes, sir. I know what I saw."

"I believe you. Go on back aloft, now. Tell no one. Mr. Lennon and I'll take care of it." Carver knew that within minutes of Smitty being relieved, the whole crew would know Jeremy Ernst had been murdered by Craig.

Peleg Carver beckoned for Richard Ernst to come to his brother. He comforted the boy and directed Younger to wrap his brother in a blanket. Reuben, the sailor from the Bronx, would help him and stay with him.

Peleg Carver and Henry Lennon then walked aft to the taffrail to talk alone.

Carver spoke. "He was a good boy—innocent. You couldn't ask for a better worker. Since—I want to hang that bastard. He killed that boy for no reason at all. Do you see it following us?"

"What do yews want me ter see? There's a wake and that big bird; that's all."

311

"There's only one bird, one albatross. Jeremy's soul's been taken. That's why there's one albatross! It's still waiting. I've seen it before, Lennon. My grandfather saw it happen. As long as that bird's there, the ship's cursed. Don't you understand? That boy's soul will never go to its reward unless Craig dies, unless he pays with his life. I don't want to wake up and see that poor boy's ghost standing by my bed. I don't want him accusing me or blaming me. The Bible tells us of Jonah. That boy was my responsibility—mine."

"Peleg, you're trembling. Besides, there was naught yews could do. He was a good lad; he'll not haunt yews."

Lennon saw terror overcome Carver's face. Carver pleaded, "Listen to me. Listen! He can't live, or this ship will founder; she's lost."

"And what about da captain? Do yews think he'll let you take revenge? Na. I know him. He'll not allow it."

"No. I'll take no chances. Do you think I care, Lennon? Do you? I'll not be cursed. I'll not bring that boy's curse down on me or my family. Besides, how long do you think it will take before the crew kills him? They'll know who did it. He's hiding in there, in the forecastle behind the wench. They'll find him, holding a heaver, the knife still in his belt. The hands know we're cursed, and those who don't believe will still want him hung. It's justice, an eye for an eye."

"What about da captain's recommendation, Peleg? What about your own ship? Ain't you going to call the captain on deck?"

"And what? He'll want to do it by the book. No, sir. There's a curse on this ship and even if there ain't, these men won't abide putting Craig in irons.

"I care more for the child in Sally's womb than I do my own ship. I'll die before my child's cursed."

Both men had forgotten that everything spoken on a ship was overheard and repeated. Just feet away, standing forward in the wheelhouse under the open scuttle, four silent ears heard all they had said. Duder and Priest had the helm.

Four bells rang.

The watch was half over and Duder and Priest were relieved at the helm, their trick over. "Did you hear all of that, Sam? Craig's murdered Jeremy Ernst?" Nicholas Priest was shocked.

"The mate's right, Sweets. There'll be a hanging, justice, or we founder and die. Believe it. See, there's but one bird now and it waits and wants Craig's soul."

It took no time for the news of the murder to spread. Both Carver and a still reluctant Lennon kept Ezra from calling the captain. Twenty heated men are hard to control, and the sound of their anger was close to that of fury. If nothing was done, Griffin would hear them and be on deck with his pistol. Duder kept Sweets back, apart from the crew.

Carver mustered the men in naval fashion, assembling them amidships and by watch. "There's been a murder; Elder's been slaughtered. There's a witness. You'll draw straws to form a jury. Not the boys, no, only men, able-bodied and ordinary.

"Now, I'll not have any of you shirk your duty. If there's to be law, if there's to be justice, who else is there but you? Look aft. Do you see that bird? There are men here who know what it wants." Carver listened to hear the older men and watched their eyes.

One portsider shouted out, "Hang the Jonah!"

"Silence!"

Carver stared the man down and silence held sway. He then said, "I'll not have mob justice! There'll be no more murder. Justice is work for cool minds, serious minds."

The boatswain passed among the two watches and had the men draw straws from his fist. Some men were reluctant to draw; others gladly did so. One man lost his composure on drawing a short straw. John Stedwin took it and gave him his own. Stedwin then looked to the first mate, who gave him permission to take the man's place.

Carver imposed silence by looking at each man, letting his dark eyes represent not only his rank but also his natural authority. "Bring Craig aft."

Craig stood there; his hands were bound behind him. His rib ached from being hurled to the deck, blood still oozed from the fresh wound on his forehead. He heard Carver clearly.

"You're to have a trial. There's a witness. You can confront him; you can ask him any question. Now swear on this Bible you'll tell the truth."

"Go to hell."

"Are you innocent or guilty?"

Craig said nothing.

"I said, are you innocent or guilty? What do you say?"

Craig turned toward Carver, smiled, and seemed to almost chuckle. He said nothing.

"Very well. You have nothing to say for or against yourself. I call Ordinary Seaman Harold Smith to testify, to tell the jury what he saw." Smitty was sworn to the truth. He told the men what he saw while looking directly at Samuel Craig. The men watched Smitty's and Craig's eyes.

Craig was surprised to hear the first mate ask him if he had any question for the witness or if he cared to make a statement. Craig remained silent; however, his face mocked Carver.

Carver again said, "Very well." He turned then to the jury and asked if they had any question for Craig or the witness. Several of the men turned angry eyes toward Craig, but nothing was asked of him or Smitty.

Priest watched Craig's face. He saw flashes of pleasure, of defiance, of pride, and of hate. The sight froze Priest's soul. In Craig he saw evil that killed for the pleasure of it. He knew it was he, Nicholas Priest, who was the intended victim and not Jeremy Ernst. Priest felt regret. The schools, his parents, all injustice real and imagined, were insignificant compared to what Samuel Craig had done. If there are some events that change men's lives, the first acknowledgment of pure evil is one, the first undeniable knowledge that it walks among us.

"Stedwin, take the jury forward of the cabin and bring me their verdict. Everybody must agree. A guilty verdict means hanging."

The word "hanging" caused several members of the jury to turn their heads sharply and look at Carver. "You heard me. Do your duty."

The men filed forward of the deck cabin. Stedwin's voice carried, and he was heard to say, "Do you have any doubts? Then thumbs up he walks, thumbs down he hangs." Stedwin and the jury returned. "Mr. Carver, he's guilty. He hangs."

Priest relieved the helm with Smallbridge, Lennon's orders. Richard Ernst still knelt by his brother and wept, barely aware that a trial had taken place and justice was to be rendered. When offered the chance to witness the hanging, he declined.

***

Craig saw Eoghan Gabriel walk to the boatswain's locker with Duder and Stedwin. He thought of holystones. They returned with a coil of fresh hemp three strand and two wooden blocks. Gabriel directed the hemp line to be wet down with the fire pump and stretched the wet line between two wing capstans. Gabriel, Duder, and Stedwin then climbed the main-mast to the main-top, laid out on the main course, and rigged a gun-tackle purchase, the tackle fall secured with a Mathew Walker's knot, the other a hangman's noose. Craig's legs started to shake as he understood what the two blocks meant; he would not plummet and die instantly. Gabriel, Duder, and Stedwin returned to the deck, bound Craig's ankles, checked the knots securing his hands behind his back, and tied his arms to his sides. "Fuck you, Duder."

"Do you want the hood?"

"Hell, no!" Craig shouted. "See that, Priestie? Who's got a pair now?"

The ship's bell rang out five times, *ding-ding, ding-ding, d-i-n-g.* Craig tried to stretch the sound of the last *ding* from a second to an hour. He turned his eyes and saw the bird. He saw Priest silently on duty at the helm. He wondered if the boy wanted to see the show. He wondered if Priest's focus was the compass card and lubber line or the shake of the main topgallant. *Are you watching? Can you even stand to?*

The deck caught the rays of the sun.

Holystoning. Holystoning. He remembered the warmth of the sun radiating from the deck. *I'm cold.*

He wanted coffee, its smell, its warmth, its flood in his throat, and asked for it. Bishop brought the coffee gently to his lips, offering the cup again. Craig smiled. Bishop nodded. Craig's eyes were wet.

Samuel Craig felt the noose tighten and felt the hangman's knot rest behind his left ear. He felt every abrasive fiber of the damp hemp. He searched to see the sky and sea, and then the albatross high above the white horse caps soaring nearly black against the brilliant gray and silver-streaked clouds.

"This ain't nothing. I ain't about to lose anything worth keeping. I'm glad it's over." He heard the albatross beckon him with a high-pitched yelp.

Carver asked, "Have you any last words? Do you want to pray? We'll say a prayer if you want it. Would you like a hymn?"

"Damn you all. You'll see me in hell. I'll be waiting for you!"

Carver answered, "You're about to die. Is that all you can say?"

The slack was taken out of the rope; the noose pressed against his neck, resting above the Adam's apple. Craig wept.

Perlie, sing to me.

The boatswain spoke. "I want you men to face aft. Put the rope over your shoulder and grip it with both hands. Don't let go. When I say run, you run aft. Run hard. I'll tell you when to belay."

No, Perlie, no.

Five men of the port watch, no boys, formed a line and turned their backs to him. Their hands curled around the line as they brought it over their right shoulders.

"Damn you! I said, damn you!"

Perlie, Mama—they...

"Run!"

Isaac Griffin heard the boatswain shout, "Run," and the sound of men's feet running, then stopping suddenly. Sleep was behind him and fear, cold fear upon him. He bolted from his chair and took his pistol from the drawer below his bunk. He ran from his cabin, ran through the cabin door, and turning windward around the after deckhouse, he saw the still-jerking body of Samuel Craig held a fathom off the deck by five silent men. He raised the pistol in the air and fired two shots instinctively, uselessly. Craig fell to the deck into the pool of his own urine beneath his feet, dead.

"What the hell happened here? Carver! What in hell have you done?" Carver and Lennon stood before their captain. The crew stood in a tight knot at the backs of the two mates. The younger men, the hotter heads, clutched the handles of their knives.

Lennon saw this and stared them down. "No! Get yews hands off those knives. There's been enough killing and murder."

Carver spoke. He tried as best he could to make a proper report. "Elder's been murdered. Craig killed him, sir."

Griffin gained his composure. He put his pistol in his belt and directed Carver to show him the body of Jeremy Ernst. He felt for a pulse, placed his ear over the dead boy's mouth, rose, and calmly said, "He's dead. What happened here?"

The men felt reassured to see the captain do this, his duty, the expected, and to acknowledge Richard, softly, warmly, by placing his hand on the boy's shoulder as if he were a son.

Carver spoke. "Look aft, Captain. The albatross are gone. They followed us since the Horn. The first one left with Jeremy, the second with Craig. There's no evil now. The devil's been paid in full."

"Nonsense! They're birds! They follow us because we dump our garbage overboard."

"Listen, Captain, my family has been to sea since England, at least one hundred fifty years. My grandpa told me about those birds, their eyebrows—cape albatross. He'd learned it from his father. Craig was a Jonah. I don't care what you do about my ship. It's in the Bible, Jonah. I'll not be cursed. I'll not have the child in Sally's womb cursed. These men know it too. Justice had to be done or the devil would take us, all hands. "

Griffin looked at his mates and looked at his crew. He saw fear. He saw anger. He saw the crew was not under his control, held in line only because of the Smith and Wesson Russian at his side.

"What did you do?"

"We gave him a trial, Captain. Smitty saw the whole thing— swore to it. We gave Craig a chance to defend himself. All he did was curse us. We drew straws for the jury—only men. He was found guilty and hung. We hung him proper too. Let him say last words. Offered him a hood. Offered to say a prayer for his soul. He cursed us. He just cursed us."

Lennon spoke. "Captain, this ain't da time. Look at them, yer men."

Griffin lowered his head. "Get that rope off him. Bring them both aft and prepare them for burial. Tomorrow, tomorrow at noon, all hands."

Sam Duder became angry. "It ain't right that the boy be buried with his killer. It ain't right at all."

"Just bring them aft and prepare their shrouds. You can keep them apart. I'll do what's right by Elder. I'll do what's right, Sam. Carver, you and Lennon go below. I have the deck. Take Younger, Priest, and Smallbridge with you. Noyes and Reuben can take the bodies aft; use a passenger stateroom for Elder. Here, take my pistol with you."

The ship's master walked forward toward the main-mast. "Gather round, now. I've words to say. Gather around me.

"All of us are in this and it is finished. Two men are dead and that's that. Can't bring them back, can't call this all back either. We have to live with it. We'll all answer to our God for what we've done, but you'll not answer to me and not now or ever.

"Listen. Damn it. I said listen to me. I mean this. We all signed on to sail this ship. I'm going to do that, and that's what I expect of you. We're all in this together, master, mates, day men, and crew. I'll not speak of it again, and neither will you. Now, go back to work."

Griffin then paused and slowly, deliberately looked the men in their eyes. His face was calm, without anger. Griffin then stood with his back exposed to his men and slowly walked aft to the cabin. One by one, the men watched and then returned to their work.

***

Griffin finished reviewing the deck log and then prepared his daily entry for the ship's log. The deck log related to the navigation of the ship, the ship's log to key events such as births, deaths, and marriages, and whatever the master felt important enough to write down.

"Ezra, ask the mates and the apprentices to step in, please."

"Aye, Captain."

The mates thought they knew why they were called, but the apprentices were surprised.

"Here's what I've prepared for the ship's official log. I want both mates to sign as witnesses." He then read aloud.

"A witness, Harold Smith, Ordinary Seaman, of New Hampshire, was questioned about the death of Apprentice Jeremy Ernst. Smith provided sworn testimony that he saw Samuel Craig stab Jeremy Ernst in the back in cold blood, causing instant death. Examination of the body indicated the wound may have broken a rib and thrust through the heart, causing both internal and external bleeding and instantaneous death.

"Craig is believed to have committed suicide when found out by the crew. He ended his own life by jumping overboard. Sea state and fog prevented launching a boat. May God have mercy on his soul.

"Richard, Jeremy's laid out in a passenger stateroom. I am sorry for your loss. I don't have words to tell you how sorry I am for you and your brother. Even if I had them, I don't know how much comfort they would be to you. All I can do now is to bury him at sea. It's a good burial, a Christian burial, a burial for a seaman. You'll see. You'll stand next to me. All hands will be there; the ship will lie-to.

"We all liked your brother. He earned the crew's respect. He was a good shipmate. That's the most we can give him, to call him shipmate and give him our respect and love. We all have lost a shipmate.

"I want you and the other apprentices to have supper with me and the mates tonight, to sleep aft too. We all understand your grief. We all share it. Go and be with Jeremy now. The men will pay their respects and want to talk to you, to comfort you. We all care.

"Don't say much. Look at their eyes. That's where their sentiments are, if they could say them. Tell them, 'Thank you.' "

319

Richard Ernst left the captain's office with the two apprentices. Priest went on deck to let Duder know where he would be. Duder acknowledged this silently and pointed aft. "There's no birds there. It's over, Sweets. See? Some things ain't understood, but they're still true."

Griffin and the mates were still in the reception area. Griffin looked at his two mates. "I think the crew's ready to follow us now. I told the crew we are all in this together and no one is to say another word about it. Peleg, I know you felt anger and fear. Damn it, give me some credit! What angers me is you forgot your duty to inform me, to call me on deck, the loyalty you owe me.

"Both of you—it was your duty to call me. I needed to have been called. We've a lazarette aboard this ship, and Craig belonged there and in irons. Someone would kill him. Who? I don't care. Who would protect him? That would have been better. Now all of us will be liars. I gave orders for you to call me and you ignored them. I may have hanged him myself if it meant this ship, keeping the crew."

Both mates heard their captain. Carver's face showed resignation. Lennon spoke up. "Captain, what about Peleg's ship?"

"No, I'll not discuss it. We'll bury Jeremy tomorrow. We'll give him a shipmate's farewell. You'll get the men ready, Peleg."

"Captain, the men will want to know what's in the log."

"Here, take it."

Griffin watched his mates leave. He opened his desk drawer and took paper and pen to write his letter to Kayleigh MacKenna. He held the pen in his hand and heard the ship's bell ring out the hour of the watch. More than thirty minutes had passed and nothing had been written except the date. He reached for the deck log, read it again and then again, and wrote:

My Dearest Kayleigh,
We've had moderate breezes and cloudy weather throughout the last 24 hours. The wind has remained steady all throughout the day and night from the north by west. It has been quite cool. All sail has been set.

The Downeaster

Unfortunately we have not been able to head up better than west by north 3/4 north most of the day. We have seen no birds or flying fish since daybreak. The two great cape albatross that have trailed us daily are no longer there. There's been a death. We've lost Jeremy Ernst. I'll bury him tomorrow. We all mourn for him.

You know my fondness for the poems of John Donne. Today the bell tolls for a boy and for all of us together. I have not the words to comfort his brother, although my heart compels me to do so. Tomorrow I will bury him according to tradition. The men will stand silently and pray. Perhaps a hymn will be sung. We all suffer at such moments and reach to each other for comfort. Perhaps the soul of this departed boy will rejoice to escape the confines of an earthly grave and feel the expanse and freedom of the sea, to soar majestically on broad white wings above all the temporal suffering below...

Griffin was momentarily startled by the sound of something being jettisoned, then what seemed to be a cheer cut short by Lennon's shouting. He shoved his chair back and prepared to go forward when he then heard the familiar grind of holystones purifying his deck.

Still standing, he picked up Melville from his shelf and turned to chapter nine of *Moby-Dick*.

"With this sin of disobedience in him, Jonah still further flouts at God, by seeking to flee from Him... Delight is to him, whom all the waves of the billows of the seas of the boisterous mob can never shake from this sure Keel of the Ages. And eternal delight and deliciousness will be his, who coming to lay him down, can say with his final breath—O Father!—chiefly known to me by Thy rod—mortal or immortal, here I die. I have striven to be Thine, more than to be this world's, or mine own. Yet this is nothing; I leave eternity to Thee; for what is man that he should live out the lifetime of his God?"

Forty-Six

Burial at Sea

Few and short were the prayers said,
and spoke we not of sorrow;
But steadfastly gazed upon the face that was dead,
And we bitterly thought of the morrow.
—Charles Wolfe

Saturday, August 24, 1872
Lat 27°27′46″N, Long 124°36′30″W

September 4, 1872

My Dearest Kayleigh,
We made good 186 miles in the last 24 hours. The wind has been consistent coming from the NNW. This has given us some time to rest, as I've not had to call both watches on deck. The ship is starting to look as if she had just been built. We've worked at painting everything above the waterline and Peleg Carver has been methodically overhauling the rigging mast by mast. Our older sails are now bent.

For being so close to the equator it's been rather cool, although it is still quite comfortable. It has been overcast but not so much as to prevent me from using my sextant to determine our position. Yesterday morning the thermometer read 67 degrees dry bulb and 64 degrees wet bulb at noon and the temperatures were again the same this noon. It does feel a bit cooler; perhaps it's the breeze.

I mentioned our two great albatross have failed to reappear. Sailors are superstitious. Perhaps it is only that these birds have learned sailors are generous with ship's biscuit or they find fish to prey upon in our wake. They were a diversion. We have headed west by north and west-northwest all day, methodically using the trade winds to close the distance to San Francisco.

I spoke to my first mate about the progress he's been making in inspecting and overhauling our rigging. He has replaced more than a few ratlines and robands. Perhaps the heavy ice from the south fifties helped rot out the line and the weight of the ice weakened them. Unfortunately, accidents befall us and the sea leads some to all men's fate. Today I will bury Jeremy Ernst, an apprentice, a life once so full of promise.

I close this noon, this day at sea with all my love...

***

The burial ceremony began when Griffin read the log entry for Jeremy Ernst to the men:

"On Thursday, the fifth of September, 1872, on board the ship *Providence*, lying-to in a gentle Pacific Ocean, Jeremy Ernst, our brother and beloved shipmate, was laid to rest."

He then spoke. "All of us knew Jeremy. All of us grieve because his life was taken unnaturally. We are less than what we were by Jeremy's departure from us. He was a good boy and would have grown to be a good man. He earned our respect by working hard and being honest. I know all of us grieve his loss and will join me in praying for him. His life had been so full of promise. We had so much more to share with him. He was our shipmate and friend."

The ship's master set the log aside and opened his old Anglican *Book of Common Prayer.*

"Lord be merciful to us sinners, and save us for thy mercy's sake. Thou art the great God, who hast made and rulest all things: O deliver us for thy Name's sake. Thou art the great God to be feared above all: O save us, that we may praise thee."

The ship's company all said, "Amen."

"We therefore commit the body of Jeremy Ernst, our brother, to the deep, to be turned into corruption, looking for the resurrection of the body when the sea shall give up her dead, and the life of the world to come, through our Lord Jesus Christ; who at his coming shall change our vile body, that it may be like his glorious body, according to the mighty working whereby he is able to subdue all things unto himself."

The ship's company said, "Amen."

Peleg Carver was a grieving man. Although he had seen this before and had lost a brother and cousins to the sea, the death of a young, promising life affected him. His eyes had begun to tear and he turned his face upward and toward the ship's wake to hide his emotions from the crew. Henry Lennon saw this and placed his hand atop his friend's shoulder.

Sam Duder led the ship in his favorite hymn, his tenor voice standing proud, a hymn he learned to sing as a boy.

> *No condemnation now I read;*
> *Jesus, and all in Him, is mine;*
> *Alive in Him, my living Head,*
> *And clothed in righteousness divine,*
> *Bold I approach th'eternal throne,*
> *And claim the crown, through Christ my own.*
>
> *Amazing love! How can it be*
> *That thou, my God, shouldst die for me.*

Forty-Seven

Approaching Landfall

Oh, I thought I heard the Ol' Man say,
Leave her, Johnny, leave her!
Tomorrow ye will get your pay,
An it's time for us to leave her!

Traditional Pump Shantey

Tuesday, September 3, 1872
Lat 37°10′00″N, Long 122°30′00″W

Isaac Griffin finished his supper in the main saloon with Henry Lennon. They were experiencing the coastal weather of Northern California. It was calm, not even enough wind for steerageway. Griffin watched the drizzle on the lights of the overhead butterfly hatch. At last the fog had cleared at noon, permitting them to see Point Año Nuevo bearing northeast some eight miles off, as calculated using a sextant and distance-off tables. They knew they were only thirty-five miles or so away from the Golden Gate.

Their circumstances both delighted and frustrated them in that it soon would be over and yet they must helplessly wait. In the last two days they had covered 171 miles and 172 miles, respectively, and today, two bells into the noon watch, they were becalmed, delayed once more. Still they saw coastal traffic, a becalmed schooner bound for Santa Cruz. The ocean was dark green and there were several varieties of shore birds flying about them, all signs of land.

No movement since four a.m. The day's run was 140 miles, thirty-five miles short of a pilot boarding, arriving at their anchorage, the bustle of agents for the Central Pacific representatives being on board to examine cargo and to inform them of where they would discharge it. They were thirty-five miles short of eight uninterrupted hours of sleep, mail from New England, a meal with good wine, fresh meat, and green vegetables, and a newspaper. Griffin looked forward to a porterhouse steak, sourdough bread, and Kayleigh's mail.

The calm remained with them until nine p.m., and then they found faint air from the south. This wind lasted the remainder of the night, and at about four-thirty a.m., the Farallones bore northwest true and Point Lobos bore northeast true. By five a.m. the pilot was aboard and then they were becalmed again until nine a.m., when the breeze once again stirred, filling the topgallants and royals but leaving the other square sails just shaking. They had way on.

Providence did not arrive in San Francisco in 110 days as planned. It was just one hundred days and twelve hours from her anchorage off the Battery in the Hudson River to passage between the heads of San Francisco Bay, 17,384 miles by log, averaging just over seven knots for the voyage. By straight line, the voyage was 16,357 miles. This voyage was accomplished despite five to fifteen hours of calm for eleven consecutive days. Although the days of the clipper races were over, one hundred days and twelve hours from New York was still impressive enough to have freight agents, ship's masters, and seamen talking. The performance was telegraphed east to Christison and Son.

Sam Duder and the other New Englanders had already indicated they would sign on for the trip back to England, as had five Irishmen and the day-men. Nicholas Priest and Edward Smallbridge looked forward to going ashore. They would get their tattoos for rounding the Horn and for being horned shellbacks. They would have money in their pockets and everything in common with generations of sailors before and after them who looked forward to an adventure ashore.

Richard Ernst had decided to stay aboard ship and finish the voyage. He knew his telegram and the captain's would send his family into profound mourning for the loss of their firstborn. Younger reasoned that his family's grief would pass and that their lives would resume their routines. Jeremy would always be remembered. There would be a memorial service and a headstone placed for him in the family plot. Younger had talked at length to his captain about the choice he had to make and decided that he would continue the voyage. He had mourned his brother's death and reasoned that delaying his homecoming would bring welcome joy to his family when he did arrive. He had been sent to sea as a boy. He would return home a man, a horned shellback and Cape Horner, prepared to run the family business with his father.

Providence remained at her anchorage for three days until berthing could be arranged. Griffin was pleased that his officers, Eoghan Gabriel, ten of his seamen including his New Englanders, Jonathon Bishop, and his apprentices had all remained aboard. Peleg Carver's wife was healthy and being cared for in his absence by her mother and sister. She sent her husband a bright and loving telegram full of strength and optimism. She urged him to continue.

Isaac Griffin was not surprised to see a U.S. Marshal climb the accommodation ladder and announce that he had come for Samuel Craig. He was certain that he was a fugitive from justice. Griffin was surprised, however, to learn that Craig—not his real name—had murdered his wife, enlisted in the Confederate Army, deserted from the Army of Northern Virginia after his first battle, and been identified as the killer of a Shenandoah Valley farmer and his wife and family by a child who had miraculously lived.

Although a judge and jury awaited Samuel Craig, they never would find him. Griffin showed the marshal and the shipping commissioner his log. The marshal said, "Shame, that bastard should have been hung. There's a reward too. Now no one gets it."

Nicholas Priest found one letter from his family, from his mother. His mother told him of how much she and his father missed him, how they had prayed for him, and how he had brought his mother and father closer together. Priest showed the letter to Smallbridge and Duder. Duder handed the letter back to Priest and said, "Sweets, shipmate, let's get you and Smallbridge your tattoos and a cold beer. Old man's going to pay us off tomorrow."

Isaac Griffin bundled the large stack of letters he had written to Kayleigh MacKenna and posted them. He then accepted hers with both anticipation and anxiety. It was not until he returned to the ship and opened her letters that he learned that Kayleigh's periods, her monthly visitor, had stopped. They were to be parents. The last of her letters revealed that she and her family were somewhere, perhaps crossing the Rockies, aboard the transcontinental train.

Forty-Eight

San Francisco

Instead of spa we'll drink down ale
and pay the reckoning on the nail,
for debt no man shall go to jail;
from Garry Owen in glory

Official Song of the
First U.S. Army
Calvary Division

Friday, September 6, 1872

Griffin's meeting with Kayleigh was everything that each could ever have expected. She took a Whitehall boat out to where *Providence* was anchored while waiting to load grain. Ezra escorted her to Griffin's cabin, and neither Kayleigh nor Griffin was seen until late that evening, when they departed hand in hand for shore, to the Lick House Hotel on the west side of Montgomery Street. Once there, they found their bedroom could wait and celebrated their union in their suite's parlor. Both embraced physical lovemaking with an insatiable passion for each other fueled by months of absence. When exhausted, they wrapped themselves in each other's arms and kissed and laughed.

Having celebrated their reunion, the couple climbed into their suite's large feather-stuffed bed, pulled the down cover over their naked bodies, and cuddled much like two drowsy puppies. Griffin was habitually slow to sleep and awoke often to assure himself he was not at sea. Wide awake, he was surprised by Kayleigh's whimpering and twisting nervously in bed. Just a short while ago, Griffin's mind would have been occupied by his ship, but this was not now the case. He could not rise from his chair, look at the telltale, and return to sleep. Kayleigh's dreams obviously terrorized her.

Griffin used his left hand to stroke Kayleigh's brow and brush her hair back with his fingers. Her hair was damp with sweat. She awoke confused and then turned on her side and held him tightly, so childlike. He stroked the base of her spine and felt the warmth of her tears on his cheeks. He removed the comforter, kissed her belly, and then drew her close to him. Silently they both passed again into sleep. He no longer heard the sound of *Providence*'s top hamper working, the passage of time marked by the ship's bell, or the muffled sounds of men on watch. Griffin's mind listened for his wife's whimpers. He had no ready answer.

That morning, prior to his wife's awakening, a Lick House bellboy delivered a note to Captain Griffin from Jim MacKenna. The note was polite, formal, but still expressed a sense of urgency. Jim MacKenna and Isaac Griffin were to have lunch together in the hotel dining room beneath the grand chandelier and skylight. Kayleigh and her mother would be shopping at that hour and the men would meet alone.

Griffin steeled himself. His natural inclination was to carry his Smith and Wesson. He thought of Jim MacKenna's threats, the charred oak, the butcher knife, and he loaded the revolver and strapped himself into his shoulder holster. Kayleigh's letters were positive about her father and his attitude toward the marriage, but just the knowledge of the pistol's presence, a bulge beneath his suit coat, might keep tempers and memories subdued.

Jim MacKenna was every bit as imposing as Griffin remembered, a big man with coarse gray hair and a broken nose. He stood over six feet tall, as stout as an oak. The fine worsted sack model suit seemed to enhance MacKenna's chest and shoulders yet still did little in the way of presenting an image of urban sophistication.

Kayleigh's father rose to greet Griffin and tentatively extended, then withdrew, his right hand first. He obviously thought to shake Griffin's hand but then thought the better of it. Jim MacKenna stood out amidst the crystal, paintings, mirrors, and marble columns of the hotel dining room, a kettle of Irish stew on a formal banquet table. His fingers and thumbs dwarfed blunt breakfast sausages and coarse-cut carrots.

"I'm sorry fer what happened between us, Griffin, and not just fer Kayleigh's sake. I know I can't expect friendship now. Perhaps, in time, that will come, but for now we'll have ter do with some respect fer each other. Take a seat, Griffin. Please. I've a lot ter say ter ya."

The men were offered menus that included hot and cold meats, game, and wild fowl and tropical fruit from South America.

"I don't think Kayleigh has ever been so happy in her life. I thank yer for that. I mean it too, not that yer'll believe me. What you don't know is how much Mary and me look forward ter spoilin' our little grandchild. 'Tis a granddaughter I'm hoping fer."

Jim MacKenna laughed and looked to see if Isaac Griffin shared his sentiment; he didn't appear to.

The big man exhaled and dropped his head, "This ain't at all easy ter say, sins of their fathers, but I'll be out with it. Kayleigh could be in terrible danger and so could you. I never meant it ter happen. Never thought it would ever happen, but I was betrayed."

Griffin cocked his head to look Jim MacKenna in the eyes. There were lines forming on Griffin's forehead, and his eyes narrowed.

"It's not the time fer that, Griffin. There's no danger t'you or my daughter as yet, but one day there will be, and I don't want yer blindsided. I'm Clan na Gael. Do you know what that means?"

Griffin replied bluntly, "No, I don't. Tell me."

"I believe in Irish independence and took an oath sayin' I'd die to free Ireland of English rule. Others, like me here and in Ireland, belong t' Clan na Gael. I joined as a boy, a killer boy. Jack O'Corkerane, the man responsible for raising money for Irish independence here in the States, has threatened t' kill Kayleigh, and me, if he doesn't get his way with yer ships. He's the head of the Clan na Gael camps in New York and Boston. He'll kill me first, though. I made sure he'd do that."

Griffin sat bolt upright in his chair and clenched the fist of his left hand. His fingers curled in his right hand but still could not close. He felt no pain but did not realize it.

Astonished, Griffin asked, "How did that happen?"

Jim MacKenna replied, "I never, ever thought it could. I never saw it coming. Griffin, they want t' use your shipping line t' smuggle men into and out of Ireland beneath the British noses. They want t' use you t' smuggle guns, explosives, and cash into Ireland too. Even talked about using you t' get Mary's brothers out of Australia."

Jim MacKenna watched the anger drain from Griffin's face, only to be replaced by shock.

"How?"

"Jack O'Corkerane knew the Christisons were hurtin' fer money and bribed the son. The Commodore has no idea. O'Corkerane wanted me t' force you t' marry Kayleigh. You two surprised me there, but it really changes nothin'. The marriage was was ter help keep William Jr. in line. He's a weak man and they know it. Now, they'd just as soon get him out of the way and deal directly with you."

Griffin slumped slightly in his chair and shook his head slowly.

"I know, Griffin. He said if she wouldn't marry yer, he'd kill her and me too. Said I took the oath and knew what t'expect. 'Tis total obedience t'death they want. Said they killed Terrence Cleary in East Boston for reneging on the oath. She can never go back to Boston and be safe again. They'll kill me first." Pride briefly flashed in his smile. "The threat's been made, no backing away from it, no letting it slide away. It would be seen as weakness and help stiffen some spines, Irish as well as English."

Griffin stared into MacKenna's eyes. "What can I do?"

"Let's finish up the meal. We need to leave, so I can talk ter ya. If someone heard me, it could mean the gallows, not that I don't deserve it."

The two men finished their meal in silence. While Griffin often regarded his meals as a necessity, he did enjoy them. The pheasant was unexpectedly good. Jim MacKenna said nothing, but the way he attacked his plate and looked at Griffin after a particularly enjoyable bite revealed that despite Jim MacKenna's past, the horrible situation he was in, he might just still be the boy he was never able to be. MacKenna had to feel shame to confess what he had to Griffin.

They left the Lick House and walked together toward the Embarcadero. Once surrounded by crowds of rough men, their voices were hid amongst many. Big Jim began.

"They'll kill me first before any harm comes t' Kayleigh. I arranged for the Clan t' avenge Kayleigh's rape. She knows nothin' about this, and neither does Mary. They won't either, yer understand.

"Three Clan na Gael men were t' do the deed, but I did it fer them—they were just lookouts. The killin' was brutal, cold and brutal. That's how I wanted it. I beat the man t' death with me fists. I watched blood flow from his mouth and ears and saw him convulse until life left him. Made sure O'Corkerane's men saw me smile. They didn't expect that. Maybe they thought there would be satisfaction or a sense of justice or even revenge. They did not expect t' see pleasure—like the devil smiles at the suffering of the damned, like he smiles at me."

Griffin bristled. "You tortured him. Where's the justice in that?"

Jim MacKenna stopped and placed his right hand on Griffin's shoulder, his face inches away from Griffin's. "Listen ter me, listen, damn it. I had no choice. I had ter send a message. Haven't yer realized that by now?

"Told those men ter tell O'Corkerane that was what I'd do ter any man that harmed me daughter. That wasn't the end of it, though. The next time I met O'Corkerane, in the Harp and Plough it was, I roughed him up a bit. Yer can never show fear. There can never be any misunderstandin'. Now, I told him face to face I'd kill him fer harmin' Kayleigh. So yer see, he'll kill me first. The bartender saw the whole thing. Saw O'Corkerane crumble like a child's doll. Yer see, he's not so fearsome now. He'll kill me first—he's too full of vengeance ter do anything else. Can't let what I did stand without an answer." Griffin nodded.

"Have yer noticed the Irish lads you shipped in New York? I hope you noticed there was no trouble with the San Francisco Shipping Masters Association? What was it? Ten dollars a head ter ship yer own men. Everyone else pays thirty dollars and more. It ain't all bad. It was me that arranged yer cargo fer the Central Pacific. That was my cargo you carried. It was me too that greased the skids with Balfour and Guthrie and the grain arrangement with the Ralli brothers. That ain't all either. This will help you and Kayleigh get yer feet on the ground."

Big Jim reached into the inside chest pocket of his sack coat and handed Griffin a folded piece of bond paper.

Griffin was taken aback. "That's the mortgage on *San Matias*. I've not asked for your help."

Big Jim laughed. "Pay up, then! Hand it back and I'll give the money to me grandkids when yer have them. I own the mortgage, Griffin—ha! Got it at a discount too, I did. I got yer by the short and curlies now, ain't I?"

Griffin smirked, then laughed, and placed the mortgage in his own coat pocket and replied, "You need to read this letter. I'm surprised you don't already know."

MacKenna took a letter from Griffin's hand. It was the report from George Priest on William Jr.'s financial dealings.

"Let's find a bar, Griffin, I want a pisco punch. The Bank Exchange's not far from here fer the likes of you and me. We'll catch a horse car if we have ter. Have yer tried pisco punch? It'll make a gnat want ter fight an elephant, they say."

Once seated in the Bank Exchange bar room, Jim MacKenna took George Priest's letter from Griffin and read it again. "I don't think it's a good idea fer ya t' spend so much time at sea, Griffin. William Jr. will drain you dry like he did his father. I hope yer also understand leavin' Kayleigh t' fend for herself ain't a good idea either."

Griffin replied, "Well, at least at sea, I've only five Irishmen to worry about. I'll take Kayleigh to sea with me, hire a midwife, and a maid to take care of her."

Big Jim MacKenna rose from his chair. "We'll need to think this

The Downeaster

through, you and me together—no talking with our women about it. And there'll be no bad blood between us, at least none that Mary and Kayleigh will ever see. If I've something needs saying t' yer, I'll say it, and yer t' me. No Mary. No Kayleigh, and no bullshitting each other. Barkeep!"

MacKenna sat and pointed to part of George Priest's letter. "There may be some value left in what Willie Jr. bought; it's stocks—he's greedy, not stupid, maybe even before his time. I know about Bessemer."

"Damn it, Jim. I'm dependent on George Priest to see this through for me in Boston. I don't want Hanna hurt—she's Kayleigh's best friend. This Irish business really messes things up, every plan I had. Do I take *Providence* to England? Hell if I know."

Big Jim rubbed his brow with the tips of the fingers of his right hand then pointed his hand toward Griffin and made a motion as if he were going to pat the table. "I'll introduce myself to George Priest. I'll buy up the holdings, but I won't pay more than market value—well, just a little more, but I want to remain hidden. Can't take a chance of anything ever being found out."

Griffin smiled. "Let's have a cigar and another punch."

"Mary's seen me in Garryowen's glory a time or two. Seein' yer with me will save us a tongue-lashing. Yer'll buy this one."

"Barkeep!"

The morning fog had rolled out past Alcatraz Island to sea through the Golden Gate. The early September sunlight, as clear as polished optical glass, warmed faces and illuminated shadows.

***

Nicholas Priest had cleaned the ship's bilge with Smallbridge and Richard Ernst. This was the foulest experience he had ever had. The bilge looked foul, felt foul, and smelled worse. Then came lining the ship's hold with wood planking, as required for carrying grain. More work below in the hold, separated from fresh air and sunlight. This, however, came to an end after supper, and Nicholas Priest found that he was refreshed despite the labor, as he could sleep all night without

335

interruption. He was also somewhat richer for the experience, as he was surprised to learn that his indenture as an apprentice did come with the wage required by the Shipping Commissioner's Act of 1872.

Captain Griffin called the boys to his reception area and asked them if they would like to attend Thompson's Navigation School while the ship loaded grain. This school could certify that they possessed the basic navigational skills required of a mate. Richard Ernst declined at first because he did not intend to be a career seaman, but eventually accepted as he would enjoy the company of his two companions and they him, while the evenings would be free for adventure ashore in San Francisco. Smallbridge discovered a photographer who had a lovely and, behind her father's back, lively daughter. The others asked if she had friends.

With time and money to spend, Nicholas Priest found himself in a small top-floor studio in a greengrocer's store near Geary and Larkin discussing tattoos, his tattoos, with Sam Duder, John Stedwin, Smallbridge, and an elderly Japanese gentleman whom Duder and Stedwin deferred to as Master Horiyoshi, master of *tebori*.

Master Horiyoshi's studio was an unusual place by Western standards, with more than a little reflection of Japanese Buddhism, a large skylight, vials of ink, a teapot, and a large handheld barber's mirror. The sailors were invited to sit around a bamboo mat on the immaculately swept floor and were offered strong green tea prior to discussing business.

Master Horiyoshi spoke a limited amount of English and the conversation essentially involved their shipmate John and the master. It was soon understood that Priest was there to get his tattoos for crossing the line and rounding Cape Horn. The master smiled, bowed, and looked to Priest to acknowledge his intent.

John Stedwin took off his shirt and showed the master the large koi fish tattoo that occupied his entire back. The master smiled and indicated that he recognized his own work. Sam Duder directed Priest's attention to the colors used: black, white, blue, and red. He also pointed out the shading of the colors; the black ink was as delicately shaded as a charcoal drawing, and a large angry sea was portrayed in the tattoo's background.

"I showed him the work so he could recognize it, and I'm showing it to you because the master's work don't come cheap and ain't quick to do, Priest."

Smallbridge added, "Looks good to me, but you go first."

The master drew his face close to Priest and sniffed. "Good, not drunk."

Having completed some of the preliminaries, the master sketched out his interpretation of the classical Neptune Rex, crowned and with his trident spear. His Neptune did bear a resemblance to the classical Greek image; however, the musculature, the hair, and the pose were very fierce and, as Duder explained, in the samurai tradition. This Neptune rode upon the back of a wingless dragon with reptile-like scales, three toes, and a beard. The background featured a roiled sea that Priest clearly recognized as graybeards, the waves breaking at the top, the upward movement of the water, and the dark abyss for the trough. Sam explained that the tattoo would be inked on Priest's left calf. Some Japanese was exchanged between Stedwin and the master, and Priest learned that the master felt a shoulder would be the more appropriate canvas.

"Does it matter, Duder?"

"Not too much, as long as the shellbacks know it's there. I suspect you'd want to keep it covered up, though, and either place works for that."

"Show me yours, Sam?"

Sam showed that his was indeed on a shoulder, but it was not at all like what the master had sketched. Duder explained that it was his first tattoo and done in New York before he knew tattooing and had experienced the Orient.

Priest looked at the master and pointed to his left calf. The master nodded that he understood but said, "Big. Not cheap."

Shortly thereafter, an agreement was reached, fifteen dollars exchanged, and Priest was asked to remove his trousers and lie down on the mat.

Smallbridge smiled. "It's gonna hurt, Sweets, but you'll get used to the pain. Ain't nothin' you can't take."

The master proceeded to grind his inks from a mixture of charcoal he called *sumi* and mix in the colors. When that was complete, he cleaned Priest's calf with hot soap and water and shaved where the tattoo would go. Then he assembled his needles. These needles were not what Priest or, for that matter, Smallbridge expected. They were delicately carved ivory needles bundled in bunches by a brass band to the end of a carved bamboo stick that was nearly a foot and a half in length.

The master said, "Draw in first, color later." The master then sketched the outline of his work on Priest's calf. Sam Duder stretched Priest's shaved skin to form a firm canvas. This sketch took nearly an hour to complete. Duder laughed. "Worst part's over." Priest knew he lied.

Priest saw the master wash his own hands and assemble his tools by Priest's side. The master sat cross-legged over Priest's calf and used a small brush dipped in an inkpot to ink his needle. He placed his left hand on Priest's calf, gripped the very top of his needle like a chisel in his right hand, and angled the needles over the thumb of his left hand so they would strike the outline the master had drawn on Priest's skin. Then, as Priest watched and Duder kept his skin stretched, Horiyoshi pushed the needle quickly through the top layer of skin in a lunging motion. Priest winced.

The first puncture hurt, but less than he had imagined it would. Priest also knew that Duder, Stedwin, and Smallbridge were watching him to see his reaction to the pain. Priest closed his eyes and breathed slowly to relax his body. Every five seconds his skin was punctured by another thrust. Duder kept the skin taut. The only stoppage came when the master wiped the blood off Priest's calf and either re-inked or changed his tattoo pens. Priest imagined he heard a *shiss* noise as the needles exited his skin.

The process ended with the master smiling toward his subject while picking up and cleaning his tools. Nearly three hours had passed. The master cleaned the blood and excess ink from Priest's

The Downeaster

calf and showed him the outline of Neptune emerging from the sea on the back of a dragon that the master had created. The outline extended from below the ankle to the top of the calf. Stedwin drew Priest's attention to the intricate detail of the dragon's scales.

Duder explained the significance of the symbols.

"Sweets, you're getting something to be proud of. Neptune shows that you are a shellback, a member of Neptune's kingdom. The dragon is *riujin*, who holds power over the sea and its tides with his magical jewels. The dragon will be finished in the same black, white, blue, and red, the four natural powers of the earth. The sea is a real snorter. This tattoo says you are a powerful man and full of good fortune."

Duder added, "John told Master Horiyoshi about you. About how you came on board all sick, how you fought, and how you've become a real shipmate to us. What he's done is choose symbols to show who you are and what he sees as your future. The master thinks you've the makings of a samurai."

Priest had observed how Duder and Stedwin treated the master with courtesy. He bowed to the master and told him, "Thank you." With that, the master bandaged the fresh tattoo, and Stedwin warned him to be careful with it. He was also told that he must come back so the master could finish coloring and shading the tattoo. He wanted the skin to heal before proceeding.

Duder explained the history of tattoos in Japan, that they had been used to punish criminals, and that the Japanese government had outlawed tattoos to please Western visitors. He said the common Japanese people have for centuries considered *tebori* to be an art and an expression of Japanese culture. The master tattooist listened, asked Stedwin occasionally to translate, and smiled. Horiyoshi spoke to Priest: "Be proud."

Master Horiyoshi had been brought to San Francisco by sailors so that he could continue to practice his art among those who appreciated it. The master, however, wished to return to Japan.

Several days later, Priest again found himself on the mat with the master, Duder, and Stedwin. Priest steeled himself for the

339

experience. It was good that he did so. The needles used by the master to color and shade in Neptune, the dragon, and the sea were considerably larger in width than the delicate needles used for outlining. Smallbridge said that he would join his shipmates later in the evening and was anxious to see the finished tattoo.

Once again Priest relaxed to control his breathing and thought of a field of freshly fallen New England snow to keep his mind away from what he endured. Then the memory of what had happened in Virginia passed through his mind. He grunted and smiled. The master stopped momentarily. "No move."

Master Horiyoshi began anew and steadied his needles with the index finger of his left hand and pushed the needle into Priest's skin with his right hand in a chisel grip at the top of the bamboo. Once again, a push was made every five seconds in a steady rhythm, only stopping to clear away the blood, ink, or change inks and needles.

When the blood and excess ink had been washed away, Priest was shown his new tattoo in the mirror. It was past midnight. He was amazed at the result and pleased with what had been done. He could easily imagine what it would be when his skin healed, and wondered what the boys at his school in Virginia would say about it. Then he smiled, realizing he did not give a damn about the opinion of those boys. He shuddered a moment, though, when he thought of his mother and how she would cry. She would surely be overcome with sorrow and a sense that she had somehow failed him. He hoped she would one day understand who he had become and what the tattoo meant.

As Priest's mind wondered about how his mother would react to him, Smallbridge burst through the door and exclaimed, "Priest, Sweets, I saw her. Sophie's at the Bella Union. It had to be her!"

Priest smiled.

About the Author

Paul Thomas Fuhrman grew up the eldest of three children in Middletown, Ohio, and graduated from Bishop Fenwick High School. He earned a bachelor's degree in English literature from Miami University in Oxford, Ohio. After college, Fuhrman spent five years, ten months, and twenty-eight days plus a wake up of commissioned naval service. He acquired the rank of full lieutenant and his wife, Donna, his salvation. Fuhrman loved bridge watches and Combat Information Center watches as well as any deck or small boat operation. He also started crewing on sailboats in the navy. His favorite ship was the *USS Tacoma* PG 92.

The sea was Fuhrman's dream from grade school on. He read about the sea, ships, and sailors in a wonderful old gothic Carnegie library on First Avenue in Middletown, Ohio.

Now ashore, arms stacked, children educated, and settled in his retirement home in Virginia, *The Downeaster* became an obsession of some ten years' research and writing and has finally reached print. It is an ambition fulfilled.

MacHugh and the Faithless Pirate

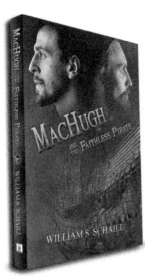

Robert MacHugh is a late 17th century Scots wine merchant and smuggler in New York who finds himself (not totally willingly) chasing pirates, perfidious French persons, angry Native Americans and others as a "favor" for a very powerful London power broker. A story filled with straining canvas, roaring cannons, spies, crooked Dutch patroons, Maroons and pretty girls, among other things.

A rip-snorting, swashbuckling adventure, that I was quickly caught up in. I liked the battle scenes, the storms and the part with the Maroons. The opening scene had a lot of atmosphere. I would have liked to know Kate a little better.

—Daniel Parrott, Former captain of the tall ships *Pride of Baltimore II, Harvey Gamage, Bill of Rights* and *Tole Mour*; professor of navigation at the Maine Maritime Academy; author of *Tall Ships Down.*

AUTHOR BIO

William S. Schaill was born in 1944 in Yonkers, NY. He has published six nautical thrillers and hundreds of magazine and newspaper articles on all subjects. He spent his junior year of high school aboard a square-rigged school ship. He majored in Spanish literature at Dartmouth College and did foreign study at the University of the Andes in Bogota, Colombia. He served as a naval salvage diving officer; devoted twenty years to educational publishing; started several other business ventures; traveled extensively and raised two daughters.

For the Finest in Nautical and Historical Fiction and Non-Fiction
www.FireshipPress.com

CPSIA information can be obtained at www.ICGtesting.com
Printed in the USA
BVOW06s1533020316

438755BV00010B/188/P